Digging Up Trouble

Digging Up Trouble

A SWEET FICTION BOOKSHOP MYSTERY

Kitt Crowe

NEW YORK

This is a work of fiction. All of the names, characters, organizations, places and events portrayed in this novel are either products of the author's imagination or are used fictitiously. Any resemblance to real or actual events, locales, or persons, living or dead, is entirely coincidental.

Published in the United States by Crooked Lane Books, an imprint of The Quick Brown Fox & Company LLC.

Crooked Lane Books and its logo are trademarks of The Quick Brown Fox & Company LLC.

Library of Congress Catalog-in-Publication data available upon request.

ISBN (hardcover): 978-1-64385-768-8
ISBN (ebook): 978-1-64385-769-5

Cover illustration by Ben Perini

Printed in the United States.

www.crookedlanebooks.com

Crooked Lane Books
34 West 27th St., 10th Floor
New York, NY 10001

First Edition: October 2021

10 9 8 7 6 5 4 3 2 1

Dedicated to D&R.
Read a book, boys, save your brains.

Prologue

"You're a blasted idiot, is what you are," the old man growled in a voice too loud for the middle of the popular downtown diner. He added a bunch of four-letter words, shocking half the occupants, who'd expected to be bowled over by good food, not the jabbering of the town's blustery curmudgeon.

"Dad, this isn't the place to discuss this," the younger man with him said between gritted teeth.

"Why? Are you embarrassed? No wonder your life is a mess. You got no grit. No backbone."

"Dad, please. Let's just have lunch."

A well-dressed man in summer casual turned in the booth behind them and cleared his throat. "You know, Gil, you might want to take this outside to discuss in private." He nodded with respect to the younger man doing his best to fight a rising blush.

"Oh, and you think *you* have a right to talk to me? You're an even bigger idiot than he is." The old man grunted. "You've been trying for years to one-up me, and where has it gotten you? Nowhere but second best, that's where." He snorted. "Couldn't garden your way out of a paper bag."

The man in the booth shut up and turned around, clearly fuming but too polite to say anything.

The woman sitting across from him at the booth shot a look at grumpy Gil. “Don’t worry about him, honey. He’s a sad little man angry at life.”

“You got that right,” Gil snapped. “My wife’s gone, and my boys are five beers short of a six-pack.”

“Dad,” the younger man choked. “Stop it.”

Gil grinned, his expression furious, mean, and darkly amused. “But hey, at least my wife’s dead in the ground. You’re nothing but dead from the neck down.”

The woman gasped, and the man with her threw his money on the table and stormed from the diner with his wife in tow.

Around them, people grumbled, but no one had the guts to speak up.

Gil turned back to his grown son. “Boy, you need to act like you’ve got a pair, unlike the rest of the godforsaken morons in this town.” He frowned before shooting a critical look at the younger man once more. “And speaking of dead and buried, I’m glad your mother is gone. At least now she can’t see the mess your life has become.”

His son got up and left.

Silence settled over the diner while the old man ignored everyone’s disapproval, seeming content that he’d said his piece and damn them all that cared.

But one patron cared an awful lot. About the dead . . . and those living on borrowed time.

Chapter One

Confection, Oregon

No, no, no. Just once I'd like to look like I wasn't the biggest idiot in town.

"Well, well. What do we have here?"

What do we have here—my least favorite sentence in existence. Confection's newest addition to the police department, Detective Berg, stared down at me as I rested on my hands and knees, trying to hide the fact that my dog had dug up a prime piece of real estate smack-dab in Central Garden—the showpiece of our downtown. Cookie had been digging way too close to the town's prized rosebush, and I just *knew* the worst of the worst would be after me as soon as Loose Lips Berg spread the word.

Discreet he was not, but Berg paid attention to detail. How the blasted man had seen me through the hedge surrounding the garden was anyone's guess. He'd rounded the shrubbery and now loomed like a thundercloud, blotting out my sunshine.

Dressed in tan slacks and a dark-blue T-shirt with POLICE printed in white letters across his broad chest and back, his PD hat, and his badge clipped to his trousers, Detective Berg looked professional enough, I supposed. Perhaps treating him like God's gift to law and order would help.

I gave him my brightest smile as I rose, brushing dirt from my knees and hoping the grass stains would wash out from my capris. Though I was twenty-seven years old, I tended to look younger with my hair pulled back in a ponytail and a tan that made my bright green eyes pop. (Or so I liked to think.) With any luck, this afternoon I looked fresh-faced and innocent. "Hello, Officer Berg."

His fake smile soured. "That's *Detective* Berg."

"Well, Detective Berg, what are you out detecting today?"

He studied me without expression, and I wondered if he'd cuff me, then jail me for being too pleasant. For some reason, though Berg had only been in town for a few months, he'd taken a fierce dislike to me, my dog, and anything resembling dirt.

"I could have sworn I saw the tail end of a troublemaking canine just minutes ago."

I subtly stepped to my left over the recently dug earth, blocking Berg's view of the fresh soil I'd repacked.

He glanced down at the rosebush and then around, and I supposed I should have been happy Cookie had taken off the second I'd yelled at her for digging. I was hoping *so hard* that she'd gone straight home.

Behind my back, I crossed my fingers.

I casually tapped my shoe over the ground. Hopefully, my weight would help tamp the sad little tufts of grass back in place.

He raised a brow. "Hiding the evidence?"

I frowned. "Evidence? I'm sorry, Detective Berg. What are you talking about?" The breeze shifted, and the sweet scent of roses and lavender filled the air. I would have breathed it in and sighed with pleasure, but I didn't want Berg to think I took him lightly.

A few folks passed by and waved, looking a little too interested in me and *the po-po*—what my best friend Teri liked to call the police. She also liked to call them *the fuzz*, *the man*, and a few other less-than-complimentary terms. But Teri has issues when it comes to authority and puts the capital C in Conspiracy Theorist.

Berg lifted the Confection PD ball cap from his head and scratched at the short dark hair that never seemed to grow. It was like the moment an eighth of an inch appeared, he chopped it off before those strands could even think about moving past regulation length.

I would know. I'd made a study of Detective Chad Berg. He made an ideal template for the hero in the secret novel I was writing. I just had to iron out a few details. And, well, not pay exorbitant fines or go to jail because of my dog in the meantime.

"Yo, Officer!" The owner of the corner taco truck, a fifty-year-old hippie with the business sense of a corporate shark, waved. "Keep the peace, my man! Protect the Confection Rose!"

Berg waved back and shoved his hat back on. He smiled at Taco Ted before glaring down at me. He had to be a few inches over six feet. I'm not short, but around him, I feel tiny. Hmm. Did I want my hero to be super imposing? Because Teri's brother was also tall but not as intense. I considered him a contender for male lead in *Lexi's Super-Secret Story* as well.

Berg frowned. "Why are you looking at me like that?"

"Like what?" Yeah, that frown line. Both hero prospects had a tendency to frown when talking to me. I'd have to add that to my character's rough appeal. And the way their brows drew close. Like an angry slash over those—in Berg's case—gray eyes. Smoky gray? Icy gray? Charcoal? Meh. I'd edited better descriptions than those back in my old life.

He sighed. "Never mind. Now let's take a look at the evidence, shall we?" He moved closer. "Step aside, please."

"Sure." I'd been standing over the sad, dead grass long enough.

"Where's the dog?"

"Her name is Cookie. And I left her at home. Why?"

He shook his head and withdrew a pad from his pocket. "I'm going to have to cite you for this."

I scowled. "For what? Walking near the garden? Enjoying the fresh scent of summer and the wonder that is Confection, Oregon?" I wasn't lying . . . exactly. Overhead, the cloudless sky showed a perfect blue seen only in postcards.

Snowcapped mountains in the distance competed with the massive pines and aspens framing the town in bursts of verdant green and brown. From Central Garden, located as we were at the base of the main thoroughfare, I could see all our downtown glory. Flowers hung in moss planters from street posts or filled large pots along the pristine white sidewalks. Not to mention the eclectic and colorful storefronts were worth a second look all by themselves.

Founded in 1906, Confection, Oregon, boasted a total of 6,048 locals as of the last census, though popular thought had us closer to 7,000 now, thanks to some stupid article in a travel magazine talking up our town.

Our main economy used to be lumber, back before we'd done our best to repopulate the forests. Now we dealt in tourism and microbreweries, second only to Bend, Oregon, our sister city farther south.

Like Bend, we're also located on the eastern edge of the Cascade Mountains, but we're farther from the Deschutes River. We're high desert, meaning we're arid if you don't count the snow in the mountains. Quick to heat up and quick to cool down. We have a lot of sagebrush and the dreaded junipers, which make allergy season a huge pain.

Confection is a tourist attraction year-round, and especially during our Sweet Summer Festival season. Everything is in bloom, and our cute little town looks like a poster for cute little towns everywhere. It's no wonder we seem to have a festival every other weekend. Cuteness equals cash.

Which was probably why Detective Berg had been keeping an eye on Central Garden, what with the recent spate of mischief going around. Still, I'd have thought a patrol officer, not a detective, would be walking the town beat.

"Everything okay, Detective?" one of our postmen asked as he strolled by carrying the afternoon's mail. "Lexi's not in trouble, is she?" He paused. "Please tell me the rosebush is okay." Now he looked horrified. Not that I might be in trouble, but that the stupid roses might be in danger.

Gah. That freakin' bush. I was up to my armpits in flower lovers.

"Everything's fine." Berg smiled. "Just making sure the town center's nice and pretty for this weekend's festival."

"Good. I hope you find whoever's been digging up the gardens around here. And Lexi, let me know when my book comes in."

"Will do," I said. "It should be in tomorrow's shipment, if I'm not mistaken."

I run Sweet Fiction, the bookstore just a few shops down from Central Garden on Main Street. I'm happy to say we have a pretty literate town, full of people who like to read, keeping Sweet Fiction in business.

Our neighborhood postman, a Civil War buff, waved his good-byes and left.

A few other locals around us said hello in passing, excited about the upcoming weekend's entertainment. Heck, even I couldn't wait to see who took this summer's "Best of" list.

When a well-known member of the Confection Garden Club—better known as the CGC mafia—walked by and asked Berg if they had any suspects in regard to the latest overturned flower beds on the south side, I thought about skipping out on my citation.

Berg smiled and turned back to me, as if having read my mind. "Not yet, but we're getting closer."

"It's not Cookie," I said quickly before he threw suspicion on me and my poor, beleaguered pup.

"We'll see about that."

But the CGC man looked satisfied. "Oh, okay then. Thanks, Detective. See you, Lexi."

Berg smiled. "No problem."

" 'Bye now." I waved, pretending I didn't subscribe to the enmity between the CGC and my book club. Sure, I could pretend I was better than that.

Berg waited until we were once again mostly alone. In a low voice he said to me, "You know why I'm out here mingling with the public and policing a *rosebush* instead of doing my actual job, detecting?"

"Um, why?" *Crap*. I had a feeling I knew why.

He leaned closer and smiled through his teeth. "Because you and that blasted dog have annoyed the Confection Garden Club, several members of which happen to be close friends of the mayor. But instead of our patrol officers protecting the town's 'treasure,' " —he inserted air quotes— "I'm on rose patrol because I apparently need to present a better face to the public." If he pretended to smile any harder, his face might break in half.

I swallowed and discreetly took a step back. "Ah. I see."

"Remember the playground last week, Ms. Jones?"

"You mean when you chased Cookie down, thinking she'd attacked two of the kids at the Maple Circle swing-n-bling?" The kids had been playing with ketchup and make-believe wounds, which Cookie had been only too happy to lick off their faces. Seeing the big bad man tackle my adorable dog had set the children to wailing. And, well, one particular six-year-old just happened to be the grandson of one of the town councilmen.

None of that had been my fault at all, as Teri had been dog sitting. Yet I had still gotten the blame.

He continued, "And how about all the complaint calls I've overheard during my time at the station? A border collie–pit mix running around town without a leash?"

He had me on that one, but I sputtered, "Hey, that could be any number of dogs in town."

"Uh-huh. Do they also defecate on Ed Mullins' yard on a regular basis?"

"She never poops there." During the day, at least. I could normally swing by at night to scoop away the evidence. But I couldn't blame her. Ed Mullins—don of the CGC mafia—didn't like dogs, and Cookie sensed it.

"How about the theft of a full roasted chicken, an apple pie, and what was the other thing? Oh yeah. A full plate of peanut butter cookies?"

I knew exactly who'd filed *that* complaint. "You know, maybe if Stefanie didn't leave her stuff out on her windowsill to cool, someone—not Cookie—wouldn't be stealing her food."

He raised a brow. "And what about Stefanie's purse?"

"Oh, well." I shrugged. "I told Cookie to fetch, she fetched. But come on, she fetched the purse because Stefanie had stolen her ball and hidden it in her purse! How amazing is my dog that she figured it out?"

"She's a menace." Berg crossed his big arms over his chest. "And so are you."

"Well I never," I fumed, secretly proud of myself for using an expression I'd been dying to use forever, and in public no less.

"Look, Ms. Jones, just take the ticket and—"

The squeal of car brakes, a loud beep, and a crash seemed to happen all at once.

"Don't leave," Berg ordered before darting to a collision outside my uncle's hardware store just off Main.

So, I waited.

Having dutifully obeyed Detective's Berg's order (for all of one minute), I rushed away from the scene of my dog's *alleged* vandalism. Time to enjoy the rest of a rare day off before Cookie *actually* dug up a prized rosebush or nicked something from the CGC mafia.

Then my klepto dog would really put me in the doghouse. No pun intended.

Chapter Two

My walk home invigorated me. It normally only took ten minutes, and the weather couldn't have been better. The sun continued to shine. The breeze kept me more than comfortable in denim capris and my tank top. And the scent of honeysuckle and lavender filled the air.

Now, I'm not that fond of the Confection Garden Club, who police the state of growing things in town, but I'm not necessarily against pretty blooms and nicely cut lawns. Though Confection is known for our sweets and spectacular views of the mountains, many also come to our town to goggle over the astounding skills our garden club has with a spade and shovel. And to gape at the grand houses in our downtown area—our mini historic district.

I left Cinnamon Avenue for Court Street, studying my neighbors' homes, still enthralled with the varied architecture. Having lived in an apartment in Seattle for a few years, I was more than happy to have returned to my hometown. The cityscape, while beautiful, had been overwhelming. The dirt, noise, and crowds tough to handle. To say nothing of the expense. My God! A cup of coffee there started at five bucks.

My apartment had been blah, like all the others, so much the same. Expensive without a view and far enough from my job that I'd had to rely on public transportation.

I'd loved walking in the pocket neighborhoods of the city, each with its own charm. Queen Anne, Fremont, Ballard. The craftsman-style homes had reminded me of Confection.

The majority of our older homes range in style from craftsman to Victorian. While we have our share of apartments and cookie-cutter subdivisions, they're few and far between. Our town thrives on variety. We also have midcentury modern homes and a few more Georgian inspired designs, and every one of those in the historic section has had to be styled and painted in accordance with the town council's House Advisory Committee.

Sounds political, I know. But Confection considers paint color and fence size to be much more important than any governmental party.

And speaking of politics . . .

I passed two standing members of the CGC—both conferring over the fence separating their yards. In the front of one home, tiger lilies and orange poppies waved around low-cut greenery and sprouts of yellow and red flowers I didn't recognize. By the neighboring walkway, a row of neatly trimmed bushes led to sculpted azaleas.

"Looks great," I said as I passed.

The older of the two narrowed her eyes at me, but the younger—still in her late fifties—smiled and waved, then turned to continue their discussion. I heard mention of parasites and nontoxic spray, then mention of Bill Sanchez's huge cucumber. And no, "huge cucumber" isn't a euphemism. Bill has won the Best Vegetable category for the past three years, ever since he joined the CGC. The man knows how to grow veggies.

Like a few of our serious enthusiasts, Bill liked to talk plants and had a home garden plot that rivaled anything I'd ever seen. But he took a back seat to the big man—Ed Mullins, the CGC president, who liked to brag about his time spent working at Portland's International Rose Test Garden, an amazing showpiece of floral beauty. Though I'm sure Ed was no more than a glorified ticket taker, I was hit by all the flowers in various states of growth and color while walking past his house. And there, upon his pristine lawn, not one pile of dog poop. Ha. Take that, Detective Berg!

Finally, I turned onto Peppermint Way, my street, and saw my criminal canine lazing on my front porch as if she hadn't escaped from my fenced-in backyard. Again. As if she hadn't almost gotten me in trouble with the law. Again. Which reminded me. I'd need to keep my distance from Berg for a few days, at least until he forgot about writing any tickets.

I strode along the front walk toward the house, content to be home. It had taken me four years, but I now knew where I wanted to be. I tried not to let it bother me that as soon as I'd moved home, my parents had decided to move away. Rather, they'd finally put all their savings to use and started touring the world, the way they'd always planned. No matter what my brother said, I knew they hadn't moved to escape from me.

I didn't think.

"Or maybe it was to get away from *you*," I accused my dog.

She wagged her tail and grinned. Adorable, but such a pain. I saw dirt encrusted in her paws. And by her side, what looked like . . . a pipe? The game Clue immediately came to mind.

"What the heck are you doing with that?" I grabbed it before she could tug it away. "Aha! It's mine now." I wielded my trophy, ignored Cookie's sniff of displeasure, and let us both inside, where I quickly wiped her paws clean.

Her dirty feet and the pipe, which turned out to be made of copper, added up to a visit I dreaded—to my neighbor's house. To call Gil Cloutier unpleasant was like calling Godzilla not small. I sighed, bit back an oath, and walked out my front door, leaving Cookie inside. In front of Gil's house near some amazing roses, I saw several mounds of dirt from what I hoped had been professionally laid pipe and not Cookie's attempts to go into plumbing.

Like his CGC buddies, Gil had a well-tended lawn and border garden, though rumor had it he leaned more toward edible plants than flowers. Not that I could tell from the giant fence protecting his backyard from us scrubby ne'er-do-wells.

From what my parents had told me, when his wife had been alive, she'd taken care of the flower beds. After she'd passed, his youngest son had taken over, and the colorful blooms had been astounding. But rumor had it the poor guy had an alcohol problem and Gil had kicked him out. Gil's older sons had moved away, one to the other side of town, the other to Portland. Even so, both rarely came back to visit. Hence Gil's focus on potatoes instead of tulips.

I sighed and trudged to Gil's front door. I had barely knocked when he yanked it open, frothing at the mouth in anger before I could get a word in. His white hair stuck out in tufts, as if he'd been pulling at it. And his rheumy blue eyes made me wonder if he'd taken sick. He glanced at the pipe in my hand and lost it.

Just my luck, a garden tour walked past my house, mouths agog as a lot of four-letter words mashed with *dog* spewed from Gil's mouth. The tour rubbernecked as they continued to walk by. Yet I noticed no one pointing at my lawn with pleased awe.

Typical.

Gil wound down, breathing hard, and grabbed the copper pipe I offered. "Get lost and keep your mangy dog off my property," he snarled before slamming the door in my face.

"Sorry again," I called weakly and scurried home, where I then chastised Cookie and decided to punish her by not giving her any treats after dinner.

So when someone knocked on my door just as I'd finished washing the dishes, I prepared myself for the worst before turning the knob.

I blinked. "Dash?"

Teri's older brother, Dash—secret novel possible hero number two—glared and stormed past me into my house.

Behind him, Teri followed. "Sorry. He's on a rampage. And lucky you, you're in the way."

I groaned. "What did I do?"

In a lower voice, Teri said, "Just go with it and I'll owe you. I swear."

I knew this song and dance. But for my bestie, I'd take the blame for her mistake and suffer the Wrath of Dash.

Dashiel Hagen was exceptionally good-looking. Fortunately for my self-esteem, he was also exceptionally annoying. The fact that he had never looked at me as anything but his little sister's best friend no longer hurt. I had gotten over my crush on Dash back in high school.

Now I only wanted to use and abuse him in fiction. Like Detective Berg—secret novel possible hero number one—Dash had that something, that quality that could easily make him a quality protagonist. He had looks and charisma. I'd seen it from a distance. If only he'd keep his mouth shut.

In a deep, sexy voice, he said, "How the hell do you constantly screw up a simple order?"

Yeah. That. *Big-time* irritating. I exchanged a glance with Teri, who pleaded with me with those stupid puppy-dog eyes in that pathetic way she had. I sighed. "I'm sorry, Dash."

She sagged with relief.

"I mean, Teri steps out for two seconds and you can't take a message? You just had to go and accept two cases of hard cider from Randall Flagg?"

"Isn't Randall Flagg a Stephen King character?"

Teri nodded. "From *The Stand*. I loved that book. Oh, maybe the Macaroons should read that one next for discussion."

Dash snapped, "Focus, you two! This isn't book club with your cookie ladies."

Teri cleared her throat. "Not cookie *ladies*. We're the Macaroons. And for the record, Alan is a book club member and a man," she added helpfully.

"Scott too," I said, not wanting to count him out.

Dash glared. "I don't care."

The name Randall sounded familiar for another reason. I frowned. "Wait. Dash, did you mean Randal Craig? With one *l*? That Randal?" I paused. "Wasn't he your nemesis back in high school?"

Dash gave me a fake smile. "Why yes, Lexi. He was. Still is. So why would you think I'd want to help him in any way, shape, or form by selling some of his brother's cider in my bar? To help that family expand their brewery so they can open up a bar downtown to compete with mine?"

"I, ah, I . . ." I glanced at Teri, who shrugged. "Because I made a mistake." I should have let him rant, but as usual, I tried to interject some common sense into the argument. "But their cider is really, really good." No lie. I'd tasted it a week ago during one of our First Friday celebrations.

"Two cases, really?"

I frowned. "Isn't that a small amount?" I could buy two cases of wine from our local grocery store. "I mean, they can't cost that much, can they? If you need me to, I'll pay for them." Meaning: Teri could pay for them.

"That's not the point." He paced as he raved, and I sat back to enjoy the show. Dash annoyed me, but I couldn't deny I liked the eye candy. And he did stop now and then to pet Cookie, who loved the very air he breathed.

Teri flopped back on my couch next to me as Dash paced and lectured.

I whispered, "You owe me so much for this."

"I know."

"Randy? Really?"

Teri sighed. "He's so cute. We're going out tomorrow."

Ah. A lie for love. I could dig it—I glanced at Cookie grinning back at me—so to speak.

Once Dash had wound down, he paused to look around him.

My house isn't that big, but it's neat and it's mine, inherited from my grandma. I have a navy-blue couch, an old relative's sea chest from the 1700s as my coffee table, and an IKEA chair that holds up well under dog fur and chewy bones. The television is on the small side, but it's a smart TV. My open-concept floor plan shows off my kitchen—a galley-style set of counters and cabinets—so I have to keep my dishes washed or my house looks dirty. A dining table plopped between the kitchen and living area denotes my space for dining. In the back of the house are two bedrooms and a third room I use as my office. Oh, and there are two bathrooms as well.

Dash would know all this, as he's been here enough thanks to my friendship with Teri.

"Your walls are yellow now?"

"Roasted Sesame," Teri corrected him. "And they've been that color for six months, doofus."

He looked around, frowning. "Really?"

"Yes, really." I shook my head. "Are you done yelling at me now?"

"I suppose." He sat in Cookie's chair, and she jumped up from her spot on the floor to sit on him as if she were a lapdog. Dash didn't seem to mind her forty pounds of lean as he stroked her. "Now we need to talk about something else."

"What now?"

"Your dog." He rubbed behind her ears, and Cookie flopped against him, showing her belly. "Detective Berg said she tried to dig up the Confection Rose. And that he thinks she's behind the digging that's been going on all over town."

That loudmouth! "When did you talk to Berg?"

Dash shrugged. "I saw him when I stopped by your uncle's place to check out the accident. Some out-of-towner tapped the back of the mayor's new Charger. Man, he was *not* happy, though he played off like it was no biggie for the tourists."

Our town mayor was a decent enough guy. He had done a short stint as a professional soccer player abroad many years ago, hence the nickname "Foot" that he insisted everyone call him. He'd also been super nice to me lately. I had a feeling he wanted me to contribute to his reelection campaign.

"Cookie isn't responsible for every bad thing that happens in town, you know." I sank lower on the sofa. "Freakin' Berg."

"But he's hot, in a mean kind of way," Teri whispered.

I ignored her and the heat staining my cheeks.

"Ed Mullins' yard was hit an hour ago," Dash continued. "I saw him on my way over. He's livid."

I groaned. "Look. I admit, Cookie can get diggy."

"Is that a word?" Teri asked.

"You mean jiggy? Does she get jiggy with it?" Dash teased as he rubbed Cookie's belly.

Her tongue hung low, and she gave him doggy love while I defended her. "You know what I mean, *Dashiel*."

He scowled. "I hate when you call me that."

Teri beamed. "She knows."

He sighed.

I continued, "Cookie digs, yes. But when I passed Ed's house earlier, I didn't see any problems, and Cookie has been inside since then. I've also had her with me when half the people complaining about holes in their yards said something. I know she digs. She stole one of Gil Cloutier's copper pipes earlier."

Teri cringed. "Oh, that had to be awful."

"It was." I glared at my unrepentant beast. "But I was super polite and apologetic when I returned it."

"Nothing more you could do," Teri said.

I nodded. "He's such an angry old guy." He'd made no secret of the fact that he didn't like me living next door or that my dog barked.

She'd barked once. At Gil's lawn mower at six AM on a Saturday. One time, that very first day I'd moved in. And ever since, Gil Cloutier and I had been enemies.

Hence Gil hating my dog and my guts, and not necessarily in that order.

Chapter Three

Dash got up to help himself to a glass of iced tea, then sat back down. Cookie waited for him to get comfortable before joining him again. Dash sipped and sighed. "Nice and cold, but it needs mint."

"You're welcome," I said sourly.

"Rumor has it Cloutier has a beef with someone in town over a small fortune he's supposedly owed. He apparently lent somebody a lot of money."

Teri shook her head. "That guy is never happy."

"Is that true about the money?" How did my neighbor have so much to spend? He drove an old car and complained about how much the town was gouging him in taxes all the time. From listening to him whine, you'd have thought he didn't have two pennies, let alone nickels, to rub together.

"I said a rumor, Lexi." Dash shrugged. "Gil has always spent money at the bar like he's got plenty of it. I know he retired with a pension from the state college. He was a commercial plumber."

"I know that."

"Did you know he thought someone had robbed his house? And that he suspected it might be one of his neighbors?" Dash gave me the eye.

I scoffed. "That's stupid. If Gil thought I had stolen something, he'd have reported it. He reports me for breathing too loud."

Teri nodded. "He once reported me for turning on your back-porch light after ten. Said it woke him and I was a nuisance. That was the last time I house-sat for you, by the way."

"Thanks so much, Teri." For getting me in trouble with not only Gil but also Dash. I was getting a headache.

Dash snorted. "You think that's bad? You just live next to him. I have to serve the man daily. He never misses a six thirty special."

"You have specials at six thirty?" Teri asked. "How do I not know this?"

Heck, I hadn't known it either. But Teri really should have. She waitressed a lot for her brother.

"No, knucklehead. What I have is a crabby customer who sits at the end of my bar, same seat every day, at six thirty on the nose, and complains about everyone and everything until he finishes his drinks." Dash sighed and ignored the rude gesture Teri shot him. "But he's a regular who pays his tab on time. I guess I can't be too choosy."

"Exactly," I boomed. "Keeping customers and business is important. You should be glad I got some new cider for you to try. You might expand your menu. Besides, helping a fellow local is the right thing to do."

Dash gave me a baleful once-over, drained the tea, then set the glass on a coaster on the table. *Darn it.* Something I couldn't rag him for later. "It's way too late on a Thursday to deal with perky blondes."

"You say perky like it's a bad word." It was a loathsome word. I hated being called perky, cute, cheerful, or any of the other backhanded compliments many in my life had handed me.

My last boyfriend had called me perky and even irresistible before breaking up with me because I was "too good for him." Translation—he wanted to get back with his ditzy ex who would do whatever he wanted, whenever he wanted. Apparently, having brains and a need to get to know my date before getting horizontal with him had been a turnoff. Go figure.

"Perky isn't always bad," Dash argued with a wink. "But when it applies to a certain little friend of my sister's . . ." He shrugged.

"I am not little." I stood.

Unfortunately, he stood as well. And had to look down to meet me eyes. *So* annoying.

"Uh-huh." He smirked, bent down to pat Cookie on the head, and said over his shoulder as he left, "And quit buying from the enemy, Ms. Perky."

I glared at the closed front door. "Your brother really annoys me."

"Join the friggin' club." Teri groaned. "But Lexi, you need to see Randy. He's so cute. And nice. Dash is right about Randy having been a jerk—back in high school. He's matured since then."

"I would hope so." Randy Craig would be thirty by now, the same age as Dash. "Is his family really thinking of opening up a brewery downtown?"

"No." Teri chuckled. "That's just what he told Dash to freak him out. Randy's a financial investor who helps with his brother's brewing hobby. But I'm with you. The Craigs' cider is really tasty. If enough people like it, they could try to open up another *restaurant* downtown, I guess." She rolled her eyes. "They don't run a brewery. It's a restaurant."

"A neat distinction." For the record, Dash considers everyone who serves alcohol at their place of business to be a competitor.

Teri cleared her throat. "Well, Randy did kind of mention they might expand downtown. But that would be years down the road. For now, he's helping his brother by sampling flavors when not working his own job."

"You know a lot about this guy who just came back to town." I raised a brow at her.

She shrugged. "I can't help it. I'm in a position where I know things. It suits me." As a county clerk in the district attorney's office, Teri had access to criminal files and court cases by day. By night, she could watch the nightlife when filling in at her brother's bar, where she heard all kinds of things. Next to my uncles, she was my go-to for anything that happened in this town.

She looked nothing like her brother. Dash's dad had met and married Teri's mom after Teri's dad died. Dash's own mom had passed in childbirth. Dash had height, sandy-colored hair, and a nice tan. He rarely burned, no thanks to Dutch ancestors. Teri looked like a younger replica of her mom, a runner-up in the Ms. Guam pageant some thirty-plus years ago. They had the same short stature, same amazing cheekbones, but different temperaments, thank God. Mrs. Hagen could be *mean*.

We spent the rest of the evening swapping stories, and one that stood out in particular centered around Cat, our other best friend, and her pathetic flirting with Officer Roger Halston.

"It was so sad, Lexi." Teri tried to sound sorry for our friend, but her laughter ruined the effect. "Cat is just . . . I have to say it. Cheesy. She's full of one-liners and bad body language. Honesty, no one winks and says, 'Catch you on the flip side,' unless they're starring in an eighties action movie."

"She did not." I couldn't help it. I laughed with her.

Cat Campbell is awesome. And an Amazon. She's six two, has pale skin that burns under the sun, freckles, and bright-red hair. She likes to call herself Strawberry Tallcake, which is corny but still amuses me even though I've heard it since freshman year in high school, when she first hit a massive growth spurt. She also happens to work with me at the bookstore. She, Teri, and I have been best friends since elementary school. When I moved away, missing them was brutal. But I needed to experience life outside Confection to learn what I really wanted.

Sixty-hour work weeks editing for too many authors and not having a social life didn't suit me.

Now that I'd been back home the past year and half, it was as if my time away hadn't happened. Even Cat's dating life had stayed the same. Lame yet amusing. Kind of like mine.

"But I like Roger," Teri was saying. "He's tall, so he's just about at her eye level and doesn't seem to mind her . . . eccentricities."

"Of course he wouldn't. He likes to eat."

Cat might be bad at flirting, horrible at accessorizing, and used to living inside her head more than in the real world, but she's also addicted to cooking shows and regularly creates what she sees on TV. She's a pretty great cook, to be honest. I'd been trying for months to convince her to make a full selection of goodies to sell in the bookstore. As of now we only offered a daily treat and a coffee bar, and that was mostly to annoy Nadine, who owns Confection Coffee.

Dash might have his nemesis in Randy Craig. I had mine in Nadine Kim.

"When I say she's got eccentricities, I'm not talking about the cooking shows." Teri raised her brows at me. "It's that ghost-whisperer thing and her addiction to horror movies that throws them."

"Well, maybe not opening a date with, 'Hey, what do you think about floating severed heads and *Chopped*?' would help."

Teri laughed. "Yeah, because that sounds awful."

Even I liked watching the cooking show *Chopped* on TV. But when Cat talked about it, it came out wrong.

Teri eventually went home. I spent my last hour before bed writing down ideas for a new take on my suspense series. The romance angle had started to bore me. Maybe because lately my dating life rivaled the dryness of the Sahara. Plus, even in fiction, I found Dash and Berg way too annoying to be sexy. Instead, I started to run with the idea of a serial killer who buried bodies in flower gardens. Not just any flower gardens but rosebushes in particular.

My first victim took on the likeness of my crabby next-door neighbor. I added him bludgeoned with a pipe for fun. Morbid, yes, but by the time I'd finished taking notes and writing a death scene, I no longer felt any aggression toward Gil Cloutier, having mentally murdered the man with words.

I washed up before taking Cookie outside. After the day's many troubles, I'd decided to lock the doggy door. Until she'd proven herself, she was going to be stuck by my side for a while.

She gave me a dirty look but did her business with a quick efficiency I appreciated. My backyard might not be CGC spectacular, but my lawn is cut, the border of sloppily planted but cheerful flowers by the back fence looks sweet, and Cookie always contains her bathroom duties to the sectioned-off area in the back corner.

I waited for her to come in, conscious of Cloutier's back-porch light on. *You don't see me complaining about* your *porch light, do you, Gil?*

Cookie continued to sniff around the lawn, ignoring any need to be in a rush in favor of fresh grass and our neighborhood squirrels, who liked to leave prints in the dirt because they could, and to screw with Cookie.

My dog rarely barks, loves people, kids especially, and has a unique intelligence that at times freaks me out. I swear she understands me. And on more than a first-grade level. She's more than poodle-smart. She never strays if I ask her not to, so the leash is really to keep people like Detective Berg happy. If only I could convince Cookie to stop digging. She'd started the bad habit a month ago, and lately she'd been getting a little obsessive about it.

"Quit digging, you." I frowned at her.

She smirked at me and pretended to dig by a tree.

"No."

She lifted her paw—because *she* decided, not because I'd asked her to—and trotted toward me.

I let her lead the way inside and wondered where she'd really come from. I'd found her on my move back from Seattle. She'd been a lost puppy sitting on the shoulder of a side road on my scenic trip through Washington. She'd been so darn cute, her bright brown eyes lively, her tail wagging with joy when I'd stopped the car and gotten out to pet her.

With no collar, tags, or even a chip to identify her owners—as I'd later learned from my veterinarian—she had been adoptable, and I'd decided to keep her. Her name came honestly, from an addiction to peanut butter cookies. Her addiction, not mine.

Had I known what a compulsive troublemaker she'd turn out to be, I might have . . . We locked gazes, and her head tilted in question. Oh, who was I kidding? I'd have kept her regardless. Though I might have invested in several leashes and serious obedience school, not those stupid DVDs that promise your dog will walk on water if you pay just $29.99 for the instruction.

* * *

The morning came too soon, but I was eager to get back to the store and Cat, if only to tease her about her girlish performance that Teri had sadly witnessed.

I'd just rolled out of bed when Cookie barked. Odd. "Hey, you did that last night too, didn't you? I swear I heard you barking at me." At zero dark thirty in the morning.

She looked from me to the hallway and back at me.

"Okay, okay. You have to pee. I get it. Hold on." I got up to unlock the doggy door, made a pit stop at the bathroom, then hurried back under my covers to warm up. I swear I meant to only spend a few seconds getting toasty before letting her out, but somehow I went right back to sleep.

I blinked at my alarm clock an hour later and groaned. "I hope you didn't pee in the house," I muttered, knowing that if she had, it was my fault. "You should have whined until I woke up."

I rolled out of bed and threw on my favorite robe. It's ratty and worn but soft and comes to my knees, so I'm not scandalizing the neighbors when I go out back to keep an eye on the canine Papillon.

I looked around for the escape artist and gaped at the *slightly ajar* doggy door. No, that hadn't been a dream. I'd given my dog license to escape and dig.

Geez, she didn't miss a beat. I opened the back door and looked around but didn't see her. But I did hear a low voice next door. Crap.

"Cookie," I whispered as loudly as I could, hoping only she would hear me. She must have gone under the fence separating us from Cloutier. I was remembering how I'd fixed the last spot she'd dug when I saw a few spots of fresh dirt, where she must have low-crawled underneath.

I swore under my breath and wondered if I should get dressed before heading over or just bite the bullet and rush over in my pj's and robe. Cloutier was not a morning person. I'd never seen him before eight, and it had only just passed seven. Seven? I needed to get a move on. But someone was outside in his yard.

Maybe I could hide by the side of the house and motion for Cookie to come home without being seen. With no time to waste, I slid into flip-flops and hustled through my side gate to a break between the fence and some high shrubbery and squeezed into Gil's yard. In the shadows, I'd be practically invisible. He likely wouldn't be looking for me there.

The good news was that I spotted Cookie in the back right away.

The bad news was that I found her sitting with a copper pipe in her mouth near freshly turned earth. What ominously looked like a grave to my writer brain. Even worse, Detective Berg and two officers stood over the big old ditch, likely plowed by Cloutier. Too big for Cookie to have dug, I hoped.

I swallowed and clutched my robe tighter, praying I could back away before they turned and saw me. But my loving dog spotted me and raced to my side, still holding that pipe between her teeth.

Berg and the others turned and stared at me. "Stay right there," Detective Berg ordered. "Grab your dog, but *do not* touch the pipe."

"Huh?"

Berg reached me at the speed of light and latched on to my arm and Cookie's collar.

"What's going on?" I started to sense I'd stumbled on something bad. "Hey, I didn't mess up his yard. I swear. If you're going to arrest me for all the yard mischief that's been going around, I'm getting a lawyer."

Berg didn't sneer or look annoyed. He didn't laugh either. Instead, he looked . . . worried. "A lawyer might be a good idea."

"*What?*" I'd been bluffing about a lawyer. "Look, is Cloutier pressing charges because of the pipe? We gave it back yesterday. And I swear she hasn't been out more than a few minutes. She was in all night long until she escaped the doggy door before I could get up to take her out. We haven't done anything . . ." I trailed off as I studied some red stuff on the pipe. I glanced back at the officers standing around what now definitely looked like a shallow grave.

Complete with a dead body smack-dab in the center of it.

Chapter Four

I felt woozy, and Berg turned surprisingly solicitous. After telling the officers to cordon off the area, he walked me to my front porch and helped ease me into an Adirondack rocking chair. Then he stood back as Cookie sat by my side.

It was then I noticed the police car parked in Gil's driveway, as well as more city vehicles parking along the street.

Berg walked to his car and returned with an unopened water bottle and a plastic bag. "Drink this."

I did. Like a robot. By the time the initial shock had worn off, I'd drained the bottle and found myself staring at the grass in my front yard. Cookie had since dropped the pipe on the porch and rested her head on my knee. I stroked her, feeling slightly better.

Berg kept an eye on Cookie as he reached down with the bag and scooped up the pipe. Then he sealed it and put it on the table next to me. He remained standing, leaning against the front of my house, his gaze on me and the street.

"Good. Now we have that taken care of." Berg pulled out a small notebook and pen. "I'm going to ask you some questions about what happened. Okay?"

I shrugged, still not sure what the heck was going on. Was I dreaming?

"For the record, I'm Detective Chad Berg."

"I know who you are." I frowned. "I'm in shock, not stupid." Oh good. Animosity had cut through the fog obscuring all sense.

His lips thinned.

Well, shoot. He had been nice to me with the water bottle and all. "Sorry. This is just so weird." I waved at the many flashing lights and neighbors beginning to clog the street. Terrific. Now we had an audience. And why was Nadine pointing at me and nodding while talking to the CGC ladies, out for their daily morning walk?

Berg nodded, checked his wrist—one of the few people who wore an actual wristwatch, not some fitness band but an archaic piece with moving hands that told time—and looked back at me. "It's seven twenty-six."

"Okay." Was that code for something?

We sat in silence for a moment, waiting for what, I didn't know. But I needed to hear the familiar, and Berg was a better choice than focusing on gossipy Nadine.

I took a deep breath and let it out slowly. "That was Gil Cloutier in that . . . grave. My neighbor. He's dead?"

"Yes."

"But I just saw him yesterday. He was yelling at me and I, ah . . ." I realized then that telling a cop about an argument I'd had with the dead guy next door might not sit too well.

"And you what?" That pen of his kept moving, like a possessed implement of justice.

Heck. He'd find out soon enough. Cloutier had never liked me, and I had nothing to hide. I sure the heck hadn't killed him. Not in real life.

Dear God. I had better never let anyone read those story ideas. I felt sick at the thought.

"Are you okay?" Berg asked, watching me like a hawk.

"S-sorry." I cleared my throat. "Not used to dead bodies."

He nodded. "You were telling me about him yelling at you?"

I leaned forward to look at the copper pipe next to me. Red with Gil's blood. "Is the pipe what did it? How he died?" I leaned back in my chair, feeling a chill that had nothing to do with the crisp morning air.

"We're not sure yet." He glanced at Cookie, still resting her chin on my knee, and cracked a small smile. "She really is a troublemaker." He sighed. "We found her sitting at the foot of your neighbor's body holding that pipe in her mouth." He lifted it in the bag to take a better look at it.

"Ew." Real-life murder wasn't nearly as exciting as it sounded when writing it. I felt a little nauseous.

He cleared his throat and put the pipe down. "So, the yelling?"

"Cookie must have been at his place yesterday, because when I got home—"

"Around what time?" The Implement of Justice started moving again.

"Ah, I guess I got home a little after you'd seen me. Maybe around four thirty? I found Cookie on my front step with that pipe. Or at least, a copper pipe like it. So, I washed it off and went over to apologize. Gil started ranting at me." I paused. "A garden tour went by. They saw the whole thing." So there'd be no point hiding that I'd talked to Cloutier. "Then he slammed the door in my face, and I went home. That's the last I saw him."

"And you didn't hear anything out of the ordinary between then and this morning?"

I frowned. "Well, after I woke up this morning, Cookie barked, and it was one of her *pay attention* barks. She never barks like that unless it's something serious. And I thought maybe she barked last night."

"Could she have gotten out last night to get the pipe?"

"No. After the incident with Cloutier, I figured it would be best to keep her with me. So I locked the doggy door."

"But she got out. We found her over the body."

"She did. I unlocked it this morning, but instead of going out with her, I must have fallen back asleep." Worst dog owner ever.

Berg eyeballed my dog.

She ignored him.

He shrugged. "Okay. Continue."

"Cookie was in all night. It was only this morning at a little after six that she woke me up. Like I said, I kind of went back to sleep. When I woke up, I realized she probably had to go to the bathroom, and I hustled to let her out, not realizing she'd already left."

"About what time was that?"

"Um, I think seven fifteen, maybe? A little after that?"

Berg gave my faded terry cloth robe a look, but I couldn't read his expression. At least I was covered. I fought a blush that threatened to rise. "I was going to sneak over and motion her to come back without Gil seeing me. I heard someone talking, so I thought Gil was awake."

"That was me and the officers."

"Um, I figured that, with Gil being in the ground and all."

He nodded, wrote a bunch down on his little pad, then snapped it closed. He stared at me again, and I wasn't sure what he saw. Heck, I didn't know what I felt.

"I might need to talk to you later. But we're done. For now."

"Thanks," I mumbled and rose to my feet, relieved to find myself steady.

Cookie stood next to me, both of us watching the chaos at Gil's.

Berg asked in a quiet voice, "Would you like me to call someone for you?"

I didn't like how gentle he was being. So different from the sarcastic detective I knew and didn't much like. "I'm okay." Not really, but that sounded much better than telling him I felt numb.

He gave me another look, one I clearly identified as suspicious.

"Wait. Do you think *I* killed him?" I goggled at the thought. "*Me?*" came out in a squeal.

"Did you?"

"*No.* Did I think him a jerk? Sure. But he's been complaining about me for a year and a half. If I was going to kill him, I'd have done it a long time ago." Oh man, had that really just come out of my mouth? I felt horrified. "Not that I would. Or did. I just meant . . ."

Berg looked like he was trying to cover a smile.

My face felt hot. My knees weak. "Why would *I* kill him?" I honestly had no motive.

"That's what we need to find out."

And that's how I learned, firsthand, what it's like to be considered a suspect by the police. On the bright side, I now had some *killer* research material for my secret book, a murder mystery based on real life.

With any luck, I'd get to write it without staring through the bars of a jail cell.

* * *

Sometime later, once again safely ensconced in my own home, I sat sipping tea in my kitchen. I'd been interviewed by the Confection PD. A suspect in a murder investigation. None of this felt real.

In a daze, I called Cat for a favor. Already an hour behind, I couldn't see myself rushing to open the store on time. I wasn't exactly firing on all cylinders today.

She picked up on the second ring. "Yaz?" Morning-speak for *yes*.

"Hey, Cat. It's me, Lexi. Can you open the store for me today?"

"Why? Did you sleep in again?"

"No." I'd slept in just one time in the last year and a half, but she refused to let it die. I mean, let it *go*. Not die. Ugh.

"Then why do you need me to open for you?"

"Can't you just do it without this being a big deal?"

"Let me think." A pause. "No."

She was really holding on to that grudge. One silly comment about her last batch of muffins being on the dry side and I was forever labeled persona non grata when it came to favors.

I sighed. "I'm sorry." For the fiftieth time. "But you asked for my opinion. And I thought they were a little . . ." Not smart to remind her of my critique.

"They were just fine," she huffed, knowing full well what I was yet again apologizing for. Annoyed she might be, but she and I usually shared the same brain. "It was a new recipe I was still working out. But my latest batch of s'more cookies is perfection. Well, it will be for those who *deserve* them." *And you're not on that list* went unsaid.

"Cat, we can argue later. Look, I was just interviewed by Detective Berg about—"

"What did Cookie do now?"

"—*a dead body* next door!"

"Who died? Please tell me it's not Bugs Bunny."

A burst of laughter surprised me. I wouldn't have thought I'd be able to laugh so soon after learning about Gil. "That rabbit left last month. Cookie scared the poor thing into Gil's yard." Gil—who was now dead. "No." I cleared my throat. "Not a rabbit. It was Gil."

"I . . . Hold on. Gil died?" When I said nothing, she gasped. "Crap on a cracker. You're serious, aren't you?"

"Yes." Why would I joke about someone dying? Had I ever before? I tend to be a little snarky, but I've never thought murder all that funny.

"Wow. Just wow. Hey, are you okay?"

"I will be. I hope."

"I'll open for you, no problem. And if you can't come in, I can cover." She was sweet to offer, but one person manning the store with our summer crowds would be a problem.

"I'll be there. Thanks again." I disconnected, put my phone down on the table, and stared at the wall, not seeing anything as I tried to make sense of my morning.

Cookie returned and cocked her head, studying me.

"Did you see who did it?" I asked her.

She didn't answer, as expected—she was a dog, after all. But a bummer all the same.

I couldn't stop images of Gil Cloutier's dead body resting in that shallow grave—*right next door*—from filling my head. I imagined him in all kinds of ways. In some images he lay covered in gore, in others covered in dirt, and in my least favorite,

Gil lay clutching my laptop with cold, dead fingers. Over his body, Detective Berg smirked at me while dangling handcuffs in one hand and a prison jumpsuit in the other.

That laptop of mine would lead to nothing but trouble, or so my last boss had said when joking about my future. But he'd been right. I needed to delete that dead-Gil story from my computer. Except . . . it had been some of my best work to date.

Cookie grumbled, startling me, and nudged at her food dish on the floor.

I glanced at the time. "Shoot. Sorry." I fed her before getting a serious move on and headed to the shower. I didn't want to be too late, and I needed to talk to someone about what had happened today. But under the hot spray of water, I relaxed and used the time to calm myself, thinking instead of reacting.

Once dressed and presentable, I took Cookie with me as we speed-walked to the bookstore. Fortunately, we didn't pass anyone, as I was in no mood for small talk. I arrived twenty minutes late, entering through the back alley.

Sweet Fiction typically opened at nine. Minutes after opening, the odd coffee drinker might drop in, followed by a steady trickle of caffeine addicts. Those who walked through our doors right as we opened did so to avoid Confection Coffee's long lines. I couldn't blame them. Our coffee was only okay, but when you're hankering for caffeine, who wants to wait?

I had just closed the back door behind me when Cat yanked me into a hug that nearly crushed me. She often forgot her own strength, like now, while hugging me off the freaking floor.

"Too . . . tight . . ." I managed while wheezing.

She dropped me so fast I nearly fell. "Oh my God. You finally did it. You got rid of Gil Cloutier!"

I scowled. "No, you idiot. Of course I didn't."

She nodded toward the front of the shop. "Wonder if they got the memo."

I walked with her into the main part of the store and gaped at the many customers looking around. Several I recognized. "Why— How— I just found out he was dead two hours ago!"

"Small town." She eased me toward the front counter. "Are you going to be okay today?"

"I think so. It's a huge shock, but life goes on." At least for me. I had bills that wouldn't pay themselves.

"Well, if you're sure." Cat didn't seem convinced as she looked me over. "You know, book club is tonight." She patted Cookie on the head and scratched behind her floppy ears.

After accepting the attention that was her due, my dog walked to her doggy bed under the counter, promptly curled into a ball, and closed her eyes.

"Wait. Book club?" I loved our book club, the Macaroons. We discussed—though I should say *I* discussed and *they* argued about—everything twice a month. Plot structure. Point of view. Author voice. The weather. Ed Mullins's roses. The eye doctor's current affair. The mayor's wife's real hair color . . .

The Macaroons could be a handful, but they always motivated me to write when I left them. They were the spoon that stirred my creative juices.

I could really use something to take my mind off my deceased next-door neighbor, not to mention help me make my word count. I was already behind by two chapters, having suffered some writer's block before writing Gil into an early end.

To Cat, I said, "You know, I think we'll keep book club tonight."

"Your funeral." Cat winced. "Er, you know what I mean."

I nodded. After situating myself with a cup of coffee and yesterday's balance sheet, I did my best to avoid the many stares. I did check out several book enthusiasts while chatting about our lovely weather and my adorable dog, who every now and again poked her head out from behind the counter.

I smiled at several unfamiliar faces who meandered in, looking for good reads.

The Confection locals who'd been circling but hadn't yet landed had a different agenda.

Trust Darcy Mason, my least favorite Macaroon, to be the first to take a shot. "Poor Lexi. Were you the one who found the body?"

Why not scream louder, Darcy? I think Portland heard you, and they're three hours away.

Everyone stopped to turn and stare. The shy tourists near the thriller and humor sections gave me subtle glances while pretending to study the shelves.

In a lower voice, trying to be circumspect, I answered, "Cookie found him, along with the police. I didn't see or hear anything. It was a huge shock."

Cat suddenly appeared and herded Darcy away, engaging her in conversation about a book series she'd been talking about last week. Now that was a true friend. I'd make sure to compliment Cat's food forever from here on out.

Two couples had been hanging near Darcy. The Donahues, Nestor and Peggy, were an older white couple who liked to hang out with the mayor, loved the Confection Garden Club, and led our town in religious celebration each Sunday. They looked shocked. The Danverses, a Black couple in their early forties, owned the flower shop across the street. *Them* I liked. Pastor

Nestor and his wife, Peggy, of the many frowns and CGC affiliation? Not so much.

The flower shop owners, at least, expressed a show of sympathy I welcomed.

"Gosh, Lexi," Julie Danvers said. "That's so awful. I'm sorry you had to see that."

"No kidding," her husband, Dave, said. "Gil was a real unpleasant bast—uh, guy, but he didn't deserve to be murdered."

"Murdered?" Darcy exclaimed, apparently not as into her conversation with Cat as she'd pretended.

Behind her, Cat rolled her eyes.

"Wait. There was a murder?" one of the tourists asked.

As one, everyone turned to me. Why? I hadn't done it. I wondered if I'd soon be accused of scaring the tourists from town. Would Detective Berg try to cite me for that too?

Darcy coughed delicately, bringing the attention back to herself. "I knew you found the body, Lexi. But I hadn't realized you were a *murder suspect*."

"Now hold on—"

"Murder suspect?" Peggy Donahue put a hand to her mouth. But instead of looking dismayed or even appalled, she leaned in closer, a horrified glee in her eyes. "Did one of *them* put you up to it?" She deliberately turned to the Danverses.

"What?" I blinked. "I didn't do anything."

Before Dave or Julie could defend themselves, Pastor Nestor nodded. "Sadly, it's always about the vegetables. Gil had some beauties this year. And I heard his garden was enough to possibly take Best Overall this summer." He nodded to the Danverses. "For a prize worth fifteen thousand dollars, well, it's enough to tempt anyone to sin."

Note: Yes, a pastor had just accused two members of his congregation of being tied to a murder. In Confection, there is no safety, even in church, when it comes to gardening.

Dave drew himself to his full height. "That's a dirty lie. Our tomatoes and peppers are always the best in this town. Gil was never our competition. No one is."

Trust the CGC mafia to make vegetables more important than a murder. Though come to think of it, people did get pretty passionate about the big Central Oregon Gardener's Purse each summer, which offered a whopper of a monetary prize for growing things. But to kill over veggies? No way.

One of the tourists who'd been pretending not to overhear left the thriller stacks and stared at me. "You killed him for his tomatoes?"

"More like his potatoes," Darcy chimed in. Again, without being asked. "I heard they were going to take the gold this year."

The tourist shook her head. Everyone else watched me with wide eyes, but no one left the shop. Cat just stared at everyone, as puzzled as I was about how to handle this. Julie started arguing with Peggy, and Dave got into a heated discussion about magical mulch with Pastor Nestor.

The shop felt overcrowded.

Suddenly, Cat shouted, "Excuse me."

The room grew silent. Everyone waited.

"We love having you here, and feel free to talk about murder and greens. But while you're doing that, how about you buy some books or coffee and cookies and support a local business?" She shot me a wry look. "I mean, some of us might need bail money soon. Help a girl out, would you?"

If looks could kill, my best friend would be . . . not dead. Gil was dead. But she'd be in for a world of hurt, that was for sure.

She winked at me and went to the coffee counter for barista duty. Muttering under my breath about loudmouthed Darcy and stupid rumors, I continued to check out customers as more filtered through the door. And more, and more.

Huh. Who knew death would be so good for business?

Chapter Five

"I can't believe how fast news flies in this town," I said at noon, wincing at my aching feet. We'd hit a sudden lull, and I cherished the quiet. Once the initial furor had died down after Darcy's accusations, we'd had steady business, selling a ton of books. No more obvious conversations about Gil, thank goodness, though I couldn't help noticing the constant speculation thrown my way.

Cat nodded. "No kidding. Gil died early in the morning, and Darcy had already heard all about it before showing up here. It'd be one thing if her husband was a cop, but he's a banker. Unless the police called the bank after finding Gil's body, which would just be odd." Cat's eyes lit up. "Oooh, maybe Darcy did it and put all that shine on you to set you up for her crime."

"Darcy? Seriously?" Thoughts of Darcy doing more than murdering a book review boggled the mind. She could be unthinking and kind of conceited, but killing someone? I didn't think she was that awful a person. Plus, it would take more energy than she'd care to expend to off my neighbor.

But one thing did strike me with fear. "Honestly, though, Cat. A murder in Confection? I still leave my door unlocked."

"I wouldn't say that too loudly around here." Cat glanced around. "We've clearly got a murderer on the loose."

I shivered, because she was right. Someone in this town had killed Gil Cloutier. He hadn't died of a chronic medical condition or freak heart attack. He'd been *murdered*. Pummeled, judging by the blood on that pipe. Bashed in the head, maybe. Technically, he could have been beaten hard enough to break the skin anywhere. I hadn't seen more than a glimpse of him in the ground.

Oh boy. I needed to stop thinking about dead bodies. "Well, I'm famished and need a break. Cookie needs a walk, so I'm going to order something from the café. Want anything?"

"A BLT combo." Cat shoved a five-dollar bill at me. "No drink. I'm on water."

Off her soda habit? "How many days has it been?" Cat loved Coca-Cola. The smell, the bubbles, the color. A four-can-a-day addict. Only her obsession with basketball made up for her consumption of so much daily caffeine. She'd played in college and a year in the WNBA before injuring a knee. Now she exercised like a maniac. At the gym, around town, and at her home. Her soda addiction and cookie baking kind of ruined her chances of being the next Ms. Universe. But only barely.

"You never did tell me what Roger Halston's favorite NBA team is."

She blushed. "Officer Halston?" She gave a poor imitation of a not-nervous laugh. "Why would I care about who he likes this season?"

"Seriously? I heard you tried to flirt with him, and it was sad."

"Shut up." Cat turned away to organize books that didn't need organizing. Then she stopped and stared at me. "Wait. How sad? Who told you that?" She muttered, "Had to be Teri."

"I'm kidding." Totally wasn't. "So a BLT, hold the Coke. Got it. I'm taking the beast."

I fiddled with getting a harness on Cookie. She hated the pink thing, but I thought she looked good in it. She looked secured. Legal-like. I clipped the leash to it, watched while Cookie yanked on it until she had a good grip in her mouth, then pretended I wasn't letting the dog walk *me* as we headed down the street to the crosswalk, where we'd cross and head back toward the café.

Eats n' Treats, Confection's most popular diner, sat almost directly across from Sweet Fiction, but during the summer the cops really enforced their no-jaywalking mandate, stressing us local shopworkers to set the example. Considering I was in enough hot water thanks to Gil being dead, I planned to do nothing to invite negative attention.

After walking Cookie to the end of the street near a small dog-friendly grass area, away from rosebushes and flowers, I waited for her to make a pit stop before heading back toward the diner. My stomach was grumbling.

Eats n' Treats serves downtown Confection with down-home cooking. It isn't about counting calories or making anything light; the owner leaves that to the organic smoothie shop a block away. No, Eats n' Treats is all about using food to fill up and feel good. The owner is also a huge proponent of engaging local farms and products to stock her shelves. That should make her prices sky-high, but she's married to a farmer, whose family owns several of the farms that produce her raw ingredients.

I'm not one to complain. A five-dollar BLT with fries is a steal. And so is the six-dollar mini meat loaf with a generous side of mashed potatoes and gravy. Not exactly a summer meal, but it can only be described as Delicious with a capital D.

Cookie and I passed a constant stream of tourists taking pictures of everything. Unfortunately, we also crossed paths with Nadine Kim—cue evil music. Nadine owns Confection Coffee and has made it her life's mission to one-up me at every opportunity. I guess our enmity harked back to high school, where I'd apparently done something to someone that offended her. I didn't care much why she disliked me, though. Sparring with her reminded me of my old job, where I'd often argued with other literary professionals who liked thinking they were right. When they clearly weren't. Being in a small town had worn away my edges. Nadine kept them from disappearing completely.

"Well, well, if it isn't our hometown murderess. A pipe, Lexi? That's so tacky."

"Listening to gossip isn't?" I huffed. "Say, is that a new hairstyle? I hadn't realized dirty and stringy was in. Kind of nasty-chic?"

She scowled, but I swore her lips quirked before she tried to hide it. Nadine seemed to like our animosity too.

"Nasty-chic?" She snorted. "Please." She ran a hand through her silky black hair. Dirty and stringy in no way described her perfect looks. Her poker-straight hair, flawless skin, and dark eyes had ensnared half the men in this town. Meh. Who wouldn't hate her just on principle?

I tried to pass, but she moved with me.

I glared. Cookie sat and smiled at Nadine. The dorky dog seemed to like her, and no matter how much I complained about the woman in my spare time, Cookie refused to listen.

"Aw, who's so pretty today? You are, Cookie." She reached in her pocket and pulled out a small biscuit. It wasn't as odd as it sounds. A lot of people in this town have dogs, and I'd seen

Nadine give doggy treats to other pups here and there. "Look what I made just for you."

Cookie waited until Nadine held out her palm before gently taking the treat and munching without apology.

"She's adorable." Nadine gave me a disdainful once-over. "Like does not always attract like."

"Quit trying to poison my dog."

"Quit killing our lovely locals."

"I'm sorry. Are you calling Gil Cloutier lovely?"

She frowned. "Well, you have a point. Still, it speaks to your lack of intelligence that you'd shoot the guy right next door."

"Wait. Shoot him?"

"Ta. Have to go. I have a *real* job to get back to. You know, the store I *own*. But you wouldn't know about that, still working for Mommy and Daddy." She tittered and deftly maneuvered around me and the line of people crowding the sidewalk, heading back to her shop.

Okay, that last zinger burned. Cookie and I headed toward the diner's front order window. After I placed my order, I followed the arrow to the pickup window in the back, down the side walkway between buildings. Entering the Eats n' Treats backyard, where picnic tables and smaller seating areas were already crowded with hungry people, I noticed a few hopeful canines, eager to rescue any food that might happen to fall to the ground.

The air smelled divine, a cross between floral sweetness and freshly baked bread, which sounds gross but was anything but. Stone tiles broke up the grassy yard, creating a crosshatch of gray and green. The clumps of flowers overflowing their containers and bordering the fence made the yard feel like a fairy haven.

Geesh. I'd have to up my game at Sweet Fiction, which boasted two modest planters of colorful peonies, something green that trailed down the pots, and some white-and-purple petunias thrown in for fun. Maybe I could bribe one of the less annoying CGC members to create something eye-catching for me. It would have to be better than whatever sat outside Confection Coffee, for sure.

I sat under a shaded table for two, annoyed I'd let Nadine irk me.

What the heck did she know? I'd moved out of the house at eighteen, attended college on a partial scholarship—thank you very much—then moved to Seattle and worked sixty-hour-plus weeks, often bringing work home, for longer than I cared to think about. I'd moved up from an intern to a major editor for one of our fiction lines before realizing I would never get anywhere but to the ER for a growing ulcer if I didn't leave the company.

Assistant editors came and went, and the rest of us underpaid, underappreciated schlubs with fancy titles continued to take up the slack before we found replacements, which often took months. Frankly, I'd tired of working so hard that I had no life. I missed my friends, my family. Time off.

Now I worked for a little over minimum wage, yes. But I had a house that was paid for, lived in a low-cost town where I knew most everyone, and had my best friends close by. So what that I didn't get many dates? So what that the police department seemed to loathe me and my dog? So what that my neighbor had been killed and everyone seemed to think I did it? (Which was absolutely ridiculous. I don't look anything like a killer. I'm sunny and perky, for goodness' sake.)

And why would they think I'd kill Gil, anyway? I scowled at the floral patterns shimmering on the tiled ground, bending off into the grass. The sunlight created its own illuminated garden, striking off a nearby suncatcher dangling from a pole in one of the flower containers.

"Shot?" I murmured, not understanding how Nadine might think that. Was she spreading rumors? Or had she heard something I hadn't? Had the pipe killed Gil or hadn't it?

I noticed two police officers taking a seat in the back, waiting for their food. And one of them wasn't a Nadine Kim sympathizer.

"Hey, Roger." I waved.

Officer Roger Halston saw me, paused, then left his sour partner to join me at my table. "Hey, Lexi," he said as he gave Cookie a pat.

I had a connection to a certain someone he wanted, so I knew he'd be ultra nice to me. Cat might be terrible at flirting and often hard to read. But Roger Halston wasn't. And he liked my best friend. A lot.

"Look, let's get this out of the way." I lowered my voice and leaned closer. "I didn't murder Gil. I had no idea he was dead until Cookie escaped." At the sound of her name, she perked up and looked at me.

When I failed to drop anything edible to the ground, she huffed and laid down.

Roger flushed. "I can't talk about an ongoing investigation."

"I know that. I would never ask you to do that. But Nadine accused me of shooting Gil, and I'm totally confused."

"What? He wasn't shot." Roger opened his mouth to say something else, then shut up. Fast.

"I didn't think so." *Nadine stirring up trouble again. Why am I surprised?* "Say, have you tried Cat's latest batch of cookies?"

He relaxed. "Oh, ah, no. I don't think so." He tried to act casual. "What flavor are they?"

"Hold on. You didn't get to try her 'S'more Books, Please' cookies? Now *that* is a crime. Next time you swing by, tell her I said you get a free cookie. And if there aren't any there, she'll need to bake you some special. We do love our Confection law enforcement."

"Yo, Halston. Order's up." His partner shot me the evil eye.

I smiled back at him with the sugar-sweet fake smile I'd perfected at age five. *But no cookies for the Nadine groupie. We don't like him. Do we, Cookie?* I looked from her to him and narrowed my eyes.

She gave a low growl. Finally back on my side.

"I have to go. Tell Cat I said hi." Roger smiled. Such a nice guy. Cat could do—and had done—so much worse.

"I will."

He left with his partner, who glared at me as if trying to imitate Detective Berg.

I ignored him in favor of my phone. Then the Eats n' Treats owner—not the teenager who'd been serving everyone else—called out my order, and I realized my mistake. I should have phoned the order in and had Cat come pick it up.

I forced myself to look chipper as I left my seat to retrieve my food at the pickup window.

"Hey, honey, how are you?" Mel was friends with my parents, so I should be glad she sounded so supportive. Except I knew she'd be ratting me out to my folks if I didn't handle this right. If they hadn't already heard. Oh man, how had I not taken care of this earlier?

I needed to manage this, stat!

"I'm good. I mean, I'm shocked by what happened to Gil. Not sure if you heard . . ."

"Oh, I did." She reached out and grabbed my hand, squeezing in sympathy. "Detective Berg was seen questioning you."

"Let me guess. Nadine told you."

"Actually, it was Bonnie Bright. We're all just so horrified. Imagine someone getting killed in Confection."

I handed her my credit card, hoping to speed up the conversation. "I know. That's what's so terrible about it. But I didn't do it."

"Oh, hon, I know that. Anyone who knows you knows you'd never hurt anyone."

Well, I wouldn't have a problem launching a verbal smackdown on Nadine. Or Detective Berg. Maybe Dash. Ed Mullins. Peggy Donahue, or Darcy and—

"Besides, Gil wasn't a small man. I can't imagine you getting one over on him at your size."

I frowned.

"When he was angry, which was just about all the time, he could fly off the handle."

I didn't know what to say to that, but then I noticed several nearby patrons tuned in to our conversation. Just what I didn't need.

I tugged the bag of food from Mel with a smile. "The food smells delicious, Mel. Thanks." After my transaction went through, I whistled for Cookie. She followed me down the sidewalk back out onto Main Street, her leash dragging behind her.

I noted Berg coming toward us and hurried to pick up the leash. "Whew. I can't believe I dropped that," I said in a loud voice, for fear he'd try to ticket me for not holding on to it.

I moved to the side so he could enter the diner. Unfortunately, he stopped with me.

"How are you doing, Ms. Jones?"

Gosh. Had it only been earlier today that Gil had been found dead? It felt like a lifetime ago.

"I'm okay. Hungry." I shifted the bag, and the smell of all that mouthwatering goodness made me even hungrier.

His stomach rumbled, and I swear he flushed. "Ah, yeah. I'm on my lunch break." He stared down at Cookie, who smiled up at him. My dog seems to smile at a lot of people she should be biting. "Good to see you on a leash for once."

She cocked her head, no longer so happy.

Before he could accuse me of anything else, I edged around him. "Well, I'd better get back to work."

He nodded, his light-gray eyes still so striking in that face that always seemed on the verge of a frown. "If you can think of anything else that might have happened between last night and this morning, let me know."

"I will."

He nodded and turned into Eats n' Treats.

I let out a relieved breath, always feeling guilty under his penetrating stare, and walked back toward the crosswalk. At the end of Main Street, I noticed a woman's silver-streaked ponytail waving through the back of a ball cap as she snapped picture after picture of the Confection Rose.

Mandy Coatney, professional photographer and member of the CGC. She seemed to be everywhere all the time with her camera around her neck. I didn't mind her, though. Her husband, Alan, was a proud Macaroon. He read a lot of books and often picked up nonfiction for his wife, who seemed partial to references on birds and trees.

Cookie and I continued back to the shop, where I found Cat ringing up another customer. Inside, I lifted the bag to show her I'd successfully hunted down our lunch.

She nodded to the back. "Go ahead. I'm still kind of full from the cookies I had earlier." She gave me a look. "They were scrumptious. And *moist.*"

Moist was not my favorite word, and she knew that. I'd edited my fair share of romantic fiction, and books with "moist" descriptions usually ended up earning reader razzie awards. Not good. At Cat's scowl, I quickly said, "Your cookies are amazing. In fact, I was just bragging about your S'more Books, Please cookies at the café."

Her scowl faded, replaced by a satisfied smile. "Go eat your lunch. I got this."

"Thanks." I took a quick break to eat, moaning at the sheer pleasure of enjoying Mel's meat loaf and potatoes. The secret was in the gravy, of course.

And speaking of secrets . . . My phone buzzed, showing my mother's name and number.

Again.

I'd missed her earlier call, apparently.

I groaned. I was not looking forward to this conversation. And I still had to get through book club later tonight. And the Macaroons were not known for their kindness when it came to sharing the ugly truth. They could be harsh with their critiques.

Then again, so could my mother. Swallowing another groan, I dialed and did my best to convince her and Dad not to leave their year of living dangerously in an RV.

Chapter Six

The day passed more swiftly than I'd thought it might. After convincing my mother Gil's death had been a tragedy and that despite what she'd heard, I was *not* a suspect, we talked about their trip through a small mining town in Arizona.

My father had helped plan their yearlong RV adventure, and they journeyed from friend to friend when not checking off popular tourist attractions across the country.

Though I missed them, I loved the autonomy of being my own person in Confection, not just Lydia and Hershel Jones's daughter.

My folks owned the bookshop and had no plans to come back and take over again, confident it was in good hands. They were actually hoping I'd buy it from them. I didn't know if I wanted to be a business owner any more than I wanted to be a full-time published author, but I needed time to figure out my future. Managing the shop gave me the freedom to just be. Now I had time to write and dream about having a life.

Even Cookie loved it here.

If only the murder hadn't happened . . .

Oddly, though, Gil's death hadn't soured me on our town. And it hadn't soured the Macaroons either, by the sounds of things.

I watched them enter the bookstore one by one, the small group vocal about Gil's death, a topic of conversation I knew we couldn't avoid.

Book club started at six fifteen, and we sat in a small circle in a back room the bookstore set aside for readings and special events. Since the book club currently totaled nine members, we didn't take up too much space. Cat and Teri had already let me know they wouldn't be able to make it tonight. We typically met on Mondays, but we'd previously rescheduled the last meeting for tonight—Friday.

BFFs Stefanie Connett and Alison Wills normally arrived together. Stefanie hailed from Texas, a crotchety Black woman who maintained a southern twang and refused to be wrong about anything. After sixty-seven years of living, forty of it spent teaching, she pretty much knew it all. As she liked to say, "I know everything. Just ask me."

Her shy friend, Alison, couldn't have been more different. A white woman from Wisconsin with wispy strawberry-blonde hair and an addiction to politics, she spent much of her days indoors, nursing her many allergies. Five years younger than Stefanie, she was a mystery buff and retired librarian who ran A Sweet Retreat B&B, our most popular bed-and-breakfast.

Behind them, Darcy arrived, not a hair out of place. The stay-at-home mother of two had a lovely manicure she showed off as she let Alan lead her by the hand to her seat. Blonde and a few years my senior, she accepted being beautiful and expected all of us to acquiesce to her. She could be sweet too, not totally a monster, but her oblivious attitude toward anything that didn't revolve around her could be tough to handle.

She'd also, more than once, tried to take over the running of the book club after my mother had turned it over to me. So maybe I had some bias against her. I didn't care how pretty or rich Darcy might be; Sweet Fiction and the Macaroons fell under *my* territory.

No matter how much Darcy and Stefanie insisted I was doing it wrong.

Stefanie snorted at Darcy. "Way to tell everyone about the murder, Darcy. And you don't have even half your facts straight! What use is that husband of yours being best friends with the mayor if you get crap wrong?"

Bingo. Darcy's info came from her hubby.

Darcy blushed. "I don't know what you're talking about."

Stefanie and Alison shared a look. Stefanie harrumphed, then sat with Alison across from Darcy.

Alan sat next to her, an easygoing retired electrician addicted to mysteries and, surprisingly, romances. Tall and lean, he wore a constant tan from his time outdoors, though he shared little gardening interest with his wife, preferring to spend his biweekly Mondays—and this current Friday—with us, talking books.

Which left just one more attendee, since I doubted Scott Cloutier would be attending. Gil's oldest son would no doubt be grieving and dealing with his dad's *passing*—which sounded so much softer than murder.

"I don't suspect Scott will be coming," Alan said, reading my mind.

"No." Alison sighed. "Poor guy. That's got to be tough. I heard he and Gil were mending fences too."

"Oh?" Darcy leaned forward. "I hadn't realized Gil got along with any of his sons."

That was news to me too. Abe, the youngest, had an alcohol problem that made him less than stable and argumentative at best. Matt lived in Portland, despite starting a successful smoothie place downtown. I hadn't seen him in Confection since I'd been back, nearly a year and a half now. And Scott and Gil had argued several times in public, though the last notable dispute I'd witnessed at the Ripe Raisin had been between Gil and Abe.

Stefanie answered, "Saw it myself. Gil and Scott were all friendly-like having lunch together last week at Eat n' Treats."

"I heard they were arguing," countered Alan.

"Nah, that was two weeks ago." Stefanie shook her head. "Last week they shared a big old pot pie."

Alan smiled. "I love Mel's pot pies. Chicken's my favorite."

Alison nodded. "Me too. Though the beef one isn't bad."

Darcy frowned. "Just because Scott and Gil were sharing lunch doesn't mean they were getting along."

"Um, well, with Gil, that's kind of what that means," Alan said, sounding apologetic. "He'd never share a meal with someone he didn't like. Or a drink, come to think of it."

Stefanie nodded. "He and Abe fought something fierce last month in the Ripe Raisin."

"I saw that too," I said, having at the time wondered why a recovering alcoholic would meet his dad in a bar, of all places.

Kay Mitchell walked through the door and scowled at the lot of us. "Really? I'm a few minutes late and you're gossiping without me? Where's the loyalty?"

And now we were complete.

A master of trivia and lover of pulp fiction, Kay never missed a meeting. With four kids and a home-based business, she claimed she needed our meetings to stay sane. I loved her. In her late thirties, funny, and fun, she always made book club more than interesting. And she loved to debate. She could talk anything to death. She claimed it came from trying to live an independent life under the long shadow of an extremely traditional, old-school Korean mother.

I'd met Eun Jung Gim, Kay's mom. She wasn't lying.

"Maybe if you showed up on time once in a blue moon, you wouldn't miss so much," Stefanie drawled.

Before Kay could defend her busy self, I cut in. "More importantly, everyone, for the record, I did not kill Gil Cloutier."

Silence.

Alan frowned. "Are people seriously suggesting you did?"

Darcy nodded right away.

I bit back a growl.

Stefanie shrugged at me as if to apologize. "A lot of people saw the ruckus outside Gil's house this morning, and that coming on top of him screaming at you the day before. You know how information flies in this town."

Alison chimed in. "Actually, someone from the CGC saw it. Peggy, I think. And she told a lot of other people, who eventually told me."

Alan nodded. "Mandy told me at lunch, but I didn't feel the need to gossip." He shot Darcy a censuring look.

Surprising. Alan was usually easygoing about everything.

Darcy didn't even have the grace to flush. "Hey, say what you want. Word is Lexi had something to do with it." She stared at me. "Your dog had the murder weapon in her mouth."

Fortunately, Cookie had a doggy date with a goldendoodle while I had book club and missed the slight on her canine character.

"*Alleged* murder weapon," Stefanie corrected. "Until the official autopsy's been done, you can't say for sure the pipe did it."

Alan nodded. "She's right."

Kay took a seat next to him. "Can someone fill me in? I've been doing summer projects with the kids and making soap all day. My brain is fried, and I missed all the good stuff."

I contained a wince at "good stuff" and excused myself to double-check the bookshop one more time. After reassuring myself that all the doors had been locked and the CLOSED sign turned over, I went into the back and sat to relieve my aching feet.

". . . because my cousin was in the tour group when they heard Gil yelling at her, that's why. Lexi has motive," Darcy was saying.

I rolled my eyes. "Oh, come on. Gil hated everyone equally. Why would I suddenly kill him when he's been yelling at me ever since I moved back here? I barely see him as it is. He's like a gnome, barely visible past his back fence and secretive as heck."

"You mean *was*." Darcy crossed her arms over her chest.

"Huh?"

"*Was* like a gnome." Alison swallowed. "He's dead now."

We all sat in silence for a moment, and I liked to think it was out of respect for Gil, much as he'd never earned it.

I glanced at Alan, and a sudden thought struck me. Someone in our town had murdered Gil. Someone strong enough to take him down. Alan had a tall, muscular build, especially for a guy nearing seventy. I'd seen him moving a wheelbarrow around, climbing up and down ladders, and doing electrical work around town. Alan could easily have overtaken Gil. But he was so nice to everyone. It felt terrible to even consider him a suspect. Though he did like crime novels.

And romance. Geez. How could I blame a guy for his reading tastes?

He turned innocent eyes on me.

Nope. Squashing that ridiculous theory right off. "Okay. There's been enough talk about murder today. Why don't we get back to our last book? We never did get to finish talking about *The Bear and the Nightingale*." Kay's chosen book, a title that had come out a few years ago.

"I can't stop thinking about it, and I already read book two, *The Girl in the Tower*. It's just as amazing," Kay said. "Katherine Arden's prose is lyrical. The use of Russian folklore and a Russian medieval setting was so different from the European folktales I usually read about."

"It was okay, I guess," Stefanie grumbled. "But none of it felt real." The woman had no magic in her soul, just sass and grit.

Alison frowned. "It was a fantasy. It wasn't supposed to be real."

"It felt real enough to me." Alan grinned. "Like that *domovoi*, the Russian house spirit that cleans up at night. After I read that, I tried leaving out a bowl of milk overnight. But the next morning the house was still messy, though our cat seemed pretty happy, sitting licking his chops next to an empty bowl."

I laughed with the others. I'd enjoyed the book immensely, always a fan of fairy tales and mythology. The author had done a wonderful job with the imagery and strong female characters. I'd planned to read the next book in the trilogy but realized if I kept reading and not writing, I'd never finish the first draft of my secret novel.

And as a former editor, I knew how important deadlines were.

Dead. Lines.

Geez Louise, could I stop thinking about death today?

We managed another twenty or so minutes of book discussion before Darcy had had enough. "Look, I enjoyed this book as much as anyone here—well, with the exception of Stefanie." To which Stefanie grunted. "But can't we return to Gil and who might have murdered him? I mean, if Lexi didn't do it—"

"I didn't."

"Then someone else did. And since Scott's not here, and Stefanie's no doubt going to choose a mystery to read before our next meeting, don't you think a real live murder might give us some insights?"

"Into what?" I asked Darcy. "How gruesome our club has become?"

"Well, yes," Stefanie answered with a grin. "Oh, relax, Lexi. Gil was a hard man to like. Yeah, I'm sorry he's dead. No one should have to go out like he did. But think. We read this stuff all the time. I bet we could figure out who did it."

Alison and Kay perked up. Alan nodded, and Darcy just stared at me, daring me to deny what the group obviously wanted.

"Fine. But we have to keep this quiet," I warned. "Detective Berg already hates me."

"You mean he suspects you," Darcy corrected.

"Same difference. The thing is, I don't want to get on the police's radar any more than I already am."

"That's probably a good point," Alison said.

Speculation turned rampant, but no one mentioned anything I hadn't already known or thought about.

Gil's sons had to be on the list. Abe and Scott had argued with him, and Matt refused to come back to see his father. Three sons, three possible suspects.

Then talk turned to the CGC and the Central Oregon Gardener's Purse. Their lofty monetary prize might turn anyone to murder. Rumor had it this year they'd gotten a few new investors, and the overall purse totaled $25,000, with the grand prize winner earning $15,000. Everyone in the competition was a suspect for sure.

I put my money on Ed Mullins, just because he treated me and my dog so abominably.

The group thought I was insane for adding his name to our list, but so what? I thought it equally ridiculous to put me and Gil's other neighbor, a hardworking single mom, on the list.

"Come on, Stefanie. She has no time to kill anyone, not with two teenagers and working twenty-four/seven." The woman under suspicion cleaned houses under the table while also working at one of the realty offices in town.

"If she has kids, she's known murderous thoughts," Kay muttered. When we all looked at her, she coughed and gave us a big smile. "I mean, anyone can do anything when given the right motivation. Heck, I bet Stefanie could have done it."

"You're danged right." Stefanie puffed up.

I rolled my eyes. The capacity to commit murder was something to be proud of?

Alison chuckled. "My best friend is fierce, all right."

Stefanie glared at her. "What? I could kill a person."

"No doubt," I said before Stefanie offered to show us the arsenal of mace, a penknife, and a whistle that she carried in her purse. I'd heard she'd once nailed our favorite postman in the face with her bag, mistaking him for an escaped convict from the Oregon State Penitentiary in Salem.

Note, Salem is nearly three hours away and the convict had been found within a day, though Stefanie had smacked the mailman two days later, still unsure about the legitimacy of the capture. Now she had to get her mail through a post office box instead of at her house.

Darcy opened her mouth to respond when Alison's phone buzzed, signaling the end to our meeting.

I smiled at her, and she smiled back. "Well, we'll have to table that discussion until Monday, when we meet again at our regular time." I turned to Stefanie. "And your book recommendation for next week? Everyone should read the first three chapters of it, but no more," I warned. All avid readers, our club could consume a book in a day. Heck, in hours, if we really wanted to. "No spoilers," I reminded them all, my gaze on Alan, who flushed.

"I said I wouldn't do it again."

Stefanie gave him a hard look before announcing an Agatha Christie novel.

"Oh, a classic." Kay clapped.

Stefanie grinned. "Yes. It's been a while since I indulged in the Queen of Crime. But I haven't read this one, surprisingly." She paused.

"Well?" I asked, ready to call it a night. I already knew what she'd selected because I'd ordered the books three weeks ago for the group.

"*The Murder of Roger Ackroyd.*"

"I haven't read that one either." Darcy nodded. "Good choice."

Stefanie looked around, as if daring any of us to have read the book before. When everyone seemed to appreciate her selection, she relaxed. "Good. It's been on my TBR list for a while."

Any book lovers worth their salt had an extensive TBR—to be read—list of books just waiting to be consumed. Which made working at a bookstore such a treat. I had access to books all over the place, often getting titles in before they were officially released.

I grabbed the stack of copies of *The Murder of Roger Ackroyd* sitting on a nearby shelf and started handing them out. As usual, I would charge everyone's accounts for the books, with receipts handed out at the next meeting along with our typical coffee, tea, and treats.

"Sorry about the lack of food tonight, guys." I sighed. "It's been a long day." Frankly, I'd been prepared for some complaints about the absence of snacks.

"Hey, from the sound of it, your day was worse than mine." Kay took her book and patted me on the shoulder. "Buck up, buckaroo. Tomorrow will be better."

Stefanie snorted. "So long as they don't find your other neighbor dead in a grave with Cookie holding a rake in her mouth."

"Stefanie." Alison clapped a hand over her mouth, doing her best not to laugh.

"Or a bloodied T-bone, more like." Stefanie glared at me. "Your dog is a menace. She'd better steer clear of me the next time you bring her. You've been warned."

"Yes, ma'am." I gave her a salute.

She patted her purse. "I'm packin', and don't you forget it."

Alan held up his hands in surrender. "None of us ever forget how lethal you are with that purse." Oh right. He'd once been beaned in the head when Stefanie thought he was accosting his wife, not having recognized him at the time.

"That's right." She sniffed, winked at me, then left with Alison.

Darcy picked up her copy. "I didn't really think you killed Gil," she admitted. "But you have to admit, it's been the most exciting thing to happen in this town for a while."

"Glad *you* enjoyed it." Because being thought of as a murderer scared the heck out of me. Innocent people went to jail all the time. And I had a snarky canine to feed!

Speaking of which, I needed to get a move on. Sherman, the happy goldendoodle, would be content to play with Cookie forever, but his owner had a standing Friday night engagement I didn't want to disrupt.

Me? I'd spend my Friday night in front of a computer while my dog watched *Pit Bull Rescue* on TV. But hey, my life could be worse. I wasn't sure how yet, but I didn't want to invite speculation. Especially with the way my luck had been running.

Chapter Seven

Since I had the weekend off, I spent Saturday morning talking Teri out of coming over to comfort me. Note to self: After being accused of murder, let family and friends know you're coping just fine. Because I hadn't, I had *more* convincing to do. So, after answering my uncles' frantic texts about my near arrest with a promised visit, I made plans to meet Teri and Cat at the Ripe Raisin in the evening.

I then hopped on my chores. I finished a load of laundry, vacuumed, dusted, and mowed my lawn, patching up the holes in the ground under the fence where Cookie had dug. By noon, Cookie demanded a walk, tired of entertaining herself outside. She scooped up Mr. Leggy, her gnawed, massacred, matted stuffed octopus. As we went on our merry way, I noticed a few front yards with loose dirt in odd places. As if someone—I refused to look at Cookie—had been digging.

Ed Mullins glared at me as I neared his home. He stood outside watering his flowers, dressed in tan slacks and a blue polo. The civilian version of the Confection PD. And like Detective Berg, he looked distinctly unimpressed with Cookie and me. Although *suspicious* would be a more accurate term.

"Good afternoon," I said, doing my best to sound überpleasant.

His eyes narrowed, and I don't think he blinked until we passed his house.

I continued down Court Street, but instead of walking toward town, I took a shortcut through one of the many trails in Central Park.

We call them honey trails, though I'm not sure why, as we don't have apiaries in the park, and I've never seen any beehives when out and about. The trails are cleared footpaths through fourteen acres of woodland that creep from Central Garden and spread south.

It was a pleasant way to spend the sunny afternoon, and I enjoyed our jaunt through the trees, lingering in the shadows while my dog sniffed and watered patches of grass. I let her do her thing while I enjoyed the coolness under leafy branches.

I waved at several passersby, ignoring a few narrowed stares that told me the rumor mill had yet to slow down. Cookie and I kept going, carefully skirting Central Garden, which would be full of those admiring the Confection Rose and the carefully landscaped flowers today.

The Sweet Summer Festival was up and running. I could hear a small brass quartet playing a chipper tune. Tents full of crafters, bakers, and shops would line either side of the road on closed Main Street, hawking their wares for eager shoppers.

The weather had more than cooperated, offering a cool breeze and clear sky, only the occasional cloud monitoring from above. Off in the distance, mountains stood sentry over the town, their snowcapped tips reminding us the weather would cool down in the evening and to layer for warmth.

I looked forward to our festival season, using Sweet Fiction's part-time help when I needed a break. And after all that had happened yesterday, I couldn't have been happier that my cousin and his college friend had already been scheduled to work today.

I managed to bribe Cookie with a treat to get a move on, and we walked over the Soda Creek bridge onto the other side of Central Park. The rich side of town. After cutting through to Lemon Loop, where many of the wealthy lived, I walked Cookie to Uncle Jimmy's house. I doubted he'd be at the hardware store today. I just hoped I'd caught him before he and Uncle Elvis hit the festival.

I knocked on the door of a lovely moss-green Victorian home, accented with purple gingerbread shingles and aqua-blue molding. The wooden railing and porch had been recently sanded and stained, no doubt by Uncle Elvis, who was the top home restoration guy in town. He specialized in woodwork, and I loved seeing his skill displayed all around Confection.

Unlike many who lived on Lemon Loop, my uncles had bought a long time ago and fixed up the house. They didn't like to think of themselves as "Confection royalty" the way their neighbors did. People like the mayor, the local doctors, and a few high-rolling techies. I loved my own quaint neighborhood, but I couldn't deny how lovely—and large—the houses were east of the park.

My uncles' home looked like something out of a magazine. Ask either one of them and they'd tell you their castle was indeed owned by Prince Charming. I wouldn't call either of them princely, though Elvis had charm down to a science. My burly, loud Uncle Jimmy? Not so much.

I rang the doorbell since no one answered my knock.

"Hold on, hold on," Uncle Jimmy barked in an annoyed voice.

Expecting a man who looked like he should be on a Most Wanted poster, complete with tattoos and a snarling expression, I was shocked when the door swung open to reveal Uncle Jimmy wearing a clown costume, bulbous red nose and frizzy red wig included.

I burst into laughter while he glowered at me and reached down to pet Cookie.

"Cookie, come in. *You*, wait until you're properly respectful."

Over his shoulder, Uncle Elvis grinned, laughed silently, and pointed at his husband.

"I can hear you!" Uncle Jimmy groused, still not turned around. He lumbered like a bear in a colorful polka-dot suit with pom-poms for buttons. His feet didn't need any exaggeration in size, though I noted a pair of clown shoes by the door. The wig hid the mane of blond hair he typically pulled back into a ponytail, that and his goatee his only claims to vanity.

After giving my dog kisses, Uncle Jimmy yanked me into his arms and gave me a huge hug. "You doing okay, girl?"

"I'm fine."

Elvis drew close, nudged Jimmy away, and hugged me tighter.

"Can't . . . breathe."

He pulled away. As usual, he looked handsome as sin, even in khaki shorts and a Looney Tunes T-shirt. Cropped black hair, bright-blue eyes, a perpetual tan, and a fit body toned from years of labor under the sun had given him the fitting moniker "Sin on a Stick." Or at least, I'd often heard the ladies in town murmur that when he walked by. But he'd been happily joined to my uncle for twenty years, married for the last ten. Off the market and glad of it.

Sometimes it pained me to think I might never have what my uncles and parents had. But then I'd remember I liked my life and my choices, and I refused to settle for *meh* when I wanted a forever love. *After* the start of a forever career. I had my priorities in line.

"You didn't kill him, did you?" Uncle Elvis asked as he shut the door behind me.

I just blinked at him. "No. Of course not."

"Pity. That would have livened up your side of the family tree." He grinned at Jimmy as he said it. Then looked him up and down. "Though this new obsessions with clowns is a step in the right direction. It's weird and kind of cute." Elvis pursed his lips. "Well, more like weird and horrifying. So creepy you can't look away."

"Thanks." Jimmy grunted and left us, shouting over his shoulder, "Coffee's in the kitchen. Go get a cup and prepare to answer some questions, niece."

I sighed and dragged myself after Uncle Elvis and Cookie, who needed no invitation to the Kitchen of Good Smells. "Do I want to know why Uncle Jimmy's in a clown costume?"

Elvis cracked up laughing. "Neither of us has developed a clown fetish, if that's what you're asking. Jimmy's filling in for Tad, who's sick today. Since Jimmy fits the costume and knows how to make balloon animals, he's been drafted to fill in at the Taffy Toys tent."

"Oh, I hadn't realized Tad was sick."

"I don't think he is." Elvis leaned closer and in a low voice added, "I think he's sick of working. But that's between you and me."

"And me," Jimmy boomed. "I know what goes on in this town, Elvis." Jimmy crossed his eyes at us and grabbed a cup of coffee for himself. I was happy to see he no longer wore the wig, the nose, or the clown suit, instead dressed like his husband, in a T-shirt and shorts.

"I think it's nice you're helping with the festival." I patted him on his meaty forearm.

"Thanks." He gave me a smile. "Now why don't you tell us exactly what happened yesterday. Because from what we've gathered, you either killed Gil to steal his prized vegetables or you did it to stop him from reporting Cookie to animal control."

Elvis wiggled his eyebrows. "I heard she was having a secret affair with him and lost it when he refused to ask her to marry him. You know how much he still mourns his wife."

I gaped.

Jimmy and Elvis shared a smirk.

Relieved they'd apparently been joking, I let out a loud sigh. "Oh, that's just mean." Bad enough people thought I'd murdered Gil. But for his vegetables or a love affair gone wrong? Gross.

Jimmy pointed at me. "You never answered our calls. And that *I'm okay, call you soon* text was pathetic."

I groaned. "I'm sorry. I missed Mom's calls too. Yesterday was just so bizarre." I told them everything that had happened.

They listened, nodding here and there, until we all fell silent.

"You're sure you had nothing to do with it?" Elvis asked again, staring at Cookie.

I goggled at him. "You really think I'm a murderer? Murderess?" Heck, I should have just gone with the neutral *killer.*

"I was talking to the dog."

Cookie went from sitting to lying down, her paws crossing over her muzzle.

"Hmm. I'm not sure if that's a confession or not."

I tried not to laugh, but between my uncles and my ham of a dog, I was back in good spirits after all the bad that had happened.

"I can't believe someone murdered Gil." Jimmy shook his head. "The guy was a complete nut, but murder's a little extreme."

"I don't know," I said, recounting for them the conversation at the bookshop. "Pastor Nestor and Peggy were quick to point fingers at the Danvers. And the Danvers, much as I like them, pointed those fingers right back. The CGC mafia is pretty passionate about their gardening."

"She has a point," Elvis said. "I've been working on the mayor's new patio. Building a trellis for some morning glories for the missus." The mayor's wife, I liked. The mayor, when not cheesing too hard on getting reelected, I could tolerate. "Yesterday I overheard her telling Ed Mullins that the judging for the Gardener's Purse this year is going to be pretty strict. They're bringing in judges from Bend and Sisters instead of using Confection's judges from last year. That anonymous donor adding twenty thousand to last year's pot is making our contest a big deal."

"So the whole pot really is at twenty-five thousand?" Pastor Nestor had mentioned that number and we'd talked about it at book club, but it hadn't really sunk in. Twenty-five grand for *plants*?

"Yep." Elvis nodded. "They'll have Best Color, Best Roses, Best Home Garden, and more. So the purse is spread out, but the main prize, Best Gardener of the Summer, gets a whopping fifteen grand. And I know some people who would certainly kill for that."

"Really? Like who?"

"The CGC has its share of competitors who take it to a whole 'nother level." He started ticking off names. "Bill Sanchez. Joe Jacobs. Dave Danvers."

"Now hold on." I knew the club members got competitive, but some of the folks he'd named were people I liked. "Bill and Dave are nice. Joe's a little obsessive but not a violent guy."

"Peggy Donahue? Bonnie Bright? Ed Mullins? What about Mandy Coatney?"

"Elvis, you just named nearly every officer in the CGC." Jimmy snorted.

"Exactly my point. Those people are rabid competitors. Which is to say nothing of all the CGC regular members and the non-CGC locals competing for a share of the prize money."

"They're *all* killers when it comes to melons and greens," Uncle Jimmy said. "But with money as a motivator, you can't just limit the pool of suspects to gardeners."

"Um, why not?" I asked. "Because only serious gardeners have any shot at winning the Central Oregon Gardener's Purse."

"Yeah, but then you have Gil's claims that someone owed him a lot of money. And plenty of folks in Confection could use a financial helping hand. Take Taffy Toys, for instance." Jimmy's eyes gleamed. The man thrived on gossip.

"Taffy Toys is having money problems?" I'd had no idea. Man, I should have come to my uncles first thing yesterday. They always knew the latest chatter in town. Almost, but not quite, as good as the Macaroons and Teri.

"That place goes through more owners." Elvis sighed. "But hey, the current store has been stable for the past three years. Maybe they'll stick it out."

"Maybe they killed Gil so they wouldn't have to pay him back." Jimmy was still running with his theory. "Or maybe Joe Jacobs took him out. I heard Gil's tomatoes—"

"Darcy said potatoes," I corrected.

"—potatoes, are amazing." Jimmy shrugged. "Who knows?" He gave me a thorough looking over. "Are you sure you're okay?"

"I'm getting better. I won't lie. It was a huge shock. I'm kind of not sure how to feel, to be honest. I didn't like Gil at all." It didn't seem like anyone in town had. "He was mean and a bully. I'm not sorry he's gone. But I would much rather he moved away than die." I swallowed.

They looked at each other and turned as one to me.

"You should move in here," Elvis said at the same time Jimmy said, "Use the guest room upstairs."

"No." I frowned. "I'm not scared, though I guess I probably should be." Huh. I wasn't scared. Why wasn't I? "I think . . . What happened to Gil feels personal. Like, someone killed him for a reason."

"Do you know how he died?" Jimmy asked. "Was it the pipe Cookie had?"

Cookie looked from him to me, apparently waiting on an answer.

"I don't know. And Detective Berg won't tell me anything if I ask."

"I'll ask," Elvis offered.

"No, keep out of it. I don't want him thinking I'm trying to get answers out of him through you. Plus, he hates me. You and I are related. I don't want him hating you too."

"What?" Elvis blinked. "How can anyone hate you? You're so sunny and sweet." He paused. "Well, sarcastic, but like, with a heart of gold."

Jimmy snickered. "Sarcastic? More like obnoxious with a side of charm. She gets that from her father."

"*Your* older brother," I emphasized. "Dad always says he's the nice Jones brother."

Elvis snorted. "He is. But nice is boring. Stick with us, kid. And you'll go far."

"Hopefully not so far she lands in jail," Jimmy muttered. "And speaking of jail, how's our son doing at the shop?"

I laughed. "Collin's great. My shop is not a prison." No, not *my* shop. "I mean, Sweet Fiction is a great place to work."

"If you say so." Jimmy shuddered. "It's just got so many books."

"Yes," I said slowly, "because bookshops sell things people *read*. And not just while they're waiting in the doctor's office."

"Or in the bathroom. You got any joke books at the shop? I don't mind reading them while I'm busy."

I cringed.

Elvis wiped a hand over his face. "No, Jimmy. Just . . . no."

"For the record, you are not invited to book club." I turned to my more literate uncle. "Uncle Elvis, you like reading."

"Comics."

Okay, he did have a well-known Marvel obsession, but personally I thought that had more to do with how Thor filled out his tights than with the stories themselves.

I conceded, "We could read a comic for book club."

He winced. "I thought you loved me. You'd actually force me to hang around with Stefanie and Alison? On purpose? And even worse, Darcy Mason? Ugh. Why not just shoot me now?"

We all looked at each other.

"Or, ah, don't shoot me, because, you know, your neighbor just died. And that might look suspicious to the police."

I blushed, not sure why. “Stop.”

He grinned. Jimmy laughed. And then Cookie rose to put her paws on the counter, staring from me to them. I swear she cocked an eyebrow, as if to ask what was so funny.

We all enjoyed more laughter, coffee, and family time before duty called.

Jimmy had animal balloons to twist and kids to scare—I mean, entertain.

Elvis had a mountain calling his name with plans to hike a trail in the Cascades with some friends.

And I had people to avoid and words to write.

No time like the present.

Chapter Eight

Several hours later

"A clown, a flirt, and a suspected killer walk into a bar . . ."

I glared at Uncle Jimmy, who wasn't as funny as he thought he was. "When I told you guys I was heading to the Ripe Raisin tonight, I hadn't realized I'd be getting an escort."

Elvis laughed at my expression. "Oh, relax. We're just making sure you get in without any bother. With all the gardening groupies hanging out downtown, it's only a matter of time before someone tries interrogating you. We wanted to make sure none of them attempt to harangue you." For some odd reason, he looked awfully pleased with himself.

Jimmy sighed. "*Harangue* is his word of the day. And no, I am never getting you one of those calendars ever again."

Elvis grinned.

I laughed, enjoying the banter. It did help to take my mind off entering a place where I was sure everyone would look at me with suspicion.

"Teri and Cat are waiting for me," I told my uncles again. "I'll be fine." I said it more for myself than for them.

"She's right." Elvis nudged Jimmy ahead of him. "Besides, we don't want our cool street cred getting downed by hanging around with someone who reads books."

"Good point." Uncle Jimmy gave me a wink before sneering. "Later, nerd."

He and Elvis walked ahead into the bar, leaving me behind.

Huh. Hadn't thought they'd really do that.

Seconds later, Cat barreled out of the bar and dragged me inside with her.

"And hello to you too," I muttered as my eyes adjusted to the dim lighting.

The Ripe Raisin was *the* place to hang out on a weekend. And on a festival night, the bar was packed.

Dash and his best friend and business partner—also working the bar tonight, I noticed—had bought and restored the place five years ago. It had been a taproom back in the eighties, then a small grocery, followed by a soda shop. Now it served both alcohol and appetizers. At one end of the space, a large oak counter supported over a dozen stools, with many patrons choosing to stand instead of sit. Booths lined the walls, complemented by a few standing tables in one area and more seating scattered around the room.

On nights when local entertainment played music, some of the tables and chairs disappeared. But not tonight, when alternative rock played through overhead speakers while people laughed and talked and drank. The lighting I appreciated, as I was able to see without being blinded by too much light or swimming in too much darkness.

Teri waved from behind the bar, the poor girl. Always working.

"I'll be at our table if you want to say hi to her. She's miserable," Cat warned. "Dash is making her work. No Randy time for Teri." She nodded to our left.

I turned to see Randy sitting with his brother, laughing at something he said. Then he sneaked a peek at the bar and let his gaze linger on Teri before tuning back in to the conversation.

"Huh. He is cute. And he has a thing for her."

"Shocker." Cat grinned.

I left her for Teri and ordered one of Randy's ciders.

"I'd get you one"—she turned to glare at her brother—"but we're all out. How about a beer?"

"Whatever's cheapest on tap."

"Right." With her hair up in a ponytail and a towel over her shoulder, she looked like the girl next door slinging alcohol for grown-ups. Teri's my age, but she's always looked younger. Just like her mom, whom I'd swear had just turned thirty but was in fact fifty-four.

"I can't believe you didn't call me when Berg questioned you," she complained as she poured me a beer. "You know I know people."

Her job as a clerk in the DA's office did put her in touch with a lot of legal eagles. But she didn't know the police all that well and liked it that way. That I did know.

"And what would you have done? Nothing. There was nothing for you to do. Except be a shoulder to lean on, which you totally are," I said, wanting her to know I appreciated her.

Back in Seattle, I'd have been on my own, with my work friends not close enough to count on for much. A shared lunch here or there, but nothing near to what I had with Cat and Teri.

"I only told Cat because I needed her to cover for me at the bookshop."

That seemed to mollify Teri a little.

"I can't believe Dash is making you work tonight. I saw Randy over there. He keeps looking over at you."

"I know." She grinned, flashing a dimple. "I keep sneaking looks at him and catching him at it. He's soooo cute. I should see if his table needs anything more to drink." She stole a glance at Dash.

Unfortunately, he spotted her glance, saw me, and scowled as he made his way to us.

I bit back a sigh.

Dash leaned over the bar, took my hand in his, and squeezed it.

I was speechless.

"Shoot, Lexi. How are you doing? You know if you need anything, you just have to ask."

I opened my mouth and closed it again, my surprise mirrored in Teri's face. "Who are you? And what have you done with Dash Hagen?"

He frowned. "What? I'm being supportive." He lowered his voice and leaned closer. "You found Gil, didn't you?"

"Well, technically, Cookie found him. But yeah, it was pretty . . . weird."

"I can imagine." He pulled his hand back. "Everyone's been talking about it. Well, about Gil and the Gardener's Purse. And then we have the festival going on too. Oh, wonderful." He didn't sound so enthused as he stared over my shoulder. "Confection's finest is here. Yo, Noah," he shouted to his partner. "Take care of your cousin."

I turned to see Berg and Halston enter together, apparently off duty. Both wore jeans and T-shirts, no police clothes to be seen.

"Cousin?"

Dash turned back to me. "Yeah. Noah is Berg's cousin. You didn't know?"

"Nope." Not my business, but I did find it curious. Was that why Chad Berg had come to our little town a few months ago? Because he had family in the area? How had I not known that?

"Anyway, if I hear anything about Gil, I'll let you know."

"Thanks." I took the beer and sipped. Not bad. "Put it on my tab, Teri," I told her.

"Sure thing."

"And an order of baked pretzel bits too." The beer cheddar dip they came with was to die for. So to speak.

"Got it." She nodded. "Dash, I'm working another hour, then I'm done. And we're even now, buddy."

"Fine, fine. I appreciate you filling in." He ran a hand through his hair, his biceps bulging.

Now that was a good move. I would go back and insert that in my book to help describe the hero as buff. *Runs hand through hair, his biceps bulging* . . . Hmm. Should I—

"What?" Dash asked, looking at his arm. "Is this where you make a crack about my puny arms? That I'm not working out as much as I used to? Because I'm getting back to it. I've just been busy lately."

"Defensive much?" I muttered and shared a bemused glance with Teri.

He huffed. "Whatever. Just try not to cause too much trouble, Lexi."

"Me? Trouble?"

He shook his head and went back to the many patrons needing a refill at the end of the bar.

"What's wrong with Dash?" I asked Teri.

"No idea. Maybe Serena shot him down."

"Serena?"

"An old girlfriend who's visiting her mom for the summer."

I didn't remember her.

"Anyway, you want to hear something interesting? Abe was by earlier. And he was drinking by himself before those two"—she nodded to an older white couple sitting at a table next to Cat's—"sat with him and started chatting. I swear I overheard him mention his dad and a treasure map."

"Seriously? An honest-to-goodness treasure map?"

"That's what I heard."

I huffed. "I'd think if Gil had a treasure worth anything, he wouldn't be—er, *have been*—living next to me."

"Right? But you might want to eavesdrop on them a little. Oh, and there's their friend coming from the restroom. He seems pretty nice."

I saw a middle-aged white guy amble up to the couple's table. He looked like a tourist, dressed in designer hiking gear and the requisite three-hundred-dollar hiking boots. Probably a city dude wanting to take a break by playing hiking enthusiast for the weekend.

"Thanks. I'll go listen in."

"Let me know what you find out. I'll bring your pretzels when they're done. And don't leave before I get to hang out with you guys."

"I'd feel more like you meant that if you weren't looking at Randy when you said it. Are you sure you wouldn't rather go flirt with your brother's archenemy than sit with your best friends in the world?"

"Shut up. And stop distracting me from my job."

"You mean the one you rarely get paid for with your bossy older brother always telling you what to do?"

She crossed her eyes. "Yeah, that one."

I smiled and left with my beer, heading back to Cat, who seemed fascinated by the tabletop and not Roger Halston, who was trying desperately not to look as if he was staring at my friend while chatting with someone next to her table.

I swear, it felt like middle school all over again, my idiot friends pretending not to like the boys they were desperately crushing on. Men. *Such* a nuisance. Someone nudged me and I tripped into . . .

"Whoa there." Two large hands on my shoulders stopped me from plowing through a large man. Detective Chad Berg. The last person I wanted to see on my happy Saturday night.

"Oh, sorry." Talk about walking into a problem. Literally.

He quickly withdrew his hands. "You okay?"

"Just fine. It's a little crowded in here." Someone had bumped me into Mr. Law and Order. At that moment, the feeling of being watched penetrated. I turned and met Uncle Jimmy's concerned look.

He nodded at Berg, who thankfully hadn't noticed. Jimmy's expression said, *Do you need a rescue?*

I shook my head and conveyed, *No, I'm fine. Do not come over here and create a scene.*

Jimmy elbowed Elvis, who looked over at me, then shook his head. Fortunately, they both turned back to each other, talking and drinking and pretending I didn't exist. Whew.

"What?"

"Huh?" I focused back on Berg. His gray eyes narrowed on me, always looking for my guilt, or so it felt. The reminder that

I still had a fictional murder file on my computer, starring Gil Cloutier, suddenly swamped me with nerves.

"You're shaking your head at me."

I blushed. "Oh, ah, just thinking I'd better hurry back to Cat before she forgets I'm here and gives away my seat." Which she looked very close to doing as Roger kept creeping closer, now smiling and making occasional eye contact with my awkward friend.

Berg followed my gaze and sighed. "Oh."

"Yeah." For once I agreed with Berg. I did not want to sit with him and Roger while Cat tried to make idle chitchat. "See ya." I hustled away, sneaking back into my seat when Roger turned to speak with Darcy and her husband, who were standing close by.

"Whew."

Cat blinked. "What happened?"

In a low voice, I answered, "While you were pathetically not-flirting, I ran into Berg. He's here with Roger, whom you're doing a terrible job of pretending not to see. Don't even think about inviting him to sit down."

Cat sighed. "Fine. I'm not prepared to fully engage tonight anyway."

Engage?

"I need to practice more before I talk to him."

No kidding. "Next time he comes in the shop, he gets a free cookie. I told him so yesterday when I ran into him at lunch."

She blinked. "You never told me that."

"I'm telling you now." I took a big swig of my drink, needing the distraction. "Think of the free cookie as an icebreaker for you two. I told him how delicious they were, and he seemed keen on getting one."

"Good." Cat tried to pretend she couldn't care less, but I could tell.

"Oh yeah, talk about the wrong guy to hit with your car," I heard a deep voice say from behind me. "Not in town two minutes before I hit the mayor's pride and joy."

A woman said, "But he was so nice about it."

I had to turn around to see: one, who had saved me from a citation from Berg Thursday, and two, the people Teri had overheard talking to Abe.

Studying the three strangers at the table, I saw right off why Teri had mentioned them. The older man seemed nice enough, laughing or smiling with the woman by his side. Yet the way he looked around him gave me the impression he wasn't as comfortable as he was pretending to be. But then, my imagination was all over the place lately.

His buddy in the Patagonia gear seemed pleasant and unassuming. The woman with them, a graying redhead, cut a trim figure in a halter top and jeans, a sweater over the back of her chair. She smiled, her lips a complementary red that went with her shirt. Pretty but also a little rough around the edges, she didn't seem to fit with her companions. All three of them, though together, looked separate. I had a tough time imagining them as friends.

"Hi," I said loudly and leaned in. "I couldn't help overhearing. So you're the ones who hit the mayor's new car on Thursday, huh?"

The wannabe hiker shook his head. "Not me. I came later. These two had the honor. Oh, and I'm Alec."

I shook his hand. "Nice to meet you. I'm Lexi."

The woman made more introductions. "I'm Anna, and this is Bob, my boyfriend. Please, join us."

I nodded and said over my shoulder to Cat, "I'll be right back."

"Sure thing." She'd already focused on her phone, once again ignoring Roger.

Alec smiled at me. "We're in town for the festival and for some amazing hikes in the mountains. You?"

"Actually, I live here. I work at Sweet Fiction, the bookshop on Main. You couldn't have come at a better time of year. It's gorgeous up in the mountains."

"And in town," Anna said with a smile. "We're from Portland. I've been to the Wooden Shoe Festival for the tulips in the spring. Lavender Valley in Mount Hood, and of course, the International Rose Test Garden in Washington Park. But the colors and blooms I've seen in Confection are incredible. I've seen more flowers and giant vegetables today than I did all last summer!"

"She's so excited she signed us up for the Confection Garden Club Flower Tour tomorrow," Bob said with a grin. "I can't wait."

"Oh, that's a great tour." And the same one that had witnessed my butt-chewing from Gil before he died. "So, can I ask, what happened with the mayor?"

"Not much." Bob took a swig of beer. "It sounded a lot worse than it was. I was parking, and my foot slipped off the brake. I scratched his bumper, I think. Totally my fault. But he told me not to worry about it and welcomed us to town. That Foot is just the nicest guy."

"He can be. But I think it was your luck that you only scratched his bumper. He just got that car."

"Good luck we'll take." Bob and Anna clinked bottles. "So what do you think of Confection? Have you lived here long?"

"I grew up here, left to work in Seattle for a few years, then came back a year and a half ago. Haven't looked back since." I smiled.

Alec nodded. "I left a small town to work in Portland. But I love the city. That's where I met Bob and Anna, actually."

"Yeah, we met at a treasure hunting club," Anna said.

My spidey-sense was tingling, but I played it casual. "What? Treasure hunting? Like deep-sea diving for treasure?"

"Not at all." Bob laughed. "We're urban treasure hunters. We check out salvage shops, thrift stores, flea markets, auctions. There are tons of places to find valuable things. You just have to sort through a lot of crap first."

"Oh. Interesting."

Anna shrugged. "It can be. It's what brought the three of us together. We're part of a local club out of Gresham. Sometimes we'll even pool our money to buy unclaimed storage sheds when they go on sale. It's fun but time-consuming."

"And it can be expensive," Alec said. "But it's all about the find. This weekend, we all decided to take a break. And then what do you know? Some guy is in here talking about treasure. Like it was fated for us to be here."

"Oh? Who was talking treasure?"

Anna answered, "His name was Abe. I think his father recently passed away. I felt sorry for him. He was crying into his beer and talking about buried treasure."

"Abe Cloutier," Bob said. "A nice kid but pretty emotional." He cleared his throat. "Though I guess with his dad dead, he had a right to be."

"Um, yeah." I didn't want to come off as unfeeling, but I needed to know more. "So, that treasure he was talking about. It was real?"

"No idea, but he pulled out a map to show us when I asked." Bob scratched his head. "Damned if it didn't look genuine. But come on. Buried treasure in Confection, Oregon? I did a little research before we arrived, and your town isn't known for buried gold, mines, or anything other than old lumber mills worth any money. And the lumber mill stopped producing over a hundred years ago."

"Yeah." I nodded, my mind stuck on Abe's map. "Abe lost his dad, and he probably should stay away from alcohol more than he does. Frankly, Gil's treasure is probably his prizewinning potatoes. Have you guys heard about how much the Gardener's Purse is this year?"

While we discussed veggies and flowers, I kept straying to Abe and his treasure map.

I wondered if Berg knew about it, and if not, whether I should tell him.

Chapter Nine

Sunday morning, I did the requisite church thing, walking Cookie and parking her outside the church. "Do *not* make me regret bringing you," I warned her. "And steer clear of the police, would you?"

Cookie gave me her trademark scowl before nosing around the back of the church. I watched her crawl under their back fence toward the rectory and left, confident she wouldn't leave a mess. She'd already done her business this morning, so the worst she might do was dig. But she wouldn't. We'd talked about that too. She knew better.

I would have left her at home except I'd left her last night while I hung with Teri and Cat at the bar. After questioning the treasure hunting visitors, I'd enjoyed time with my friends and those amazing pretzel bits. Dash had a surefire winner there.

Yum.

A church bell rang, so I hurried inside and took a seat in the back along with the rest of the infrequent attendees, whom I'd once heard Peggy call "those unruly heathens." Obviously confusing us with the parents-of-small-children crowd, who'd been partitioned behind Plexiglas to the side. We infrequent attendees were way short of unruly, doing our best just to stay awake on a Sunday morning.

The church is nondenominational, and though Pastor Nestor can be a horse's butt about gardening, he's actually pretty welcoming to any and all who choose to worship. Seriously. He doesn't care about your background so long as you shake hands when called to so do. Giving to the collection plate doesn't hurt either.

I saw plenty of visitors along with our regulars as we sat through a lecture about giving back to the community and living each day to the fullest. And then Pastor Nestor mentioned praying for our dearly departed, Gil Cloutier, and said a few words to Scott and his wife, who sat in the front pew.

The church had a long moment of silence, during which a few sniffles could be heard. Fake tears or not, I couldn't be sure. Gil hadn't liked many people in town and hadn't been shy about sharing his feelings.

That Scott and his wife had put in an appearance at church meant something. Like me, Scott often slept in on Sundays. I only knew that because Teri attended Sunday service religiously—*ha, see what I did there?*—and liked to gossip whenever new people came.

She said she attended services to try to be a better person and to keep her folks happy, though she'd privately confessed to me her addiction to Sunday pancake breakfast.

The pastor gave a short but surprisingly moving speech about Gil's finer qualities. I had no idea my neighbor had regularly donated to a homeless shelter and often given his homegrown vegetables to the church.

The service ended with a song, and we all stood and sang with an energy I didn't normally hear on those rare occasions when I attended, not counting Christmas.

After the service, I made my getaway and searched out back for Cookie. To my surprise, I found Scott in the back as well, crouched and petting my dog.

He saw Cookie look my way and smiled at me. "Hey, Lexi. Sorry I missed book club Friday."

"Oh, Scott. Please. You had a lot more to worry about than book club." I paused. "I'm so sorry for your loss. I know you must have heard that I was, um, there that morning when the police found your dad. But I had nothing to do with any of that. I swear. I was just out looking for my dog."

He stood and stuffed his hands in his pockets. I couldn't see much of Gil in Scott, except for the blue eyes. "I know, Lexi. People in this town just like to gossip. Don't let it bother you."

Relieved that Scott didn't blame me, I asked, "How are you holding up?"

"I'm confused. When I was younger, we were such a close family. All of us. But as we got older, and especially after Mom died, Dad just got bitter. He was always so angry all the time." Scott sighed. "I miss the man he used to be. We'd almost started to connect again. He was trying. But then something would set him off." Scott shrugged. "And now he's dead. I still can't believe someone killed him. Maybe a robbery gone wrong?"

I hesitated to bring up the map, but I wanted to know. "Well, someone mentioned Gil had a treasure map. Maybe someone wanted whatever Gil buried?"

Scott gave a short laugh. "My father? A treasure? He had a pension from work but not much else. A treasure map?" He snorted with amusement. Until his face lit in understanding. "Ah, wait. I bet that's it. When we were younger, Dad would stop us from getting bored by making up these silly maps and having us hunt in the yard. It kept us busy and out from under him all the time. But that was twenty years ago." He shrugged. "The best thing I ever found were some beads and Bottle Caps—the candy kind."

"Oh yeah. I used to love those." We took a moment to relive our sugary pasts. "Have you seen Abe or Matt lately?"

"I haven't talked to either of them in a while. But we're meeting with Dad's lawyer for the will tomorrow. I guess I'll see them both there." He paused. "I thought Abe was doing better, but I heard he was at the Ripe Raisin recently. Man." Scott frowned, looking like he was trying to hold back tears.

"I'll let you go." I put a hand on his arm. "We're having book club tomorrow night as usual, if you need a break. You're always welcome, and if there's anything I can do to help, just say so." I figured I should let him know about Stefanie's choice. "But we are reading a mystery now. Not sure if you want to read about fictional crime after . . . well, after what happened with Gil."

"Thanks for the warning." He smiled through watery eyes. "Stefanie's selections are always a kick. What did she choose?"

"An Agatha Christie. *The Murder of Roger Ackroyd*."

"Huh. Interesting choice. I think I've read that one."

"Well, whatever you do, don't mention that to Stefanie."

His wife exited the church from the back. Seeing us, she smiled and made her way toward us. She stopped to pet Cookie, then stood and offered a hand. "Hi, Lexi."

I took her hand and gave it a gentle squeeze. "I'm so sorry, Jan."

"It's so sad. And just when Scott and Gil were starting to reconnect."

Which was what Scott had said.

I nodded. "I was telling Scott that if you guys need anything, please let me know."

"We will." Scott put his arm around his wife and gave a somber smile.

Jan looked down.

I left them, Cookie by my side.

We'd just reached my car when Dash appeared. "Well, well, if it isn't Miss Trouble."

"What do you want?" I waited for Cookie to stop begging Dash for kisses before letting her in the car, protected from the sun by the shade from nearby trees. I kept the door open, blocked from closing it thanks to Dash standing in the way.

"First, you're welcome for not charging you and your girl gang for all the pretzel bits and beers last night."

"You mean, you finally comped your sister by feeding her and her friends. There's no such thing as free labor, Dash."

He shrugged. "Whatever. I'm teaching her responsibility."

"She's twenty-eight, doofus. Try again."

"She owed me. Now we're even." He paused. "So what do you think about Scott and Jan?"

"What about them?"

Dash crossed his arms over his chest and leaned against my car. Still in the way unless I wanted to close the door on his leg. "They aren't the churchgoing type."

"Neither am I." I frowned. "Neither are you, come to think of it. What are you doing here?"

"Looking and listening." He nodded. "I know why you're here."

"To get closer to heaven."

He smirked. "Yeah, right. You're a twice-a-year attendee, if that."

"Takes one to know one."

"Nah, you feel guilty about Gil."

I growled, "I told you I had nothing to do with what happened to him."

"Hey, I don't think you wanted him dead or anything. But you're a softy."

"Blow it out your— Oh, hey, Mrs. Hagen."

Dash's mother passed by, walking next to her handsome husband. She smiled at Dash before glaring at me. With two fingers, she pointed from her eyes to mine and said something in Chamorro before strutting away in heels that still only put her at her husband's shoulder.

Dash rolled his eyes.

"What did she say?"

"You don't want to know." He let his grin out. "Something about doing my best to stay alive next to you."

Teri's mother had never liked me. "She still hasn't forgiven me for daring Teri to experiment on her hair our junior year, huh?"

"Nope." Dash chuckled, then pretended to cough when Pastor Nestor neared us. "Oh yeah, so sad about Cloutier." Once the pastor left, he leaned closer and said, "Look, Scott and his dad weren't close, no matter what he's trying to pretend. Gil used to spout off about his conceited jerk of a son, and he wasn't talking about Matt or Abe. Abe has his problems, but he's never acted like he's better than half the town."

"Scott does that?"

Dash nodded. "Since he made a fortune creating that app five years ago, he's been investing big-time in his company and not quiet about his many successes."

"Funny, he never acts superior at book club." I'd always found Scott polite and kind.

"Well, maybe he only feels the need to preen around other guys."

"*Preen* is a big word for you, Dash. I'm impressed."

He rolled his eyes. "Oh, please. You think because you edited for some bigwig publisher, you're better than me."

"No, I think I'm better than you because I'm smarter, prettier, and all around nicer."

"She really is," Teri said, joining us. She linked her arm through mine, and we stared at Dash.

In a low voice, I recapped for her, ending with, "He was just telling me not to trust Scott."

"You shouldn't. He's too smarmy."

"Isn't that too big a word for my sister?" Dash said with a huff.

"Not at all. She reads."

"I read."

"Books, Dash."

He opened his mouth and closed it. "Recipes count."

"So do news fliers, I guess."

He grinned. And boy, but he did have that handsome glow going on. The sun made his head that much more golden.

"My point," Dash emphasized in a low tone, all seriousness again, "is to keep an eye on the Cloutiers. If Gil did die because of that stupid treasure map Abe was crying about yesterday, then my money is on one of his kids, not the CGC or a random mugger."

"Mugger?" Teri snorted. "Mugging him for what? Tomatoes?"

"Potatoes," I automatically corrected. "But why did you mention a mugging, Dash? Is that what the police are investigating?"

"I heard a few things last night. Noah and his cousin talking in addition to something Roger let slip. They think the murder was intended for Gil and only Gil, so you shouldn't be worried you might be next," he said to me.

"I wasn't, but thanks." I frowned. "I can't believe any of his sons would hurt him. Gil was unlikable, yes, but he was their dad. And from what the tourists who hit the mayor's car said, Abe was crying in the bar over Gil's death and that supposed treasure map."

Dash watched me, but I could tell he wasn't looking at me so much as he was looking through me while his brain went far away. "I've seen that map. It's real. No idea if it was really Gil's or just something he made up, but Abe has something. The police already talked to him, so I hear."

"What did he say?" I asked.

"No idea." He glanced at Teri. "You hear anything?"

"Nope. The DA is handling the case himself, and he's been really quiet about details. Trust me, I've been trying to get any info I can, but I got nothing so far." She winked at me. "Why don't you cozy up to Berg for some info?"

Dash frowned. "To Iceberg?" He barked a laugh. "Good luck with that. That guy is a robot. Even Noah gets annoyed with him, and he gets along with everyone."

"So it's not just me then." That made me feel better about always being on Berg's bad side.

"Nope. Well, maybe." Dash scratched his cheek. "But that probably has more to do with Cookie getting the guy in trouble." He grinned. "I still laugh at the ketchup swing-n-bling incident."

Teri chuckled. "Me too."

Cookie grinned from her spot in the car.

I cleared my throat. "Not that I don't appreciate the help, Dash. But why so interested in Gil's murder?"

"Did you just hear yourself? Someone killed one of our own in Confection. There hasn't been a murder here in . . . well, since before we were kids."

Teri nodded. "It's true. I looked it up. That it was your neighbor who died . . . We're worried for you, Lexi."

"Thanks, but I'm good."

"You can stay with me," Teri offered.

"With you and Cat? In a two-bedroom apartment no bigger than a shoe box? No thanks."

"That's rude." She glared.

"I'm just being real. Besides, my uncles already tried to strong-arm me into staying with them. I told them no yesterday. I'm fine at home. I agree that someone targeted Gil; it wasn't random. I'm not worried. Unless the police try pinning the murder on me. That *does* scare me."

Dash nodded. "It would scare me too. Trust me. I'm keeping my ears open for you."

"Me too." Teri squeezed my arm. "Now, if we're all done talking about death, can we please go to the annex for pancake breakfast? I'm famished."

"I knew that's why you came today," Dash muttered.

"Oh, please. I came because Mom nagged me into coming. Same with you." She turned to me. "And speaking of my mom, you might want to steer clear. She's been warning me you're trouble." Teri sighed. "She's never going to let go of my rad junior-year haircut."

"You got that right. Wait. Did you just say *rad*? Are you channeling Cat now?"

She laughed. "Do you know she spent last night, after we got home, texting with Roger? I'm telling you. She's so into him."

"On that note, I'm out. See you two idiots later." Dash left before I could thank him, then punch him for being obnoxious.

But one thing was certain. I had more questions than answers about Gil's relationship with his children and a need to talk to Abe about a treasure map that might or might not be real.

And no idea why I thought it was any of my business. I really should leave all this investigating to the police.

Yes, that made much more sense. I would totally do that.

Cookie gave me a small growl, the one that said, *Hey, don't forget about me.*

As if I could.

"Teri, if I go with you, Cookie's going to want to come too."

"She's welcome. Mom's in charge of pancake breakfast this week." Teri reached for Cookie's leash on the floor of the car. She clipped it to my dog's collar and started toward the annex. "Coming?"

Cookie didn't look back at me, suckered in by the word *pancake.*

"Yeah, yeah." I stomped behind them and did my best to forget about murders and angry neighbors. I had more important things to worry about.

Like pancake breakfast and my hungry, hungry pup.

Chapter Ten

Monday morning at seven, I took Cookie for our daily walk. It was nice. Normal.

The lawns we passed hadn't been disturbed. No mounds of dug-up dirt. No angry CGC mafia. No suspicious neighbors eyeing me like Jason Vorhees mowing through summer campers on *Friday the 13th*.

We passed a few people but no one who seemed to care about a woman and her dog.

Of course, I'd taken an alternate route today, cutting through Central Park to walk Lemon Loop. We had nearly come full circle when I saw Darcy's side yard, immaculate as always. The grass had been trimmed, the bushes pruned, and the many roses bordering the side of the house looked vibrant and smelled amazing when the wind blew.

Except . . . there, under the largest rosebush, I spotted dirt.

Son of a gun.

I'd done pretty well putting Gil's sad demise to the back of my mind after church yesterday, doing my best to pretend I didn't need to worry about it. The police would catch their criminal, and my life would go on as usual.

But more digging made me paranoid. I glanced around and, not seeing anyone nearby, walked onto Darcy's pristine lawn to study the hole in the ground. Whoever had dug had gone a good foot deep. They hadn't tried to hide the evidence well either.

Heck, if I were digging around town, I'd at least fill in the holes before leaving.

Cookie nosed closer, forcing me back a step.

"Hey," I whispered. "Watch it."

She ignored me and pushed deeper into the bush.

"Easy, you'll get hurt," I continued whispering, not wanting to get caught on private property. "Those roses have thorns, you know."

After looking around, I tugged Cookie with me off the yard.

She gave a small growl, dog-speak for *Pay attention*. I glanced down at her and saw something in her mouth.

For once she didn't make me play tug-of-war, depositing a scrap of fabric in my hand.

"Huh. Must have been caught in the bush." I studied the yellow scrap, what felt like the thin cotton of a T-shirt, maybe? Or a rag? There was an odd pattern on part of it, not paisley but something that could have been a spaceship. I felt like I'd seen this before, but I couldn't remember where.

Probably on Darcy's husband, considering it was his yard. Heck, for all I knew, Darcy or a member of her family had been playing in the yard and run into the rosebush, losing a piece of T-shirt. Yeah, probably one of her kids, if that pattern was a UFO.

Still, I tucked the fabric into my pocket and continued on our walk.

We finished without fanfare, enjoying the crisp Monday morning that should heat up to a lovely eighty-five degrees later in the day. Sunny with a few passing clouds. That I could handle.

I made it in to work early, went over some orders I'd been putting off, and spent a pleasant morning selling books. Cat showed up at noon, following her later Monday–Wednesday schedule, bearing a tray of new S'more Books. Please cookies. Huh. She must really be eager to feed Roger, who I had a feeling would stop in today.

I sipped a mediocre hazelnut latte as I stood at the counter, my journal open wide. We were slow, so I studied my story notes and realized I had a huge problem with my current work in progress. I had some plot holes big enough to drive the mayor's new car through. Gil's death had shown me that my death scene was too obvious, pointing out the killer too early in the story. There was no mystery, no tension. A too-easy capture of the bad guy.

If only life imitated art.

Since Gil's death, I'd steered clear of writing any more violent scenes. Which reminded me to definitely delete what I had on my computer later. No sense in being stupid by keeping a fictional account of Gil's murder to make me look guilty. And yes, I still felt ghastly for having written Gil's death. But in my defense, I hadn't thought anyone would actually kill the guy.

I closed the journal—which had no mention of Gil in it whatsoever—and tucked it next to my purse, on the shelf under the register.

Cat had started a new batch of coffee brewing and was cleaning up the food counter.

"Lookin' good," I told her.

She slid the tray of cookies behind the glass counter top display and tucked away the cleaning supplies. I liked that we gave customers a chance to browse while caffeinating. As a java addict myself, I always appreciated a hot cup, no matter the time of day.

Cat rounded the coffee counter, dusting her hands together. "Not only do those cookies look good, they taste great."

"I'll bet." I smiled. "So how did your Sunday go? I went to church and met up with Teri." I told her all about my Sunday, including my talk with Scott. I felt no need to keep my voice down, as we only had one customer wandering about. A common lunch slump.

Cat nodded. "I thought about going to church." She paused. "Not that I would have gone. Sunday's my one day to sleep in. It takes time and energy to bake like a dream."

"Of course."

"Although I did see Roger Sunday afternoon. I was at the gym, working out, when he showed up."

By the faint blush on her cheeks, their meeting had gone well. "And?"

"We have a date this Wednesday. Nothing serious," she hurried to forestall further questioning. "Just a friendly dinner at a place in Bend." She rattled off the name of a decent eatery in the foodie town.

"Fusion cuisine? Nice."

She nodded. "Roger's into eating good food, not fast food. That he likes my baking is actually a huge compliment."

"I don't think it's just your baking he's into."

She blushed harder.

I laughed. "At least you have a date. Teri's still dancing to Dash's tune, not Randy's. I have no idea why she always caves when he asks for help at the bar."

"Well, on Saturday, it was because Mike left him short-handed. He's having problems with his girlfriend. With the other two servers on vacation, Dash was swamped."

"Makes sense, I guess."

"Plus, Teri owes him for a loan he gave her not long ago."

"What? I didn't know that."

Cat nodded. "You didn't hear it from me, but she was a little tight for rent two months ago. Remember that handbag she bought?"

"The one she swore wasn't the real thing?"

"It actually was."

And worth a cool five hundred dollars. Teri had a bad habit of buying expensive shoes and purses she couldn't afford. But she hated our lectures on financial sensibility, so I tried to confine myself to one or two a month.

Cat sighed. "Yeah. It cost a fortune. I wanted to cover the rent for her, but I couldn't afford to."

"I could have lent her the money." I didn't have millions, but I had savings put aside.

"Teri swore me to silence or I would have told you."

"I heard nothing. I know nothing." I turned a pretend key over my lips.

"She felt awful having to borrow from Dash, but I'm hoping it taught her a lesson. At the time, it was a big deal. But it blew over fast. I don't like arguing with her."

"Oh, hey. That explains why you two were sniping at each other constantly a few months ago. It was about the purse, not about you leaving your shoes all over the apartment or not taking out the trash."

"Well, it was about those too. She annoyed me, so I was being petty by being a bad roommate."

"Touché."

Cat smirked. "I can do petty like nobody's business." She watched me. "Do you ever wish you had a roommate?"

"Angling for the job?"

"No thanks. Teri and I get along well, with the exception of the purse incident that shall not be named. Besides, you're too anal-retentive for me."

"Excuse me?"

"You heard me. You like everything just so. I get it. You've lived on your own for a long time. Sometimes I wished I did too. But I like having Teri to talk to. Don't you ever get lonely?"

"Me? Nope." I did, but I didn't want to sound pathetic. "I have Cookie to listen to me." We both looked at my dog, sacked out and lying on her back, her paws in the air as she snored lightly on her dog bed behind the counter. "And I have you guys. All the gossip, none of the drama."

"That's true." Cat nodded and lowered her voice. "Then again, none of *our* neighbors are dead, and we haven't been accused of anything. When it comes to drama, you currently rule." She gave me a look. "You'll hate to hear it, but I think you might look good in prison-orange."

Not something I wanted to think about. "Did Roger say anything to you yesterday about the case?"

Our only customer approached with a book, so I smiled and rang her up. I waited until she left before continuing the conversation. "Well?"

"Again, you didn't hear this from me."

"Spill it!"

"Okay, okay. Apparently, the pipe Cookie found had nothing to do with Gil's murder. He was stabbed."

"Not with the pipe?" Could you actually stab someone with a pipe? I had no idea.

"No. The pipe had blood on it, so it must have fallen in Gil's grave. Or where he was murdered. Huh. I wonder if Gil was killed inside the house before being placed in the backyard grave."

I shivered at the thought of anyone putting my neighbor in the ground. "Someone dug a hole for him? I'd assumed he was digging up pipes in his yard, where Cookie originally found the copper pipe. Or else that he'd been planting something."

"From what I heard, they found him in a man-sized hole. Though they can't be sure who dug it. But they do know he was stabbed."

"With a knife? Do they know what kind?"

"Roger told me it's weird. They're not exactly sure it was a knife. But they ruled out the pipe for sure. He might have known more than he told me, though." She paused in thought. "He's not supposed to share details, but come on, it's me. Who am I going to tell?" She blinked. "Well, you, of course. And Teri. Maybe Dash, if he asked."

Relief that I had to be officially off the suspect list made me light-headed. "So they know it's not me? I mean, they don't think I had anything to do with it, right?"

"I can't say for sure, but Roger knows you're innocent. Same as the rest of us who know you. And I think Berg, though Roger isn't sure what Berg really thinks. The guy keeps his thoughts and feelings close, you know?"

I nodded. We let the silence fall between us before I asked, "On another note, are you coming to book club tonight?"

"Sure am. I even read the first three chapters. It's not bad."

A ringing endorsement. Cat didn't normally enjoy mysteries unless they had a lot of gore in them. A horror fan, she had particular tastes.

"Outstanding." I handed her a twenty. "If you grab us lunch, I'll pay."

"Awesome."

"Get me a club sandwich, would you?"

"I'll be back soon." Cat left, practically skipping out the door.

I drew my journal out, opened it, and sighed. Sunday I had gone to church, enjoyed a pancake breakfast, and written a few chapters I'd need to scrap. How to make the murderer less obvious?

I withdrew the bit of fabric from my pants and placed it on my journal, wondering about my continual problems with my story.

Was it the plot or the characters and their motivations? Or was it something else?

Granted, I'd been shocked by Gil's murder. But three days later, I felt less bothered by it, as if that traumatic morning, finding my dog over a dead body, had happened to someone else. Then too, Cat's date bothered me. But why?

Did I feel jealous? I sat with the emotion. No. I wanted Cat happy, and I had no designs whatsoever on Roger Halston. But her question, did I ever got lonely, made me think.

Especially because Teri had been crushing on Randy Craig for a while. And with Cat starting to date Roger, that left me the odd man out. I knew my friends would never desert me for guys, but still. Relationships changed all the time. And I was the only one in our group without a social life. Well, except for my furry companion.

"It's just you and me, Cookie."

She didn't stir.

I sighed, frustrated and not sure why. I pulled my notebook closer and went over plot details, trying to fix the problem. By the time Cat returned with our food, I'd checked out another customer and jotted down some new ideas to bridge the issues in my story's structure. I'd never understood authors who could just write without any prior planning.

Pleased I wouldn't have to delete more of my manuscript than I'd thought, I enjoyed my sandwich and the company and spent the rest of my day chatting with book lovers.

* * *

By ten to six that evening, I had already set the table in the back room of the shop, laying out a nice little spread. We had coffee and hot water for tea. Mini sandwiches and chips catered by Eats n' Treats. Cookies—handmade by Cat. And as a special treat, just in case Scott arrived, I'd purchased some truffles from Choco-NOW, Confection's best sweetshop.

I loved when we hosted book club, mostly because I could expense our food to the bookstore. I was all about thrifty spending, though you wouldn't know it by the way I'd been blowing my grocery budget. No more Eats n' Treats lunches for me for a while.

As I welcomed everyone back, including Teri, I was pleased to see Scott walk through the front door.

"Hi, Scott. So glad you could make it."

He smiled and followed the others into the back room. "I needed a break. I'm looking forward to book club tonight."

And the Macaroons were once again complete.

Stefanie, Alison, Alan, Darcy, Kay, Cat, Teri, me, and Scott. Nine book lovers ready to talk about a murder. A fictional one, of course.

I glanced at Scott, watched him smiling and talking to everyone, a library copy of *The Murder of Roger Ackroyd* in his hand, and figured we should get started. He'd been warned ahead of time and had the book. He knew we'd be covering a murder mystery. Yet . . . I sidled next to Stefanie, seated and eating a generous helping of food.

"Hey, Stefanie?"

"This is terrific. Mel is on top of her game." She held up a half-eaten roast beef sandwich.

"Yeah, she's great. Look, Scott's here. He knows we're talking about a murder mystery. Just go easy, okay?"

"On account of Gil?"

Her loud voice drew a few sharp glances.

Stefanie sighed. "Sorry. Yeah, yeah. I'm not a complete insensitive clod."

That remained to be seen.

Alison joined her.

"Alison, put some food on your plate." Stefanie groaned. "This isn't another one of your diets, is it? I swear, John will think you're sweet with or without your extra ten pounds."

Alison turned beet red. "Honestly." She huffed and put her coat and book on the chair next to Stefanie, leaving a seat between them.

"Oh bother." Stefanie sighed. "Everyone's so dang sensitive these days."

It took everything I had to keep a straight face. Not talking about death with a man whose father had been killed wasn't like tiptoeing around prickly do-gooders. And Alison had been battling her weight for years, losing over a hundred pounds in the past eighteen months. To think she might be a little touchy about her weight only made sense.

Heck, I didn't know many women who *did* like to talk about the scale.

I turned and saw Teri watching Stefanie and Alison and trying not to laugh. I joined her by the food table.

Teri grinned. "I swear, Stefanie has no filter. I love her."

"I do too, but tonight we should all be a little bit careful about how we talk about the book, you know?" I shot a subtle glance at Scott.

Teri's expression softened. "I'll sit next to him for support."

"Good call."

We continued to mingle, making small talk as we normally did. Sure, book club centered around book discussion. But we generally liked one another. Even Darcy, who couldn't help herself. She typically meant well, even if she did have foot-in-mouth disease. A lot like Stefanie, actually.

I neared Darcy, only to hear her telling Kay and Alan, "I can't believe we got hit too. It was a small hole, but I almost fell into it when I was chasing the dog out from nosing in my roses."

"Cookie didn't do it," I blurted.

The three of them turned to me, Kay with a grin on her face.

Darcy paused with a chip to her mouth. "Are you sure?"

"Positive." I swallowed. "I, ah, we were out on a walk this morning around Lemon Loop. It was beautiful."

"It has been a gorgeous day." Kay nodded.

"Well, when we were passing your house, I noticed something near one of your rosebushes. Looked like a pile of dirt, the same as I've been seeing around my neighborhood. I've been really careful to keep Cookie with me since Friday morning. I know she didn't dig there, or in any of the other spots around town." Well, with the exception of the Confection Rose that one time.

Alan frowned. "What do you think it is, Darcy? Moles, maybe?"

"Could be." She shrugged. "But it seemed like kind of a large hole for a mole."

"Rabbit, maybe?" Kay offered, and chewed into a raspberry truffle. "Oh, Lexi, I love these. Choco-NOW?"

"Yep. Got them fresh today. I thought it would be nice to have them if Scott came. A special welcome back just for him."

"That's sweet." Darcy smiled. "I'm sure he knows you had nothing to do with Gil."

"I know that, Darcy," Scott said loudly.

Everyone drew quiet.

"Sorry, Scott." Darcy blushed. "I didn't mean—"

"Hey, it's okay. Everyone's talking about it." He sighed. "It's not something you can ignore, and it did just happen. But for the record, I know Lexi, and Cookie, had nothing to do with Dad's . . . passing."

At her name, Cookie sat up from where she'd been lying down and gave a soft grunt.

The group laughed, the tension broken by my canine cutie.

Scott grinned. "Now, if she'd been after a tray of peanut butter cookies, I might have to rethink my suspicions."

"You got that right." Stefanie shot my dog a nasty look.

Cookie scooted closer to Cat for protection.

As we continued to chat about anything but Gil Cloutier's death, I settled down, pleased to find myself back among the familiar.

We started our three-chapter book critique.

It went well. At first.

And then Stefanie tried spoiling it for us.

"It's such a fun novel," she was saying. "The narrator, Dr. Sheppard, is quite the unreli—"

"Stop right there," I interrupted. "We are *only* discussing the first three chapters. So we can't know much about anyone just yet."

Stefanie frowned. "Well, I . . . fine."

Alison cleared her throat. "I like that Dr. Sheppard is well versed in poisons, much like Agatha Christie. As a nurse and apothecary assistant in World War I, Dame Christie had an extensive knowledge of poisons, which appear in many of her books as the murder weapon."

"True." Alan nodded. "I'm also a fan of Hercule Poirot, the detective in this novel."

Kay said, "You know he hated women. And in fact, Agatha Christie didn't like him. She wanted to kill him off in several novels."

Stefanie harrumphed. "Yeah, well, *I* like him." *Because you're both a bit cantankerous*, I thought but didn't say. "And this book is considered to be one of the best crime fiction novels ever written."

"That's true," Alan said. "I've only ever seen the television version with David Suchet, who's the one and only Poirot, in my opinion."

"I have to agree," I said, because I loved the Agatha Christie televised series. It was a toss-up as to which sleuth I preferred, Miss Marple or Hercule Poirot. Hmm. I still didn't know.

Alan added, "But reading the book is a much better experience than TV, I have to admit."

"Exactly." Stefanie slurped her coffee.

"I like that the story is in Dr. Sheppard's point of view," Darcy said. "In a lot of the Agatha Christie books, it's third-person point of view. But here, we only know what Dr. Sheppard knows."

"And then we have the lead-up to their dinner. And all the gossip that flows between Poirot and Dr. Sheppard's sister." Alison nodded, enthused.

"It's pretty good," Cat said. "Plus, the chapters aren't that long."

"Of course *that's* why you like it," Teri muttered. "Look, I didn't read past the third chapter, I swear. But I'm intrigued. There's a lot of talk of poisons, and something's going on with that Ralph Patton guy, who's supposedly engaged to one woman but walking in the woods with someone else. And he needs money."

"Well, when it all comes down to it, that's why people kill, isn't it?" I asked. "For money or for love."

"Or for both," Scott said. "But I have to say, I'm intrigued too. I love what I've read so far." A small pause. "*And* I'm ready for a bathroom break."

We decided to take a few moments to stretch our legs, during which I grilled Teri about Randy and learned they had rescheduled their second date for Wednesday night, since their Friday outing hadn't happened. She and Cat tried to figure out who would get the apartment Wednesday night in the event of an "extended date."

Listening to them bicker and bargain made me doubly glad I had no one but Cookie for a roommate, even if I didn't have any "extended dates" of my own.

I saw my dog staring at Stefanie's purse on the floor, under her chair. "Cookie." She glanced up, and I added, "Don't even think about it."

She sighed and lay back down, resting her head on her paws.

The rest of the meeting progressed without one mention of Gil's death, thank goodness, and suspicions about what Agatha Christie might have meant by giving us a story from the doctor's point of view instead of Poirot's.

After we broke up, I was still musing on how well Agatha Christie introduced suspicion and interest so easily. How she could make a simple turn of phrase so ominous.

I gathered my purse and Cookie's leash. But I couldn't find my journal.

Odd. I checked all over for it—under the register counter, in the tiny office, and even the back room, though I knew I hadn't brought it in with me. No joy.

Uneasy and hoping no one read into my notes if someone indeed had taken it, I headed home with Cookie.

On the way, we passed Mandy taking pictures of downtown in the fading sunset. She must have some kind of project due. I didn't normally see her around town so often.

She waved.

I waved back and continued toward home.

But it took me a long time to fall asleep that night, as I was disconcerted about Darcy's hole in the ground and my missing journal.

Chapter Eleven

One thing I'm not is stupid. At least, I don't like to think I am. Last night, I'd sadly deleted my killing of Gil Cloutier from the computer. Though I hated to lose the words, I would hate even more for those words to be used against me in a court of law.

Tuesday proved a real return to normal. It surprised me how quickly people could adapt and ignore that which made them uncomfortable.

Gil had been killed four-plus days ago. I still heard mention of it now and again, but suspicion had definitely turned from me. I kept hearing people talking about a popular news segment featuring a new trend of murders for hire in Salem. Now everyone seemed to think someone had hired a hit man to take out Gil. Motives stretched from knocking him off his gardening pedestal for the Gardener's Purse to a secret love affair with some (unlucky) woman in town.

As long as everyone kept my name out of it, they could ruminate to their hearts' content.

While working, I slid back into my old routine—stocking new releases, packaging some of our new mail orders, and checking out a swell of customers. *And* I found my journal in the back room where we'd had book club. I still didn't know how it had gotten in the back room. But no one had ripped any pages out or written in it. It was as I'd left it.

I tucked it into my purse and kept my purse under the counter by the register, locking the cabinet just to be safe. I ate a lunch I'd brought from home, swapped bad-date stories with Cat, who tried to pretend she wasn't agonizing over tomorrow night's date yet could talk of nothing else, and had a lovely walk with Cookie after the lunch hour.

The weather remained ideal for doing anything and everything outdoors, so I forgave all the customers who didn't show up in the early afternoon, enjoying the many who came in after three to browse and enjoy some delectable cookies. And I don't mean my dog.

Cookie, for her part, didn't whine too much about being kept inside. As someone recently suspected of murder, I found it best to keep myself and my dog away from discovering any other evidence at a crime scene. No way I was letting my canine miscreant out of sight. She'd been stuck in the bookshop with me all day except for our post-lunch walk, and she'd been way too interested, yet again, in the Confection Rose.

Unfortunately, I didn't realize how much she'd been waiting for a shot at freedom.

On Tuesdays we closed at five, and with ten minutes to go, since no one had stepped in, I started closing early. I had nearly finished with everything except shutting down the register. Cat opened the front door to the store as she was leaving. "Hey, I'm heading out. Want to grab a bite to eat at our place? Teri's cooking. It's stir-fry night."

"Oh. I love her stir-fry. Sure. Just let me— Cookie!"

My dog darted out the door and raced down Main toward Central Garden. The little idiot even paused at Cinnamon Avenue, making sure it was clear before crossing. Several people standing nearby smiled and pointed. Until Cookie closed in on the Confection Rose and started digging.

Oh God.

I rushed and found her, dragging her away just as a shadow loomed over me.

"I got her. I got her," I said, panting, winded from my mini sprint. Luckily, Cookie hadn't disturbed too much earth. I pointed to the large section missing from the rosebush way underneath and looked up, expecting to see Cat.

Instead I looked into the face of a fuming Detective Berg. "Oh, uh, well, uh . . ."

"You're coming with me, Ms. Jones."

"No, wait. I just got here after her. There's no way she dug that deep that far back. You saw her."

"I have no idea what you're talking about. This concerns Gil Cloutier. We need to talk at the station."

"What?"

He hauled me up by my arm and firmly escorted me to his car, parked in front of the bookshop. "Please get your things. Including your journal."

"My . . . *What?*" I took the purse Cat handed me.

Cat stared from me to Berg. "I tucked the journal inside for you. I'll take Cookie."

Cookie whined, wanting to go with me.

"Cookie, go with Cat. I'll get you when I'm done with Conan." I glared at Berg, who ignored my annoyance. "Thanks, Cat," I managed before Berg shoved me into the back seat. Okay, he gently pushed me into it, taking care not to bump my head. But I felt manhandled all the same.

As he drove the minuscule distance to the courthouse, I sputtered, "What the heck is this about? I didn't do anything. And neither did Cookie," I added before he could accuse my dog of a grievous offense.

Berg didn't answer. And that made me nervous.

We pulled into the parking lot. He turned off the car and turned around to look at me. "What did you do?"

"What the hell are you talking about?" Hold on. "And how did you know about my journal?"

He firmed his lips, frustration cooling his glare. Man, Dash had been right. "Iceberg" suited the menacing detective. He left the vehicle and opened my door. This close, he felt dangerous. Too tall, too muscular, too cop-like for my peace of mind.

I shrank back instinctively.

He sighed and helped me out of the vehicle. More like tugged me out, but he did it gently. "Come on. I won't bite." Under his breath he added, "But I can't say the same about your dog."

"Hey!"

We entered the police department at the rear of the courthouse. Small, with a whopping total of ten people, eleven including the administrative assistant, the Confection PD nevertheless did everything by the book. They acted professional, never a hint of misconduct, and treated everyone fairly.

Which made me really, really anxious. Berg wouldn't have yanked me down here if he didn't have a reason.

"Okay, what's going on?" I tried to dig in my heels.

He finally released my arm in the middle of the main office. Two patrol officers and the secretary watched with big eyes.

"Some evidence has come to light implicating you in the death of Gil Cloutier."

"What? But the pipe didn't kill him."

Berg scowled.

Shoot. Me and my big mouth.

"I mean, did it?"

He walked to a door, opened it, and gestured me inside.

I walked in and sat down.

"Do you want a lawyer present?"

"Are you going to read me my rights?" I goggled. On the one hand, I found this insider look into law and order fascinating. Talk about great research for my book. On the other, I was freaking the freak out.

He nodded to my purse. "Please open that. Spill the contents on the desk."

"I don't have to do that."

"You don't." *But if you refuse to cooperate, you look guilty.* I swear that's what he was thinking.

I sighed. "Fine." I dumped my purse. My wallet, a few dog biscuits, a bottle of strawberry hand sanitizer, a pack of tissues, a stale pack of gum, a bottle opener, and a roll of doggy bags fell out. On top of my journal.

My journal that he drew toward him while watching me with keen eyes.

Oh shee—ooo—t.

I groaned and covered my eyes. "Go ahead. Read it. I have nothing to hide." Oh yes I did. I'd made notes about why several murders couldn't happen. Granted, I hadn't mentioned Gil in my notebook, but one idea had spurred another, and I had one of my bad guys trying to kill another with a hand shovel, since I'd remembered how Gil used to carry his precious trowel everywhere with him.

Cheese and rice, this ain't nice.

Berg's face grew grimmer the more he read.

He looked up at me. "Are you prepared to talk to me without *a lawyer*, Ms. Jones?"

"I, uh—"

He shot me another look I couldn't read before saying, slowly, "Because *you have the right* to remain silent. Anything you say can and will be used against you in a court of law. *You have the right* to an attorney—"

"I want a lawyer."

He nodded, continued reading me my rights without any extra weird emphasis, and scooped everything on the table back into my purse. "I'll get you a phone. Wait here."

He stood and left with my purse.

I sat, stupefied, then less puzzled and more intrigued. My journal had gone missing last night. And the only people in the bookshop had been the Macaroons. So who had ratted me out, and why?

When Berg returned with a phone, I immediately called my uncles. Elvis answered and said he'd phone his friend for me. Amy Redston was an attorney who practiced family law but had in the past defended criminals. Lovely.

Now we waited.

Berg watched me, and I felt like an ant under the microscope. I watched him back, waiting for him to sit. He didn't, remaining standing with his back against the two-way mirror, his huge arms crossed over his huge chest.

"I didn't kill anyone," I blurted and ripped my ponytail holder from my head. A strand had caught on the elastic, giving me a killer headache.

"I'm not asking you any questions without your lawyer present," he stated, watching me comb back my hair.

"Fine. I'm not answering any. I'm just talking. And I find it really interesting that last night at book club, my journal went missing. The same journal I'm writing notes to myself in because I'm writing a book." *Seriously, Iceberg? Do I really look like a killer?*

His eyes narrowed, but he didn't speak.

"You can ask Cat and Teri. They've known I've been working on this for over a year."

He raised a brow.

"Since I got back to town a year and half ago, as a matter of fact. I used to edit for a large publishing house. Well, I quit my job, came home, and am trying the writer thing out. But that means I need to draft my story, and that means taking notes."

And writing a piece of fiction whereby I mentioned killing Gil Cloutier.

Could they read deleted files? Oh my gosh. Should I go home and destroy my computer? Would I need to smash the hard drive to make it unreadable? Oh no. Had I emailed myself the story? Sometimes I did that to back it up. Would it be on a mail server somewhere, in electronic limbo?

Berg cleared his throat, and I whipped my gaze to his face. He asked, "You okay?"

"Can I have some water?" My anxiety shifted to anger at the ridiculousness of being considered a murder suspect. "You know, so you guys can take my prints and match them with the bazooka that killed Bigfoot?" I snapped.

He tried to mask a smile, but I saw it. "I'll be right back." In a lower voice, he added what sounded like, "Try not to incriminate yourself further," but I couldn't be sure.

I fumed in silence, rolling my fingers across the tabletop. I wondered if they'd ever cuffed anyone to the chair. If I tried to leave, would I find myself locked in? Or worse, in shackles?

Before I could wonder myself into a panic, the door opened. Amy Redston walked in, a middle-aged white woman wearing a Hawaiian shirt and baggy shorts. She wore her dark-red hair in a cacophony of curls, the ends dyed purple, her cheeks freshly sunburned. Not one thing about the woman screamed "lawyer," yet her steady blue gaze set me immediately at ease.

Then she looked me over and sighed. "So how much damage control do I need to do? What did you say before I got here?"

"What?"

Amy sighed again. "Tell me."

I mentioned all of it except killing Gil on the computer, not relieved by her many sighs and eye rolls or the way she slowly dragged her hand over her face.

"Dear Lord. No more talking unless I say so. Not a peep."

Berg entered with a notebook and folder in hand. His lieutenant followed.

"Hello, Ms. Jones," the lieutenant said, dressed in a pair of blue slacks and a crisp white shirt that set off his medium-brown skin. A handsome, older, and very dignified man. "Detective Berg has a few more questions for you. I hope you don't mind if I sit in."

I opened and closed my mouth before looking to Amy.

She sighed. Again. I wanted to ask if she had a medical condition. "You can answer," she said.

"I don't mind if you sit in." Though I wondered what he might have done if I'd told him to get out.

Berg took over. "Your journal is very . . . interesting . . . to us."

I liked it. The interior pasted-down end papers had unicorns stabbing ogres who bled rainbows. Yet the outside of the journal was a flat red. Kind of like me. Normal on the outside, a mess within.

"That's not a question," Amy said.

Berg ignored her. "Ms. Jones, can you please tell us what all your references to death and killing are about?"

Sounded self-explanatory to me. I glanced at Amy, who nodded.

"I'm writing a book."

"About killing Gil Cloutier?" the lieutenant asked.

"No, about killing and getting away with it."

The lawyer smacked her forehead.

"I mean, I'm writing a mystery. Well, a romantic suspense that's turning into a thriller, kind of. But not really a thriller." I thought about it. "More a mystery, I think. There's a murderer, but it was too obvious who did it. So I had to really think about how to increase the tension."

Berg and the lieutenant stared at me.

I flushed. "It's still a work in progress. But seeing what happened to Gil made me realize I can't have the killer be caught too early or I'll lose the reader. If there's no intrigue, it's boring."

"It's a fictional novel she's writing, gentlemen," Amy cut in. "Not reality. My client, despite evidence to the contrary, is not so stupid she'd write about murdering her neighbor and leave her journal out for anyone to see."

I turned to Amy with a frown. "Hold on. Evidence to the contrary?"

Out of the corner of my eye I saw Berg roll his eyes. His lieutenant had yet to blink.

The lawyer stared at me. "Did you kill Gil Cloutier?"

"What? Heck no. He was a mean old man and continually grumpy. But I'm no killer."

"At least, not in real life, is that it?" Berg asked.

"Right. And I really am writing a book. You can ask my friends. They know." I thought about it. "But how did you know? I haven't told anyone about it. Not even the Macaroons."

"Who are the Macaroons?" the lieutenant asked.

"Sweet Fiction's book club. Are you a reader? You're more than welcome to join us. We meet twice a month to discuss books. We're currently reading an Agatha Christie. Not my choice," I hurried to add, lest he think I wanted to discuss murder for fun.

"I see." The lieutenant leaned back. He pushed the journal toward me. "Care to comment on your more recent notes? The ones dated near Mr. Cloutier's death?"

I leaned forward to read what I'd written. Most of it involved ramping up tension and clearing up some point-of-view spots. "Well, I'm sticking with third-person point of view. Unlike *The Murder of Roger Ackroyd*, I want my narrator to be reliable."

"Another murder?" the lieutenant sat up straight. "Who's Roger Ackroyd?"

Berg murmured, "He's a character in an Agatha Christie novel, sir. Not a real person."

Amy snickered, then pretended to cough when the lieutenant glared at her. Probably not the smartest thing to do, considering I was being questioned as a suspect.

"Oh, of course." The lieutenant cleared his throat.

I swore Berg was suppressing a smile but couldn't be sure. His face read like a granite slab of I'm Not Telling.

"How did you know about my journal?" I asked Berg.

"What?"

"Well, I've never shared with anyone that I'm writing a book except my best friends. And I know Teri and Cat haven't said anything. I was keeping it secret."

The lieutenant pounced. "Why?"

I sighed. "Because if I can't finish the book, I'll look like a loser. And considering I used to edit some pretty big names, that would be majorly embarrassing. Plus, if I do publish the book and people don't like it, I don't want them to pity me for having no talent, when my mistakes will likely be the result of being a beginner. And yes, I've given this a lot of thought."

Berg nodded, saw the lieutenant glance at him, and quickly looked down at his notes.

"But I'm curious," I continued. "Because I keep my journal private. I had it last night at book club, tucked away next to my purse under the register. I didn't see anyone take it, but that journal went missing until this morning. Someone must have taken it to read it, so who told you about it?"

"That doesn't matter," Berg said.

It mattered a lot to me. I had a narc close to home. A rat. It appeared the Macaroons would need an extermination. Huh. Great line. Oh, I should use that in my book.

Berg cleared his throat, and I realized I was pulling a Dash, staring through Berg while my thoughts were miles away.

"Sorry. Just thinking . . ."

"About?"

"That treasure map of Gil's." I leaned over the table, staring at Berg. "What do you make of that? Abe talked about it at the Ripe Raisin on Saturday. And someone's been digging all over town. Maybe whoever killed Gil is after the treasure." I paused. "That could mean Abe is next." Or that Abe was the killer, but I didn't want to throw stones. Not here in front of the po-po. "Are you protecting him?"

The lieutenant and Berg exchanged a glance, then the lieutenant stood. "Thank you, Ms. Jones. We'll be in touch." He left.

"Are we done here?" Amy asked.

"Not yet." Berg went over, yet again, my timeline before, during, and after Gil's death. We discussed the spat the day before he died. The copper pipe, Cookie, the barking she'd done the night before Gil's murder, everything and anything related to my dead neighbor.

I was exhausted after another hour of wasted time when I could have been at Teri and Cat's eating dinner someone else had made.

Amy must have had enough, because she groaned and stretched. "Okay, Detective. You don't have any evidence to charge her, so we're walking."

I stood, eager to leave. But I had one more question. "Did Gil die by a stab wound made from a knife? Or maybe by a spade?"

"A spade?" Berg's expressionless face grew more wooden, were that possible.

"You know. A small garden shovel. A trowel."

"Where did you hear that?"

"I didn't. But I remembered Gil never let his prized garden trowel out of his sight. It was his wife's, and he never gardened without it." I studied Berg. "If you didn't find it, then that would be my bet for the murder weapon. It's got a rosewood handle. I only know that because Gil used to wave it at me when he was yelling about something I or Cookie allegedly did." I sighed. "I didn't like him, Detective, but I didn't want him dead. I really hope you can find who did this."

"I do too." He nodded at me. "Don't leave town."

"I'll postpone my trip to Bermuda," I drawled.

"She's kidding," Amy said, before Berg could wipe away his scowl.

"Good. And if you hear anything that you think might help us with our investigation, let us know." He walked us out, his large presence impossible to ignore, a shadow that refused to go away. "Ms. Jones, be careful. And keep your dog from digging up any more yards or you *will* be fined."

We had reached the exit. He turned and left without another word.

As the door was shutting, I yelled after him, "It wasn't Cookie! And if you don't take all the digging seriously, that's on you!" Not the cleverest thing I could have said, but I didn't like how everyone found it easier to blame my dog than do a little "digging" of their own into why someone wanted to excavate around town.

I stood for a second, blinking at Amy. A lawyer whose time I had used. Oh man. What would she charge me? With my luck, a bazillion dollars an hour. "So, ah, thanks for coming to help. What do I owe you?"

"I owed Elvis for some work he did. Consider it paid." She nodded to the building behind me. "But leave the investigating to the police. And no more writing about murder for a while, okay?"

"But I'm writing a story. Not about Gil; it's fictional."

"All the same, I'd delay for a while. Better safe than sorry, and you definitely don't want them dragging your computer into forensics and digging up anything questionable. I can only imagine your search history."

"On poisons, guns, rigor mortis . . ." I cringed. "Okay, okay. I'll take a break. But I might still take notes. In code."

She sighed. "It's your life. Behind bars or in Sweet Fiction. Your choice." She nodded to me and left.

I realized I'd have to put my story on hold while this mess got sorted. *Dang it.*

I trudged toward Cat and Teri's, despondent and unsure of where to go from here.

But as I cut through Confection Park by the courthouse, I overheard two CGC members saying some very interesting things about the recently deceased Gil Cloutier . . .

Chapter Twelve

"So then Joe tells him he's a shoo-in to win the fifteen-thousand-dollar grand prize. But Bill argues that there's no way Joe can top Bill's outdoor home garden. Although, he says, maybe if Gil were still alive, he—Bill, I mean—might lose. Apparently Gil's been hiding one heck of a garden next door. I'm saying that, not Bill." I paused to take a sip of my drink. "Then Bill says, but not this year, and not with Bill's award-winning tomatoes, onions, and peppers. And his flowers too. But Joe's determined *he's* going to win," I said around a mouthful of spaghetti.

Teri had changed her mind about stir-fry, wanting a lot of leftovers.

I don't know if it was being in the police station forever or the stress of being viewed as a suspect again, but I'd never had a better dinner.

Cat and Teri just stared at me.

We sat in their kitchen, Cookie under the table, while I regaled them with the events causing my delay to dinner.

Teri frowned. "I still want to know who told them about your journal. That's so weird."

"I didn't tell them," Cat said. "Not that you asked. I just wanted that out there." Her cheeks turned pink. "You know, since I'm kind of seeing Roger. And he's a cop."

"No. Is he? I had no idea." Teri stared at Cat, wide-eyed. "Wow. How about that? I'm sorry. You said you're dating? *You?*"

Cat snorted. "You are *such* a pain in my a—"

"Ladies," I interrupted. "Let's think. Last night, I locked up the bookshop after everyone arrived for book club. I put my journal by my purse under the register. The cabinet wasn't locked, but no one but me and Cat ever goes behind the register."

They nodded, and I continued. "There were nine of us at book club last night. Eliminating the three of us, that leaves Stefanie, Alison, Darcy, Kay, Alan, and Scott. When we took that bathroom break, anyone could have snooped and found it. I stayed in the back room talking to Teri the whole time."

"My money's on Darcy. She's a busybody." Teri nodded.

"I was thinking it might be her too. She was the one telling everyone I killed Gil after we found him."

"She's nosy and gossips too much, but I don't know." Cat frowned. "I can't see Darcy stealing your journal, then ratting you out to the cops."

Teri and I looked at each other and said as one, "I can."

Cat shrugged. "Maybe. Or maybe it was Stefanie. Or Alison. Those two plot together."

"Yeah, but if it was Stefanie, she'd help me hide the body." At the looks they shot me, I flushed. "*Hide the body* is an expression. *I mean* she'd tell me to hide the journal and figure out a way to make someone else look guilty."

"That's true." Teri nodded. "And Alison does what Stefanie says, so I'd count her out."

"Alan? Scott? I don't see Kay turning me in." I sighed. "But maybe Scott is doing his own investigating. He somehow saw the journal, took it to read later, then turned me in to the police."

"I don't know." Teri shook her head.

"Dash says he's annoying and arrogant."

Cat frowned. "I've never heard Scott being arrogant. I mean, we all know he's loaded thanks to those apps he developed. Heck, he has a house on the north end of town. Lots of land and a big old updated farmhouse. I once helped Mel cater a party there. The house is massive and looks like it should be in a magazine."

"So we know Scott has money. That doesn't mean he stole my journal."

"It doesn't mean he didn't steal your journal." Teri shrugged.

"Then what does his being rich have to do with anything?" I glared at Cat. "You're distracting us from—"

"From what? Your dinner? Let's face it. One of the Macaroons stole your journal and tried to set you up as a murderer."

"Murderess," Teri corrected. "That sounds more violent."

"Oh, it does." Cat nodded. "Okay, murderess. And that's not cool, because you could get in real trouble if the idiot police—not Roger—believe you did it."

"I have a feeling Berg might not be out to crucify me." He'd made a minor remark about me trying not to incriminate myself. And he'd hinted pretty strongly that I should have a lawyer. "Then again, I have no idea what Iceberg really thinks."

Cat and Teri grinned.

"Dash called him that. It fits."

Teri tapped her chin. "It does, but then you have to think about what it would take to melt all that ice." She wiggled her brows, like a goof, and had us all laughing.

Secretly, I wondered what it really would take for the guy to relax a little. Did Berg ever date? Did he have a social life? His cousin worked at the bar, and Noah had always been nice to me. Of course, that didn't mean I had to like Chad Berg by association.

"See? She's thinking about him." Teri elbowed Cat.

"Stop. I'm just wondering if he's hiding all that niceness that his cousin has. Noah's good people."

"I don't know." Teri scowled. "Noah has been acting pretty bossy at the bar lately. He's taking his cues from Dash, and I'm getting tired of it."

"Right." I twirled more spaghetti on my fork and realized Cookie had been pretty quiet. Too quiet.

I took a quick peek under the table and groaned. "Who gave her meatballs?"

"No one." Teri gasped. "Cookie Jones. You get out here right now, young lady."

Cookie darted from the table with food in her mouth. A normal dog would have immediately eaten the meatball. Not Cookie. She liked to savor her purloined goods.

I watched with Cat while Teri did her best to capture my dastardly dog, who managed to evade Teri long enough to chew and swallow the stolen meat.

"Now, Cookie I can see murdering someone," Teri muttered. "Like she murdered my meatballs."

I tried to hold back a laugh. But my dog had tomato sauce on her mouth. I motioned to my lips, and Cookie licked her own, erasing the evidence.

Cat watched us and shook her head. "I swear that dog's smarter than you are. It's uncanny."

"It's weird." Teri did that move her mom did, pointing two fingers at her eyes, then reversing them to point at Cookie. "I'm watching you, Cookie."

My dog whined and hurried back to my side, trying to hide behind me.

"Nice try. But you got caught," I told her. "I've taught you better than that."

I mulled over my words, wishing I could put the mystery of Gil Cloutier and my journal behind me. But I couldn't. "You know, I think it's time I talked to Abe. And maybe to Joe and Bill. They certainly didn't seem to mourn Abe, more concerned with winning the Gardener's Purse."

Teri continued glaring at my now-repentant dog. "Well, at book club, we did say people murder for love or money. In Gil's case, I'd lean more toward money."

"Me too," Cat agreed. "But if you're going to talk to Abe, make sure to be gentle. He's not the drugged-out monster people make him out to be. He's actually a decent guy, just trying to get his life back together. From what I've heard, he was doing pretty well until his dad died. I feel sorry for him."

Interesting. "How do you know that?"

"My friend, Juanita, works at the shelter, and we talk. Abe used to be a regular until he moved into that halfway house. But he actually pops in now and then to help out. He's always loved my cookies."

"Ah." A Cat fan. "Can you ask Juanita if she's seen him lately? I need to talk to him."

"Sure. But be careful. I have a feeling Berg will have a meltdown if he thinks you're interfering with his investigation."

"She has to," Teri said. "I'd tell you to let the cops handle this. But Lexi, they're blaming you for Gil's murder. I think you need to protect yourself." Teri's eyes gleamed with excitement. "Just think of it. I can help with info I get from the DA's office. Cat knows everybody and can bribe them with baked goods. And you can keep your ears open by watching and listening to who says what at the bookshop."

"If you were really smart, you'd put the Macaroons to work for you," Cat said. "You know those guys know everything that happens in this town. Especially Stefanie and Darcy."

Teri shook her head. "Yeah, but one of them might have told the cops about her journal. Who can she trust?"

"I say she can trust Stefanie." Cat turned to me. "I'll figure out where Abe is."

I nodded. "Teri, see what you can dig up at the courthouse. And Cat, while you're looking for Abe? Lean on Roger a little." She turned pink again. "Your big date is tomorrow night, right? Try to weasel some info out of him, like you did at the gym. But don't risk your new relationship, okay? A question or two about me would be normal. Roger won't suspect anything, I don't think."

Cat grinned, excited. About investigating or the date, I couldn't say. "I won't. I'll be slick about it."

I grimaced. So did Teri. Fortunately, Cat didn't see us, focused on her plans to Mata Hari the heck out of Roger Halston.

"Well, I think it's a plan." I took my plate to the sink and washed it. "Teri has the DA's office. Cat has Roger and Abe. And I'll start compiling what we know. But I'm going to have to keep any notes on the murder here. I can't have Berg linking me to something else suspicious."

"Good call." Teri nodded. "Do you want me lean on Stefanie, to try to figure out what she knows?"

"No. I'll do it. She ordered a book that just came in, and I'll bring it by tomorrow. Cat, you'll need to cover for me at the store for a bit."

"No problem."

"So, we have a plan." I felt like the ringleader of a circus and prayed I wasn't going to come off as a clown. Yet, imagining how great this might translate to the written word did excite me. Especially because I would be pausing my writing career while waiting for the police to catch a killer. Helping them a little couldn't hurt, could it?

* * *

"Are you out of your mind?" Stefanie asked me the following day, tucking the book I'd brought her under the cell phone sitting on a nearby table.

We sat on her back porch, overlooking a butterfly bush filled with flittering hummingbirds. Stefanie had a lovely little craftsman-style cottage. A one-floor home, painted navy blue with white shutters, it even had a white picket fence squaring off her lush, green lawn. Her back garden, like most of the homes south of Cinnamon Avenue, looked like an explosion of color. She spent much of her time gardening but had no urge to belong to the CGC, claiming they were too cliquey and annoying.

I agreed with her, but then again, *everything* annoyed Stefanie: Alison living too far away (two streets over, not even a quarter of a mile), Confection Coffee's house brew being too pricey since Nadine now charged an extra quarter (making it 75 cents) if you didn't bring your own cup, and my Uncle Elvis's motorcycle being too loud and distracting for our cute little town, because, "for God's sake, we aren't a motorcycle gang kind of city."

Uncle Elvis drives a cute, sporty Vespa. The royal-blue scooter tops out at forty miles per hour and embarrasses my Harley-loving Uncle Jimmy to no end.

"I'm not crazy," I found myself saying. "I want you to swear, on the state of Texas, that you had nothing to do with turning me in to the cops."

Her eyes bugged. She opened her mouth, then snapped it closed. "You wait right here." The screen door banged shut as she entered her house. She returned holding a neatly folded Texas flag. She held the flag in one hand and placed her other on top of it.

In a solemn voice, she said, "I hereby swear, on the great state of Texas, that I did not touch your goofy little journal."

"Hey."

"What? I saw you write in it once. It has unicorns in it. With fangs." She frowned. "I told you I don't much care for fantasy books."

I nodded. "Fair enough. You can put the flag away now."

"I think I'll keep it close." She sniffed. "It always makes me feel better."

I studied her. "Why did you move out here, anyway? I've always wondered."

"Well, my husband had family out here. So we raised our children, then stayed when we retired. After he passed, I'd made so many friends and had put down roots. Texas has my heart, but I'm also a proud Oregonian." She narrowed her eyes at me. "And I'm no rat."

"I didn't think so, but I had to be sure." Oddly, I believed Stefanie. Not just because I knew her as more of an instigator than a tattletale, but because she held Texas as sacred as some folks held their religion. Heck, to Stefanie, Texas *was* a religion.

"Well, I guess I can't blame you." She took another suspicious look around her yard.

I bit back a laugh. "I kept Cookie at the store. Cat has her."

"Good. That mutt."

I chuckled. At her look, I swallowed the rest of my mirth. "So, well, I need your help."

"I'd think so."

"You're a real crime afficionado. You know how mysteries work." I had debated how much I wanted to tell her and decided I might as well go all in. "You know I used to edit books when I lived in Seattle. I mostly edited romance and women's fiction, though I did help out on a few thriller novels." Which had been a blast. Don't get me wrong, I loved working with romance authors, especially the romantic suspense titles. Who doesn't love falling in love? But the whodunit parts stayed with me long after the reads.

Stefanie nodded, her gaze surprisingly intense.

"When I quit my job and came home, I decided to write my own mystery."

"Okay."

"The thing is, I wrote some notes about murder—in general—in my journal, which makes me look like a bigger suspect, especially after Cookie found Gil's body and that bloody pipe."

"Which has already been established not to have been the murder weapon," Stefanie said.

"Right. Word is Gil was killed by something sharp." I paused. "Maybe a knife." I really needed to know more.

"Interesting. Go on."

"Well, someone at book club—it had to be a Macaroon—took my journal, returned it, then told the police about it. Berg and his lieutenant questioned me yesterday." I filled her in on everything I knew so far about the murder, including my suspicions about Abe and a treasure map.

"You know, you have a pretty good list of candidates for the murder. Hold on." She grabbed her cell phone off the table next to her chair and dialed.

I frowned. "Stefanie, I'd hoped to keep this between—"

"Ali? Get your butt over here. We have a real murder to solve!" Stefanie cleared her throat. "And keep that quiet, you hear? We're in the back." She hung up.

I sighed. "I wanted to keep this between you and me."

"You'll want Alison too. She's got better ears than I do about what goes on in this town. And trust me, she'd never read a private journal and blab. She's got secrets of her own." Stefanie winked. "A dead body or two buried in that old house, I suspect."

I blinked. "*What?*"

Stefanie laughed. "I'm kidding. But I can tell you Alison and I were together all night at book club. Even mad at me, she likes to stay close and rant at me until I apologize."

"Quiet Alison rants?"

"Huh. Nothing quiet about that woman. It's all a front."

"If you say so."

Alison lived two streets over at her B&B, A Sweet Retreat. She arrived in minutes, and from the look of her, she'd run the whole way. Seeing me, she smoothed down her hair and walked up the back stairs. In a pair of light-green capris and a floral T-shirt developing some sweat stains, she looked like she'd been through a storm, the hair not floating around her face sticking to her sweaty forehead.

"Oh, hello, Lexi."

"Hi, Alison. Thanks for coming."

"No problem." Then quiet, conservative Alison gave Stefanie a firm look and demanded to know, in the firmest voice I'd ever heard her use, "So did Lexi kill him or not? And what are we proving? Her innocence or someone else's guilt? What's the verdict?"

I just stared. Huh. I guess I didn't know the people in this town as well as I thought I did.

Chapter Thirteen

I stared from Stefanie to Alison, ready to go over the whole mess again, but Stefanie did the honors instead. In concise words, she filled in her best friend on the case.

The case. As if I were playing at being a detective. More like Inspector Clouseau than Sherlock Holmes, to my way of thinking, Clouseau being a comedic goof who always—accidentally—got the bad guy.

"Right." Alison leaned against the porch railing, deep in thought. "I'm a retired librarian, so I know how to do research," she said to me. "When Gil died, Stef and I discussed it. We didn't think you had it in you to murder him."

"Had it in me?" Why did I feel insulted that the pair thought I didn't have the moxie for murder?

"Which leaves us with too many suspects." Alison shared a glance with Stefanie, and the two nodded. "You have the CGC, because they're all super competitive. Plus, this year the Gardener's Purse is worth a lot of money. And despite what you might think, not everyone's as flush as they say they are. That prize is definitely worth murdering for."

"Seriously?" What the heck? "Who's lying?"

"We'll get back to that." Stefanie nodded at Alison. "Go on."

"Right. Then you have Gil's boys. None of them got along with him. Personally, my money's on Abe, but Stefanie doesn't think so."

Stefanie shook her head. "I think Scott might have done it."

"What? Scott?"

Stefanie sighed. "I know. He's an unlikely suspect. That's why my money's on him. I'm voting for the underdog."

"What about Matt?" I offered.

Alison answered, "An interesting choice. Do we know for a fact he was in Portland at the time of his father's murder?"

"Nope." Stefanie shook her head. "We do not."

Fascinated to see who else they'd come up with, I asked, "Who besides those guys are on the list?"

"Gil said whatever was on his mind. He irritated a lot of people. Not just his sons or the CGC wanting to knock him off for the Gardener's Purse. He said plenty to folks in town about whatever was bothering him at the time. Heck, we caught him at the Ripe Raisin once ranting about his neighbor and her teenagers. It was ridiculous, but she was there and overheard him talking about the twins. She laid into him but good."

Alison nodded. "As soon as we heard Gil had been murdered, Stef and I talked about who might have killed him. You were way, way down on our list. Sadly, it's a pretty long list."

I just stared at her.

"What?" She grinned, no longer appearing timid or mousy. "I like to keep a low profile in public, especially since I dally with politics."

"Yep. She's smart. No dirt on the quiet, respectable Alison Wills, the real puppet master in Confection." Stefanie smiled at her friend. I was starting to get scared. "Whereas I'm the loudmouth of the group. Oh, don't try to tell me I'm not."

"I wasn't going to."

She grinned. "When you get to be my age, you call it like you see it. I'm not into politics or needing people to like me. I don't give a rat's tail." Her grin faded. "Gil was a jerk. No talking around it. But he was one of our own. Lived all his life in this town, and he'll be missed for that alone. Every town needs a jerk."

"But we already have Chad Berg." I chuckled at my own joke.

Alison shook her head. "Detective Berg isn't so bad. Now his boss is a horse's patoot. That Captain Know-It-All is just like his father. Please."

"Alison isn't fond of the chief," Stefanie confided, as if I couldn't have figured that out on my own. "In any case, you need our help. We're just starting to get the Macaroons right. With Lydia gone, we've had to mold you into a proper bookshop owner and club host. And we're finally getting there."

"Wait. What?" Getting where?

Alison interrupted, "The point is, we don't want a murderer in our lovely little town. My business is thriving. Stef's flowers are amazing, and her tutoring business has been growing."

I stared, wide-eyed, at Stefanie Connett. "You teach little kids?"

"Teenagers mostly."

Who the heck hated their children that much that they sent them to Stefanie? I wanted badly to ask but held myself back.

"We want this criminal captured. The fact he—or she—is targeting you isn't good, Lexi." Alison looked troubled.

"I know. It makes sense, though. Gil was my neighbor. He was spotted tearing into me the day before the murder. I'm a likely suspect."

"But was the murder planned or spontaneous? Did Gil's killer just snap? Or did the killer plan his death for weeks and months before? That makes a difference in how we move forward. In any event, we still have to be careful, because if he killed once, he'll kill again." Alison said half apologetically, "And I'm using *he* as just a placeholder. I'll be happy enough to learn a woman killed Gil."

"Not really happy," Stefanie amended and said to me, "You know what she's saying."

Did I? I shook my head. "I think we *all* need to be careful. Someone in book club is out to get me. Or at least wants the police to suspect me."

Stefanie shrugged. "In their defense, you did look guilty from what you wrote in your journal. You can't necessarily blame the person who turned you in. Anyone reading that might think you really did kill Gil. They did their civic duty by telling the police about the journal."

I sighed. "I guess."

"But be careful. Suspect everyone." Alison nodded. "Well, except us and Cat and Teri. But everyone else, be careful."

"Right." I paused, wanting to ask them about my theory tying the dug-up yards around town to Abe's supposed treasure map and possibly Gil's death. But the cops didn't seem to buy into that theory, so I decided to sit on it, find out more information, then bring it back to my new sleuth team.

Stefanie stood and nodded to Alison. She then turned to me. "Okay, get out. We'll talk again, soon. But not at book club."

"Yes, it's too public, especially not knowing who ratted you out," Alison said. "Plus, our next get-together is too far away. The Macaroons don't meet again for another two weeks. We'll need to share our info sooner than that. And we don't want the police to track us."

"Track you? Why would they?"

"Our involvement must be kept secret." Stefanie frowned, and I could almost see a cartoon bubble with the words *conspiracy theorist* in neon over her head. She reminded me of Teri, for sure. "We'll contact you through your friends. I have their numbers from book club."

Alison nodded. "Good idea."

"Um, okay." How was I losing track of the conversation? From investigating a murder to secret phone trees? Had I fallen down a rabbit hole or what? "I'll talk to you two later."

"You mean, *Teri* will talk to you later," Stefanie emphasized.

"Right. Teri. After you get some info on Gil and his sons."

They both nodded, like crime-fighting bobbleheads.

I left before I caught more of the insanity. On my walk back to work, since we still had another two hours before closing, I had just passed Peppermint Way when I saw Mandy Coatney standing in front of Gil's house on the sidewalk, her camera, as always, hanging around her neck.

I waved, catching her attention.

She hurriedly snapped a few pictures before heading my way.

To my bemusement, she looked sad, as if she'd been crying.

"Are you okay?"

She blinked and smiled through watery eyes. "Allergies. I ran out of my pills and can't stop tearing up. It's awful." She sniffled. "What are you up to? Not at the bookshop? Did you close early today?"

"Cat's covering. I was taking a quick break, needing a walk in this gorgeous weather."

We chatted about the weekend festival and book club, about how much Alan enjoyed being a part of the Macaroons.

"He told me he thinks the Macaroons need more boys." She smiled. "Though not a boy, I'd love to attend, but I just don't read enough. And honestly, during our growing seasons, I spend most of my time trying to capture the perfect picture."

I knew she'd once won some major awards for her photography, even getting *National Geographic* to publish a photograph or two. "You've been shooting up the town, huh?"

She laughed, and I realized she was a lot prettier than I'd realized, always having seen her with a camera hiding her face. "Yes, so to speak."

"Have you seen anything out of the ordinary lately? Maybe something that stuck out to you, around the time Gil died?" Okay, that was pretty direct, but what harm could it be to ask?

"I see a lot of stuff out of the ordinary around this town," she murmured, looking down at her camera. She looked up at me. "Everyone has secrets. And that's not a bad thing; it just is."

"I don't have any secrets." Not now, since someone had told the police about my *secret* novel. "But I get what you're saying. Just because we're a small town doesn't mean we should be up in everyone's business all the time."

"Right." She studied me, and I wondered what she saw. "But if I knew anything about Gil's death, I'd definitely tell the police." She teared up. "I can't believe anyone would kill in our town. It's so . . . savage. So wrong." She wiped her eyes and gave a watery smile. "Not allergies now. Poor Gil."

"Yeah."

She left with a quiet good-bye, but I stared at Gil's house, wondering why Mandy Coatney seemed to be all over town lately. And why I got the sense she knew more than she'd said.

* * *

I returned to Sweet Fiction to finish out the workday, telling Cat to leave early since she'd covered for me. "Plus, you need to get ready for your date."

She blinked. "What? I'm ready."

"You're wearing that?"

I looked her over, from her Hello Kitty skull-and-crossbones T-shirt to her knee-length ripped jean shorts and Converse sneakers. Yes, it did indeed feel as if my friend was twenty-eight going on sixteen. "Well, uh, you do look nice, but . . ."

"Oh, just spit it out." She glared at me, her hands on her hips, doing her best impression of an Amazon.

"I'm just— Well, I think that . . ."

"I look terrible?" Cat's insecurity was so odd. To me, she was a beautiful woman with a big heart. She cooked like a dream, was in fantastic shape, and never failed to help out when needed. Yet she'd never had much luck with guys, despite going on a ton of dates. It was as if she wouldn't let anyone close because she didn't feel she deserved it.

Or maybe that was me projecting. Again.

I put my failed engagement to the back of my mind and concentrated on Cat. "Let me ask you something."

She seemed to brace herself. "Go ahead."

"You like Roger, don't you?"

"Sure."

"Why?"

She blinked. "Well, he's cute, has a great job, and doesn't live with his parents," she said drily.

"That's always a plus."

"And he likes me." She sounded amazed by that. "He never tries to change me. He, so far, accepts me as I am."

"And he should. But that doesn't mean you can't try to impress him a little. You're in the getting-to-know-each-other stage. When you both take a little more care with your appearance. You don't eat broccoli at dinner because you don't want the green stuff hanging from your teeth. You don't fart in front of each other." Which I still thought should never be acceptable in a relationship. "And you never kiss without fresh breath. All beginning-relationship things."

"So, okay." She paused and looked herself over. "I should dress up?"

"Just a little. Nothing too sophisticated. You want him to like you as you are."

"Ha-ha."

I grinned. "I'm just saying I know you have nicer clothes than these. If you're trying to test him, to see if he'll dump you because you don't look your best, I guess you can. But isn't it nice when he tries to impress you? It shows he cares, at least a little. Would it be so wrong to put on your nicest shorts and sandals? And maybe a tank top to show off your arms? Or a vintage T-shirt with a story behind it?

"You said he likes good food, right? Most places for a date night have diners wearing fancier clothes than Hello Kitty. I'm just saying. Don't change yourself. But a change of clothes wouldn't be remiss."

Ha. Take that, Uncle Elvis! I had used *remiss* in a sentence. I'd have to text him about that later.

Cat sighed. "Okay. Teri said something similar to me the last time I asked her, but I thought she was just being a pain. She's pretty prissy about clothes."

"She is. But she's not wrong. You don't need a five-hundred-dollar purse, but maybe jean shorts that aren't ripped? And a T-shirt that doesn't sport a bloody knife and skulls?"

"I guess. But at the gym, Roger liked how I looked. I saw him checking me out. And let me tell you, I had a pretty good sweat going on then."

I snorted. "Of course he likes you. You're like Xena Warrior Princess but with red hair." Cat had a toned body I'd kill to have. Unfortunately, I remained slender only because I had a weird metabolism. The luck of a genetic draw. On the exercise front, I liked hiking, but only in the cooler months. I had an aversion to sweat. Thus, my muscles remained "mealy" according to certain statuesque redheads.

"I am pretty strong." Cat made a muscle.

I shook my head. "I'm done with you. Go home, shower, put on your very dating best, and knock Roger's socks off. Well, after you pump him for information on the Cloutier Case—capital Cs."

She saluted me. "I'm on it, Skipper."

I cringed. "Skipper? Isn't that Barbie's flat-chested younger sister?"

Cat snickered. "If the shoe fits."

I stared down at my front. I liked the way I looked. I was proportionate, could lunch at Eats n' Treats a few times a week and not freak about gaining ten pounds, and liked my blonde hair. I wasn't amazing in the looks department, but I was pretty enough.

The door jingled as Cat left. I was still staring at myself when a deep voice startled me out of my introspection.

"Ms. Jones? Everything okay?"

Of course it had to be Berg witnessing me check myself out. I did my best to not flush. "Um, fine. Thought I had a stain on my shirt, but I don't." I glanced up and saw him in regular clothes. "Off duty?"

"Yeah." He studied me.

I studied him right back. Then a thought struck. "Hey, are you staking me out?"

"What?"

I frowned. "Are you watching me? Trying to catch me in the act?"

He let out a loud breath. "The act of what, exactly?"

"I don't know. Something illegal?"

"And just what would that illegal something be?"

"Not murder, I can tell you that." I crossed my arms over my chest.

Cookie suddenly remembered she had a duty to protect me and crept out from her sleeping spot behind the register. My threatening pooch then gave a huge yawn as she stretched, sat, and smiled up at Berg.

His lips quirked. "Actually, I came in to look for a book."

"You . . . oh." Deflated, I looked around. "What genre?" Yes, that sounded much better than *I didn't know Neanderthals could read.*

"I like crime fiction."

"Really?"

"Yes. Why? Is that a problem?"

Man, his eyes were really gray. Icy, yet warming as he talked. Or was I imagining things? Was he setting me up by being, not pleasant, but normal, in order to get me to confess everything? Not that I had anything to confess . . .

"Ms. Jones?"

"Oh, please. Enough already. My name is Lexi." I frowned at him. "It's not a problem that you read. I'm just surprised that you'd be dealing with crime all day, then want to relax by reading about it some more."

"Good point. But I like to read fiction for fun. What happens on the pages isn't real."

"They do say reality is stranger than fiction, I guess."

"I am open to other things. My life doesn't always revolve around crime." He sounded defensive. Hmm. Maybe I was coming across as badgering my customers. That wasn't a good habit to get into.

I'd humor him. "Can I interest you in a romance?"

He just stared at me.

"No? How about science fiction then? Fantasy? Horror?"

He blinked and deliberately turned away from me, heading to the nonfiction area of the store.

"Oh, okay. You want some nonfiction. Biography? History?" I followed.

He perused the shelves without looking at me. "I'm not sure."

Realizing he probably wanted to shop without an audience, I relented enough to direct him around the store. "Right. So science fiction and fantasy is over there. Next to it you'll find the stacks of romance and women's fiction. Thrillers and mysteries are there. General fiction is there. On the tables you'll see popular fiction and current best sellers. And there, on the far wall, is a selection of books by our local authors."

Berg followed my directions with his gaze before looking back at me. "Is that where your alleged book will be soon?"

Just when I was starting to warm to the detective who claimed to like books. "Nothing *alleged* about it. As soon as you coppers figure out who really killed Gil, I'll be back to writing. And you be nice, or you'll find yourself—"

"Dead?"

"I was going to say written into my book as the idiot cop. You know, the dunderhead who misses all the obvious clues and has to be saved by the intrepid heroine?"

His lips quirked. "Intrepid, you say?"

Strangely enough, something about that expression struck me, and I couldn't look away from Iceberg and his laughing but not laughing face.

He stared back.

I didn't know what I would say next, but then I didn't have to worry about it. Dash walked through the door and immediately glued himself to my side, glaring at Berg.

"Yo, Berg. What are you doing here? Harassing Lexi again?"

"Uh, Dash, I—"

"I'm here for a book, Hagen." He glanced from Dash to me and raised a brow. "I didn't realize I was interrupting anything."

"You're not—"

"She's a friend of my sister's, so lay off." Dash wrapped an arm around my shoulders, vibrating with tension. "Got a problem with that?"

Berg gave a short laugh. "Please. Am I supposed to find you threatening?"

I gawked, not having anticipated a fight for my attention. Thrilled at first, I gradually realized I had nothing to do with the building testosterone in the bookshop. Especially since the guys seemed to have forgotten all about me as they tried to outglare each other.

I squirmed out from Dash's hold. "Okay, fellas. I'm closing up in half an hour." Screw it. We weren't that busy and I wanted to go home. "Dash, either buy a book or get out. Detective Berg, same goes for you."

Dash had the nerve to scowl down at me before stalking to the magazine section. I happened to know he had an addiction to *Men's Health* and *All About Brews* magazine.

Berg glared at me.

"What?"

He muttered, "My name is Chad, not Detective Berg. Not when I'm out of uniform."

Out of uniform took on a literal meaning that had no business being in my brain. It took a moment for me to nod and return to the register counter, pretending to be normal.

Yep. Red on the outside, unicorns eating ogres on the inside. That was me in a nutshell. Way beyond normal.

Berg brought a biography on a real-life detective I'd read and enjoyed, beating Dash to the counter by seconds, though not on purpose. I didn't think.

"You'll like this," I told Berg. *I mean, Chad.* "It's really good."

"Yeah, it looks good." He watched me as he paid, his gaze intense.

"Now what?" I growled.

He smiled back—*smiled,* talk about lethal—taking his time while Dash made impatient noises behind him. "Appreciate the help, Lexi." He slid his change into his pocket, turned, and made a wide circle around Dash. On his way out, he said over his shoulder, "Keep your nose out of my investigation, and you won't have any more trouble from me. Unless, of course, we find the murder weapon in your backyard."

The door shut behind him.

I gaped and asked Dash, "Do you think that was a veiled threat to plant evidence?" Berg had called me Lexi. What did that mean?

Dash sighed. "I think he meant for you to stay out of his way and let him do his job. He's a conceited dictator with authority issues, but he's good at his job, or so Noah tells me."

"Great." I stared at Dash. "So why are you here? You do know this is a bookstore."

"Very funny. Ring me up, Ms. Perky."

I growled and took his money. "Here. Enjoy being fit and drinking beer."

He grinned. "Thank you. I will. And for the record, I just wanted to make sure you were doing okay. Teri told me she and Cat had plans to be out tonight while you had nothing better to do than sit home with your dog." He reached down to pet Cookie, who mysteriously appeared at his side, looking for love. "I thought I'd swing by and check on you before I head in to work." He glanced over his shoulder. "Seems like I wasn't the only one."

"Don't worry. I have his number." Plant evidence in my yard, indeed. I'd go home, where Cookie and I would do a thorough sweep.

Dash's eyes widened. "His number?"

"What? Oh, not his phone number. I mean, I know what Detective Law and Order is all about."

Dash frowned. "I'm not sure you do."

"Huh?"

"Go home, would you? It's five o'clock."

I let out a relieved breath. "Quitting time."

He waited while I quickly locked up and joined me and Cookie as we walked out the front door. At the corner of Main, we parted ways.

" 'Bye, Dash. Behave tonight."

"Please. Where's the fun in that?"

I watched him leave, a flirty swing in his step. I swear, the guy did things like that just to irk me. But I did like watching him . . . walk away. I grinned down at Cookie and, seeing no one near, let her off her leash as we walked home.

No one bothered us, and I appreciated the cool evening as the birds chirped and the trees whispered in the breeze that brought the scents of roses and lilacs to me.

Which reminded me . . . I stared down at my dog. "What were you looking for by the Confection Rose yesterday, Cookie?"

But she made no move to revisit the scene of her earlier crime, so we went home.

I made dinner. I fed Cookie. I stared at my laptop, wishing I could write and knowing I should take a break.

Instead, I stared through my window at Gil's house. It remained empty. The windows dark.

After a last sad glance at my laptop, I turned on the television and watched a movie. As I ate popcorn and did my best to tune in to a woman blamed for a murder she didn't commit, I wondered how Teri and Cat were doing. Why Dash had been so nice lately. And what Berg really meant by telling me to call him Chad.

Chapter Fourteen

Starting out my Thursday on the heels of a nightmare had not been pretty. I kept seeing Gil Cloutier lying in a grave next to my dog, who held his femur in her teeth, a pipe where Gil's thigh should be.

Around the grave, Gil's sons were sobbing, while Cat and Roger stood with their basketball-playing children. Berg and Dash stood on either side of me, holding me off my feet with a hand around each of my pigtails while I squirmed and screamed, "I didn't do it! I didn't do it!"

So disturbing.

After I showered, I dressed in a sporty skirt and lime-green tee with my favorite walking sandals. A bit of lip gloss, mascara, and a spritz of floral perfume and I was set for work.

Cookie grabbed Mr. Leggy, and we set out for the bookshop. Today I decided on a garden tour of my own along the way, and we looped down Mocha Drive, past Pixie Apartments, where Cat and Teri lived, and down Court Street, which ran parallel to Main. On my way, I passed Ed, Peggy, and Bonnie—three CGC heavies—on a walk.

They glared at me with suspicion as Cookie and I passed. I waved and wished them all a good morning, but only Bonnie waved back.

Along the way, I kept my eye out for more upturned grass and mounds of dirt, but I saw nothing out of the ordinary. Which reminded me, I needed to talk to Abe today. I'd get Cat to arrange a meeting or I'd find him myself.

Neither of my friends had texted me last night, not that I'd hoped—er, expected—to hear from them while they were socializing. But I had to admit I couldn't wait to hear how their dates had gone. And if Roger had spilled any more beans.

And speaking of beans, once in the shop, I was happy to fire up the coffee machine before Cat arrived, living up to my perky namesake since I'd had so much sleep last night. With the exception of my little nightmare, I'd had more than ten hours of shut-eye. Sad what a lack of a love life could do for a girl's health.

I put a few books away I'd missed at closing yesterday, unable to stop reassessing my visit from Berg. I couldn't exactly think of him as Iceberg anymore, though *Chad* felt a little too personal. Fascinating to see so much animosity between him and Dash, though. I needed more information on that tense relationship, and I had a feeling Dash would be less than forthcoming about it. No matter. I'd get the truth from Teri once I saw her again.

I pulled out my phone and invited her to the bookshop to share lunch. A glance at my bologna sandwich and yogurt in the office minifridge convinced me to host a business lunch, courtesy of Sal's Smoothies, the vegan place around the corner that made the best pesto wraps. Plus I knew Teri liked them.

After sending Teri a text, I finished straightening up, made myself a coffee, and took Cookie out for another quickie pit stop down the street.

I waved to Uncle Elvis as he zipped by on his scooter, likely on the way to a job.

See? When in Seattle, I never used to run into people I knew when not working. And when at the office, I typically interacted in business mode. Oh, I'd had friends. It wasn't like I lived a monastic life in the big city. But none of them gave me warm fuzzies. None of them were family. While dating had been a lot easier in Seattle, I'd never felt as if I had found a home with anyone there. And I'd tried.

Here, I felt at home just by walking down Main Street.

Cookie finished sniffing and headed back toward the shop. I followed with her leash in hand but not attached to her collar.

As I walked, I noticed the couple I'd spoken to at the Ripe Raisin walking hand in hand across the street. Bob and Anna, I remembered. Wow. Had they been here all week? I loved Confection, but just how much sightseeing could a person do in our small town?

Anna saw me and waved. I smiled back.

She jaywalked with Bob to greet me at the entrance of the bookstore. "Hey, Lexi."

"Better not let the police see that," I warned with a grin. "They're very happy to issue jaywalking warnings and tickets during the summer season."

"Oh, whoops." Today Anna wore a pair of shorts with butterflies sewn onto the pockets, a bright-purple T-shirt, and colorful sneakers. I absolutely loved her fashion sense. "We won't do that again. We're just excited to be taking the garden tour today."

Bob slung an arm around her shoulders. "She means taking the tour *again*. We spent last weekend hiking and didn't get to see as much of the garden tour as she'd wanted."

"Had to get back to the city and our real jobs," Anna said with a sigh. "But I convinced Bob to take off early from work so we could head back here for an early weekend."

"Good idea. So your friend didn't come back with you?"

"Nah. Alec had to stay behind." Bob grinned. "He's an office jockey. I'm my own boss, so I come and go when I please." He looked me over and nodded. "You too, huh? You own the bookshop, right?"

"Well, I manage it. My parents own it, but they're on a much-deserved vacation traveling the country."

"That sounds nice." Anna nodded and said to Bob, "Maybe something we can do someday, right, hon?"

"Sure, babe." He squeezed her shoulder, his hand curled like a claw.

I watched them, something in the gesture touching on a memory that refused to fully surface.

Cookie gave a short growl around Mr. Leggy, which she refused to drop, and my mind wandered.

"Cute dog." Anna leaned down to let Cookie sniff her hand first. Smart. When Cookie wagged her tail, Anna crouched to ooh and aah over my canine conniver. "She's a sweetie. I love dogs. How old is she?"

"Two, maybe. I found her on my way back to Confection, alone on the side of the road." *You sad, pathetic thing.* Ha. My dog was eating up all the attention. "She was just a tiny puppy then."

"I think she's adorable." Anna laughed at Mr. Leggy, which Cookie had yet to drop. "And she has a pink friend. So cute." She rose and grabbed Bob's hand.

He stood there, looking awkward. Probably not a dog person, though he smiled at us encouragingly.

"Well, I'd better get in so I can open up. You guys enjoy the tour. Again." I smiled.

They waved and walked down the street, no doubt toward Nadine's coffee shop, where the garden tour normally gathered to meet. Surprisingly, the tour did a fantastic job of swinging by all the participating home gardens and outdoor spaces, giving histories on not only the old homes but also the town itself.

I had to give credit where credit was due. Darcy had been instrumental in getting the tour up and running. She occasionally still picked up a tour to run herself, probably to get a break from having her kids underfoot all day. Hey, I'm just repeating what she's mentioned at book club, not trying to malign her or anything.

The morning at work passed without incident. Cat insisted she'd share news with both me and Teri at lunch, which made me feel a little better about her keeping so quiet about her date. Yet it was killing me not to know, having to wait.

And she knew it. She kept smirking at me while I watched the time slowly tick away.

By noon, I'd had enough. "I'm grabbing our lunch," I called as I whisked Cookie with me down the street.

We passed Confection Coffee. Fortunately, Nadine appeared to be nowhere in sight.

"Where are you off to so fast? Trying to avoid the police?" Nadine called just as I turned the corner off Main.

So close, and yet so far.

I turned, my pleasant face on. "Shouldn't you be back at work? I hear the boss is a real pain."

Her smile soured. Score! "Who said that?"

"Why would I tell on your poor slaves—I mean, employees? You'll just whip them back in line."

"Very funny." Yet she didn't look as amused by our repartee as usual.

"What's your problem?"

"Aside from you?" She knelt and pulled a treat from her pocket. "Not *you*, Cookie. *You* I like."

My traitorous companion left me for Nadine and her biscuit, happily chomping while Nadine stroked her fur.

I watched, curious. Nadine seemed annoyed, and for once, I wasn't the cause of it.

"Not that it's any of your business, but someone broke into my shed last night and made a mess, stealing half my tools. Then they destroyed the roses I'd finally gotten over their aphid problem. Just when I finally had them healthy again!"

Like me, Nadine wasn't one of the CGC. A gardening enthusiast, however, she did her best to grow things. Also like me, she didn't have a knack for it.

"Before you start whipping out accusations, we didn't do it." I nodded to Cookie. "Ever since Gil, we've been together all the time. And if she's not with me, she's with Cat or Teri."

"I know." Nadine sounded glum. Normally I liked her knocked off her precious perch on the cusp of arrogance, but not like this. "I'm bummed about the shed and roses, and about there being this much trouble in Confection. Our town used to be so nice. You could leave your door unlocked or your bike in your yard and not worry someone might steal it. Now we have vandalism all over town and a murder to deal with."

"Vandalism?"

She stood and wiped her hands on her back pockets. "You can't tell me you haven't heard about someone tearing up all the yards? The gardens? It's ridiculous. They hit me last night and the Salters a few nights before that."

"Seriously?" I blinked. "I know Ed was blaming Cookie for a lot of digging, but she's actually innocent. Well, she did dig around the Confection Rose last week, but I got to her before she could do any damage. Though come to think of it, I think someone else did the digging first. She was probably rooting around for whatever they might have buried." Or dug up.

"Buried?" Nadine's eyes narrowed on Cookie. "Like a body?"

"Not in the holes I've seen. They're normally not bigger than the size of a bowling ball, I guess. But I haven't heard of anyone having property damage. You should report it to the police."

"Thanks, Mom. I already planned to."

Annnnd our little truce was over before it could properly begin. But hey, at least she wasn't blaming me for breaking into her shed.

"Well, don't let me keep you from avoiding work," I said brightly. "I'm sure you've got a ton of tourists needing your time and attention. But then, hard work is probably something only a lowly employee—not store owner—would understand. Because we peons do all the grunt work while you do nothing but chat up your customers and take all the credit for a successful business."

Her scowl made bumping into her worth it. She turned and left.

"What? No good-bye?" I called after her, snickering at the gesture she shot me over her shoulder.

Continuing to Sal's, I gave a quick glance around, wondering if maybe Matt Cloutier had stopped by. He had started the first smoothie shop here in Confection and had steadily grown one store into a small franchise. I wondered what Gil had thought of that.

I picked up my order from a pleasant employee and hurried back to the bookshop, stopping briefly by a grassy area for Cookie to do her business. Once back at the bookstore, I headed into the back room and spread out our small feast. Veggie wraps, small salads, bottled iced tea, and a few eggplant meatballs with marinara sauce as an appetizer. Yum.

"I put the CLOSED sign out," Cat said as she entered. "Just for half an hour."

Sometimes we closed for a brief lunch, though not often. We had a little plastic clock where you could set the clock hands announcing when you'd open again. We had until one to eat and share news.

The back door jingled. Teri soon hustled in, throwing herself into a chair next to me. "Ah, lunch."

We all grabbed plates and divvied up the food. "Come on, guys. I'm dying here. Tell me how last night went," I demanded while eating.

Cat answered between bites. "It was awesome. Roger loved my outfit. I went with a non-ripped pair of shorts and a green blouse." She said *blouse* as if it were something hideous, but I'd seen that shirt before and knew it looked good on her.

"Your shoes?"

Cat sighed. "Strappy sandals Teri picked out."

Teri beamed.

"Anyway, Roger told me I was pretty. We talked about food and recipes for like over an hour."

"Great." I kept waiting for her to get to Gil.

"He loves basketball. I mean, he's really into it! He played in college a little, did you know that?"

Teri put down her cup. "We're so happy your date went well. But what did he tell you about Gil?"

"Oh, right."

I had to force myself not to roll my eyes.

Teri did it for me.

"Well," Cat said, "apparently, it wasn't a knife that killed Gil. The weapon had an odd shape. Like a V, so something that's sharp and wedged. Gil died sometime last Thursday night, around midnight, maybe."

"I bet he died when Cookie barked," I mused.

"Probably. She hears everything."

Cookie mumbled, a whiny kind of growl that told us she was indeed paying attention. She lay under the table, waiting for the opportunity to gobble up anything we dropped.

"Anyway, Roger told me you're not really a suspect, though that journal didn't help any."

"Did he say who dropped it off?" I asked.

"They don't know."

"Yeah, right," Teri muttered. "They know everything. He's just not telling you. Freaking cops." There was that Teri-paranoia I knew and loved.

Cat ignored her. "Roger said Berg found a note on his desk telling him to look at you. The note was dropped off anonymously at the front desk. No help there."

"Too bad they can't dust it for fingerprints."

"Why would they? The crime still points to you, kind of," Teri pointed out.

"Thanks." I turned back to Cat. "So, the real question we all want answered is . . . did you guys make out after the date or what?" What I really wanted to ask—*did you ruin things with Roger because you asked too many obvious questions about me?*

"We totally did!" Cat squealed.

I relaxed. I had a feeling Roger was as clueless as Cat and probably hadn't noticed her grilling him. That or he was so enthralled with her he didn't care. Regardless, I liked the guy even more, because he'd been kind to Cat and had the good sense to like her for herself.

"I take it you'll be going out again?"

She nodded. "I'm making him dinner Saturday night." She blinked at Teri. "Um, that's if I can have the apartment."

"She can stay with me if Randy's busy," I told them.

Cat high-fived me.

Teri sighed. "Sure. Fine. Make plans around me and about me."

"Oh, like you're bothered." I studied her. "*Are* you bothered?"

Her wide grin made us all laugh.

"Randy and I had fun. He's so smart and handsome. I stared at him all night long."

"I'm sure he stared back. He was ogling pretty hard at the Ripe Raisin last Saturday."

"Darn right." Teri winked. "Sadly, he knows nothing about Gil or the murder. But he did tell me he saw someone running around two nights ago, which would be Tuesday night. Randy was checking out the Confection Rose. There were other people around, though not that many. And he saw someone skulking at the corner of Court and Cinnamon Ave. When he walked closer to investigate, they'd disappeared."

"Could have been kids. Tourists walking near Confection Park."

"Could have been but wasn't. Randy said he saw the person running away from him before he or she disappeared."

"Vanished?" Cat's eyes grew wide. "I knew this town had ghosts."

"No, weirdo. They darted through some trees, and Randy lost them as they headed into the park."

Confection Park, not to be confused with Central Park, sits to the west of Main Street. Bordered by the Court Street municipal buildings, Soda Creek, and a grove of thick trees, the park is home to a baseball field and acres of grass, enough to house our town sports teams. The parks and recreation department has a building there as well, where they store soccer nets, lacrosse nets, and baseball gear. The only thing they don't have is goal posts for football, which is played at the schools.

I wondered whom Randy might have seen and if it meant anything. Or had some random passerby who wanted privacy run away?

"Will you be seeing Randy again?" Cat asked Teri.

"I might." She frowned. "He was sweet, but I didn't like what he said about Dash."

Cat and I leaned forward, and I asked, "What did he say?"

"Some not-nice things."

"Uh-oh. Did he not understand your insane family loyalty?"

"I don't think insane is a good description."

I blinked. "Seriously? Your mother still hates me for something that wasn't my fault ten years ago. Dash is her precious baby boy, and she insists she meet anyone he dates more than twice. Also, as much as you complain about Dash working you to death, you drop everything to help if he needs it."

"Well, he helps me too," Teri said.

"What exactly did Randy say?" Cat asked.

"That Dash takes me for granted. That he works me too hard. That I should stand up to him more."

"You've said as much to us," I exclaimed. "A bazillion times, in fact."

"I know," Teri snapped. "But then he called Dash a jackass."

"And?" I waited. "It's true. He is."

Teri gaped, and I had to laugh at her expression.

"Oh, please. You know he is. You should have heard him with Berg yesterday."

"What? What happened?" Cat wanted to know.

Teri shut her mouth. "Yeah, what happened?"

"Berg came in to buy a book. And he was . . . well, not exactly nice, but not a *jackass*," I said for Teri's benefit.

Cat snickered.

"Then Dash came in and darted to my side, defending me when I didn't need defending. He and Berg kept posturing until I ordered them both to buy a book or leave. Berg bought a biography and Dash bought two magazines."

"Health and beer?" Teri asked.

"Yep."

"Was Berg checking you out?" Cat asked.

"I think so." But in what manner, exactly, I wasn't sure. He hadn't seemed to be angling for anything personal, though he had told me to call him Chad.

Yet I couldn't rule out the possibility he was trying to lull me into trusting him by being less antagonistic. Something I'd do. But then, I'm sneaky like that. Hmm.

"What's that look?" Teri asked, staring at me.

"I don't know what Chad's game is, but I'll find out."

"Oh!" Cat finished her veggie wrap, and we had to wait for her to swallow her food. "Speaking of finding out, I talked to

Juanita. Abe is due at the shelter later today if you wanted to talk to him. He's scheduled to help out."

"Perfect. Thanks. What time?"

"Six, I think. He's serving dinner."

"I'll be there."

"Want my help?"

"Nah. I'll take Cookie. She disarms with cuteness, then I go in for the kill."

"Sounds good."

We both turned to Teri.

Cat quirked a brow. "Now how about you tell us what your real problem is with Randy?"

"And don't lie," I tacked on. "We'll know."

Teri sighed.

Cat and I shared a knowing glance. Time to help our friend in need before I interrogated my number-one suspect in Gil's murder—his son, Abe.

Chapter Fifteen

I waited outside the shelter, sitting at a picnic table with Cookie. She'd left Mr. Leggy behind, fortunately, because she had a habit of dropping him when something interested her, then became obsessed with finding her lost toy.

Lunch had been fun. I'd missed my friends, which made little sense because I saw them all the time. Heck, I worked with Cat. But with them branching into boy country, I felt lonely. Lunch had made up for that. Teri, that little goof, felt intimidated by Randy because, for once, she didn't know if she out-prettied him.

Teri was used to being the gorgeous one in all her relationships. Like Dash, she was seriously good-looking. She was also actually a low-maintenance friend and deserved to be neurotic about something in her life. With Cat, it's her self-esteem due to her height. With Teri, it's about her looks.

I'd told her she was being an idiot, which caused a small fight I'd enjoyed. Then Cat and I had reminded her that she was so much more than her looks and she needed to realize her worth or no one else would.

Lessons I kept taking to heart. *I'm a good writer, and people will love my work.* Meh. No wonder Teri had looked so irritated with me. Even my own pep talks were annoying.

As I waited to talk to Abe, I watched Cookie sniffing at the small green area outside the shelter. The large parking lot looked more than half-empty, only a few cars littering the space. Yet Juanita had told me the shelter was nearing full capacity. Curious. Typically, the folks needing a place to bed down in the summer camped out, leaving plenty of space for newcomers. It was the winter months that saw no room at the inn.

Abe exited the side door, saw me, and smiled as he approached. I stood to greet him.

A nice enough guy, pale from spending much of his time indoors, Abe stood a few inches taller than me. Thin but not emaciated, he'd put on some healthy weight. His blue eyes, the same color as Gil's, seemed clear. Not a bad-looking man if you could discount the jittery tension in his frame.

"Hey, Lexi. You're lookin' good."

"I have to say the same, Abe." A pause. "I'm so sorry about your dad."

He didn't cry, but I saw him tense. "Yeah. He was an ass, but I loved him."

"I think we all say that about our families," I joked. "You have met Sam, right?"

His grin returned. "Your brother's a trip. When's he coming back to town?"

"Oh, Mr. Popular is living it up in Seattle. His work in cybersecurity isn't getting less busy."

"The cybercop of the century." Abe snorted. "I knew I should have taken those coding classes more seriously."

"No kidding." I sat at the picnic table, and Abe sat with me. "Can I ask, does this look familiar to you?" I pulled out the scrap of fabric Cookie had found.

His eyes lit up. "Hey, that's mine."

"Yeah?"

He pulled out a bandanna from his back pocket and matched it to the yellow swatch of fabric. He stroked his fingers over it, and I noticed his first and middle fingers crooked at the tip, the digits not straight but with a permanent bend at his fingertips. Another thing Abe and his dad had in common, because I'd seen Gil's middle finger more times that I cared to admit during my tenure on Peppermint Way, and it too had been crooked even when standing straight and tall at me.

"It's weird," Abe was saying. "I pulled this out of the laundry the other day and found a piece missing. Must have caught it on something."

I studied him, looking for the truth.

"What?" He frowned.

"Abe, my dog found your dad last week. The police keep asking me questions about his death. I didn't kill your dad." I decided to test him. "I don't think you did either."

His eyes filled. "I didn't, no matter what my jerk brothers say." He scowled. "Can you believe they had the nerve to ask me if I killed him? My own dad?" He swore for a while, and I let him get it out. "I mean, come on. I might not have liked him a lot. Hell, no one did. But to kill him? Why would I? Not for any kind of inheritance, that's for sure," he muttered.

"That's right. You guys had the will read the other day."

"Yeah. Dad left the house to me, because I have nothing. But it's not like either Matt or Scott wanted it." He didn't sound bitter, just matter-of-fact. "He left some big investments to Matt and a few sentimental things to Scott."

"No money to Scott?"

"Scott's already got wealth. You know he created that gaming app that went nuts. The house he has here is just one of several." I definitely heard the resentment there. "Oldest brother, most successful, has everything going for him. What does he need from Dad he doesn't already have?"

"Matt's doing well too, though, isn't he?"

"I guess. He and Becky are engaged, and Sal's Smoothies is expanding to San Francisco, last I heard."

"That's great for Matt." And his fiancée, whom I'd never met. "Hey, Abe, how come you don't work at Sal's? I don't mean to pry, but it seems to me Matt would do better having family managing the place rather than a stranger."

Except Abe was a recovering alcoholic who'd last been seen crying into his beer at the Ripe Raisin. *Great thinking, Lexi, you big dope.*

Abe just looked at me, and I tried to pretend my cheeks weren't on fire.

He sighed. "It's no secret I'm a booze hound. Or I *was.*" He ran a hand through his hair. "Lexi, I've been clean for eight months. When I found out Dad died, I ran to the bar and demanded a drink. Dash and Noah served me. I felt drunk as hell, but mostly that was my shock at hearing my dad had died. When Dash helped me home, he told me they'd only given me nonalcoholic beer." He snorted. "I'm a moron who got drunk on fake beer." But he smiled, looking relieved. "I was close to falling and they didn't let me. I'm so glad about that. But man, it's been so hard lately."

"I'll bet." I patted his shoulder. "I'm glad you're getting by, sober."

"My sponsor has been helping a ton. And I've been going to meetings a lot."

"Good." We sat in silence, and I watched him stroke his bandanna. "Can you tell me how Cookie found that torn fabric near Darcy Mason's house?"

He stared at me. "What?"

"She was nosing around Darcy's roses and found it."

"Huh. That's weird." He studied it.

"Abe, are you the one doing all the digging around town? Is this about your treasure map?"

He flushed. "I can't believe I told anyone about that. It was supposed to be a secret."

My heart raced. "So it's real?"

He paused before nodding. "Don't tell, okay?"

"I won't." Though pretty much everyone already knew.

He groaned. "I said that at the Ripe Raisin, didn't I? Now everyone knows."

"Um, yeah. They probably do."

"My dad used to make maps for us kids. That was our thing, the treasure-hunting Cloutiers. That was years ago. But what people don't know is Dad had another map. A special one with a real treasure. He marked spots all over town. I've been looking."

"Digging."

He flushed. "Yeah, a little. But I put the dirt back after I dug. Except someone's been digging after me, leaving a mess. At first I thought it was weird. Now it's just creepy."

"What?"

"Yeah. I thought about telling the cops about it, but to them I'm just Abe's drunk kid who's got issues. If I tell any of them I'm digging around town, they'll throw me in jail for property damage or something worse. Officer Brown told me he's keeping an eye on me." Abe scowled. "Screw him. It's so hard to be sober all the time. People who've never had a problem with addiction don't understand."

"I'm sorry, Abe."

He nodded. "Thanks. And thanks for being sincere about my dad. A lot of people in town have been saying they're sorry, but I can tell they're not." He grimaced. "I know my dad was a pain. He used to complain about you and Cookie when I'd come over, and for the dumbest things. For a light on. For having a dog. For her staring at him sometimes. Dad was weird."

Tell me about it. "He had some quirks for sure."

"I visited him a lot the month before he died, you know."

"I didn't know that."

"Yeah. He felt bad because we never got along. Heck, he only tolerates Scott because Scott 'made something of himself.' But he's not friendly with Matt, which is why Matt's fine to live three hours away."

"Matt has a successful chain of smoothie shops that's growing."

Abe shrugged. "Maybe, but he's not a millionaire yet."

"So you're saying your dad liked Scott because he had money?"

"Nah. Scott's majorly annoying, even to my dad. But they got along, I guess, because Scott doesn't like to rock the boat. Me? I pretty much capsized it." He wiped his eyes. "But Dad changed. At least with me. Last month, he started talking to me a lot more." Abe looked away, twisting his hands. "Gave me his map. Told me to keep it a secret," he muttered. "Bang-up job I did there at the bar. But I was grieving. Not an excuse, but, you know."

I nodded.

"Then there were these people asking me questions. Nice enough for out-of-towners. They were talking about real live treasure hunting, and the guy kept asking to see my map, which I'd left out on the bar. So I showed it to them. They thought it was cool."

"Did you tell them you'd been digging around town?"

"Heck no. And anyway, I stopped digging. My dad was trying to reconnect with me, and the treasure map feels like he's still with me, you know?"

"I'm so sorry for your loss, Abe. I didn't like Gil much, but only because he yelled a lot."

"He was pretty ornery." Abe grinned. "He used to call himself that. I was like, Dad, you sound like you're a hundred years old. Ornery? Cantankerous? Who talks like that?"

"Gil Cloutier," I said drily, ignoring the fact I'd mentally described Stefanie as cantankerous not long ago.

Abe laughed. "Yeah. He wasn't a great dad, but he was *my* dad. I miss him." He started crying again, and Cookie put her head on his leg.

He sniffed and smiled down at her. "Oh hey, Ms. Cookie. I didn't see you there."

She sighed.

He petted her and relaxed. "Sorry. I keep getting teary and can't for the life of me understand why. It's not like me and Dad were super close."

"But like you said, he was your dad. You cry all you want. You earned it."

Abe smiled. “Thanks.” He clutched his bandanna. “And thanks for the missing piece of my headgear. I don’t know how it got by Darcy’s house. Hell, I don’t even like her. She looks at me like I’m gum under her shoe.”

I snorted. “She looks at everyone like that.”

“Yeah. But I am glad you brought it to me. Man, this town is nuts for flowers. If they think I tried digging near anyone’s roses, I’m toast.”

“Tell me about it.” I glared at my dog.

She ignored me, soaking up Abe’s attention.

“Um, Abe?”

“Yeah?”

“You said you’d stopped digging around town. When did you stop?”

“Ah, let’s see. Today’s Thursday. So I stopped Monday, after the will. My heart’s just not in it anymore.”

Yet someone had dug around at Darcy’s. Someone who wasn’t Abe.

“Well, thanks for seeing me. I just wanted a chance to let you know I was sorry about your dad. And that I had nothing to do with it.”

“I know. Thanks for stopping by, Lexi. And you too, Cookie.” He smiled at my dog.

She licked him, and we walked away. But as I glanced over my shoulder, I saw Abe looking at me. I couldn’t read his expression, but it seemed a lot less than friendly.

* * *

By the time Cookie and I returned home, the hour had reached seven thirty. I was starving, and Cookie kept shooting me dirty looks.

"I know, I know. I said I was sorry already." We had just reached the front door when Cookie growled. Not her friendly, pay-me-attention growl. The one that signaled danger. "What?"

She cocked her head, staring at the door, and growled again, this time showing teeth,

I unlocked the front door and let myself in. Looking around, I saw nothing out of the ordinary, but Cookie darted all over the place, sniffing and acting pretty suspicious.

"Weird dog."

I made a tuna sandwich and helped myself to some chips. Before eating, I fed Cookie some precious wet food, making a mental note that I needed to go shopping because I was getting low on groceries.

Cookie whined as she looked around for Mr. Leggy. Despite being insanely intelligent, more than a dog should be, she had some kind of weird amnesia when it came to her toys.

"Doofus, Mr. Leggy is at the bookshop. You'll have to play with T-Rex instead." I pulled her stuffed neon-blue Tyrannosaurus rex from her bin and handed it to her. She sniffed, ignored it, and fetched Gooey the Extraterrestrial, a fuzzy yellow alien, from the pile instead and sat on her dog bed by the couch, cuddling with it.

After dinner, I read a little bit, because hey, what is life without reading. Then I decided to go through some emails before getting to bed. And, well, maybe writing just a little bit. But not about my mystery. I'd write a page on a new character, fleshing her out. I just couldn't afford to stay away from my story.

Sadly, the more I didn't write, the easier it became to procrastinate writing.

Except I couldn't find my laptop. And I'd left it right on top of my desk in the study.

My heart started racing. Nerves flared, and I shivered, feeling stupid for not having paid more attention to Cookie upon our arrival.

Outside, the sun had set, and the darkness now made my home feel less cozy and more creepy.

I rushed around the house, turning on every light, and looked for anything else that might be missing. But no, my jewelry—cheap as it was—and my secret stash of cash remained in place. No missing documents, credit cards, nothing.

But my laptop was gone.

I hurried to my back door. It wasn't locked.

Ever since Gil had died, I'd been making a point to lock up when I left for the day. That included locking the back door.

The missing laptop freaked me out, but I would have been more panicked if I hadn't saved my story by emailing it to myself, minus the Gil parts, of course, which I'd deleted. The story was safe. Great.

But the back door being unlocked?

Had I left without locking up? Now I started second-guessing myself. Still, the missing laptop hadn't walked away by itself. Which meant someone had been in my house when I wasn't home.

I grabbed the phone and made a call, hugging Cookie as I asked the police to send someone out to my address. Stat.

Chapter Sixteen

"It doesn't look like anything's missing," Detective Chad Berg said as he scratched his head and looked around my house.

I hadn't expected him to show up when I'd asked for help, but apparently he'd been in the area. And as I was tied to Gil Cloutier, he was the go-to guy for related incidents, whatever that meant.

"I know what it looks like. But I'm telling you, I locked my doors when I left today, and my back door was unlocked when I got home. My. Laptop. Is. Missing," I spaced out. "It didn't leave on its own."

"Hmm. Any reason a thief would have wanted a look at the laptop?"

I started to answer before noticing the suspicious glint in Berg's eyes. "What exactly are you implying?"

"Nothing at all," he said smoothly. "Just wondering why someone would break into your home and take only the laptop."

I was so, so, so glad I'd deleted that part about killing Gil. I squared my shoulders and did my best to look him in the eye. I hated looking up to meet his gaze. "I have no idea why someone would steal my computer." I then added, "Just like I have no idea why someone would dig all over town looking for Gil's treasure."

He frowned. "This again?"

"Yes, Detective Berg. This again. Think. Who wanted to kill Gil?"

He sighed. "You mean, more than half the town? You have someone specific in mind?"

I growled, "Abe has a treasure map that Gil gave him. Someone has been digging holes all over town, and it's not Abe."

"According to Abe," he said drily.

"No, Abe did dig those holes. But he filled them in. Someone is going all over town digging them back up. But looking for what, exactly?" I asked him, musing on what it might mean.

"What do you mean, Abe dug those holes? Did he say he did?" Berg looked serious.

"Uh, well . . ."

"Alexis Jones, what exactly do you know?"

He'd whipped out my whole name. *Ohh.* "First of all, I'm not intimidated."

He stepped close and glared down at me with those icy eyes. Combined with his Confection PD uniform of khakis and that short-sleeved blue shirt that showed off his massive arms, I admit I was starting to feel intimidated. And I hated feeling small.

I tried to stand taller and thought I saw a smirk. "Are you laughing at me?"

"Crime is no laughing matter."

Huh. He seemed serious.

"Of course, if you'd rather talk about this down at the station with your lawyer present, I'm happy to oblige."

"Such a jerk," I muttered.

He raised a brow. "What's that?"

Cookie wiggled between us and backed me away from Berg, who did flash a small smile at her antics.

"Fine. I talked to Abe yesterday. Not about any crime," I said to forestall his accusations. "But I wanted to let him know how sorry I was about Gil's death."

"And?" Great. Now he looked interested.

"And he admitted he has a treasure map his dad gave him. That Gil started reaching out a month before he died. Did you know Abe inherited Gil's house? Matt got some money, I think. And I'm not sure Scott got much of anything."

Berg watched me, listening, finally.

"Anyway, Abe told me he had been digging around town, following the map. He believes Gil buried something. But Abe filled in all those holes. So who has been digging them back up? Because that interests me."

"And it shouldn't."

Shoot.

"Because this is a murder investigation, and you, last I checked, are not a licensed investigator."

"I'm a PI."

He blinked.

"Well, not officially. I mean my character—"

He loomed. Seriously glared down at me and stuck his face in mine. "You will *not* involve yourself in this investigation, Ms. Jones. Especially if someone is actually targeting you. We'll look into the laptop. Now stop asking questions and go back to your bookshop. You too," he said, pointing to Cookie, who bared her teeth. "I'm not intimidated."

She blinked at him and hid her fangs.

He nodded. "Good. Now, lock both your doors and let me know if you think anything else is missing." He glanced around. "And if your laptop happens to turn back up on its own, let me know that too."

I walked him out and paused. "Wait a minute. What do you mean, turns back up on its own?" My eyes widened. "You think I did this myself? Why?"

He shrugged. "For attention? To become a bigger part of the investigation for your book?"

"My book? Investi— Oh!" I stomped back inside and slammed the door behind me. "Jackhole!"

"I heard that," he yelled and walked away, as I saw through the front window. After watching him get into his car and leave, I called for backup.

Teri and Cat arrived in no time, spare clothes in hand. Sleepover-protect-Lexi night was well under way when Dash showed up, demanding an explanation.

"I told you Berg is an idiot," he muttered for the umpteenth time as I shared my story.

Dash checked out my back door and frowned. "This feels loose. I wonder if someone tampered with it."

"Unless they had my spare key, I doubt it."

He looked at me, turned on the back-porch light, then went outside. He returned holding my spare key.

"You told him where it is?" I asked Teri.

Dash sighed. "I looked under two flowerpots before I found it. Not difficult, so anyone who wanted in could have let himself—"

"Or herself," Teri interrupted.

Dash rolled his eyes. "Or *herself* inside. Lexi, this is getting weird."

Cat nodded. "Dangerous."

"Totally dangerous," Teri agreed. "And instead of being helpful, sexy Berg acts like a tool. Don't worry, Dash. We got this."

Dash frowned. "What do you mean, 'sexy Berg'? There's something sexy about a guy on steroids with no personality whatsoever?"

"Oh, ho, someone's jealous of those biceps," Cat murmured.

He glared at her. "I am not. I'm just as buff." He flexed.

Which had Cat reassessing his arms. Then the pair started comparing dead lifts and gym routines, so I turned to Teri, who looked simultaneously fascinated and irritated with them. "Teri, something's going on."

"Tell me about it. Maybe it's something in the water." She sneered at Cat and Dash. "I swear, some people live their lives for the gym. I find it sad."

I glanced from Cat and Dash to Teri and grinned. "Randy likes the gym, doesn't he?"

"He does," she groaned. "I'm not a workout kind of person, Lexi. And he wants to spend our next date *exercising* together. And not in a good way. At the *gym*. What the heck is that about? I'd rather get his-and-hers manicures."

"Meet him in the middle. Go for a romantic walk and stop in at Cookie Crumbles for ice cream on the way."

She brightened. "Good idea." As she watched Cat and Dash, she said, "But now I'm extra worried for you. It was bad enough your next-door neighbor died. Then someone ratted you out to the cops. Now they've broken in and stolen your laptop." She looked in my eyes. "Is there anything on there that would be bad for you if anyone else read it?"

"Nope." I added in a lower voice, "Not anymore."

"Oh boy."

I whispered, "I kind of killed Gil in my story after he yelled at me. It was therapeutic. But I deleted it after he actually died."

Her eyes looked huge. "How did you kill him?"

"I started with a pipe, then a garden trowel, and moved up to a chainsaw, actually. It was bloody and felt really good." I looked up to see Cat and Dash gaping at me. Apparently, I needed to tone down my loud whispering. "Oh, stop. It was fictional. Plus, I don't have the strength to chop him into tiny pieces and string him up in the tree in his front yard. Then to clean up all that blood so that nothing was left? That's a lot of work. If I do ever kill someone, it will be an easy cleanup."

Dash blew out a breath. "Well, that's true. You are lazy."

"This is why no one likes you," I muttered.

Cat nodded. "She is lazy. She's neat but not as tidy as she'd have you believe. Lexi, when's the last time you cleaned your bathroom?"

"Just before you two came over, actually."

"I rest my case."

Dash shook his head. "Okay, I'm leaving you two and Cookie to watch over Ms. Perky."

"Stop calling me that!"

He walked to me, pulled me to my feet, and dragged me into a super hug. And wow, was he strong.

When he pulled back, he frowned and lifted my chin to close my mouth. "There. That was a power hug. Try to stop getting involved in murder, fictional or otherwise, okay? I'm outta here. I have a bar to run." He left the three of us staring after him.

"What was *that*?" Teri shrieked, staring at me.

"What?"

"That hug," Cat said, blinking as if amazed. "That looked way too friendly, if you get my meaning."

I frowned. "I don't."

"I do!" Teri leaped to her feet and danced in place, instigating my dog to do the same. Except Cookie didn't dance in place. Instead, she zipped around the house at Mach 10.

"Teri, stop being hyper. Look what you did to Cookie."

Teri laughed. "I love when she gets the yips."

"The zoomies," Cat corrected. "Watch. Four more times, then bam, she'll be dog tired. Get it?" She grinned. "*Dog* tired?"

Right as rain. Cookie did four more laps, then detoured to her dog bed, where she flopped, panted, then closed her eyes. In minutes, she was snoozing.

I shook my head. Unfortunately, the yips had not deterred my friends.

"Lexi, seriously, Dash was hugging you in a very nonplatonic way."

"I'm the one he was hugging. Shouldn't I make that call?" Nothing he'd done had been inappropriate. I thought it was nice.

"Say what you want, but he had a weird expression on his face." Cat looked at me.

Huh. "How did he look?"

"Like this." She made a weird face.

"You look constipated."

Teri laughed. "You do, Cat. But still, he did look all mooneyed and kind of confused. I know my brother. That's his 'hot for a chick' look."

"Oh, please." Yet part of me reveled in the handsome dork finally seeing me as something other than his little sister's friend. "Look, crushing is nice, but we have more important things to worry about."

I told them both about my conversations with Abe and Berg.

"Huh." Teri and Cat exchanged a glance, and Teri said, "I think this calls for popcorn."

"Darn it. I'm out."

Teri grinned. "That's why we brought some." She nodded to Cat, who grabbed a paper sack I'd missed earlier. In it were an abundance of snack foods and soda, none of which was good for any of us.

Cat chugged some cola—apparently off the wagon—as we tried to figure out who might be messing with our town and its most upstanding citizens, meaning me.

Teri handed me her phone. "You need to talk to Stefanie."

"I'm on it." I texted Stefanie with a time to meet the next day. She texted back, and we arranged for a Friday lunch. I wondered what she and Alison had found out about the Cloutiers. After meeting with Abe, I wanted to believe he'd told me the whole truth. But something held me back.

Hmm. I'd need to make a new list. I'd need to print out . . . I sighed. No more laptop.

"What's wrong?" Cat asked, guzzling caffeine. Not that we needed any to stay up.

"I just realized I can't print anything. No laptop."

Teri slung an arm around me and pulled me down onto the couch. "You poor kid. Here. Let's watch a few revenge movies to make you feel better." She flicked on my television and scrolled through Netflix.

I smiled, a fan of the vigilante-who-gets-back-at-the-bad-guys trope. Cat settled in, thrilled for some ultraviolence from actor-crush Jon Bernthal. Except Teri had put on a different version of the show we wanted to watch.

"Whoa." Cat sat up in the plush chair I liked to read in. "This isn't *The Punisher*."

"It is," Teri said. "It's the movie with John Travolta and—"

"Stop! Get this off!" Cat screeched. "I want the latest series, not the movies. Those blow."

"You mean you want the one with Thomas Jane as the Punisher?" I asked.

"No, no, no."

God, I loved messing with Cat. She was too easy. "Does Roger know you're fixated on dark justice?"

"Not yet," she grumbled. "I'm easing him into my passion for horror movies and cooking shows."

"So no ghost hunting yet?" Teri asked, happily munching on some caramel corn.

"Well, I might have mentioned how much Halloween is my favorite season."

I cocked a brow. "You love Halloween because of the scares, not the candy. And that's aside from you believing in ghosts."

She shot me a superior look. "Ghosts are a lot less scary than vandals, thieves, and killers. As many times as I've tracked the spirits in this town, the police have never called me in to be interviewed about murder."

"You have a point." I glanced at my own ghost protection, a snoring dog lying in the most uncomfortable-looking position ever. "Get Jon Bernthal on the TV, Teri."

She clicked the remote, and the series exploded on the screen.

"That's what I'm talking about." Cat gave us a smug smile and went back to her chips and soda.

But while I watched a Marine with a grudge mow down some baddies, I couldn't stop thinking about what might have happened to my laptop. And what might next be coming my way.

Chapter Seventeen

I found out the next morning when I let Cookie out to go to the bathroom. As I stood in the backyard, soaking in the sun, I noticed Cookie going crazy in the yard.

"What the heck?" I yawned, conscious my ratty bathrobe was all that stood between me and the light breeze of a cool June morning. My pj's were too short and thin to provide much coverage against our cold sunrises. Yet I knew that by noon today, the temperature would hit the mideighties. Living in Central Oregon could be so challenging. I never got to pack my jeans or jacket away. Because it had been known to snow in June. Seriously.

"Cookie," I called as she darted to a few spots near the fence separating my yard from Gil's. *Oh man. I'd better get over there before she crawls under it again.* No telling what she'd find if she ended up at his house. Another body? A different pipe dipped in blood? Or worse?

Though what could be worse than another dead body?

I hurried to her side and noticed mounds of misplaced earth. "What the heck?"

"Yo, Lexi. What's up?" Cat yelled from the house.

"Shh," I shout-whispered back. "It's too early for noise."

"Please. Most of the world is up by seven. And it's already"—she checked her fit-watch—"seven thirty."

She had a point. Plus, I wouldn't be getting any complaints from my neighbor.

"I— What are you wearing?" I sure hadn't noticed that last night.

She grinned and spread her arms wide, showing off a long sleep shirt and nightcap that made her look like the reincarnation of Sister Mary Clancy, a nun I'd once crossed paths with at my aunt's funeral many, many years ago. I shivered at the remembrance.

Cat twirled, the headpiece not a wimple but a long black cap with a white band to hold it in place on her head. And the black gown wasn't so much a habit as a formless sack. "Like it? I call it 1850s hipster nun."

I snorted. "Come here." When she joined me, I pointed out several spots where Cookie had sniffed. "Someone's been in my yard looking for something." We investigated closely, but I saw no scraps of fabric, footprints, or anything resembling evidence of trespass other than dirt. "I didn't check last night."

"Bummer. We should have." She looked around the yard with me, but we saw no other signs of an intruder. "Are you going to tell Berg?"

"What for? He'll end up accusing *me* of doing the digging. Or worse, he'll accuse Cookie." At her name, Cookie trotted over to me. She sniffed at the ground, then pawed at it, digging with zeal.

I sat back, for the moment giving up on trying to keep her from getting so dirty. "Why would anyone come here? Do they think Gil buried something on my property?"

"It would seem so."

I wanted to ask more questions, but I couldn't take my gaze from her pajamas. "Why are you wearing that?"

"Well, it's a funny story. I was at this costume shop and saw this nun outfit. Last year, actually. But feel it. The material is so soft."

"So you wear a costume to bed."

"Just to sleepovers. Don't worry." She huffed. "I haven't shown Roger yet."

"So not at the sleepover part of the relationship yet, eh?"

She blushed. "I just started dating the guy. Geez."

I laughed. "Some advice: don't show him the nun outfit. Ever."

"You're no fun."

"I'm . . . What the heck?" I accepted the treat ball Cookie placed at my feet and shook the dirt off it. The treat ball had been missing for months. I'd inadvertently left it outside and Cookie had decided to hide it. Apparently, she'd buried it under the fence.

I shook it and heard nothing. I could only pray any leftover treats hadn't turned to mold. If they had, I hoped they'd at least be easy to clean. From looking at it, the treat ball looked like one piece. But with a secret twist, I opened it.

And found a note.

I stared, eyes wide.

"Holy crap. Cookie found buried treasure!" Cat leaned down and scratched behind Cookie's ears. "Who's a good girl? You are. Such a good girl."

Cookie was in doggy heaven.

I pulled the note out and read in the worst chicken scratch ever: *You weren't the best neighbor. Not even close. But I'm pretty sure you can't be as dumb as you look. Roses have thorns you know. It's all in how you hold it. Now get off my lawn.*

I stared up at Cat and whispered, looking all around me to make sure no one saw, "I think this is from Gil."

"*What?*"

"Shhh." I tucked the note in my robe pocket and put the treat ball back together. Then I knelt in the grass and started filling in all the holes with dirt. "Help me." I had to shove Cookie away a few times, because she was pretending not to know I wanted to fill in the holes, not make more. By the time I'd finished, I looked like I'd rolled in muck. And Sister Not a Nun wasn't much better.

"We'd better hurry up so we're not late to the shop," she said.

I nodded. Teri had already left for work, so Cat and I battled it out for the rest of my meager hot water supply. Needless to say, I had the quickest shower on record and shivered through five minutes of hell. But I'd shampooed and washed off all the dirt I'd accumulated.

After dressing in jean shorts and a cute T-shirt with unicorns—no teeth or ogres—I joined Cat in the kitchen. She made herself a bowl of cereal while I wolfed down a banana and yogurt.

"Are you going to tell Berg about what you found?"

"Are you kidding? He'll assume I killed Gil for burying that in my yard. Or because Gil thought I was stupid."

"The note says, 'Not as stupid as you look.' "

I gave her *a look*.

She grinned and plowed through her Frosted Mini-Wheats like a champ.

"I have to talk to Stefanie at lunch, but I don't want to close the bookshop. I want to seem like I'm going about my normal routine as much as possible. Can you cover for me?"

"Yeah, but maybe you should meet at her place. She's loud. No way you can hide whatever comes out of her mouth by simply going in your office or the back room of the bookshop with her."

"Right." I looked from Cat to Cookie and back.

Cat sighed. "Yes, I'll take care of the pooch while you visit with the Mystery Maven. You do know she's calling herself that now, right?"

I snorted with amusement. "If it fits. Anyway, I'll tell you guys what I find out later."

"Ah yeah. About that." Cat slurped up her cereal and fidgeted.

"Just tell me."

"I kind of have a date with Roger tonight."

"I thought it was tomorrow." I'd secretly made plans for a really cool sleepover tonight with my best friends. I wouldn't admit it to them, but I'd been both relieved and excited to have company last night. Not that Cookie wasn't great, because she was. But Teri, Cat, and I hadn't been hanging out in the evenings like we used to.

"Well, it is. And tonight. He texted me earlier—he knows I'm an early bird—and asked if I wanted to go bowling tonight. I said yes." She looked at me. "But I can cancel." She gave the fakest laugh. "Bowling is boring."

"Oh, stop. You're a terrible liar." I ignored her blushing cheeks. "Go have fun with Roger. But hey, if I get an urge to write, can I borrow your laptop?" I smiled to show it didn't bother me at all that she was deserting me for a dude. Not that she was, but I was feeling pretty melodramatic this morning. "I hope to do some brainstorming."

"Sure, sure. No problem." Her wide smile made me feel terrible for even considering the fact she was ditching me. My best friend had a life. She should live it. Period.

"And before you ask, wear whatever you want. It's bowling. Besides, maybe something clingy will distract him. You know you hate to lose."

She rubbed her hands together, her blue eyes sparkling. "I truly do. But so does he. Hmm. I'll have to think on that."

While she thought about how best to crush Roger without emasculating him, I grabbed Cookie and left for the bookshop, promising Cat she could show up all kinds of late if she whipped up a bunch of blueberry muffins. I knew she had a batch already mixed and ready to bake at her place.

I needed to hurry so Cookie and I could open up on time. And ran into Bill Sanchez and Joe Jacobs, of all people, arguing at the corner of Cinnamon and Main.

"You know I can't do that," Bill was saying in a mean voice. "I won't do it."

"You will or I'll tell them," Joe shot back. "And if they find out, you'll never—"

They both shut up upon seeing me and Cookie.

Bill pasted a smile on his face. "Oh, hey, Lexi. How's it going?"

Joe cleared his throat. "Good morning."

I would have stuck around to question them but was running way behind. "Sorry, late to open up," I managed as Cookie and I ran by them.

They laughed good-naturedly, but now I had more questions. Like, what had they been arguing about? Joe sounded mean. Bill sounded meaner. And hadn't the pair been talking about winning big-time prize money, now that Gil was dead, just three days ago?

I opened the store and hurried through my morning routine. Cookie, fortunately, forgave me for rushing her sniff-and-pee time and jumped to Mr. Leggy, her comfort in any situation. While she snuggled up to the pink octopus, which really needed a bath, I finished putting the coffee on and neatened up the shop.

Gil's note had burned a proverbial hole in my bag, and I stuffed it under the register, locking the cabinet and tucking the key in my pocket.

The morning passed with a god-awful slowness. It felt like every minute that ticked by took an hour. Cat arrived a little after ten with warm muffins that made my entire being happy, which made up for having so few customers on an oddly slow day.

Bob and Anna peeked in right before I was due to take off to meet Stefanie and Alison for our secret meeting.

"Oh, hey, you two. How was the garden tour?" I asked.

Bob pretended to hang himself behind Anna, and I did my best not to laugh.

"I see that, Bob," she said, not turning around. "Actually, the garden tour was fantastic. Our guide this time was Darcy, and she said she knew you when I mentioned how nice some of the local Confection people were." Anna smiled. "Darcy knows a lot about this town."

"She does." *She's amazing; just ask her.* I cleared my throat. "So, what's on the agenda for today?"

"More sightseeing. Maybe a trip to Bend or Sisters, though I don't think we want to drive too much today. The weather's gorgeous. I was hoping for a picnic actually, so we might forgo window shopping and head up the Cascade Lakes Byway."

"It's a beautiful drive." I wished I could go. But I had a murder to solve. No scenic trips for me. "Todd Lake and Sparks Lake are good choices. Or you could trek to Paulina Lake, a personal favorite. That's a terrific place to hike with a seven-mile loop on the lower end. I usually avoid the other trail because it's so steep." *Usually?* I was such a liar. I had hiked the Paulina trail once over five years ago to impress my younger brother. And he'd laughed at my pathetic attempt to outhike him the whole way while I did my best to breathe and walk at the same time.

I ignored my inner honesty, pasted on a smile, and pretended not only that I liked to hike rough trails but that I loved Confection Coffee, and yes, Nadine was a sweetheart.

They left, and Cat laughed at me. "You and Nadine are besties now, is that it? She's a sweetheart, I think you said."

"Sweetheart, my a—"

"Well, niece, how are you today?" Uncle Jimmy boomed as he entered and startled me half to death.

Cat smirked. "Hey, Jimmy."

"Cat. Lookin' good as always." They flexed at each other. Gym rats to the bottom of their souls.

I ignored them and tried to skirt my uncle. "Well, I'm on my way out, so—"

He grabbed my arm and gently-not-gently ushered me outside. "I'll walk with you. 'Bye, Cat."

I heard her laughter as the door shut. The traitor.

"All right, Lexi. You talk while I escort you to wherever you're going."

Shoot. I'd toyed with the idea of involving my uncles in my investigation. They knew the skinny about everyone in town. Elvis was worse than a stoolie trying to make a deal, full of information and willing to share. But if I told them I was investigating Gil's murder, they'd worry. Especially if they learned my home had been broken into last night.

"Ah, well, I'm kind of in a rush, so . . ."

Jimmy smiled through his teeth. He really did look a lot like my dad when my dad got mad. Same low brow, same blazing brown eyes, same glare and gritted jaw. Oy. "How about we talk about why Fred wants to know why you need your locks changed?"

"Fred's a blabbermouth." Had I said I liked living in a small town?

"Yeah, and he gets the majority of his business through me. Talk, girlie. Or I'll make you," he growled.

Several passersby stared at the menace oozing from my uncle while I smiled and pretended I wasn't being dragged by a giant with attitude. But no one stepped in to interfere.

Mailman Rodney saw us, a mailbag over his shoulder, and smiled. "Loved that book, Lexi. Thanks. I'll have to order the next when it's available."

"I have another you might be interested in," I said as my uncle hauled me past.

"Great. I'll stop by next week." He waved.

Even Taco Ted nodded and smiled as my uncle pulled me past Central Garden.

No one seemed to care that I'd have a dent in my left arm before long. "Ow, ow, ow. Okay, I'll talk."

He let go, and I rubbed my arm, glaring at him. Which had no effect. He just raised his eyebrow at me and waited.

"Now I see why you and Dad had so many fights when you were kids."

He laughed.

"You're annoying," I mumbled.

"What's that?" He leaned close. "I didn't hear that, niece."

I swallowed. He made me feel five years old and in trouble. "Not here." This time *I* dragged *him* with me away from the masses. Past the Confection Rose, we cut through Central Park and over Soda Creek.

Once away from everyone, I shared. "So yeah, someone read my journal and narced me out to the cops, but there was nothing but fictional research in the book. Berg and his lieutenant had no choice but to let me go."

He patiently walked by my side. "I know all that. Elvis told me." He paused. "*You* never did."

"Oh, ah, because I knew he'd tell you."

He snorted, clearly disbelieving. "Why are you changing your locks?"

Crap. I had to tell him. He looked genuinely worried. "Because I swear someone broke into my house yesterday and stole my laptop."

He jerked me to a halt. "*What?*"

"Shh." I looked around and, seeing no one nearby, explained, "When we got home last night, Cookie smelled something odd. I ignored her, which is my fault. Then I realized my laptop was gone. I know I locked my back door before I left, but I found it unlocked. Dash pointed out I might have been burglarized by someone using my spare key."

He covered his eyes. "Please tell me you don't still keep it under the small red pot."

"Not anymore."

"Lexi."

"Uncle Jimmy."

He growled.

I frowned back at him.

A jogger cleared her throat. "Excuse me."

We parted so she could pass, then moved back into position to glare at each other.

"Do you want to help me or lecture me?" I asked, exasperated when he continued to stare.

"I can do both." He nudged me to continue walking. "Where are we going, anyway?"

"Stefanie Connett's house."

"Why?"

How could I tell him without him getting his feelings even more hurt? If I mentioned she was helping on the investigation I hadn't asked him to help solve, he'd get bristlier than he was now.

"Well, see, she's our Mystery Maven. The ultimate authority on mysteries in the Macaroons."

"And?"

"And she knows Gil's family." Not exactly a lie. She knew them better now, after having dug into their business. "Plus, Alison is a retired librarian, and you know those librarians have godlike power when it comes to research."

He nodded.

"The plan was to find out what they knew about Gil's family. Cat and Teri are digging where they can, Cat into Roger Halston—he's into her—and Teri at the DA's office. And you guys . . ."

"Yes?"

"I was coming to visit you and Elvis after I visited Stefanie. You guys need to get me gossip on everyone who might be a suspect."

He watched me out of the corner of his eye, and I put on my best and brightest hopeful expression, praying he bought it. "I had planned to email you about it but decided I shouldn't have any traces to my investigating on my computer or cell phone. I've been contacting Stefanie through Teri."

"What? Why?"

"Because Berg will get all up in my—er, he'll get upset if he learns I'm investigating. He told me so."

Instead of taking my side, my uncle nodded. "He's right. It's dangerous."

"What? But—"

"But then he doesn't realize your uncles will protect you."

"I don't need protection."

"So you stayed alone at your place last night, is that it?"

By the look on his face, he knew about my guests. "Not exactly. Teri and Cat stayed over."

"And Dash put in an appearance. He told me so earlier this morning. I admit, I was a little upset I hadn't heard from you about all this. But since you had clear plans to talk to me and Elvis after you met with Stefanie and Alison, I'm fine with it." The look he shot me told me he didn't believe a word I'd said.

Blasted Dash and his big mouth.

"What do you think Stefanie will have to tell us?" he asked.

"I don't know. But I'm hoping I can put it together with what I learned from Abe. And the note Gil left me."

That shot his eyebrows way up. I let him read the note, and we shared our confusion.

I couldn't wait to see how Stefanie and Alison responded.

Chapter Eighteen

"Now that's something," Stefanie said, rereading Gil's note. "I recognize Gil's handwriting."

"I do too," Alison said.

We sat in Stefanie's kitchen, enjoying sandwiches and lemonade Alison had brought over.

"How do you know his handwriting?" Uncle Jimmy asked Stefanie.

"Saw him writing at the post office once. You can barely read it. See?" She turned the note toward us.

Alison nodded. "And I used to see him at the library years ago. Gil and I ran in some of the same circles back in high school."

"Oh." Funny, I hadn't realized Alison had grown up in Confection.

"Yeah. He, Mandy, and I were friends at one point. Then Mandy graduated and went away to school, where she met Alan." Alison shrugged. "We all moved on, drifting apart."

"I saw her crying outside his house the other day. She said it was allergies. I don't know."

We all considered Mandy's odd crying.

"Right. Another point to consider." Stefanie nodded. "Well, we dug into Gil and his boys. And wow, did we unearth some interesting tidbits."

"Oh?" I leaned forward at the same time Jimmy did.

Stefanie's eyes twinkled. "Motive, my dears, is something all the Cloutier boys have for killing their father."

Alison nodded. "It's some pretty juicy information. Even I was astounded, and I know things about the people in this town you wouldn't believe."

"Is that so?" Jimmy smiled.

Alison blushed. "But that's for another day. Stefanie?"

"Right. Well, we know for certain Abe was here in town when Gil died. Abe has a job doing janitorial work at the high school and the shelter. He also volunteers at the shelter, and according to my sources—"

"Ahem. *My* sources. The director's mother is an old friend," Alison confided.

Stefanie glared. "Fine. *Alison's* sources tell us that Abe has been doing well at the halfway house for the past six months. Now, since our source wasn't in bed with Abe, and she didn't monitor him all night, she can't be a hundred percent sure, but she considered him home when his father was killed."

"But definitely in town," Jimmy said.

Stefanie nodded. "Next we have Scott, who lives here. Also in town, though I couldn't get close enough to see if Jan could confirm an alibi."

Alison said, "According to the police, Jan said he was with her all night."

"How do you know that?" I asked.

"Well, my cousin works at the parks office, and she heard two officers talking while they were making rounds, and one of them mentioned how he couldn't believe we had a murderer in our happy little town, but it's always the ones closest to you that do it. And his friend said Scott didn't, because his wife alibied him."

"Huh." Alison had some sources, all right. I wondered how many times her friends had overheard me talking about something and reported back.

"But that's not the real juicy part." Stefanie grinned. "Matt, who lives in Portland, was here."

"He was?"

"Yeah. And he wasn't alone." Stefanie tittered, an honest-to-goodness menacing giggle.

My uncle and I both leaned back from the table.

"You're chortling," Alison said.

"I know, but this is just too good." Stefanie paused for dramatic effect, which wasn't necessary, because I was already dying to know what she'd learned. "Matt was seen arguing with someone Friday night over in Sisters."

I blinked. "You have eyes in Sisters?" A small town to the north of us, Sisters had just shy of three thousand people and lovely little shops and restaurants. But it took nearly an hour to get there because we had to navigate the mountains. "Were you in Sisters and saw him or something?"

"No. A friend of mine runs a B&B there, and she and I like to talk. I mentioned how sad it was that Gil Cloutier had died, and how it was a good thing his sons had alibis, because we all know to look at the family of a murdered one first."

"Yeah. Family. It's love or death, for sure," Jimmy murmured.

I elbowed him.

"Why was he in Sisters?" I asked.

Stefanie's grin put me in mind of that creepy Cheshire cat from *Alice in Wonderland*. The one with too many teeth. "The question isn't why, it's who was he with."

"Okay already. Who was he with?"

"Jan." Boom. Stefanie sat back and watched for the fallout.

"Jan? So what? He came back to see Scott, and—"

"I don't think you understand," Alison said kindly. "Matt was with Jan. Not Scott, *Jan*. And they were checked into the B&B."

Jimmy whistled. "Holy moly. Does Scott know?"

"We aren't sure," Stefanie said, exchanging a glance with Alison. "But that means Scott's alibi isn't a sure thing. And neither is Abe's, really. Though he should have been at the halfway house, no one can be sure he didn't slip out and come back."

"Wow." I blinked. "Matt and Jan are having an affair?"

"And that's not all." Alison, apparently, was up to bat. "I know some people who know some people."

"I'll say." Jimmy looked impressed.

Stefanie and Alison beamed.

"Alison?" I prodded.

She continued, "My cousin's nephew is an accountant and friend of Scott's. He does Scott's books. Apparently, Scott isn't as well-off as he pretends."

"Hold on." I had to make sense of this. "So Matt and Jan are having an affair."

"We'll throw an 'allegedly' in there to make you feel better, how about that?" Stefanie said.

"And now you're telling me Scott is hard up for money? So, what? He killed his dad to get an inheritance Gil never had? Heck, Gil left his small investments to Matt, the house to Abe, and Scott got nothing but some leftover sentimental stuff, according to Abe."

"Scott was supposed to get a map," Stefanie said.

"A . . . Wait. Abe's treasure map?" I gaped. "Seriously?"

"I can't say for sure, but I think, yes." Stefanie nodded. "Alison, didn't you say Paul mentioned the will and said—"

"Hold on." Jimmy frowned. "You two expect us to believe you know what was in Gil's will?"

Alison gave a shy nod. "But that's completely by accident. I know a lot of people in this town, and I'm tight with a lot of the B&B community. Paul Abbott is meticulous about keeping his clients' confidentiality. But I was at Eats n' Treats, waiting outside for some takeout, when I overheard him on his cell phone. He was talking very quietly, but I heard him all the same."

"What did he say?" I whispered, in awe—and a little frightened, I'll admit—that two of the Macaroons had such an extensive intelligence network in our town.

"That there was no contesting it. I think he was talking to Scott, because Paul was apologetic and nice and wanted to help, but Gil had made sure to leave everything to his boys for a reason, and that Scott would be pleased if he accepted what he'd been left. Because it was worth far more than he might think."

"Huh." The hamster on the wheel inside my brain was sprinting as I pondered this new info. "So really, any of the Cloutiers are candidates for murder."

"Yep." Stefanie sighed. "The news is hot, all right, but it's not as helpful in narrowing down suspects." She brightened. "Unless we're talking *Murder on the Orient Express*."

I recognized the Agatha Christie title. "Not *The Murder of Roger Ackroyd*?"

"Nope. Our current read is terrific, but our point of view is skewed." She looked me up and down. "Unless you really did kill Gil?

"No. I did not."

"Bummer."

I rolled my eyes.

"But what if all the Cloutiers offed their dad?" Stefanie asked. "Abe to find the treasure, Scott because he wants the treasure too, and Matt because somehow Gil found out about the affair and was going to tell Scott?"

"That's reaching, don't you think?" Jimmy grabbed another sandwich. "I don't know. I just don't see any of them killing Gil."

I added, "From what Abe told me, he and his dad were getting along before Gil died."

"Then what was that argument about?" Alison asked. "A lot of people heard them yelling at each other in a public place."

I needed to talk to Abe again. "I don't know. I'll find out."

"Do that," Stefanie said at the same time Jimmy said, "The hell you will."

We all looked at each other.

"How about if I take a friend with me and meet Abe in public?" I asked my uncle. Twenty-seven years old and I had to get permission to meet a murder suspect? Geesh.

He stewed for a few seconds.

"Come on, Jimmy," Stefanie cajoled. "You know the girl has to figure this out. Besides, I think she might have a knack for it. She's writing a mystery, you know."

Shocked Stefanie would defend me when for so long she'd been critical of how I ran the bookstore and the Macaroons, I could only stare when she winked at me.

"Well, okay."

"You're not the boss of me," I grumbled under my breath, but I knew how fast he could call my parents, and I sure didn't want them here interfering and possibly putting themselves in danger.

He continued, "But you have to constantly have someone with you. And, well, I guess you should know that the Cloutiers aren't the only ones with issues."

"What do you know?"

"I expect it's about the Danvers," Alison said, looking sad.

"What about them?" Was I the only one in this town who had no idea what really went on with my neighbors?

"They owe a substantial amount to the bank," Jimmy said. "Dave tried expanding too fast too soon, and plans fell through on their shop in Bend. That put them in a bad place financially. The three of us were talking about it at the last CoC meeting."

"COC?" I knew the CGC, but I didn't think the COC had anything to do with our gardening mafia, though it sounded familiar. COC? Celery, Okra, and Cucumbers?

"Chamber of Commerce. You know, the meeting you keep avoiding?" Jimmy shook his head. "Your father used to go."

"Oh, that." Yeah, and Dad had told me that he typically went to eat and drink with friends, rarely talking business, mostly talking fishing tips.

Jimmy sighed. "I told Dave not to do it, but he and Julie were close to going under. The bank wouldn't extend any more credit, and I wanted to help but can't afford to without dipping into reserves I don't want to touch."

"Smart not to." Stefanie nodded. "You gotta keep the hardware store open. No way I'm driving all the way to Sisters or Redmond when I need nails."

Alison hushed her.

"Wait." I was still confused. "You told Dave not to do what, exactly?"

"Borrow money from Gil."

I blinked. "Seriously? Why would Gil lend Dave and Julie money? And how would he have money anyway?" Heck, the guy had lived next door to me. It's a nice neighborhood, sure, but nothing like Lemon Loop.

Jimmy shook his head. "All I know is the Danvers had a lien on their business, but the last time I saw them, right after Gil died, they didn't seem stressed at all. When I mentioned it to Elvis, he told me Julie told him they'd figured their money problems out."

"How come you never told me any of that?" I asked, trying not to sound accusing.

Jimmy scowled. "I don't like gossip."

I choked on the sip of lemonade I'd taken. "Seriously?"

He flushed. "Well, we don't talk about people we like."

Stefanie's eyes narrowed. "You ever talk about me?"

I cut that avenue of conversation off before it could get started. "Great. So we have a whole lot of people who might have wanted Gil dead. What if he loaned money to other people besides the Danvers?"

"What if he did?" Jimmy shrugged. "Look, I don't want to point fingers, and anyway, the police are investigating all this. Berg knows."

"How do you know?"

"Elvis was at the Danvers' shop fixing some of the shelving in the store and overheard Berg questioning them."

"But you just said they don't have much money, and I know Uncle Elvis doesn't work for free."

"No, but he likes flowers. He fixes stuff for them, and when they can't afford to pay him, he gets free bulbs and blooms." Jimmy smiled. "I like them at the shop too. Everyone always comments on how nice the hardware store smells. Like fresh flowers."

"It really does," Alison agreed.

Stefanie shrugged. "Yeah, but what's really important is that you guys always have what I need."

"We aim to please, ma'am." His smile widened. "Especially when it's to help such lovely ladies like yourselves."

Stefanie chuckled. "Oh, Jimmy. Such a scamp."

He winked.

I wanted to throw myself in front of a bus. While the older people in the room flirted, I couldn't stop my creeping dismay. Instead of narrowing down our suspects, the list continued to grow.

Who else had Gil lent money to? And had any of them wanted to kill him?

More importantly, how the heck could I get that information without attracting the attention of Chad Berg?

Chapter Nineteen

I left my uncle and my Macaroons. Oddly enough, after talking through suspects, Jimmy had lightened his protective stance. It was once again okay for me to walk by myself in broad daylight.

Thank goodness.

Annoyed at life in general, I stomped my way back toward the shop, cutting through a honey trail, not wanting to see anyone while I stewed. How had I not asked Abe what he and Gil had argued about in public? Yep, dropped the ball on that one.

But Uncle Jimmy keeping the Danverses' secrets from me was odd. He loved to gossip as much as Elvis. Although he had only ever shared information with me about people we both disliked. And really, what business of mine was it what the Danverses did?

Except I was trying to solve a murder here.

I kicked at the ground, missing my laptop. I needed to write all this down and look at it like the cops did on TV shows. A murder board. That's what I needed.

I continued through the park, trying to let the sunny sky and slight breeze perk up my mood. Hmm. Who could help me learn about financial information? I would have asked Alison, but she and Stefanie had decided, along with Jimmy, to focus on the Cloutiers, digging deeper to see exactly where the men fell on the patricide scale.

I needed to regroup.

As I neared the bridge over Soda Creek, leading me toward Central Garden, I heard voices and instinctively stepped behind a nearby tree.

"I know, honey, and I believe you, but so many others don't."

That was Peggy Donahue, the pastor's wife and CGC hit woman.

"But it's not fair." Sobs, sniffles, and one whopper of a nose blow. "He was really a good man deep down. He didn't deserve any of this. And neither do I."

I knew that voice. But from where? I had to know, so I peeked around the tree. Unfortunately, someone saw me.

"Oh, hey, Lexi. Beautiful day, eh?" Taco Ted grinned as he walked past me on a perpendicular trail. "Taking a quick break before I head back. Still got some taquitos left if you want 'em." He continued on.

I turned to see Peggy glaring at me and Mandy Coatney, of all people, trying to hide evidence she'd been crying.

"Eavesdropping, Lexi? Really?"

I ignored Peggy. "Mandy, are you okay?" What did Peggy believe that others didn't about Mandy? And why was Mandy so upset about Gil?

"I-I-I can't." She sobbed and ran away.

Peggy and I stared after her. To my surprise, I saw concern on Peggy's normally stern face.

"Should you go after her?" I suggested.

"I'm not dressed for a sprint." Peggy pointed down at her trendy flats, which complemented her Sunday finest. "I'm actually getting ready for our Friday ladies' luncheon." Peggy sniffed. "Why are you hiding in the woods? Following me?"

"I wasn't following you. I was looking at a chipmunk." Wow. Worst lie ever. I cleared my throat. "I've heard the rumors too. But like you, I don't believe them."

Peggy opened her mouth to say something condescending, I was sure, then sighed instead. "Poor Mandy. She's really torn up over Gil."

I nodded. *Keep talking, Peggy. Fill in the blanks for me.*

"Before she met Alan, she and Gil were so in love. They made a cute couple. Then they had a pregnancy scare."

"I didn't know that."

"Not many do." Peggy shook her head. "Mandy's mother had a conniption. She made sure Mandy stopped seeing Gil. It turned out to be a false alarm, fortunately. But then Mandy went away to school. Gil pined for her, you know. It was sad." Peggy sounded like a decent human being. And that floored me as much as Mandy and Gil's secret history.

Peggy glared at me. Ah, kindness over. "And if you repeat one word of that to anyone, I'll make you sorry."

"Sorrier than I am that I stopped to talk to you?" popped out before I could stop myself.

Peggy gaped. "So incredibly rude. Just like your mother." She stomped off.

"Thanks, and have a nice day," I called after her.

Wow. Today was the day for revelations. The Cloutiers all had motive to kill their father. Gil might have been a secret loan shark. And one of the Macaroons, easygoing, fun-loving Alan

Coatney, might just have had a reason to murder Gil. Jealousy over his wife's ex-lover, perhaps?

Now that stunned me. But like everything else I'd been learning lately, the idea had merit.

I needed to talk to Mandy and Alan. And Dave and Julie. And Abe again.

A familiar face neared as I hurried past the Confection Rose. Him I did *not* need to talk to. At all.

"Excuse me, Ms. Jones. I need a moment of your time."

I groaned. Loudly.

Unfortunately, Detective Berg paid no mind to my attitude. "How are you doing? Not working today?"

"I was on a break and have to get back."

"But you left the shop with your trusty sidekick, so it's in good hands." Berg had dressed in his Confection PD casual. The brim of his ball cap shielded his eyes, though I could feel his stare lasering into me.

"Yeah, yeah. Do I need a lawyer?"

He blinked. "Ah, no. I just wanted to see how you were doing."

"Any word on my laptop?"

"Not yet." He looked me over carefully. "You seem tense. Are you okay?"

I did my best to keep it together, but I was unraveling. I needed to cross someone off my suspect list! "Do you have any idea how messed up this town is?"

"Yes."

"I mean, Abe is digging all over the place. And he's got a shadow doing the same thing. Matt's sleeping with Scott's wife. Scott is having money problems. Gil was a loan shark."

"A what?"

"And it seems like half the town wanted to kill him. Bill and Joe are hiding things. And so is Peggy."

He scowled. "Peggy Donahue?" He pulled out a notebook and pen from his back pocket.

Man, had I let everything fall out or what? I sucked at the notion of *discreet*. "Forget I said anything."

"Oh no, Lexi. You and I need to talk."

"I'm not investigating anything," I said clearly. "But people have been talking around me. And I have no idea what you people know or don't know."

He pushed back the brim of his cap. " 'You people'?"

"Police people," I snapped. "You accuse me of killing my own neighbor. Meanwhile, people are lying and sneaking around town. My laptop was stolen! My house was broken into! And my yard—"

Stop. Talking.

"What's going on?" Berg asked, his voice calm, deep, authoritative.

I took a few deep breaths, trying for calm. "I did *not* kill Gil Cloutier."

"I know."

"I— You do?"

He nodded. "Now why don't you fill me in?"

"Why don't you fill *me* in?" I planted my hands on my hips so I wouldn't give in to the urge to strangle him.

"I can't discuss—"

"See? This is why no one likes you."

He blinked.

"I have to go. I have a job to do." I left him standing there, staring after me.

I felt like a total idiot. Having a meltdown in front of the guy investigating me for murder had been incredibly unwise. Not that I'd planned it, but still. Yet he'd said he didn't think I'd killed Gil. Hmm. I should mull over that bit.

I arrived back at the shop and entered to see Cat and Officer Halston chatting at the register. No one else was around but Cookie, who came out from behind the register to greet me.

"Hi, Roger. Cat, I have a headache. I need to take the rest of the day off. Can you cover?"

She waved around her. "It's been dead like this all day. Go ahead. I was just telling Officer Halston about—"

"Great, great. Well, I need to go." I hurried to get my purse and Cookie's leash. She grabbed Mr. Leggy, and we headed back to the door. "Oh, and Roger, did you get a chance to try Cat's cookies yet? They're amazing."

"Oh, right." Cat blushed. "You get one on the house."

"Thanks." He blushed right back.

Cuteness overload. I left before I blurted I'd dreamed about their basketball babies. Cookie looked up at me as we raced back to the house, a question in her eyes.

"I can't handle all the not knowing. It's time to find some answers. You, my friend, are my trusted safety companion. So after we dump Mr. Leggy, we're talking to Abe, Julie, Dave, Mandy, and anyone else on my list . . . that I don't have. I need a list!"

By the time I arrived at my front door, I was out of breath from all the walk-running I'd been doing. So many thoughts jumbled in my mind that I had to write them down or explode.

An hour later, I'd had a refreshing ice water with lemon and calmed down. Cookie had gobbled up a treat. My list—in a separate notebook I'd make sure to stash at the girls'—took up two pages, and I'd returned a text to Teri. She'd seen something interesting in Gil Cloutier's online background. After arranging a "share brunch" at my uncles' place the next morning—confirmed by both Uncle Jimmy and Uncle Elvis in a joint text—I pondered whether to drive or walk the two miles to the halfway house in hopes of talking to Abe. Instead of calling and possibly giving him a chance to avoid me, I figured to pop in unexpectedly and hope he'd be there.

I looked at Cookie, feeling more balanced that I had earlier. "Well? Do we walk or drive?"

She grabbed her leash and set it at my feet.

"Right." I could use the exercise to clear my head anyway.

We left the house, Cookie on her leash should Berg be ready to jump out at any moment and arrest me for dog walking without a license, and skirted downtown by taking Court Street. We passed Peggy's house, then Bonnie's house on the way, where more holes lined their front yards right near their flowers.

If I believed Abe that he'd stopped digging after his dad died, that meant someone else had been digging. And continuing to dig, because I was pretty sure Peggy would have accused me of vandalizing her property if she'd known about it, especially after I'd been rude to her in the park.

I hurried with Cookie in case Peggy or Bonnie tried to flag us for digging. We reached the courthouse and turned onto Nutmeg Avenue. We'd just passed Sal's Smoothies when I ran into Bill Sanchez grabbing some carryout. Bill, a pleasant enough white guy in his late thirties/early forties, typically greeted everyone with a smile. He owned a small software company and did more than all right for himself. A given, considering he was a standing member of the CGC. Though they appreciated talented gardeners, they appreciated pedigree and money even more.

"Hi, Lexi. Say, have you gotten in any new books on modern horticulture?"

"Didn't you order one the last time you came in, Bill? I checked the orders this morning, and it's not in yet. But it should be by Monday, I'm thinking."

"Oh, that's right. You emailed me that." He sighed. "My mind's on so many things lately."

"Especially with one of our own dying," I said, watching him for a reaction.

Bingo. Guilt rented space across his face. A big old billboard of remorse.

"Sad stuff, that."

"Yeah. So, can I ask you something?" I moved with him out of the way of the door.

"Sure." He clutched his takeout bag like a lifeline.

"Was it worth it? You and Joe? It's wrong, what you did."

He turned sheet white. "Wh-what? I didn't do anything."

"I know, Bill." I had no idea what I was talking about, but pretending had worked with Peggy. Would it work with Bill?

"You know . . . You kn-know . . ." His face crumpled. "Oh, God. I can't believe it's come to all this. I don't want to be out of the CGC. I love the club." He looked stressed to the max.

CGC business, hmm?

He glared at me. "Who told you? Joe, I suppose. Well, *he's* the one that ruined everything. Not me."

"Um, Bill? It's okay."

"No, it's not." He looked miserable again. "I'm a stand-up guy. I'm not a cheat."

I'd been expecting to hear that he wasn't a murderer, but okay. "No, you're not."

He nodded. "Gil was in it to win this year. I'd seen his garden. I have no doubt he would have taken the grand prize."

I said nothing, listening.

"I swear. I had no idea we were even related. How the heck could I know? I was adopted!"

"Bill?"

"But Joe said if I didn't do it, he'd tell everyone and they'd kick me out. It might not seem like a lot to you, but I love the Confection Garden Club. Growing things is my passion."

"Bill, it's okay." Yep. Now I was completely confused.

"No, it's not. Joe's ruined everything." Bill's face grew red, and he left with angry steps, muttering, "He's gonna pay one way or the other."

I was even more confused now than I'd been earlier. What the heck had Bill and Joe been up to? For some reason, I didn't think it had been murder.

What did Bill being adopted and being kicked out of the CGC have to do with Gil's murder?

My head ached. Before I hunted down Abe, I decided to treat myself to an energy smoothie.

And because it was Friday, I got a doggy smoothie for Cookie. A coconut, blueberry, and peanut butter concoction that sounded gross but disappeared down her throat in three seconds. I swear, I don't think I'd ever seen Cookie suck up food so fast, and that included her obsession with Teri's meatballs.

We finished our trek to the shelter, only to find that Abe wasn't due in that day. But as luck would have it, I found him at the halfway house.

"He's in the back," the lady at the front said. "Go on in."

"Thank you." I headed back to a near-empty TV room to find Abe and Matt talking, their expressions intent.

They paused when they saw me.

"Hi, Abe. Oh, I didn't realize you were busy."

Matt nodded to me. "Hi, Lexi."

I'd met him once a few years ago on a visit back to town. I hadn't met him through Gil, though. Instead, I'd seen him at Sal's Smoothies for some promotional thing and introduced myself as the granddaughter of Gil's neighbor. I thought it pretty neat to know someone who had their own smoothie chain.

"Hi, Matt." I kept imagining him and Jan in a torrid embrace. *Oh, big points for* torrid. *Take that, Elvis.* "So sorry you had to come to town under such sad circumstances."

"Yeah." He glared at Abe before turning back to give me a melancholy half smile. "But I did miss the town and my brothers."

"And Jan too, hmm?"

He froze.

Abe smiled with triumph. "I *told* you if you kept screwing around, you'd be found out. And now you have been. Ha!"

I considered Abe. "You knew?"

He nodded, not questioning the fact I had no right to be in his personal business.

"Did your dad?"

Matt flushed. "It's none of your bus—"

"He did. That's why he and I had a huge argument and why everyone thinks I killed him. Which is just crap." Abe glared at Matt. "I loved Dad. He was an ass, yeah. But he was my dad too. I haven't had a thing to drink in eight months and ten days. Dad and I were talking, Matt. So why the hell would I kill him now?"

"Maybe because you stole his map and he wanted it back!"

"Wh-what?"

Oh my gosh, this was getting good. I was getting answers and didn't have to do anything more than wait and watch. Cookie sat next to me, staring, and we listened as the truth spilled out.

Chapter Twenty

"Yeah, genius. Dad knew someone had stolen his map. He tried to blame me, because he saw me on a brief visit I made a month ago."

"He saw you with Jan," I said, putting the pieces together. "And he was going to tell Scott."

Matt nodded. "He was furious. Told me I was ruining Scott's marriage. Please. Scott hasn't been into Jan in years, too busy with his work. Jan is tired and grieving. They lost a baby last year, did you know that? No, because Scott keeps everything to himself. Heck, Jan getting pregnant was a huge deal because she's wanted a kid for so long. But big brother barely had time to . . . ah, to make a kid before he dove back into work. Jan was lonely. Sad. We talked. Things happened."

"Yeah, they happened," Abe sneered. "But then you made a mistake and Dad found out. Damn, Matt. I knew about you guys since February. A friend told me he saw you and Jan. And he said you seemed more than friendly. So I started watching Jan more, and her weekend trips suddenly made sense."

I didn't understand. "Did Scott not notice?"

"No," Matt snapped. "He didn't. And he wouldn't care if he did either."

"But Dad did." Abe clenched his fists. "He didn't want you guys messing with Scott's head. Scott needed to fix some problems at work, and he promised he'd pay Dad back the money he'd borrowed."

"Wait." There it was, that windfall Gil had been expecting. Maybe not from the Danverses after all? "Did your dad have a habit of lending out money?"

Matt snorted. "You've met the guy, right? Did he strike you as the altruistic type?"

"No, but then I wouldn't have thought he'd help out the church either, but he did."

"Because he's friends with Pastor Nestor," Matt explained. "A CGC buddy. Those people are like a cult. They share everything, including enemies."

Abe scoffed. "They're not that bad."

"They are," I said before remembering to censor myself. I cleared my throat when both brothers stared at me. "I mean, they can be a little standoffish. I know Gil loved the CGC. All its members do." I paused. "Do you know anything Bill Sanchez and Joe Jacobs might have been into?"

The brothers looked confused.

Abe shook his head. "No."

"I don't live here, remember?" Matt said, his sarcasm not appreciated.

"I know, which makes me wonder how you could come back to town so many times to see Jan and no one noticed."

Matt swallowed. "Well, ah, we used to meet in Sisters sometimes. At a special place." The B&B Alison had mentioned, I'd bet.

"And once or twice lover boy couldn't stay away," Abe muttered. "Had to come into town to get his freak on."

Matt dove at him, and the pair crashed to the floor and started rolling around, punching and swearing. Cookie barked once until I gave her a look, then she quieted and ran back and forth in the room, keeping an eye on the brawling brothers.

I hurried to lock the door, needing to stop them before we all got kicked out. I'd already learned so much, and I had more questions.

"Guys, stop. You'll get Abe in trouble." Nothing. "Come on, you'll get *me* in trouble. Matt, be the big brother here."

Still nothing but grunting and pathetic wrestling moves. And there, the odd fist that flashed out and hit nothing.

I rushed between them and got a fist to the cheek that knocked me back on my butt. Hard.

At once, Cookie raced to my side and stood over me, growling at the Cloutiers. I cupped my cheek as tears rushed to my eyes. "Shoot. That hurt!"

Matt pushed Abe away and knelt by me, apologizing first to Cookie to get her to calm down.

"Cookie, it's okay," I told her. "Easy, girl."

She still bristled, but she let Matt get closer. "God, Lexi. Are you okay?"

Abe rolled to his feet, his gaze stricken. "Oh man. I didn't mean to. I'm so sorry."

"I'll forget all about this"—maybe because I'd end up with a concussion—"if you tell me *exactly* what that fight was about with Gil, Abe. Because I'm hearing that maybe one of his sons killed him, and it's sad and wrong. I know I didn't kill him. I want to know you guys didn't kill him either."

Matt and Abe stared, wide-eyed. "*I* didn't kill him," they said as one, then chagrined, apologized to each other.

"I fought with Dad two days before he died," Matt confessed, which I could tell surprised Abe.

"You were in town then?" Abe asked.

Matt nodded. "Since before Dad died and after. I've been staying in Sisters."

"What does Becky think?"

Matt blew out a breath. "We broke up last Christmas."

"*What?*"

"Did Gil know?" I asked.

"Not then. But he knew last Wednesday. It's taken me and Becky a while to part as friends while staying business partners. But we're making it work."

"No kidding?" Abe blinked at his brother. "Seriously?"

Matt nodded. "My relationship is—*was*—part of what Dad and I fought about. I'm in love with Jan. She's in love with me. Dad didn't want me to see her anymore. He wanted me to come home and help Scott with his business, as if I know squat about tech. Look, I know what Jan and I started was wrong." He closed his eyes for a second. When he opened them, he looked at *me* as if searching for acceptance. "But sometimes love just is." He turned to Abe. "Do you care? Not about Dad. I mean, about me and Jan."

"Not really, no."

This family needed help.

"Scott doesn't know, does he, Matt?" I asked.

Matt shook his head. "I don't know how he'll react when he does. Jan and I were going to tell him last weekend. But then, with Dad . . ."

"Ouch."

Matt nodded. "Dad was mad at me for backstabbing Scott, as he saw it. But he has no idea what Scott and Jan's relationship has been like."

"What has it been like?" I asked. My cheek was throbbing now. Cookie leaned close to lick me.

"Lonely, sad, apart." Matt sighed and sat on the floor facing me. Abe sat next to him.

I looked at them, seeing similarities. Heck, even those bent fingers. Odd how genetic similarities could manifest. My brother and I could pass as twins though I was three years older. Yet neither of us looked much like Mom, which had caused years of fun speculation.

She still insisted we belonged to her and not any long-lost millionaires.

"So you told your dad that you and Jan were going to be together and that you and Becky were over," I stated, to which Matt nodded. I looked at Abe. "And you fought with your dad for the same reason?"

Abe sighed. "Dad wanted to tell everyone about Matt and Jan. Like, in public, to embarrass them. And probably Scott too, for not knowing the truth. Who knows? Dad was a big believer in tough love."

Matt nodded. "Though he softened a lot as he got older."

Abe agreed. "I did get the feeling he was just sad about it all. He told me last month that he was sorry he wasn't a better dad. That maybe if he'd been with his soul mate, he wouldn't have been so screwed up. But what can you do?" Abe's eyes grew shiny. "Mom died so long ago. Cancer sucks."

Matt nodded and threw an arm around his brother.

Abe continued, "Look. I'm a lot less than perfect, so I try not to judge. If Matt and Jan are happy and Scott doesn't care, then why should Dad get in the middle of it? That's what I told him. And he told me Scott would care if he knew. That I didn't care about the family and I should get my head out of my butt and act like a freaking Cloutier."

I highly doubted Gil had said *butt* or *freaking*. I also had some doubts about whom Gil might have been calling his soul mate. His dead wife, whom he still missed? Or Mandy Coatney, the one who got away? But I nodded at Abe to keep talking.

"Anyway, people saw us argue. It was weird, because Dad and I had been kind of getting along. Not that we were tight, but he seemed like he wanted to be around me more. Said he wasn't getting any younger and that things were happening. And blood should stick up for blood. So long as it wasn't bad blood. Weird, right?"

"What things were happening?"

"I don't know. I thought he was referring to the Gardener's Purse. Rumor had it Dad was going to win some big money."

"How could he know he'd definitely win, though?" I thought again about Bill and Joe and their comments about the prize. "Did he have an in or something?"

"An in?" Matt frowned. "Oh, you mean, did he bribe the judges, a way to ensure the prize?"

"Yeah."

"No. Not that I know of. My dad had a green thumb all his life. And he claimed that after he met my mom, he was complete. That the love he had for her made everything grow."

"Gil said that?" Hard to believe.

"I know." Matt gave a sad smile. "Dad had a poet buried deep inside. Way deep."

"Well, he did use that garden shovel your mom gave him all the time. The one with the cherry-stained handle and sharp green spade. Said if Cookie ever dared put her mangy teeth near it, he'd rip them out one by one."

Abe sighed. "Good old Dad. A monster to a puppy but in love with our mother's ghost."

"Huh." Matt blinked. "That trowel, that's not the one Mom gave him. Hers is in a shadow box in the living room on the mantel. It's part of some award she gave him about being the best gardener in the family. Yeah, they could be sappy like that."

"Then what was the deal with the garden trowel he used all the time?" Abe asked. "Because I always saw it with him in the yard. Always."

"Yeah." But it hadn't come from his wife? Had it come from Mandy, maybe? And did Alan know about it? Or was I speculating on fiction again?

"You need help standing, Lexi?" Abe asked as he stood and reached a hand down to me.

"Thanks." He pulled me to my feet, and for a moment I was dizzy as the blood rushed from my head. "Whoa. Stood too fast."

Matt swore. "Your cheek is going to bruise. You need to ice that."

Abe raced away to get something cold.

Cookie watched Matt with suspicion.

"I'm so sorry, again, about you getting hurt" He sighed. "Abe and I have some healing to do. It hasn't been easy. My dad is—was—a mess at best. Scott and I were never tight. And with Abe drinking, he was hard to talk to. But I think we're going to do better now." He gave a ghost of a smile. "Sad that Dad's passing might bring us closer together, huh?"

"Yeah." I cleared my throat. "But you and Jan . . . What do you think Scott will say?"

"Honestly? I think he might already know. He's been so stressed, even before Dad's death."

"I had noticed that, but I thought it was just him being awkward at book club."

"That's right. He's a Macaroon, isn't he?" Matt chuckled. "Jan thinks it's cute. It's the one normal part about Scott, that he likes to read. Otherwise he's been distant with everyone, her especially."

Abe returned with an ice pack, which I immediately put to my cheek.

I hissed at the sudden pain of the cold, then relaxed as that cold started numbing my sore cheek.

"Well, I guess I found out what I'd come to ask."

"Which was what we argued about with Dad?" Matt looked from me to Cookie.

"Yeah." I nodded to them as we all walked out the front door.

"We want to find out who killed Dad, Lexi," Abe said. "I get why you do too. Being accused of a murder has to be awful. But losing our dad, that's even worse."

Matt nodded and slung an arm around Abe's shoulders. "It really is."

* * *

On my walk home with Cookie, I did my best to pretend I wasn't nursing what would soon turn into a shiner. Oh my gosh, Uncle Jimmy was going to flip. I needed to hide this before someone saw and told on me. Again, nice to live in a small town where people cared. Not so nice that they cared a little too much.

I cut across the field from the library, hoping to take a shortcut by way of Lemon Loop and a trail through Central Park.

Unfortunately, just as I had nearly passed the corner of Cinnamon Ave and Lemon Loop, where the Ripe Raisin perched, ready to serve the masses, Dash exited. He saw me and froze.

I dropped the cold pack by my side and walked faster, Cookie right next to me.

"Hold on, Lexi. I'll walk you back." He took a few steps in my direction.

"Nope. Gotta go. Bathroom emergency. Sorry." I started running.

Unfortunately, Dash caught up with little effort. "Hold on. You can go in the bar and . . ."

He pulled me to a stop and gently pushed my hair back, which I'd been using to hide my cheek.

I don't think I've ever seen Dash so angry. "Who did this?"

"Oh my God. Stop. If someone had hit me, do you really think I'd run away in tears, with my killer dog by my side? Or would we be buried in my assailant's intestines and covered in gore?"

He blinked. "Er, good point. I think." But he had yet to look away from my face. "I bet it hurts." He prodded the flesh over my cheekbone, his touch tender. I still flinched. "Oh yeah. That's gonna leave a mark."

"I can't let my uncles see this. They'll put me under house arrest or call my mom and dad. And I like not having my parents over my shoulder all the time." All true. I did miss my folks, but here I'd finally become Lexi Jones. Not just Hershel and Lydia's sarcastic spawn.

Dash sighed. "Okay. Then you're coming back to my place where I can doctor you. And we'd better move fast. I think I hear your uncle's scooter."

We hurried down Lemon Loop, past Bill Sanchez's house, I noticed, until we hit a honey trail. We took it the long way, over

Soda Creek, and eventually reached Cat and Teri's complex. Dash's house being right down the road, we made it to his cottage in no time.

I hadn't been inside in months, not since the last time Teri, Cat, and I had raided his stash of man-candy.

Dash lived a bachelor's life, but he had nice taste. His house had been decorated in grays and whites with splashes of color, mostly blue and orange. Neat but not as "anal-retentive" as I was, he nevertheless had a house I deemed livable. A big-screen TV sat over the fireplace on one wall. Comfy furniture and black tables gave the living room a contemporary feel, and he placed me on his soft, cushy couch, grabbed a dog treat for Cookie, and left to grab something for my eye.

Exhausted by my day, my punch to the face, and our marathon walk to get back to safety unseen, I promptly fell asleep, Cookie leaning against my side, her dog breath in my ear.

Chapter Twenty-One

When Dash shook me awake, I blinked up into concerned brown eyes.

He stared at me and brushed my hair back from my face, his fingers so incredibly gentle. "That looks painful."

"How long did I sleep?"

"About two hours." He shrugged. "I didn't want to wake you, but I have to get to the bar. I needed to make sure you were okay first." He put an ice pack wrapped in a towel over my cheek. "How's that?"

"Good." I must have been groggier than I thought, because I'd swear Dash had that look in his eye, the one Teri and I had long ago identified as the pre-pucker-up. It was both pleasing and weird to see it as he looked at me. But I blinked, and he looked normal again, so maybe I was imagining things.

"So, well, do you want me to call Teri?"

"No." I shifted and felt dog breath on my neck. Cookie had curled into my side on the couch, lying half on me.

Dash glanced down and smiled. "She's protecting you. Or she's just tired. Could go either way."

I snorted. "No kidding." But I stroked my dog's soft fur, loving her no matter what. "Thanks for bringing me back here, but I'm really fine."

"You're really not. I know you're still freaked out about that break-in at your place. I would be too. And if you still haven't gotten the locks changed . . ."

"Um, not yet. Fred texted he'd come by tomorrow, first thing."

"Then you should stay here. I'll be out till two AM. You know where everything is."

"Huh? How would I know that?" Color me a snooper, but I'd thoroughly gone into every drawer and cabinet with my friends the last time we'd invited ourselves over for chocolates while Dash was busy working.

He gave me a look. "I know it was you three who stole all my Guy Day candy."

Guy Day—a day in Confection when we celebrate our men. I told you Confection has a bazillion festivals.

"But you hate chocolate."

"Not milk chocolate." He glared. "I was saving that stuff."

Tons of candy from admirers he'd been cultivating for years. "Well, we were only trying to save you from some love handles we know you wouldn't want."

He immediately looked down at his waist, and I did my best to hold back a snicker.

"Such a pain." He sighed at both me and Cookie, who defied physics to crane her neck and study Dash, upside down. "Stay here. No one will mess with you. You can use the spare room. Sheets are clean. And I have some food in the fridge and snacks. Just went shopping."

I didn't want to go back home, to be honest. "Thanks, Dash." I paused. "You sure I won't be invading your love nest?"

He barked a laugh, which had Cookie scrabbling off me to get to the floor.

"Sorry, Cookie." He curled a lock of my hair around his finger. "Love nest. I guess you really are a writer. 'Cause that's some strange fiction you got there." He let my hair go and stood, still chuckling. "Love nest. Heck, Lexi. This has never been a nest. It's a pad. A love *pad*."

"Because that's more manly?" I asked drily.

"Yep." He grinned down at me, his dimple showing.

My heart raced, but I ignored it. "Whatever. Thanks again, Mr. Love Pad. I really do appreciate it."

"No problem." He turned to leave.

"Wait. I probably won't see you when you get back, because no way I'll be awake at two in the morning. I'm having a meeting at my uncles' tomorrow. You're invited. Eleven o'clock for brunch. We're talking about the investigation."

"You mean the investigation you aren't supposed to be doing or Detective Chad Berg will lock you up? That investigation?"

"That one. Yeah."

"I'm in. See you tomorrow, and call if you need anything." He started to leave, then stopped, turned, and bent down to me. After a brief kiss that barely grazed my good cheek, he left with one last piece of warning, "Have a good night, and stay out of my room."

Cookie and I watched him leave. Then we looked at each other. "So that's like an invitation to check out his room, isn't it?"

She cocked her head.

I took that as a yes, and after stealing a shirt I meant to sleep in, we returned to the living room to scrounge up some dinner.

* * *

I had planned to eat before taking a brief nap, still sleepy after a heavy two-hour slumber. I also meant to move some of Dash's pillows on his bed to make it look like I'd obviously invaded his privacy, but closing my eyes for just a second turned into another nap until eight. Admittedly, I hadn't been getting the best sleep, stressed and unnerved as I was by the intruder. But Dash's house felt safe, and I guess subconsciously I knew that.

I heated up the leftover meat loaf and mashed potatoes his mother had made. I knew Mrs. Hagen had made it because she had been born with an inability to make anything taste bad. She just couldn't do it. She even made brussels sprouts and grits taste good. And I hate them both. Plus, though Dash isn't a bad cook, he's not great unless it comes in a box with instructions.

Savoring Mrs. Hagen's leftovers, I enjoyed a few sitcoms while Cookie made do with some leftover canned food I'd given Dash a few months ago when he'd watched Cookie for me. Rather, he'd begged to use Cookie to lure in a cute tourist for a double-dog date, and who was I to stand in the way of love and a night off of dog duty?

The hour reached ten, and though I'd had more sleep during the day than I normally did, I started to wind down. I dragged out the journal I'd been making notes in and added a few more. That would keep until tomorrow when I met the others at my uncles' place. They loved company, and having everything in their house would more than make up for the unintended hurt I'd caused Uncle Jimmy.

I rubbed my stomach, taken with the worn softness of Dash's shirt. Guy T-shirts always felt more comfortable than my own clothes. Not that I was a connoisseur of men's clothing, but I'd had a few boyfriends in my twenty-seven years of living. I washed up, using my finger as a toothbrush, and after taking Cookie out back to do her business, we went back inside and sacked out.

* * *

The next morning arrived bright and early. A glance at my phone showed I'd slept in until eight. I felt like a hedonist, especially because Cookie continued to let me sleep, snoozing on the floor by my side in the bed Dash had bought for her last Christmas.

After doing a quick washup, I wrote Dash a thank-you note. I would have popped my head into his bedroom to say thanks, but one, I didn't want to wake him, and two, that just felt a little too intimate. I folded his shirt and set it back in the center of the bed I'd made. Then Cookie and I set off for home.

Fortunately, we didn't pass anyone who might perceive my early return as a potential walk of shame. And God knew I had no intention of making a big deal about spending the night at Dash's. I'd mention it casually in passing to Teri and Cat. Because if I looked at all uncomfortable about spending the night at his house, I'd never hear the end of it. Teri was still convinced that one day I'd marry her brother and be tied forever to her family.

Yeah, um, not gonna happen.

After arriving home, I'd just managed a shower, change of clothes, and makeup to hide my bruise, now turning a deeper blue, when someone knocked at my door.

"Fred," I said as I opened it to allow the locksmith inside. "Thanks for coming."

"Sorry I couldn't get here yesterday," the older man replied. "With all the vandalism around town, folks are jumpy and changing locks like crazy."

"There've been that many break-ins?" I only knew of Nadine's shed being trashed.

"No, but people are panicking anyway. And who am I to tell them no?" His eyes twinkled. "Good for business." His mirth faded. "Though from what I hear, you really do need this."

"Yeah." I sighed. "Someone stole my laptop."

"Ouch. Is it insured?"

"No. But you can bet my next one will be."

"I hear you."

While Fred got to work changing the locks on my front and back doors, I went outside to see if any new holes had been dug. "Hey, Fred, have you been hit by the hole bandit?" I asked as he worked on the back door.

"Nope. But then, I don't have a lot of flowers out front. Just some bushes."

Hmm. Did that make a difference? Did everyone who'd been hit have flowers?

"But then we're north, near the schools. From what I'm seeing, pretty much every yard that's been dug up is either in the center or south of town. They're calling whoever did it the Rose Bandit on the local news."

"I hadn't heard that."

He looked up from my door and grinned. "Yep. Was on last night. Rose Bandit. Only in Confection."

"I bet the CGC is livid."

He nodded and returned to the lock. "I heard Ed Mullins complaining about it yesterday at the coffee shop. A few of his buddies were there too. Everyone's hot about the yard vandalism, but they can't agree if it's to do with the Gardener's Purse or something else."

"You got me."

He shrugged. "I'm not into gardening myself. And I haven't been affected, so I don't really have an opinion. But after what happened to Gil Cloutier and then someone destroying property, I fear for our town."

"I'm sure the Confection Police Department will catch the bad guy."

"I sure hope so."

Once Fred finished, he left Cookie and me with enough time to straighten up around the house before leaving. I had just finished putting away some clean laundry that had been living in my clothes basket for a good week when I happened to peek into my office.

"What the heck?" I stared, wide-eyed, at my laptop. It sat in the middle of my desk as if it had never been gone.

I called the police to report it had returned, and they said someone would get back to me.

But I was one step ahead of them. I put on some winter gloves, then opened my laptop and powered it on. I looked through as many files as I could but saw nothing missing. Fortunately, I'm the paranoid type, and all my banking and financial websites had manually inputted passwords, since I'd always feared something like this would happen.

But as I scrolled through my documents, looking at my story to see that glorious creation that had taken me over a year to put together, I saw something disturbing.

At the end of the document, someone had typed, in bold letters, MIND YOUR OWN BUSINESS OR WE'LL TAKE A LOT MORE THAN YOUR COMPUTER.

Proof I hadn't just imagined my computer had been gone!

A knock at the door had me jerking to my feet.

Cookie gave a warning bark at me to get up before racing away. When I reached her, I found her sitting expectantly, her tail wagging at whoever stood behind the door.

I peeked through the window and saw, of course, Chad Berg standing there.

I opened the door and stared at him.

He looked me over, noting my gloves, and nodded. "Good. You didn't touch it, did you?"

"Not without these on. And they left me a message." I nodded for him to follow me.

I showed him my computer, pointing out the warning. "And before you think of accusing me of making any of this up or typing this myself, I didn't. Go ahead. Dust it for prints. I'm clean."

Berg tilted his head, looking at lot like Cookie did when she found something interesting. "You could of course have typed this message with gloves on."

"I . . . Well . . ."

"And your prints are likely all over it anyway because it's your computer, unless of course the thief wiped everything clean."

"Crap."

He smirked. "But I'm sure you didn't. If you want, I can take it in for prints. Only problem is if they're not in the system."

"Huh?"

"If whoever it was doesn't have a criminal record or has never had a job requiring a background check, we'll have nothing to match them to."

"Oh." Bummer. I hadn't thought about that.

"Also, they gave your laptop back. I'd bet we won't find any prints. One thing for sure with who we've been dealing with—they aren't stupid." He looked back at the screen, sat down in my chair, and scowled. "But this is a definitely a threat, any way you look at it. When exactly did you notice the laptop's return? Last night? Today?"

"I wasn't here last night."

"Where were you?" He kept his gaze on the screen, looking for more clues, I guessed.

"Is that relevant?"

He looked up at me, opened his mouth, then closed it, his gaze narrowing.

On my cheekbone.

"I hadn't realized you wore that much makeup," Berg said, his voice tight.

"I hadn't realized you notice what I wear." *Oh, snappy come-back, Lexi.*

"I do my very best to keep you and your dog in my sights at all times," he said drily. "Now, do you want to explain who hit you?"

I gave a fake laugh. "Hit me? No way. If anyone had hit me, I'd have busted him or her up. I'm lethal with these fists."

I held them up, expecting him to laugh. But his sober expression worried me.

"Would you like to make a report?"

"Nah." I sighed, glancing at my laptop. "You're probably right. I doubt it has any prints we could use."

"I meant for assault." Berg remained seated, being very gentle all of a sudden.

"I'm . . . What?"

He looked from my bruise into my eyes. "Who hit you?"

I groaned. "Look, you can't tell anyone."

He raised a brow.

"It was nothing illegal, not an assault or anything. I tried to break up a fight and got whacked in the face. My own fault." I looked down at Cookie, who looked back at me in agreement. She'd been smart enough to stay back from the fighting Cloutiers. "When I was heading home after getting smacked—accidentally—trying to avoid my uncles, I ran into Dash. He let me stay at his place, since he was working late. When I got home this morning, I didn't see anything at first. I was probably here a good hour and a half before Fred came over and changed my locks."

"Good. And then you saw your laptop?"

"Yeah. I poked my head in my study, and it was sitting right there." I pointed to the computer.

Berg kept staring at me.

"What? I'm telling you the truth."

"Huh." He shrugged.

"What does that mean?"

"Nothing at all."

Yet somehow I felt judged.

Berg wrote down some more in his little notebook. He scrolled back through my story on my computer, and I realized I should probably stop that before he got to some of my notes about male posturing, gray eyes, and whether I wanted my hero to have too many muscles.

I darted in to minimize the screen.

"I was looking for clues."

"Yeah, well, you can read them when it's published." I moved back when he stood.

Looming over me, as usual. Before I could step back, he put his hand under my chin.

I froze while he tilted my head to the side.

"You did a fairly decent job, but that bruise is going to get darker." He let me go, and I did my best to look normal and not like I was about to jump out of my skin. "You're sure you don't want to press charges?"

I started to feel like a victim, and I was anything but. "No, thank you." I stepped back. "Now, if you'll excuse me, I have a date with pancakes and my uncles."

He gave me a half grin. "When you do, make sure you tell Elvis to slow down, or next time Roger will have to ticket him."

"The Vespa won't go over forty."

"Yeah, well, he was doing thirty-five in a twenty-five." Berg shook his head. "Only in Confection."

I walked him out. "Thanks for coming by." *I guess.*

Once on my porch, he turned and gave me his serious police stare. "Lexi, I can only tell you so many times to keep your nose out of Gil's murder. There are some dangerous people who don't mind killing to get what they want. You need to take that warning to heart."

"I will. I mean, I do." It did freak me out, I'd admit. But that only told me I was close to something someone didn't want exposed.

"You won't." Berg sighed. "But I'll make sure I said I told you so when I'm hauling you off to jail."

"Nice threat, Officer."

"That's *Detective*," he said with an icy smile, his eyes bright. Definitely more like diamonds than smoke, that color. "And it's not a threat. It's a guarantee." He shook his head. "I want you, your friends, your family, and your boyfriend to stay out of this investigation. Last warning."

"We're not— Wait. What boyfriend?"

He left without answering.

I stomped back inside to fix my makeup, then grabbed Cookie and headed over to my uncles. For once I'd be early.

Boyfriend? What boyfriend? It took me a minute. He had to mean Dash. What a laugh. My social life had taken a back seat to my career a while ago, and now it was even farther back, locked in the proverbial trunk, pushed there by a murder and a mystery.

I seriously needed a cup of coffee. "Come on, Cookie. Time for the Macaroons to get some answers."

She woofed, and we were off.

Chapter Twenty-Two

"Lexi, I need you to grab this."

I hurried to Uncle Elvis to take the second plate of bacon he handed me and set it down in the dining room just off the kitchen. I placed it on the buffet that took up the long wall under a large antique mirror. The expansive round table, I noted, easily sat eight, and they hadn't needed to use the leaf to make extra room.

My uncles lived to entertain, as evidenced by the buffet spread, grandly set table, and floral arrangement that looked professionally done.

"Yep, Dave and Julie did that," Uncle Jimmy said as he saw where my attention had wandered. "That was a bonus for Elvis fitting them in on a project right before Memorial Day. He was waiting for the right occasion to pick it up."

"Nice." I grabbed a pitcher of orange juice while Stefanie added a bottle of champagne to the table.

"Mimosas for everyone," she said with a satisfied grunt.

Alison shook her head. "My diet is never going to succeed around you people."

I chuckled.

"Alison, stop worrying about life and start living it." Elvis poured her a glass of bubbly with a splash of orange juice and handed me a coffee. "Now, who are we still waiting for?"

Cat and Teri stopped chatting with Jimmy long enough to join us at the table.

Teri looked around. "That would be my late brother. He texted that we should start without him." She paused, her eyes sparkling as they landed on me. "He said Lexi never woke him when she left, so he's behind this morning."

Everyone stopped what they were doing to look at me and my red face. "You are so dead," I muttered.

Even Cookie laughed at me before taking a bone back into the kitchen, where she watched Jimmy plate a few more trays with warm regard.

Time to nip this gossip in the bud. "Okay, for the record, I stayed at Dash's house last night—while he was working in the bar—because I wanted a break from everyone and everything. No offense," I said to my friends and family.

Stefanie harrumphed. "I know all about wanting my own space. Don't apologize. People are annoying."

Alison chuckled. "Some more than others."

She had my uncles laughing. Cat and Teri, however, were staring at me.

"Oh, stop." I yanked them to the side of the room and in a low voice explained about the bruised eye and why I'd avoided my uncles. "Now stop gossiping about me," I warned Teri.

"I will, I promise." She stared at my bruise. "Not bad, but you're a little heavy on the concealer. Changing the subject, my date with Randy went really well."

"Mine too!" Cat grinned so wide I feared her face might split in half.

"Breakfast! I mean, brunch!" Jimmy bellowed. "Come sit."

We all sat around the table, leaving a space next to Teri for Dash.

I clinked a fork against my glass for attention. "Before we begin, I just wanted to say thank you to my favorite uncles—"

"Only uncles," Jimmy said.

"—for hosting our first ever mystery brunch."

We all toasted Elvis and Jimmy.

"Now, before we get started, I wanted to tell everyone that my locks are officially changed. Also, I will no longer keep a spare key under my small red flowerpot."

"Thank God," Elvis muttered.

"*And* my laptop is back."

Everyone started asking questions at the same time Dash arrived. He hurried inside and sat next to his sister. "What did I miss?"

"Well," Elvis started. "After Teri told us you spent the night with my niece, Lexi informed us she had her laptop back and Berg threatened to throw her, and all of us, in jail."

Dash conveniently ignored any innuendo, disappointing my uncle, no doubt. "You got it back? How did that happen?" he asked as he gladly accepted a cup of black coffee from Jimmy.

"Let's get our food and eat and I'll explain," I said.

I followed the others to the buffet, heaping my plate full of the delectable dishes lined up so prettily. I felt like we were eating at a fancy B&B, and Alison apparently felt the same because she said as much to my uncles. Scrambled eggs with chives, a potato casserole, avocado toast, a mango chutney to go with spiced chorizo, and the mountain of applewood-smoked bacon and mini homemade bagels and herbed cream cheese sat in trays and serving bowls with even fancier spoons and tongs. To round out the meal, sliced cheeses, prosciutto, and salmon pâté and crackers sat at the very end of the spread.

I filled myself to bursting, enjoying the laughter and teasing as we all ate and talked about who and what we'd seen over the past week. So many tourists. The mayor grandstanding all over town with visitors. A few closely competitive soccer games at Confection Park with our summer soccer league. And of course, the morbidly curious who had been passing by Gil's house in large numbers.

I hadn't realized, since I had been spending my days at work. But Alison mentioned she'd seen a lot more people on garden tours and walking in our neighborhood than usual.

"Yeah, out here too," Elvis said. On the other side of Soda Creek, the Lemon Loop area had its share of garden gazers. But Gil's death had brought a surprising number of visitors from our neighboring towns. "I know because I asked where they were from. A lot coming from Bend and Redmond, actually."

"Interesting." It also made it that much easier for the bad guys to blend in. "So, let's recap a bit about what we know. Abe and Matt are probably in the clear. Abe argued with Gil on Matt's behalf. Matt was already in town, spending happy time with Jan."

"Happy time?" Dash said under his breath. "With Jan?"

I cleared my throat and glared at him. "We also know Gil lent money to Scott, who might be having money problems."

Stefanie nodded, her arms crossed over her chest as she leaned back to give herself some room at the table. I knew the feeling. I'd eaten so much I wanted to bust.

"But we aren't sure about who else Gil might have been giving money to," I continued. "We also have Bill and Joe sounding suspicious. Something's going on with those two."

Alison frowned. "That concerns me."

"Me too," Jimmy said. "Wouldn't have ever thought of Bill as a cheater."

"And Gil and Mandy?" I asked. "What do you guys think of that angle?"

"What?" Elvis asked. "That they had a secret love child who died and Mandy's been pining for Gil all these years? I don't buy it, or the fact Alan might kill out of jealousy. He's one of the most laid-back guys I know."

Jimmy nodded. "Yeah. I don't see Alan hurting anyone, frankly. But Gil and Mandy being more than friendly does explain seeing them interact in the past. Gil was always a jerk, but not with her."

"So sad." Teri sighed. "Imagine them being in love and having that ripped apart because of a baby that wasn't to be."

"We're sure that baby wasn't born and given away?" Stefanie said, out of the blue. "Because think about it. A secret love child who comes back to get revenge is the perfect plot in any made-for-TV movie."

"She's got a point," Cat said, slurping her mimosa. "But you need to add 'crazy' in there to round out the plot. It's always a *crazy* love child with notions of vengeance. Never someone who just wants to meet their long-lost parents."

Dash rolled his eyes. "Yeah, um, no. Someone killed Gil for either money they didn't want to pay back, to get him out of the way because of the Gardener's Purse—which is my bet—or because they want whatever he buried according to his treasure map. Not a secret love child, a lost love, or because he was a mean guy."

"Which begs the question, what happened to his trowel?"

Everyone turned to me.

Elvis raised a brow. " 'Begs the question?' Who are you? Ms. Marple?"

"I wish. But don't change the topic, Uncle Elvis. I think it's beyond odd that no one is concerned Gil's trowel is missing. He never did any gardening without it."

"How do we know it's missing?" Cat asked. "Roger never mentioned any evidence at the crime scene. He won't talk about the case much. And I doubt Detective Berg told you anything, Lexi."

Teri cut in. "No, but I was listening pretty hard at work yesterday. They don't have the trowel. And the DA wants it found. They think the trowel made the stab marks on Gil's body."

We all sat in silence, pondering that.

"Well hot damn," Stefanie said with gusto. "We finally have a murder weapon."

"And a note from the deceased," I added for dramatic effect, pleased when several jaws dropped. Well, just Uncle Elvis's and Dash's, since they were the only ones who didn't know. But still.

I pulled it out from my pocket and read it aloud in a deep, crabby voice, to simulate Gil. " 'You weren't the best neighbor. Not even close. But I'm pretty sure you can't be as dumb as you look. Roses have thorns you know. It's all in how you hold it. Now get off my lawn.' "

"Sounds totally like Gil," Stefanie said. "Convoluted and angry."

Alison agreed.

Uncle Jimmy asked to see the note again. I handed it to him and watched him and Elvis look it over.

"Fred said something interesting today," I told the group. "Apparently, most of his neighbors in the north of town aren't having any issues with yard vandalism. Just us south of Central

Garden. And only those places with roses. Then you have Gil talking about roses and thorns." I was missing something. I could feel it. His note was cryptic. A message for me, obviously. "What did he mean about 'It's all in how you hold it'? That's code, right?"

"I'm still confused as to how you found this," Uncle Jimmy said.

"After my place got broken into, I went outside with Cookie and found someone had dug near the fence where Cookie used to dig to get to Gil's. Her dog treat ball was down in the hole, and the note was inside."

"But you never saw the treat ball there before? And whoever was digging just ignored it?"

"I guess." That bothered me too. "Another thing that's curious, there are no rosebushes on either side of the digging in my yard. So why dig there?"

Jimmy looked thoughtful. "Gil's yard is amazing, but it's mostly shrubs, decorative trees, and his garden. He doesn't have a lot of flowers in his yard either. Yet there was a hole there."

Dash coughed. "More like a grave."

I cringed. "Yeah."

"Well, this just keeps getting more interesting." Elvis wiggled his brows. "Tell you what. We'll look into the Danvers for you. And Mandy and Alan. We're friendly with them. We can feel them out for answers."

"Good. We still need to figure out if Scott had an alibi."

Teri nodded. "I'll dig at the DA's office some more. Discreetly," she said, before I could warn her to be careful. "And technically, we don't have an alibi for Abe—who stole Gil's map, remember. Big red flag there. Also, Matt might have been with Jan, but we don't have sure times on any of the Cloutiers. Only the police do, and I doubt Berg will be forthcoming with any of us." Why she looked at me when she said that, I had no idea.

"Right."

Jimmy leaned into the table, staring at me. "Hey, what's that on your face?"

Crap. I'd rubbed my cheek, not thinking, and no doubt messed up my concealer. "Oh, I tripped and bumped into a door when Cookie yanked her leash yesterday. I put some makeup over it to cover my clumsiness."

He nodded, buying the explanation. Elvis, however, frowned, especially when Cookie grumbled at me. Apparently she didn't like being a scapegoat.

Time for a diversion. I stood. "I hear there might be cheesecake to top off brunch. Is that true?"

Everyone cheered.

Off the hook, I dashed into the kitchen and grabbed an amazing-looking New York–style cheesecake I'd spotted earlier. After we cut slices and dug in, I tuned in to Stefanie and Alison's conversation.

"I still think we're missing something," Alison said.

"Me too. There's a big plot twist coming our way. More we're not seeing." Stefanie frowned.

"I think there's a lot we're not seeing," I said, butting in. "But until we have concrete proof of alibis, we need to keep on our toes."

"Good point." Stefanie sighed, took another bite of dessert, then stood. "Well, as much as I want to stay for more food, I'd best be going. Got a lot of chores and more mysteries to solve." She winked at me. "I finished *The Murder of Roger Ackroyd*, by the way. Wonderful book. But not helpful . . . unless *you* killed Gil?" she said to me.

I blinked. "What do you mean?"

"Spoiler," Teri said drily. "The narrator is the murderer."

Cat swore. "Darn it. I hadn't read that far yet."

"Thanks a lot, Teri." I sighed. "Just don't spoil it for the rest of the Macaroons."

Alison shrugged. "We've been texting. It was such a good read, a lot of us finished early. Alan, Kay, and Darcy are done."

"I'd love to talk about it, but we don't meet until next Monday. And Scott might not be done yet."

"Fine, but we're wasting time when we could be diving into another murder." Stefanie blinked. "Although we're kind of doing that now, aren't we?" She grinned. "But this is real."

"Real dangerous," Jimmy, the wet blanket, reminded everyone. "If they killed once, they probably won't hesitate to do it again."

"He's right." I nodded. "We should work in pairs for accountability. Cat and I will work together, since we're already together at work. Dash and Teri. Alison and Stefanie. And Jimmy and Elvis. We always check in with each other, right?"

Everyone nodded.

"Then go forth and prosper."

"That's a Star Trek reference." Elvis frowned. "Not appropriate for a murder investigation. Don't you have anything more mystery-like?"

"I love it when a plan comes together," Dash suggested.

"Isn't that the A-Team? From the eighties?" Cat asked. "How about 'I'll be baaaaack'?"

"From *The Shining*?" Teri grimaced.

"No, that's from *The Terminator*," I cut in. "You're thinking 'Heeeere's Johnny.' "

"There's a murder in *The Shining*," Cat said in her defense.

"He's possessed and tries to murder his family." Teri grimaced. "The terminator kills people because he's a robot from the future. Try something less evil."

A furry foot trampled on mine under the table, inspiring me. "Jinkies! It seems like we've got another mystery on our hands!"

Elvis grinned. "Perfect. We have our own Scooby right here, don't we, Cookie?"

She trotted out from under the table, where she'd been hiding, and looked up with a guilty grin, a piece of bacon hanging off a whisker.

"Right." I sighed. "Well, gang, try to steer clear of Old Man Withers, and we'll reconvene when we've got more to share."

Alison and Stefanie left.

Dash nodded for me to join him at the front door on his way out. "Are you okay?" He glanced at my cheek.

"Fine. Thanks for letting me stay over."

"Anytime." He looked over my shoulder and shook his head. I followed his stare to my friends, who were making kissy faces at me. "It's like they're eleven years old all over again."

"More like eight," I muttered.

"Well, I'm out of here. Got stuff to do before work."

"Don't you ever take time off?"

"I could ask the same."

I waved my hands around me. "I'm here, aren't I? Collin and Lee-Ann are working this weekend at the bookshop."

"Be careful. I know you'll get up to some kind of trouble with too much time off."

I grinned. "I'll be good. Scout's honor."

He scoffed. "Like you were ever a Scout. And on that note, I'm gone." He paused. "You can always stay over if you need to. Just find me at the bar and I'll get you a key."

Before I could thank him, he left.

I stayed with my friends to help clean up, but my uncles kicked us out after Cat bobbled yet another of their favorite serving trays.

"Love you," I called as we rushed out the door. Once away from the house, I said to Cat, "And thank you for nearly dropping that tray."

"There was no danger of that happening, but Jimmy was on my nerves." She sighed. "I can see where your pickiness about cleaning comes from."

"No kidding," Teri agreed. "Now enough about murder and Lexi and my brother."

"There is no me and your brother," I reminded her.

"Let's talk about our dates. Cat, you go first."

Cat started talking, and talking, and talking. So I listened, pleased for her and for Teri, who'd also had a fabulous time with a potential new boyfriend. Cookie trotted alongside us, pleased to be out and about after a morning of bacon bits.

But while they blathered about their men, I made plans to clear up a few more uncertainties about the case. Because I really needed to get a clue to help me scooby-dooby-doo, or I might never scrub the thought of murder out of my brain.

Chapter Twenty-Three

After dropping Teri and Cat at their place, I decided to spend my sunny Saturday afternoon walking off my brunch. Avoiding the crowded downtown area, not having a reason to go there since I had the weekend off, I instead sauntered around the neighborhood, enjoying the beauty all around me.

Though I didn't particularly want to spend my free time burying my hands in dirt while endeavoring to make things grow, I did like getting ideas on how to better the look of my house while also scouting for patches of dug-up earth.

I stayed on the southwest side of town, my neighborhood in particular. I enjoyed our varied architecture, especially the cute craftsman- and Victorian-style homes in rich colors. I noticed what seemed like everyone and their mother out working in their yards. Then I realized the judging had seriously started for the Gardener's Purse.

Passing another garden tour, I waved at Darcy, then again later at Darcy's cousin.

The yards with big yellow ribbons attached to fences showed their involvement in the contest. There were a lot more than there'd been last year. But with a huge monetary prize, I wasn't surprised. Three people stood with clipboards at Ed Mullins's house while Ed paced nervously behind them, supported by Bonnie and Peggy.

I wondered who would win this year, and if any of it had to do with Gil's murder.

As I ended up on the south end of Court Street, I realized I'd passed Stefanie's house and paused just outside the Danverses'. A big golden bow had been tied to their fence as well. No surprise there. I knew my uncles had plans to talk to them, but I couldn't help myself.

Dave knelt in the front, weeding, his T-shirt sticking to him and his shorts smudged with dirt. He glanced up to see me, smiled, and stood. "Hi, Lexi. And Cookie."

Cookie gave him a hello grumble. She liked the Danverses, same as I did.

"Hi, Dave. Sorry. I don't mean to distract you."

He wiped his forehead, sweating under the sweltering sun. "Not at all. I'm happy for the break. Want to come see something amazing?" He crossed to open the front gate of his three-foot-tall wrought-iron fence, which framed his glorious blooms.

"Do I! Cookie, you be nice." I looked from her to Dave and decided to err on the side of caution. "I'm going to leave her right here, outside the fence."

"Okay." He looked relieved but pretended not to be.

"Cookie, stay. And don't make trouble," I warned as I looped her leash around a pointed fence topper and clipped it to her collar.

She lay down with Mr. Leggy and waited, staring around her. We both knew she could escape without much effort, though she pretended to be bound to humor me. My very own canine Houdini, and I still had no idea how she managed her tricks. Some assistant I was.

I followed Dave into his front yard and stared. I had no idea how the judges decided who would win the many contests in the Gardener's Purse, but I would have easily given the Danverses the gold just looking at their front yard.

The colorful blooms of roses, lavender, poppies, marigolds, daisies, and more blanketed beds that were curved around the border of a lush green yard. I could see the lines of mowing Dave had done, his yard pristine, not one off-colored blade of grass or dandelion anywhere to be found.

The scents of rose and lavender tickled my nose. A few hummingbirds ventured close to bubblegum-pink phlox and purple coneflowers. And to the side, a bubbler burbled, attracting birds and a few butterflies.

"This is incredible," I said in awe, standing in a real-life Disney background. I swear, if a bird landed on my shoulder and started singing, I'd order my fairy godmother to turn Cookie into a horse and ride off to find my prince.

Dave gave me a pleased grin. "And this is just the front."

I followed him around the side, through another gate into his backyard, where four raised cedar beds served as a barracks for a platoon of green and growing vegetables that would make the purveyors at our local farmer's market weep. All the veggies had been labeled by date and type, all in rows, fertilized and watered through drips and overhead sprinklers affixed to raised hoops, which could be covered in cloth and lowered over the beds during cold nights.

"There's no way you're going to lose this year." I couldn't take it all in. They had tomatoes, green beans, peppers of different colors and sizes, potatoes, green onions . . . And there, strawberries and blueberries. "This is *incredible*."

"And yet we only took fourth place last year in Best Overall Garden." Dave sighed. "Competition's pretty fierce, so we really stepped up our flower game this year. Gil was the one to beat, I have to say. He focused on the vegetables. Not only did they look great and grow healthy, the taste was extraordinary."

"I never noticed." Honestly, anytime the CGC gathered next door, I kept my distance. "The most I ever saw of my neighbor was him shaking a fist at me for breathing too loud."

Dave chuckled. "I'm sad he's dead but not sorry he's gone. He wasn't a nice man."

"I know." I paused, trying to segue into what I wanted to know. "So, well, I was curious."

"About?"

"You didn't like him, but someone told me he lent you guys money?" I made it a question, not a statement of fact.

Dave blinked. "*Gil?* Gil Cloutier, lend us money?" He started laughing and didn't stop until Julie came to see what was so funny. "Lexi thinks Gil lent us money."

"For what?" Julie looked puzzled.

"Well, I might have overheard that the flower shop was having some trouble, and the bank wasn't being cooperative." I hurried to tack on, "You know how the CoC is. People talk."

Julie shrugged. "It's true. We were having some money problems. Oh, hush, Dave. It was no secret we couldn't make the Bend store work. We tried to grow too fast, but we learned."

"We did. It looked like we might lose the Confection store for a while." Dave shook his head. "But we managed. We ended up getting a small loan."

"From my mother," Julie clarified. "Not Gil. He would never have given us, or anyone else, a cent. That man was bitter to his very end."

"No kidding." Dave took Julie's hand in his and squeezed. "We've worked hard to make a go of this town, and we're doing it. But with little help from anyone else. Well, not until we joined the CGC last year." Dave smiled. "They can be a little overbearing. Like Nestor and Peggy."

"And Ed," I added.

Dave laughed. "And Ed. But when it comes to gardening, they're actually good people. Nestor's conceited, and his wife's awful, I'll just admit it."

"Dave," Julie admonished.

"She is, and you know it. Heck, they accused us of killing Gil for his potatoes."

Julie grimaced. "I'm sure they didn't mean it."

"Trust me, we *all* know Peggy's awful," I said.

Dave snorted. "She is. Yet they've helped us tremendously. Ed offered to hook us up with his finance guy. When finances were tight, Bonnie filled in for a few days when we had trouble getting a new person to work in the shop. And despite Nestor acting like a horse's ass, he's actually been very welcoming to both of us at church, when not competing for the Gardener's Purse. They're not all bad."

"What about Bill and Joe?"

Julie piped in, "I like Bill. He's a sweetheart. Smart, in his head a lot, but he really—forgive the pun—blossoms when he's talking gardening. Joe is more standoffish but always polite. He's also a little competitive."

"*A lot* competitive," Dave said. "He lost to Gil last year for Best Home Garden and Best Confection Veggie. But he said he was going to kill it this year." He paused. "Not literally, mind you."

"Right." At least I could strike the Danverses from my suspect list. Thank goodness.

In a much better frame of mind, I chatted with them some more before heading out to grab Cookie, who lay in front of the fence on the sidewalk in the same position as when I'd left her.

Julie opened the gate for me. "Lexi, you should check out Joe's garden. Trust me, you'll be impressed."

"I think I will. Thanks, Julie. Good luck this year!"

"Thanks. We'll take all the luck we can get." She smiled.

I stroked Cookie, who had gotten to her feet, and unclipped her leash. "Okay, Cookie, let's go swing by Joe's. I have got to see his garden."

She grabbed her toy and walked with me back toward Pixie Apartments. I texted my uncles, letting them know not to worry about the Danverses. Cookie and I cut through Central Park toward Lemon Loop, where Joe lived. If Julie and Dave were impressed, I had a feeling Joe's garden had to be out of this world.

Who knew the CGC really did have a reason for so much posturing? That their arrogance was, kind of, deserved?

Cookie and I enjoyed our traipse through the shadowed woods, the sunlight warming but not overly hot when tempered by broad oaks and aspens overhead. We passed a few squirrels Cookie ignored and a cute chipmunk I had to warn her to leave alone.

We came out on Lemon Loop, and I made a left to take us past Bill's house on the way. I walked slowly, seeing all the yellow ribbons on fences and noting who did and didn't have a chance to win. Admittedly, the homes on this side of the creek had vast gardens and lawns that looked professionally maintained. But few had front yards of the Danverses' quality.

Until we reached Bill's house.

The software guru had a large, detailed Victorian in dark and light blues. The posts supporting his portico had been carved by hand. I could tell, and if Uncle Elvis were here, he'd gush about the quality of craftsmanship.

The wraparound porch had a clean teak stain, the porch swing and table and chairs inviting you to sip a glass of lemonade while swinging and watching the clouds skip through the sky. The house looked twice the size of mine, and the front yard had boxwoods squaring off the lawn, two large pines providing some shade while off on either side of the house, blooms in blues, yellows, and whites gave ample framing to the glorious Victorian. I swear, all the flowers looked even, none of one kind taller than its brethren. So that the effect was a blanket of blue, then yellow, then white with clusters of ferns and ivy around the shady base of the trees.

On either side of Bill's large front door, which had an impressive stained-glass insert in a geometric design, two overflowing containers boasted more color in purples, blues, and yellows with trailing green down the sides.

Okay, so I finally had some sincere garden envy.

I hoped to see Bill so I could question him again, but I didn't notice him anywhere about. Continuing on my mission to talk to Joe, I turned the corner and walked a few more houses up the street to Joe Jacobs's midcentury modern home. Gorgeous yet much different from Bill's, Joe's house had been designed in clean lines. Gray concrete siding interspersed with dark-brown horizontal planks and black framing around the windows complemented the plethora of green surrounding the house. Like a mix of big city and wild forest in our own little town of Confection.

The home had been designed by some big name from Portland ten years ago. I only remember because my parents had been on the housing committee at the time, and it had been a huge, hairy deal that Joe had torn down a crumbling three-story to build it.

Everywhere at Joe's I saw green and white, but that lack of color didn't detract whatsoever from the glory of the home.

Impressed, because Joe didn't seem like such a fancy type of guy, I saw the yellow ribbon tied to a large oak out front and looked at his walkway, lined with different shades of green foliage leading to his open front door. I paused but didn't hear or see him nearby. Odd.

"Joe," I called out.

Nothing.

I looked at Cookie, who looked back at me. She dropped her octopus and made a mad dash for the front door.

"Crap. Not again." I started after her but froze when I heard my name yelled.

I turned to see Detective Berg rounding the car he'd just parked. Great. Now he'd ticket me for Cookie being off her leash and trespassing. No more than one sighting of the detective a day was my new motto.

"Are you following me?"

He rolled his eyes. "I'm following a lead, thank you. What are you doing here?"

"I was just talking to the Danvers while out on a walk. They told me if I wanted to see an amazing garden to check out Joe's. But it's weird, because his door is open and he's not answering. I was going to go see if he was okay when Cookie bolted inside."

"Of course she did."

I glared. "She's a concerned citizen."

"She's . . . Oh hell."

I turned back to see what had Berg's eyes so wide. Cookie held a mini hand rake—or cultivator, I think it was called—in her teeth, the ends coated in black soil. But it wasn't the dirty tines on the cultivator that concerned me. It was the bloody paw prints my dog left as she growled and went back inside.

Berg hurried to follow her. "Stay here." He pulled a gun from the holster at his belt. Wow. How had I missed the fact he had a gun?

I had no intention of hanging back, though I did prep 911 on my cell, ready to make the call should Berg need backup. I didn't want to contaminate any evidence, so I walked only where Berg had into the entryway, avoiding bloody paw prints.

"Is Joe okay?" I called out.

"No. Call 911. He's dead."

I couldn't believe it. A *second* murder? Seriously? I made the call. "Hi. This is Lexi Jones. I'm at Joe Jacobs' house on Lemon Loop. Um . . ." I had to back out to read the number next to the door. "Four-four-two Lemon Way Loop. He's been murdered."

A pause. "Murdered? Are you sure?"

"No, but Detective Berg is here, and he told me to call. There's blood . . ."

"Roger. Help is on the way." The dispatcher disconnected.

I stood in the doorway, looking but not seeing anything. Well, apparently Joe wasn't the murderer after all. My mind went directly to Bill Sanchez and stayed there.

Berg hurried back to me, Cookie on his heels. "Can you please get the rake from her mouth? But don't touch it. We need to get clear of the house."

I followed him to his car, where he dug a large evidence bag and plastic gloves out from the trunk.

I looked down at Cookie and in my firmest voice said, “Cookie, drop.”

She looked at me and sat but refused to let go of the cultivator, so I explained, “It’s part of a murder investigation. Detective Berg needs it.” I nodded to Berg, who came to stand next to me, holding open the bag. He didn’t look pleased, to say the least.

Then I spotted Mr. Leggy. I hurried to grab it and held it to my dog. “Trade.”

She looked at Mr. Leggy, me, and Berg. With a doggy sigh, she walked to him and deposited the cultivator in the bag.

Grabbing Mr. Leggy, she took a spot in the shade with the pink octopus in her mouth and sat like a sphinx.

Berg stared at her, surprised. “She’s an odd dog.”

“She’s super smart, you mean.”

“Yeah.” Berg looked at her then shook his head. “Right. Look, I need you to stay here, out of the way, while I canvass the rest of the house. If anyone but the police department comes near, you keep them out.”

I brightened, finding one silver lining in today’s death cloud. “Are you deputizing me?”

“No. Just keep everyone out.”

I saluted him, and he sighed heavily before walking away. At the door, he stopped to put on some disposable booties and gloves, then disappeared inside the house.

It didn’t take long for the cavalry to arrive. Police cars, their sirens on, of course, and more police vans showed up. I waved to Roger, whom I recognized right away. He wore civilian attire but had come out anyway. He waved back, his serious face indicating I should leave him alone to do his job. What looked like a forensics team entered the house with gear while a few other officers in uniform cordoned off the area.

Roger came over to me. "You're a witness?" He glanced down at Cookie. "Ah, I see bloody paws. Is she okay?"

"I hope so. But I think the blood is from inside the house. Detective Berg is in there. He told me to wait out here. But, um, it looks like you guys are going to be a while. Can Cookie and I go home? We didn't see anything."

"Hold on." Roger walked a few steps away and made a call, returning moments later. "Can you give me a statement before you go?" He had his phone out. "I'm going to record you, okay?"

"Sure. Basically, I came to see Joe's garden. I called out for him because his door was open, but I didn't see him nearby. Then I started to walk toward the house when Cookie bolted inside. Detective Berg found me before I'd taken a step up the walkway. When Cookie came out with a cultivator, that rake-y thing, in her mouth, she had blood on her paws. But no blood on the cultivator, just dirt. Berg has it in his car in a baggie."

"Right. So you never went inside?"

"Well, I stood in the hallway after Detective Berg went in, and I stood where he had. But that's as far as I went. I really don't know much. Berg told me to call 911 and that Joe was dead. He's really dead?" I'd just seen the guy yesterday.

Roger nodded, his eyes sad. "I'm afraid so. You should go home."

"Wait, Roger." I mentioned the odd conversation I'd overheard between Bill and Joe and how Bill had reacted.

"He really said he'd make Joe pay?"

"Pretty much." I hated to put suspicion on someone who didn't deserve it, but with Joe dead, Bill was certainly the guy I'd look into, were I the police.

"Thanks. I'll pass that to Detective Berg," Roger said. "Before you go, hold on a sec." He left and came back with some water and a towel. But before he could touch Cookie, a frantic guy in a blue jumper came over. "Wait, wait. Let me look over the dog."

We waited while he lifted Cookie's paws, washing them and looking for anything at all between her toes. Like a lady, she remained calm and let him inspect her without issue. He found nothing but a blade or two of grass.

So we left and headed home, the day just as sunny but nowhere near as bright as it had been.

Chapter Twenty-Four

By Saturday evening, I'd already informed my brunch buddies about Joe's death, though my uncles had already known thanks to the many sirens that had screamed down the street.

Feeling less than safe, even in my newly locked house, I thought about spending the night at Dash's again but then realized I couldn't let fear rule me. Instead, I needed to think about why Joe would be dead. Reason, not fear, would settle my nerves.

Fortunately, neither Berg nor I had shared the news that I'd nearly found the body, so no one was pestering me for more details than I wanted to handle.

"Cookie, why kill Joe?"

She gave me a doggy shrug before loping out the back door into the yard.

The evening hadn't cooled down too much, so I'd taken my dinner out onto my small back porch. So pretty outside, with birds still giving the odd chirp, the dusk starting to turn the sky from a bright blue to a cotton-candy pink merging with candy-apple red.

And now I wanted something sweet to eat.

Using my new notebook, not the unicorn one known to the police, I jotted down some ideas.

Bill and the Central Oregon Gardener's Purse. He'd been arguing with Joe recently about something pretty serious. Both men had made comments about finally taking the prize, now that Gil was out of the way.

But murder? Money did make a terrific reason for killing. Yet Bill had a lot of money, didn't he? But how much was too much? Or too little, in some cases?

I had enough to make ends meet with a little left over for savings and fun. But I had nowhere near what those on Lemon Loop had. Would I consider murder to get more?

The almighty dollar just didn't interest me the way it did some.

But Joe . . . had he been blackmailing someone? Maybe Bill? Was the murder all about a grand gardening prize? Or had Joe maybe stumbled over someone dangerous and been killed for it? To protect a secret treasure, perhaps?

Which brought me back to the Cloutiers.

Though I didn't have evidence, I didn't think Matt, Abe, or Scott had killed their dad—or Joe—either. Something more was at play here. Like Stefanie and Alison had said, I was missing something.

I sensed that the digging around town was tied to Gil's death in some way. And Gil's cryptic note: *Roses have thorns. All in how you hold it.* Hold what?

I wished I had more answers than questions.

Which made me wonder how Detective Berg was getting on. What had killed Joe? I had no idea, though I knew it involved blood. At least Berg had been on hand when Cookie had discovered the body.

Cookie seemed to have no problems after walking in Joe's blood. My dog chased a butterfly around the yard, then trotted to the tree in the corner and stared up at a chittering squirrel. Great. Mr. Peabody was back. No love lost between the dog and squirrel. Cookie really needed to stop aggravating the poor thing. Because Mr. Peabody had one heck of an aim with acorns.

I sipped a glass of wine, feeling jittery. The plot thickened, the murder mystery in my cozy little town growing as motives and alibis grew more complex. What if Stefanie had been right and Gil had a secret child he'd never known who'd come back to haunt him?

I thought about all three Cloutier men but couldn't catalog any similarities to anyone I'd seen in town lately.

Something scratched at my mind, a detail I'd missed. Like a hard slap of writer's block when I couldn't write because I'd made a mistake in my work and my subconscious refused to let me continue until I'd fixed it.

This was no *The Murder of Roger Ackroyd*. I was a very reliable narrator, at least in that I hadn't killed anyone. But someone had. And I'd bet that same someone had killed both Gil and Joe. Then again, what a whopper of a tale it would be if we had *two* murderers in town.

Zoinks! I laughed at myself for being so dramatic and enjoyed the rest of my wine, the sweet breeze, and the fading sunset while clearing my mind and watching my dog play.

Tomorrow would come soon enough.

* * *

Sunday morning I decided to forgo church, not looking forward to talking to anyone about Joe's death or seeing Mrs. Hagen glare at me for my many sins.

I slept in, did a few writing exercises to keep myself in the game, and focused on satire and fantasy fiction instead of crime.

Fleshing out characters helped me to see goals, conflicts, and—there was that blasted word again—motivations.

Sitting at my dining table with the sliding glass back door open, I watched Cookie nosing around the yard with a sigh of contentment. I had just finished a half pot of coffee, bacon, and eggs—my own nod to brunch as the hour reached noon—when someone knocked at my front door. Expecting one of my friends or my uncles, I was startled to see Scott Cloutier waiting with flowers.

Flowers?

"Hi, Lexi. Can I come in?"

"Sure, Scott." I stepped back to allow him to enter. Cookie had followed me to the front door, but seeing Scott, she gave a nod and trotted back outside.

Scott looked tired, his face drawn, though he'd dressed in khaki shorts, boat shoes, and a plaid, short-sleeved collared shirt.

Dressed in simple shorts and a pink tank, my hair up in a haphazard ponytail, I likely looked a wreck. But I was home and comfortable and didn't much care.

"Would you like some coffee?" I asked. I'd been considering putting on another pot.

"Sure. Thanks." He looked around. "This place is really cute. Did you decorate it yourself?"

"Yeah." I dumped out the half inch left over in the pot to make new. I poured in the water and ground the beans before saying, "My grandma died and left the house and some money for me and Sam. He took the money. I took the house."

"It's really nice."

Not nearly as nice as his, I'd bet. While the coffee brewed, I moved back into the dining area, where Scott lingered.

"These are for you." He held out a bouquet of summer daisies, lilies, and some blue stuff mixed in.

"Thanks." I blinked. "But, ah, what's the occasion?"

"An apology." He made some bland comments about our great weather and the increase in revenue in downtown sales, something he'd discussed with a few Chamber of Commerce members.

He blew out a breath as the coffee timer beeped. "Can I get a cup?"

"Sure." I took out some flavored creamer, half-and-half, and sugar and sugar-alternative packets and set them near the coffeepot.

"Wow."

"I like to caffeinate daily. I'm serious about my coffee." I put the flowers in a glass vase and added water, setting them on the counter while Scott fixed his cup. I got myself another and sat at the dining table with Scott.

We sipped coffee and watched each other.

"I'm the one who gave your name to the police," Scott blurted.

"Oh?"

He groaned. "It was at book club last Monday. On my way to the bathroom, I kind of snooped and found your journal. I took it home and read some things that made me, ah, cautious."

I could only imagine. "I'm so sorry, Scott. Most of what was in there I wrote prior to Gil passing. I'm writing a mystery." I explained my goals and prior work in editing. "Gil's dying made me think about incorporating fact into fiction. But I'm so sorry you had to see that."

"I am too." He sipped his coffee, and I noticed he had no crook in his fingers like Abe and Matt. Yet he clearly resembled

Gil, in looks if not temperament. Apparently that little crook didn't pass down to every male member of the family. "But that's what I get for snooping. I've just been so lost about Dad. About Jan." His voice hitched.

Oh crap. He did know about Jan.

"Scott . . ."

"I, well, I've been having some problems in my marriage. My business. Then with Dad . . . I've been trying to put myself back together. I don't think Jan and I are going to work out, unfortunately. She doesn't understand how hard I've been working to give her what she wants. But at least my business was getting better, and Dad and I were actually developing a relationship. He told me he loved me." Scott's eyes were wet. "He hadn't said that in over fifteen years, Lexi."

"I'm so sorry." I put a hand over his, wishing Scott good vibes. The poor guy.

"I had no right to look at your journal." He sniffed, so I left to grab a box of tissues and handed him one.

He blew his nose. "Thanks. I'm sorry for prying. But when I read what you wrote, I thought you might have had something to do with Dad's death. I told the police. Left an anonymous tip and returned the journal to you. I should never have done that."

"I understand."

"I've just been driving myself crazy trying to figure out who might want to kill my dad." He sniffed and drank more coffee, settling himself. He turned a hopeful gaze to me. "Do you have any idea who did it? It seemed like you were looking into his death."

"I am a little. I have some idea, maybe." I sighed. "Not really. It's either family or a stranger. A CGC rival for the Gardener's Purse? Abe wanting the treasure he's been following? Matt's jealousy of your dad's affection for you?" I would have mentioned Jan as a reason for Matt to kill but didn't want to add to Scott's pain. "I'm not sure. I do think whoever did it is tied to all the digging around town. Around rosebushes," I mused, still stuck on Gil's note.

"My dad wanted me to have his map. Abe finally handed it over yesterday. Apparently, he stole it from my dad. They argued about it and . . . other things."

Yeah, that stolen map still bothered me. Yet I didn't get the vibe that Abe had killed his dad.

Scott continued, "But the map's a bust. I've seen that stupid thing before." An odd tone entered his voice before he broke down in tears again. "God, I wish Dad and I could have looked for treasure together one last time. No matter what we found, I'd have treated it like gold."

I patted Scott on the back, wishing I could do more. But nothing I could say would bring Gil back.

"It's so funny, you know?" He blew his nose again. "Dad wasn't likable. Seriously. I hated him at times. But that's because he'd had such a rough life. Mom dying of cancer. His parents dying when he was just out of trade school. I don't think he ever had a good example of how to be a family man."

"Maybe not, but he raised three boys who aren't so bad. Are you close with your brothers?"

"Not so much." His lips twisted. "Just like my dad, I guess. A mess with interpersonal relationships."

"Did your dad have any family besides his parents?" I'd never seen anyone visit while I lived here. But maybe Scott knew of a secret half-sibling?

"Not that I know of." He shrugged. "It's so weird. I've gone over and over who might have done it. Even I have a motive."

"You do?" I hadn't expected him to admit that.

"I borrowed money from Dad a while ago, when the business was having problems. Dad has—had—a nice little nest egg from his job. He never went anywhere or bought much of anything but plants." Scott snorted. "When I needed the money, he gave it to me with no strings. I had just paid him back. The debt settled, we were trying to figure out how to be close, you know? After nineteen years, I was finally going to get my dad back. I was fifteen when Mom died." Scott shook his head. "Then someone killed him."

"That's so sad." Time for me to pry, delicately. "I remember your dad mostly when he'd yell over the fence at me for something, and he'd wave that trowel around and point it at me. Like he was digging at me with that little shovel." I gave a small laugh. "He was gruff but consistent. I always knew where I stood with Gil. You know, I kind of miss him." I really didn't. At all.

Scott gave a weak smile. "Oh yeah. His pride and joy. Mom gave him that trowel and started him on gardening. They used to grow things together. He put the thing in a shadow box over the mantel when she passed, to always remember her. The one he waved at you was from a friend in town, I think. A Christmas gift a few years ago, maybe?" He frowned. "You know, he loved that shovel. Even had it engraved." Scott looked lost in thought.

"Right. Well." I paused, not sure what else to say.

Scott looked up at me. "I have a favor to ask."

"Sure. Anything."

"Would you mind if we had book club tomorrow night? I know we aren't due to meet until next Monday, but I could really use something fun to get my mind off everything."

"Even though we're discussing a murder mystery?"

"Even though." He grinned. "I read the book. I know who did it."

"I know too. Unfortunately because my friends have big mouths."

He laughed, and I felt good for having lifted his spirits.

"Book club tomorrow night it is. Six fifteen."

"I'll be there. Thanks, Lexi. You're a sweetheart." He stood.

"Yes, I am." I laughed and stood with him.

He gave me a brief hug before taking his cup to the sink and leaving.

I sat back down and stared at my new incognito journal, having plenty more to add.

Abe had lied about getting the map from his father. But he'd also handed it over to Scott, who'd verified that the map led to no treasure. Scott knew he and Jan weren't doing well, but did he know Matt was sleeping with his wife? Man, talk about a big old can of domestic worms.

Funny, though, how two of the three Cloutier brothers had that weird bend in their fingers. Why was I so fixated on that tiny genetic detail?

And then it hit me. I'd seen that same quirk before. Someone else with a weird crook in their finger. But where? And what did it mean, if anything?

Chapter Twenty-Five

Monday morning passed swiftly. My cousin, Collin, and Lee-Ann had done a great job the past weekend selling a bunch of books, and they'd left the shop neat and tidy. Collin took after my uncles a lot, easygoing with a great sense of humor. He was super responsible and flexible on hours. The perfect employee, really, as well as the perfect cousin. A year ago he'd recommended his friend, Lee-Ann, and I knew I'd sincerely lucked out with my part-time employees. I loved having the college-age help around, in the summer especially.

Cat came in late Mondays and Wednesdays. But today she called in to take some extra time off, working hard on a new recipe. I needed to remain busy, so I told her to stay home. The foot traffic kept me on my toes, which I appreciated.

The Macaroons had all responded to my text last night about having book club a week early. I was actually looking forward to it, wanting to talk some more about Gil's death. And now with Joe passing and the whole town ablaze with new rumors, I had a feeling the club would want to discuss more motives. Maybe Scott would be able to contribute, which could help him with his grief.

I'd at least finished *The Murder of Roger Ackroyd* last night. "Great book, right, Cookie?" I asked my faithful companion as she dozed under the register. Too bad I hadn't killed Gil. Because my being the narrator and the killer would make for a fantastic twist.

My writing exercises had helped a lot, and I was chafing to get back to my mystery. But lawyer Amy had been emphatic that I should steer clear of writing about more crime. Hence dropping my journal off at my uncles' this morning prior to coming in to work.

They planned to talk to Mandy and Alan later, and I knew I could count on them to get me some answers. I still couldn't believe Jimmy and Elvis hadn't tried to force me to stay at their place after learning about Joe.

Joe Jacobs. I shook my head. Berg would definitely talk to Bill. Especially since I'd told Roger about Bill and Joe's argument. But why kill Joe? Had there been any dirt piles in his backyard? Did Joe have roses back there?

I should ask Berg about the roses. But maybe not until he's had time to deal with Joe's murder.

The bell over the door jingled.

Taco Ted walked in and flashed me a jaunty wave. "Yo, book lady. Can you hook me up with some treasure hunting?"

"Sure can." Interesting topic for Taco Ted. "Can I ask what brought on the interest?"

"Well, I know Abe was wandering around with his dad's treasure map for a while. That got me started, and then a few tourists were talking about it, and it sounded pretty cool. I was thinking of starting a club around here after trying geocaching in Portland with the people I met."

"It wasn't Anna and Bob, was it?"

"Yeah." He smiled. "That's them. They were checking out the garden tour and stopped by for some ah-may-zing fish tacos. I had them on special last weekend. Anyhow, Anna and Bob started telling me all about how they go to flea markets and buy auctioned storage sheds. Then Anna mentions her buddy who likes geocaching. That's where people use GPS to hide and seek stuff. The geocaches. And think how many outdoorspeople we have here with the mountains so close. Much more fun than checking out the city, right? Although Anna promised me a blast if I come out in July."

"No kidding. That sounds like fun."

"Yeah. We got friendly." He wriggled his eyebrows. "They stayed over last week while I was out and about helping with my cousin outside town at his ranch. Nicest people . . ."

I showed him to a small section where we had maybe one or two books on treasure hunting. "Use that computer to look up any titles you might be interested in, and we can order them."

"Cool." He fired up the laptop I had on a tall counter near an information desk, the sign clearly marked overhead.

"So, ah, Bob and Anna were here all week?"

"Not Anna. She had to head back to work. But Bob has been in and out when not working, and he's still here. Dude's a monster fix-it man. Helped patch up my water heater. I think he used to be a plumber or something before he opened a pawn shop."

"Huh. You make interesting friends, Ted."

"You know it." He grinned at me, and I felt the good vibes from several feet away. Our town had a few people like that, good souls who would give you whatever you needed whenever you asked. Just because.

I wished I could be nicer. But hey, I was what I was. A not-so-perky blonde with attitude. "Let me know if you can't find what you're looking for on the computer."

"Will do."

I returned to the counter and continued to check out people, many of whom felt the need to ask me about Joe and Gil and whether I knew anything about the murders. Apparently, word had trickled out that I'd been on the scene when Joe was found dead. Lovely.

The day flew by, and I didn't have much time to wonder about Bob and Anna taking so much interest in our town, though I kept them both on my "must investigate further" list.

At six, I finished ringing up Darcy. She'd bought a few children's activity books that looked awfully cute.

As soon as the last customer left and I turned the sign over to CLOSED, Darcy gasped.

I jumped and turned to face her. "What's wrong? What happened?"

She squealed. "Oh my God! I can't believe you found *another* dead body! You're like a magnet for dead people." Her eyes shone with excitement.

Though I hated myself for it, I felt the same enthusiasm. As if a new dead body might point clues toward Gil's murderer. Gah. What was wrong with me?

"Did you see Joe's body?" Darcy asked, quieting down. "Was it gruesome?"

"You know, I'm surprised you didn't see him first. You were running garden tours on Saturday, right?"

"I was." She stared at me, her eyes growing wider. "What if we showed his house with him already dead inside? Oh wow. Wait. We passed Joe's. Hmm. Let me think. Had to be around noon. Definitely before two, because we had a picnic—me, Dex, and the kids—up at the cabin."

"Yeah. I passed you guys on Saturday not long before I met the Danvers and then went to Joe's house. I have to say, his garden was amazing. I mean, his house is gorgeous. Same with Bill's and Dave and Julie's. I don't know how anyone can judge a first-place winner with so much gardening expertise."

"I know." Darcy nodded. "That's why they went to such extremes to get impartial judges from other towns. The benefactors for this year's Gardener's Purse aren't messing around."

"No kidding." I grabbed my journal and purse and locked them under the register, the key tucked away in my pocket. "Hey, can you help me out?"

"Sure."

"Can you go down to Eats n' Treats and pick up our goodies for tonight?"

"I'd love to." Darcy looked beautiful, glowing with that find-a-killer enthusiasm matched only by her love of a good sandwich. Though she did at times annoy me, I had to admit she had a knack for making me think.

I took her purse and purchases and put them in the back room on her usual seat. While Darcy left to grab our goodies, the others started filtering in. Stefanie and Alison paused for a moment.

"Got some news to share," Stefanie muttered before continuing into the back.

Teri and Cat entered, and Teri rushed to my side and whispered, "Holy crap. Did I find out something incredible today at work."

"It'll have to keep until we're done." Though I couldn't wait to learn what she'd found out.

She crossed an invisible key over her lips before tossing it away.

Cat rolled her eyes. "Yeah, like that's ever kept you quiet."

"Big mouth. You should talk." Teri glared. "Why would you tell Randy how much I enjoyed our date?"

"Um, because you did?"

"But now he thinks I like him more than he likes me."

Cat frowned. "What?"

"It's a power hand, doofus. You keep your feelings close and don't let the guy know you're into him. The more he hunts, the better your relationship progresses."

Cat looked at me. I shrugged. "I'm not even going to pretend I know how her mind works."

"Amateurs." Teri huffed and walked past me into the back.

"Thanks for today," Cat told me. "I made a new batch of brownies that is going to rock your world."

"Chocolate. Yum." I stared down at the covered tray she carried. "And you brought them?"

"Sure did." She grinned and added in a low voice, "Teri wasn't lying. What she found out definitely explains why someone might have killed Gil." The tease left me hanging as she walked away without explaining.

I called after her, "Seriously? You suck."

Kay entered with a cheery grin. "I'm so excited we're meeting again. I really loved the book."

"Me too. Go on in. Cat brought a new brownie recipe."

"Yes." Kay fist-pumped, then lowered her arm and in a more sedate voice said, "I mean, hurray. I hate to be so peppy considering another of our townies just died. I can't believe it."

"No one can."

She nodded and joined the others, hefting two insulated drink containers, one of hot coffee and the other of hot water. Since she'd offered to bring them courtesy of Confection Coffee, I hadn't turned her down. No way was *I* going to Nadine's to grab beverages.

I waited another ten minutes. Darcy had returned with the food, and I knew Cat and Teri would help set everything out. To my surprise, Uncle Elvis appeared.

"You did say comics counted," he teased. "I want to see what book club is about. Mind if I sit in?"

"By all means." I gave him a kiss on the cheek and slapped him on the butt as he passed.

"Watch it, grabby."

I laughed and watched the clock.

By six thirty, I decided I'd waited long enough. Neither Scott nor Alan had arrived, but we had to start sometime.

I hustled back so we could talk about the book and everything else that had happened in the days since we'd last met. I had a feeling tonight would be one of our best meetings yet.

Chapter Twenty-Six

"Lexi, we have to know." Cat's eyes were glowing. "Did you kill Joe Jacobs?"

"Stop it. Of course not."

"Yet you were there when they found him," Darcy quickly announced.

"I thought we were here to talk about *The Murder of Roger Ackroyd*?"

Kay snorted. "Yeah, right. The doctor did it. Okay, next. Lexi, what the heck is going on? I heard Detective Berg grabbed you off the street and jailed you overnight."

Darcy cut in, "Well, I heard she's been digging holes all over town and got into a fight with Abe over his map." Darcy pointed to my cheek. "See? The bruise is still there."

And still sore. Darn it. I thought I'd done a good job touching up my makeup before the gang had arrived.

Elvis stilled. "What?"

"Okay, hold on. Everyone, calm down." I grabbed a plate of food and balanced it on my lap as I explained things. "First of all, I haven't killed anyone. I accidentally got hit when I tried to jump in to separate two grown men from fighting. A dumb move on my part."

"I'll say," Kay said. "Heck, when my boys are fighting, I usually leave them to it until the loser cries and signals his defeat. Hey, they're ten and eleven. They can handle it."

I should have had Kay in on the investigation from the start. She had survival skills. I looked over the group and came to a decision. "Something you guys should know. I'm writing a book. And a lot of what's happened to me lately spirals from that."

I explained, in great detail, everything—with the exception of Gil's note. That I kept to myself and our core group of investigators. But I included the sordid details of writing my mystery and using Gil's investigation to further plot bunnies.

"Oh wow. We're going to have our own author soon." Darcy seemed more excited about that than our investigation, which surprised me. "You know, I was an English major."

Alison coughed loudly to cover whatever it was Stefanie said. I saw Stefanie roll her eyes and mentally agreed.

"I know, Darcy. And yes, it's exciting. But it's also scary, considering the stuff I'm writing has nothing on our reality."

Elvis nodded. "We'll talk about that bruise later."

I swallowed a groan.

Kay turned to me. "You never said anything about a book or about looking into Gil's murder. Heck, Lexi. We can help you. We dissect books for fun, and we know all about plots and conflicts and character tropes."

"We're already helping her," Stefanie said before I could gently explore the topic.

Darcy frowned. "What?"

"What she means is I had reason to believe someone had stolen my journal and reported me to the police." I went on to tell them about Scott's confession and how I was sorry for doubting any of them.

"Oh my gosh. Real subterfuge," Darcy squealed. "This is so much fun."

"Darcy, Gil and Joe are dead," Kay reminded her.

"Yes, but it's thrilling too. Sad, very sad," she tacked on hurriedly. "But come on. Gil was a tyrant at best. And Joe was a little too smug for most of us." She turned to me. "So we're in now, right? The Macaroons are not just a book club. We're a murder mystery club."

"A secret one," Elvis said, "because Detective Berg is not going to accept anyone outside the police department investigating. And Darcy, Lexi had her home broken into, her laptop stolen, and someone left a threatening note on it. You have kids to protect."

"And I have a dog to protect," I said with a nod at Cookie, who sat by Teri's side, watching her eat before Teri slipped her a small piece of meat. "Teri, stop it."

"Oh, ah, sorry." She flushed. "But she's hungry."

"It won't kill her to wait until we get home for dinner."

Elvis patted his lap, and Cookie hurried to sit by him. "She's so mean. You poor thing."

I sighed. "Right. Well, if we're really going to bag on the book . . ."

Everyone nodded.

"Then let's get back to our investigation." Once they were all caught up on what I knew, we started going around the room.

Stefanie stood to speak. "Well, we know Abe was, in fact, at the halfway house when Gil died, because I talked to a few of the residents, and one of them confirmed it. The poor kid worked a double janitorial shift and sacked out early. And Matt was with Jan."

Kay gasped.

Darcy nodded. "I knew they had something going on."

"Silence, please." I had to keep a handle on the group or we'd devolve into Darcy's exclamations and Kay's disbelief after every revelation. "One at a time."

"Right. Sorry." Darcy motioned for Stefanie to continue.

Stefanie frowned back at her. "That's all I got."

"Nothing on Scott?" I asked.

"No," Alison answered. "But I still don't think he did it."

"He did seem pretty torn up about his dad's death yesterday." I'd give him that. "Right. So, Teri? You found out something, I take it."

Teri was bursting at the seams, her knee bobbing. "Oh my gosh, yes."

It seemed as if the entire room leaned in.

"I was moving some files and had to go into—" She cut herself off and stared pointedly at Darcy. "This can't go any further or I could get in big trouble."

We all looked at Darcy.

"What?" She put a hand on her chest. "I would never betray a confidence."

"Please." Stefanie huffed. "You tell Dex everything, and he spills his giblets like a holiday turkey pooping out stuffing."

I slapped a hand over my face.

Elvis burst out laughing, and I heard a few giggles from Teri and Cat.

"Stefanie, that's just not true."

"Darcy, it is," I had to say. "But if you promise to keep this just in the Macaroons' circle, Teri will tell us this earth-shattering news. And again, you cannot tell anyone about it. One slip and you're out."

"Out?" Darcy's eyes widened.

"Out of the Macaroons," Stefanie said before I could. "Trust in this club, and each other, comes first." She turned to Elvis. "So think hard before you want to join. You do have to read books, Elvis. Without pictures."

"I know." He sighed. "Fine. I'm in."

We all looked at Darcy.

"I won't tell a soul. I promise," she said emphatically. "On my word as Mrs. Confection 2017."

I mentally rolled my eyes, though several others weren't so circumspect.

"Great. Now that's settled." I looked at Teri.

We all did.

"Right," she said. "I happened to be filing some paperwork when I spilled a file at work and papers went everywhere. Guess what I saw? A printout of a Claude R. Cloutier with a record."

"Wait. Claude? Is that Gil's real name or something?"

Teri shook her head. "No. Gil is short for Guillaume. He was French. Apparently, there's a Claude Cloutier who was arrested in California for first-degree robbery and aggravated assault. He did fifteen years in prison for it."

We all stared at her as we digested her news.

"So, you're telling us one of the Cloutiers has a record?" Dang it. I should have had Berg take my laptop to get it dusted for prints.

"It could be blind chance that Gil and this Claude guy have the same last name. But my bet is they're related."

"And he stole something and buried it and now he's come back to find it," I said.

"But then why kill Gil?" Elvis asked.

"Because Gil knew where it was hidden?" Alison suggested.

"Or Gil had it when Claude went to jail," Kay offered. "Then Gil hid it. Claude gets out of jail, comes back to find it, has an argument with Gil, and kills him for it."

"For what?" Darcy asked. "Gil never acted like he had money. And if he had something worth killing for all these years, why not use it? Spend some serious cash, have the best garden in Confection?"

Stefanie said, "Well, rumor had it he *did* have the best garden in Confection. Which is why Bill Sanchez killed him for it."

"Bill?" Kay blinked. "I like Bill."

"He and Joe have been arguing lately," I told them. "And Bill wasn't happy with Joe. But angry enough to kill him? And if it's related to the Gardener's Purse, why dig holes all over the south of town?"

"He's digging around prizewinning roses," Elvis said.

"True." Cat looked pleased to offer her two cents.

I wanted to laugh but didn't, caught up in our shared enthusiasm for the investigation. "I still don't buy it. No. The digging is related to Gil's death."

"What about Joe's?" Kay asked. "Or did Joe kill Gil, and the Cloutier brothers then killed him in revenge?"

Stefanie scowled. "That's crazy talk."

"Show me proof they didn't."

Stefanie argued with Kay. Alison piped up and had Darcy firing questions at her. Elvis looked highly entertained as he sneaked chips to Cookie, who munched like a freight train, while Teri and Cat kept trying to figure out who Claude Cloutier might be. A hidden love child or Gil's secret twin?

"Okay, everyone. Quiet, please." I had to shout to be heard. "We haven't yet gotten to Elvis. Uncle Elvis? Do you have anything to share?"

"As a matter of fact, I do. And you're not going to like it."

We all grew very quiet.

"What's said here can't go any further."

We all nodded.

"Jimmy and I have been looking into allegations that Mandy and Gil might have been involved."

Darcy gasped.

I shot her a warning look to quell her into silence.

Elvis continued, "Turns out Alan knew all about Mandy and Gil's relationship back when the two were in high school. Gil and Mandy fell in love. Mandy got pregnant—no, it wasn't a false alarm. But the baby died before it could be born. Apparently, Mandy had complications, likely due to all the stress she'd been under. So Mandy was sent away by her parents. In college, she met and fell in love with Alan. They're a lovely couple who share no secrets. In fact, Alan and Gil were fishing buddies."

"I knew that," Kay said loudly and blushed. "Sorry for yelling. My husband loves to fish, and he used to tell me how fishing makes the strangest friends. Alan and Gil, he told me, were an odd pairing. Because Alan's so nice and Gil's . . . not."

I felt a little relief to check Alan off my list. "So Alan had no reason to kill Gil?"

My uncle shook his head. "None. He's not here tonight because he's depressed. He and Gil were supposed to go on a big fishing trip in John Day."

Kay nodded. "John Day River has incredible smallmouth bass fishing after March. My husband's a fan."

Elvis agreed. "I've heard the same. Anyway, Mandy's been upset about Gil dying because they still loved each other, but *as friends*. And Alan, too, lost a friend and fishing buddy. Cross them off your list."

"Good. It's not them or the Danvers. Though Joe could have killed Gil, he had no reason to unless we think he did it to win the Gardener's Purse?" I asked the room.

Stefanie shook her head. "Sure, it's a possibility, but Joe had money. He didn't need to win the prize purse. Though I'm sure his ego needed stroking. So maybe he could have killed Gil to win just to be the best. But it feels wrong."

Alison nodded. "I agree. I don't think Gil's or Joe's murders had to do with the CGC or the Gardener's Purse. Not with this new information about Claude. Teri, can you find out who he is?"

"I have to be careful about accessing crimes outside the state. I don't have access to that database." She frowned. "But I can try."

"Just be careful," I reminded her. "We're not supposed to be investigating at all. The only reason I started was that I got accused of killing Gil."

Stefanie glared at Cookie when my dog took a step in her direction. "But you have to admit, it's helping with your own murder mystery."

"True." I watched with amusement as Cookie gave Stefanie a wide berth and sat by me. "So, Macaroons, we're investigating low-key. Uncle Elvis, great info. Can you ask Mandy if she's seen anything at all that might have struck her? Because I've seen her all over town taking pictures. I wonder if she captured something that might help us."

"Good point. I'll ask her tomorrow. I have some work to do at their neighbors'."

"Great." I looked to Teri. "Teri, please don't get in any trouble. But if you can find out more about this Claude, I'll—"

"We'll do it," Alison said. "I have resources."

I didn't ask. "Great. Then you and Stefanie have Claude R. Cloutier to research."

Stefanie grunted her agreement.

"What can I do?" Darcy asked.

"Can you maybe feel Dex out?"

Cat guffawed.

I shot her a look. "I *meant* see if he knows of any odd financial transactions concerning Gil or his sons. Or anyone else with the last name of Cloutier. Nothing that would let him know you're looking into things. But maybe you could ask if he's heard any rumors of money problems with people in town."

"I'm on it." Darcy quivered with excitement.

"Kay," I said, "same goes for you. Any information on anything pertaining to our case, let us know. And because you live up north by Maple Circle, can you do a run around and see if anyone at all has been having their yards dug up? Especially people with rosebushes? I don't think so, but that would at least eliminate a possibility."

"Perfect. I'll have my boys do some searching. Keep the little buggers busy." She grinned. "This is going to be fun."

"It's dangerous too," Elvis said before I could.

"He's right." I nodded. "No one can know what we're doing. No one. Not spouses or friends or friends of friends. If they aren't a Macaroon, they don't have a need to know what we're doing."

Stefanie grinned. "I like the way this girl is thinking. Exactly. Only us Macaroons are in a need-to-know status."

Everyone looked pretty pleased about our new exclusivity.

"Hey, what about me?" Cat asked.

"You keep making brownies," I told her. Everyone laughed.

But after everyone had left for the night, I kept her behind and asked her to keep an eye on Roger. To maybe see if she could find out anything else. Like if the same weapon had been used to kill both Joe and Gil. I knew what I thought, but I wanted proof. Because I had a sneaking suspicion that information would prove more valuable than anything else in solving this case.

Chapter Twenty-Seven

Tuesday morning, I realized it had been a week and a half since Gil's death, though it felt like much longer. I kept hearing about Joe's murder, and speculation ran rampant about how and why he'd died. It didn't help that the police refused to let anyone know the specifics of *how* he had died, only saying that the department was ruling it a homicide.

Cat was selling her super-fudgy brownies today alongside a new blend of Sumatra, and we had quite a crowd up through lunch. Darcy and Kay managed to swing through, neither with any new information, but not for lack of trying. In just the fifteen hours since we'd disbanded last night, Darcy had peppered her husband for rumors about financial misdeeds and debts, of which he had little to say. Apparently, Gil hadn't been loaning money out to anyone but his son, and we kind of already knew that.

Kay, on the other hand, had come through with her four children to let me know Operation Diggy was about to get under way. Her older boys, six through eleven, were adorable. But her daughter cried too much to tell if she was cute. Even Cookie shied away from the sobbing toddler.

After sugaring up her kids, Kay left to continue our amateur investigation.

Cat and I watched them leave.

"Are we sure it was a good idea to invite all the Macaroons in on this?" she murmured.

"Too late now. You know when Alan gets wind of this, he's going to be all in. He's our noir guy, after all."

"Yeah." Cat sighed. "I feel kind of useless. I didn't bring much to the table last night."

"You sure did. Those brownies are to die for." I paused, met her amused look, and rephrased. "I mean, not to die for, but to beg until you're hoarse for."

"Awkward save." She helped a few coffee and treat customers while I checked out several romance afficionados—my favorite people.

Unlike a lot of snooty independent bookstores, Sweet Fiction stocked everything for our readers. Erotica, romance, and all kinds of fiction most literary types considered "pulpy" were our bread and butter. I figured a billion-dollar industry like romance should have a ton of shelf space in the shop, and we'd seen nicer revenue since making the change when I took over.

By the time Cat and I had a break, the hour had reached noon. Roger, Cat's hottie, entered in his police uniform. Unlike Berg, he definitely looked like a patrol cop in his police blues and Batman belt. Okay, not Batman, but he did have a cool holster on his hip.

"Hi, Cat. Lexi." Roger smiled.

I smiled back. Behind Roger, Cat nodded at him and gave me a thumbs-up she quickly hid when he turned to face her.

She offered him a wide, cheesy grin. Uh-oh. "Hi, Officer Sex—"

"Cat," I said loudly, to stop her from embarrassing her almost-boyfriend, who'd already started to turn red. "Enjoy your lunch. I've got the shop." Cookie grunted as she padded out from under the register and gave Roger a sniff. "I mean, Cookie and I have the shop. Get out of here."

Roger grinned. Cat followed him out, walking through the front door when he stepped back to allow her to precede him.

"You know, Cookie. I like him. He's such a gentleman with her."

Cookie huffed. A yes, I think.

An older woman carrying four novels approached the counter. "You're right about that. Roger's a good boy. I taught him in sixth grade, you know."

"Mrs. Campbell, how are you?"

Well, heck. Now the cat was out of the bag, so to speak. Cat's grandma grinned at me, her own six feet diminished to five ten thanks to her stooped posture.

"I'm doing fine, sweetie. Now ring me up. I've got some werewolf nooky with my name on it waiting for me."

I chuckled as we talked about the current series she was reading. When I told her I had edited that author, I attained superstar status and an invitation to hold the next Paranormal Lovers Unite book club at our store. I told her I'd see what I could do about getting the author to sign a bunch of her newest series to Mrs. Campbell and her shapeshifter lovers.

"You get those books here and I promise I'll have at least twenty of us here to buy. See if I don't."

I knew a lot of our more senior townsfolk liked to shop at the used bookstore in Sisters or ordered off the Zon, and I couldn't blame them. A lot of us lived on a fixed income. Personally, I liked to refer people to the library, where I got a ton of my own reading material. But I also loved it when people came into the store. Not just for them to buy something, but because interacting with them made me feel like a part of the town.

Gil hadn't had that in years. Or maybe he had, though his contributions to the community came from the CGC. I still didn't care for Peggy, and Ed would never get my vote for Mr. Congeniality, but after seeing the magic Bill and Joe—rest his soul—had made with their yards, and the Danverses too, I couldn't in good conscience ignore their talent.

I snacked when customers weren't looking, enjoying some carrot sticks today in an effort to get my eating habits back on track. Between noshing a lot lately and gorging at my uncles' on Saturday, I was gaining a pudge I'd been adamant I couldn't have due to my genetics.

Sucking down water helped because I needed to hydrate, especially with today's forecast predicted to reach eighty-eight degrees.

Once the store emptied, I left with Cookie for a brief fifteen minutes to give her the walk she deserved. And who did I see when we walked by the Confection Rose but Mandy Coatney.

My phone pinged, and I glanced at it to see a message from Uncle Elvis informing me Mandy wanted to talk. Seeing her right now, I texted him back. *Got it. Thx.*

"Hi, Mandy. We missed Alan last night."

She gave me a genuine smile. "He was sorry to miss it. But we've both been down with Gil's passing." She studied me. "Elvis told me you know about me and Gil. Our past, I mean."

"I do."

"Alan really liked Gil. Then again, there aren't many my husband doesn't like." She huffed a laugh. "He really is too nice."

"That's what I tell him."

We grinned at each other.

Then her smile faded. "I like to think I'm a nice person too. But I've been having a real problem lately." She paused. "Gil's death hurt, and I tried to work through it, taking all my pictures and trying to push through the pain. But heck, Lexi, I forgot half of what I took, to tell you the truth. When Elvis asked if I'd seen anything that might niggle at my mind, I went through my camera again. And I saw something." She paused. "Oh, hold on. I need a shot of that." She snapped a few photos of a nearby bird perched in a tree.

I had half a mind to yank Mandy to me and shake her until she told me what she'd learned. But I kept a tight rein on my patience and let her lead. She finally stopped taking pictures and nodded for me to come closer. I tugged Cookie with me, ignoring her whine because I wasn't going to let her pee on one of the rosebushes near us.

"Not there," I said under my breath and got a canine stink eye for my trouble. "Sorry, Mandy. You were saying?"

She held her camera out to me, and we looked at the images she scrolled through. "There. Can you see?"

I peered closer. "What am I looking at?"

She fiddled with the camera and showed me again. "That."

I focused and saw Scott Cloutier on the side of his father's house holding something in his hand. Maybe a garden trowel? I couldn't tell. My pulse raced. I looked for a date. "When was this taken?"

She looked closer. "Sunday the seventh, right after Gil died."

"Have you told anyone about this?"

"No. I didn't want to get Scott in trouble, not when we all know how half this town jumps to conclusions." Yeah, I heard a touch of bitterness there. And rightly so. Heck, even I'd wondered if she'd been having an affair with Gil. She continued, "But I've been wondering, and it's been really bothering me. It looks like Scott's holding Gil's prized trowel. He never let that thing out of his sight." She bit her lip. "Lexi, I gave it to him."

"What?"

"The trowel. With the rosewood handle. See the back of the blade, that pledge of 'forever friends'—see the *FF*?" She showed the picture again, though I couldn't make out the initials she was talking about. "Gil loved his wife. No question. But he was my first love, and I was his. We never forgot each other. He told me he'd always treasure that trowel. I gave it to him on the anniversary of our first date a few years ago, when he was feeling low, missing his wife and realizing all he'd lost by not trying harder with his kids. That trowel reminded him I'm still here. That Alan is still here too." She took a shuddery breath and paused to level out. "The only way Scott could have gotten that trowel was if he snuck into Gil's house. He always kept his tools and gardening equipment neatly in the basement. I *know* the police hadn't cleared the house by the time I took that picture."

"Heck. Have they cleared the house by now?" I didn't know. I could have sworn the police tape had been taken away, but did that mean the Cloutiers could come and go as they pleased?

"I don't know. But I do know Scott shouldn't have that unless he took it from Gil's house. And when would he have had time?"

"Unless he was there when Gil died and took it then and was maybe returning it?" I said what she didn't.

We stared at each other.

"It's yours now." She fiddled with her camera. "I texted you the image. You handle it. I don't want to hurt Gil's children. But I don't want the truth to go unknown either."

"Thanks, Mandy. That's really brave of you."

She shrugged. "I've also taken pictures of a lot of holes dug near rosebushes, if you need those too. And two shots of Bill and Joe in a heated argument. They weren't getting along so well lately, and I'm not sure why. They're usually best of friends."

"Keep all that in case the police want to see it. And thanks again. Tell Alan we expect to see him next Monday night. Uncle Elvis has started attending."

"He'll be glad for another man to show up." Mandy grinned, looking as if a huge weight had lifted off her shoulders. "Thanks, Lexi. It's a relief knowing you'll handle this."

"Sure." I glanced down at Cookie, who started to tug at the leash. "I guess Cookie is telling me we need to head back."

"Take care. If I think of anything else, I'll let you know. I need to have another look at the pictures I took anyway. The town plans to put them on their website."

"How exciting."

"Yes." She waved at us before snapping a quick picture of me and Cookie standing near the Confection Rose. "Great shot. 'Bye!"

We headed back. Cookie took to wandering around the store, greeting people and asking for some petting. I focused on catching snippets of a mystery I'd been reading when not needed by customers.

The lunch hour came and went. As did another hour.

Cat showed up, breathless, at two.

"Well, well, slacker. Nice of you to make an appearance."

She blushed, but only a few people were around to notice.

"Funny." She tugged me with her back from the register, giving us a poor illusion of privacy.

"Well?"

She kept her voice low as she bent to whisper, "You're not going to believe this, but Roger told me they think they know the murder weapon that killed Joe."

"And?" I swear. All these people today with amazing news that took forever to share.

"The wounds were shaped in a V. Made by a gardening tool. Like a hand shovel." A trowel. Like the one that had killed Gil.

I let that sink in, then told her what Mandy had told me.

"Holy crapola!"

Considering she'd become a regular potty mouth of late, I appreciated her holding back. "You said it."

"But we can't be sure it's the same one, right?"

"I—" I smiled at the customer who approached the counter. "Hold that thought."

I made small talk that took forever as I rang up Rodney, who was ecstatic about trying out some alternative history books. A Civil War buff, he hadn't yet read any fiction about what might have happened if the South had won the war. Or if there had been no war at all because the Native Americans realized what schmucks the whites were from the get-go and kicked us out of their country.

"I've heard of Harry Turtledove before, but I've never read him. I can't believe what I've been missing out on."

Hurry up, Rodney! Go deliver the mail, why don't you! "Yeah. These books are older but still pretty popular with history buffs. We also have some great political thrillers I think you might like, set in different time periods. Oh, and you really should try James Rollins, just because he's a fabulous writer and I can never put down his thrillers." Great. Now Rodney had me wasting time blabbing.

"Sounds right up my alley." Rodney smiled. "I'll start with these and be back."

He chatted some more. Oh my gosh, I felt like I was stuck in an eternal loop of sllllooowwwnnneeeesss.

Rodney finally left.

Cat grabbed me. "Why are you holding back? Quit making small talk and finish what you were saying. This is *huge*."

"I know." I looked around. One older man remained in the shop, but he left soon after Rodney did.

Cat marched to the door and turned the sign to CLOSED and locked it. Then she stomped back to me. "Okay. All of it. Tell me."

"Mandy had pictures she hadn't looked at. She was taking them all over the place, but sad about Gil, she hadn't looked at them until Elvis asked her to. Well, she saw Scott with Gil's trowel—maybe, but that's what I'm thinking it was—which is something only Gil should have had. Or at least the police should have had, since it would have been at his house at the time of the murder."

"So maybe someone stole it before Gil died." She chewed her lip. "Sorry I was late, by the way. We were, uh, hanging out."

"Is that a euphemism for sucking face?" At the sight of her blush, I laughed. "Ha. I thought so."

"Hey. I'm making huge sacrifices to get you information."

"Yeah, sure."

She grinned. "Anyway, so we have proof Scott might be involved."

"It's really looking that way. I can't imagine him having that trowel. Gil wouldn't have given it to him. Apparently, Mandy gave it to Gil as a present a few years ago when he was having a tough time. And he, Mandy, and Alan have been pretty friendly since. Well, friendly for Gil is like being friends with a rabid dog who only growls and doesn't bite."

We both glanced at Cookie, who sat between us, watching us.

"So now what?" Cat asked.

"Now we wait and see what else everyone else comes up with. Teri might be able to get more info on Claude Cloutier. Kay will let us know if she finds any digging north of town, which I doubt. And I will call Detective Chad Berg and let him know what Mandy told me."

"That's brave of you."

"I know. But like you, I'm willing to make the big sacrifices."

Cat stared at me as if I had two heads. "You're going to suck face with Berg?"

As if we'd conjured him, Detective Berg knocked on our door, making us both jump.

"Maybe if we don't answer, he'll go away," Cat said.

"I can hear you," Berg called through the door. "And I'm waiting for an invitation."

"For what?" I said, loudly enough to be heard.

"To suck face. Or come in and ask you some follow-up questions. Either one works for me."

Chapter Twenty-Eight

I hurried to unlock the door and stepped back when the epitome of the Confection PD entered, dressed up in his khaki finest. He wore a smirk I didn't trust.

"I was, that is, you didn't hear—"

"I heard plenty," he said, and I worried that he might know Roger had been talking. A lot. "I know how to work a suspect. Don't worry. You can keep your lips to yourself. Just move them when you talk, and we'll call it even."

My face threatened to catch fire. "What do you want? Speak, Detective."

Cookie had the nerve to bark, which made Cat and Berg laugh.

"Not you, Cookie," I murmured, trying to get a handle on my embarrassment.

"I want to know what you can tell me about Bill Sanchez and Joe Jacobs."

"I already told Officer Halston."

"I know. But tell me." He glanced at Cat.

"She stays."

"I can see that," he said with forced patience. "Ms. Jones, I—"

"You need to see something first." I showed him the picture Mandy had sent me. "See? That's Scott Cloutier holding what looks like Gil's most prized possession. A garden trowel Mandy Coatney gave him three years ago, I think. Or maybe two years ago, I forget. The point is, Gil would never give that away. To anyone. So how did Scott get it?"

"I need you to forward this to me." Instead of waiting, Berg took my phone and texted the image to himself. His brows drew close as he continued to study the picture. "When was this taken?"

"The date stamp shows last Sunday, June seventh. Gil was killed on the fifth, right?"

"Right." Berg finally gave my phone back.

"And Mandy's been taking all kinds of pictures. She might have more that can place your perp near Gil's house."

"Perp?" Berg asked as he looked at me. "What did I tell you about staying away from this investigation?"

"Oh boy," Cat muttered. "Come on, Cookie. Let's go do stuff away from here."

Cookie gave a soft rumble of assent, and the pair deserted me for the kid section.

"I know what you're up to, Lexi."

"Oh? What's that, *Chad*?"

His eyes narrowed. "Your friend is pumping Roger for information. And you and your network of spies have been all over my town digging up dirt. Literally *and* figuratively."

"Ha. First of all, Cat is the least devious person I know. If she's pumping Roger, it's not for information." I paused, realized that might have come out wrong, since Berg choked on a laugh that seemed to surprise him, then hurried to continue. "Besides which, I have no network. I do have loyal customers, however. Did you like the crime novel you bought?"

"Yes, but I'm not here about books."

"But we're a bookstore." Pause. "Chad."

Every time I said the guy's name, he got a funny look on his face. It was comical.

"I know that. *Lexi.*" Huh. Now I felt funny. "But I'm worried that you're going to get hurt—"

"Aw, thank you for caring, Detective."

"—while screwing up my case," he bit out between his teeth. "Butt out, for the last time. Next time I talk to you about . . ." He wiped a hand over his face, drew in a deep breath, and let it out slowly. "Tell me what you know about Bill and Joe."

I did my best not to smirk, worried he might really throw me in jail just to make a point.

I cleared my throat and, in a polite voice, answered. I told him all about Bill and Joe's tension, threats, and CGC competitiveness.

"So is Bill a person of interest?" *Come on, Berg. Give me something.*

"I'm not talking to you about the case."

"Scott is the one who gave you that anonymous tip about my journal."

He smacked himself in the forehead. "Am I making a sound? Is anything coming out of my mouth? What about *Do not engage* do you not understa—"

"I just thought you should know."

Berg glared down at me. Gosh. Was the guy growing?

"How tall are you, anyway?" I asked.

"Six three," he said absently before once more focusing on me. "Why?"

"No reason."

His phone buzzed, and he frowned when he looked at it. "I need to go. Please, stay away from Gil's house and this investigation, including anyone named Cloutier."

"That's going to be a little tough, since I live right next door."

At his scowl, I conceded. "Fine. I'm out. Bam. Don't care what happened, won't ask any more questions about anything." I wanted badly to just blurt out Claude's name to see Berg's reaction but decided against it. I'd pushed as much as I dared for the day.

Instead, I watched Berg answer a call on his way out the door, his movements growing faster as he got some news no doubt not intended for civilian ears.

"Well, that was painful," Cat said once he'd gone.

I went to turn the sign back to OPEN before slinking back to the register. "You're telling me."

"For the record, your face was ghost pepper red."

I groaned. "My cheeks felt that hot. Why did you have to ask if I was going to suck face with Berg at the worst possible time?"

"I don't know. I like to think of my timing as a gift." She started laughing. I joined her.

Because in retrospect, that had been pretty funny . . . though it would have been funnier if it had happened to someone else. I'd just pretend another person had bantered with the police department and its six-foot-three hunk of manliness.

"He's starting to grow on me," I admitted.

"Like mold?"

"Just like mold."

We snickered and got back to work, and Cat told me all about how special, handsome, and amazing Roger was turning out to be.

Cookie sneered at all the gushing and went to look out the front window.

I wanted to do the same but had to be a good friend, so I stayed, nodded, and listened. And I mostly paid attention. Except when she mentioned Claude again.

"Wait. He said what, exactly?"

"Oh, I forgot that part."

"*Cat.*" I glanced around, but our customers were circulating far enough away for our discussion to continue. "What about Claude?"

"Apparently, Claude is Gil's brother, but it doesn't seem as if any of Gil's kids knew him. They've been questioned but have no knowledge of any of Gil's or their mother's relatives. Their phone records don't show evidence of any collusion either."

"Oh, *collusion*. Nice. You get five points for that word."

"Ha. Take that, Elvis." Cat grinned.

While thinking about Claude, Gil, and Scott, I finished my shift and took the doggo home. We had a nice meal of ravioli from the can for me and a special serving of turkey cutlets from the can for Cookie.

Then I forced my brain to shut down and simmer while I watched some sitcoms streaming on my laptop before going to bed early. Because boy, did I need the sleep.

* * *

Wednesday morning proved to be both profitable and long. Cat came in at ten with some orange-cranberry muffins that melted in my mouth and sold out within an hour. So she went home to make more. Kay texted me to let me know they had found no holes near rosebushes or elsewhere, so the culprit wanted only what had been buried south of Central Garden.

I'd bet money that Abe's map had little X marks corresponding to all those southerly holes.

And rosebushes had something to do with that buried treasure. *Roses have thorns*, Gil's note had stated. *It's all in how you hold it.* What was Gil always holding? That trowel. I knew I was onto something. But what would I do with that information? I needed to find something that might very well be a murder weapon that had killed two people.

As I walked home after work that night, Cookie by my side, I felt a little woozy at the thought of trying to confront Scott about the murder weapon. No way. I might be nonsensical sometimes, but despite what *some* in law enforcement might think, I wasn't stupid. The police could handle Scott and any other murder suspects.

My phone buzzed, and I looked to see a new text from Mandy. Following the text—*Look at this!!!!*—came a few images of Scott inside Gil's house and on the property several days after Gil had died. Oh man. It sure wasn't looking good for Scott.

I immediately stopped walking to forward the texts to Berg, since I now conveniently had his contact number. *It's Lexi*, I told him. *Mandy sent these. I'm not intruding on your case. Going home now. Not investigating anything.*

Good, don't came immediately.

"Such a jerk," I muttered.

Cookie and I had started up my walkway when a hand landed on my shoulder.

I screamed and jumped a mile.

"Sorry, sorry. I called your name," Bill Sanchez said, and took a step back. He glanced at Cookie. "She heard me."

I glared at my dog. "Well, maybe she should have told me."

Cookie sniffed.

"What's up, Bill?"

"I wanted to talk." He twisted his hands. To my surprise, he looked less than well groomed, his sandy-brown hair disheveled, his pale face blotchy from stress. "The police have been asking me all kinds of questions."

"Not my business, Bill."

He stepped around me to keep me from walking toward my house.

I started to feel uneasy and glanced around. For once, no one seemed to be near. Not one nosy neighbor out glaring at me. Really? Not one?

"I think you maybe misunderstood. Peggy told me you found Joe and that the police were talking to you and you mentioned what I'd said about Joe needing to pay. But Lexi, I didn't kill him." He sounded stressed.

"Okay. I believe you." I really needed to get away so I could text for help. I didn't want to be in this situation. Bill had height and muscle on me. Not much, but enough to kill me and bury my body while my lazy dog watched with glee. Why had she not warned me of Bill approaching?

"You don't understand." Bill took my hand and squeezed. Not too hard, but not letting me go. "Joe and I have been best friends for years. But it wasn't until I joined the CGC that I really felt a part of something. I'm not great with people."

"I see that," I muttered, and tried to tug my hand back, but he refused to let go. "Bill? My hand?"

"Oh, sorry." He let me go then, which made me feel better. But he still stood too close. "Joe and I have been trying to get Best Home Garden for the past three years. But Gil kept edging us out. When he died, Joe thought he could take the win. Heck, I thought so too."

Oh my gosh. Was he really going to confess to killing Gil for gardening cred?

"Joe wanted to win. But if you've seen the Danvers' garden, you'd know that wasn't a sure thing. Except he thought he could if something were to happen to Julie's prized rosebushes."

"Were you the one digging all over town?" Had I really been so far off the mark?

"What? No. And I never did mess with their garden. I'm not a cheat."

He'd said that before.

"I didn't mean to—" He cut off midsentence, and I realized Cookie too had shifted her attention to next door. "Did you see that?"

"See what?"

He stared at Gil's. "Someone's in Gil's house. And they shouldn't be." Bill headed for Gil's.

"Hey, wait. You can't go in there." Could anyone else? The crime scene tape had vanished. Maybe one of Gil's sons was inside. I rushed after Bill while wondering what I thought I was doing, but I at least had the sense to redial Berg and yelled as soon as he picked up, "Send help to Gil's!"

Cookie joined me, and we reached Bill as he entered through an unlocked front door and paused at the entryway. The sun hadn't yet set outside, but the interior of the home looked dark. Until Bill flicked on a light.

I stared in shock, along with Bill, at the mess in Gil's home. Though I'd never been inside, I doubted Gil would trash his own house and live that way while alive. Pillows had been ripped, sofas as well. Books lay scattered, figurines smashed, and above the fireplace, the shadow box supposedly holding Gil's other trowel was missing, the box in pieces, shards of glass everywhere.

"What happened in here?" Bill whispered.

"We should call the police."

Instead of waiting, Bill continued into the house.

"I shouldn't go. This is where the idiot heroine gets herself killed, right?"

Cookie glanced from me to Bill and took off after him.

"Dang it! Cookie!" I chased her down the stairs into—what else?—a creepy basement.

Unfinished and filled with stuff, Gil's basement had a lot of junk and old mementos scattered on shelves and in piles on the floor. Yet this mess, as opposed to the one upstairs, looked like deliberate stacks of attempted organization rather than a thief rummaging through his things.

Bill turned to me and tugged on a string, giving the basement faint illumination not coming through the small high windows at ground level. "I feel so bad about how it all happened. I need to confess."

"Uh, Bill? Maybe save that for the police."

"Police?" He blinked at me.

"You didn't mean to kill Gil, did you?"

"What? Kill Gil? I didn't kill him. But Joe had plans for his garden. For all their gardens. And he was blackmailing me to make sure they all lost. You think those small holes dug by a few rosebushes are bad? Imagine intentional root rot, aphids, and vinegar tampering with award-winning flowers and veggies."

"Huh?"

Bill sighed. "Joe wanted us to both win, to prove we deserved to be in the CGC. See, Joe never thought the town accepted him on account of tearing down the historic home he bought to put up something newer and better. Ed Mullins never let him forget he was just a new guy."

"Joe's been in Confection for ten years."

"I know. And I've been here for eight, but they were always friendlier to me."

"I'm sorry, but what does this have to do with Gil and Joe's deaths?"

Bill sighed. "Nothing. But it's related to my death."

"*What?*"

"My forthcoming end with the CGC. A death of sorts."

I was having trouble following. Why did I care about this?

"You see, Joe has been digging into all the top contenders for the Gardener's Purse. And he found out that my aunt is one of the Gardener's Purse judges. But I had no idea. I'm adopted and never knew my birth parents or their relatives. Anyway, Joe found out, and it was a big deal because my aunt is a judge this year, which means an automatic disqualification for me, in addition to the CGC judgment. They were pretty specific about kicking anyone out who tried to cheat to win, and Joe was going to make it look like my aunt and I were in on her judging if I didn't do what he said. And he had plans to ruin anyone he thought might win." Bill rubbed his face, and I noticed something odd.

One of Bill's fingers had a crooked end. Just like Abe's and Matt's. Like Gil's.

Holy Mary Fan and Fairy. I'd just found Gil's brother, the armed robber and aggravated assault guy who was spiraling out of control. And I was trapped in Gil's dark basement with him.

All alone.

Dear God. I really was too stupid to live.

Chapter Twenty-Nine

"Bill, or should I say, *Claude*." When in doubt, go on the offensive. My heart threatened to burst out of my chest. And where the heck had my dog gone? I heard her somewhere in the basement but couldn't take my gaze from Bill.

"What?"

"Why, Bill? Why kill Gil and Joe? Not just for CGC fame. It was for whatever Gil buried, wasn't it?"

Bill frowned, still playing innocent.

"I know, Claude. I see your finger."

"What finger?"

I held up my hand and pointed to my index finger. "The tip is bent, just like Abe's and Matt's."

"What are you talking about? I broke my finger three years ago on a climbing trip, and it never healed right."

"Sure you did." *Shut up, Lexi.* Yet I couldn't stop myself. "Did you and Scott plan it together? Or did you fall into partnership by accident? What are you really here for?"

Before he could answer, something made a soft thud, and he fell forward at the same time Cookie started barking. It was her mean bark, not her playful sound.

Scott took Bill's place. "Hi, Lexi."

"Scott. How could you?" I leaned down to check on Bill. In the movies, people pass out and fall down all the time. But really falling to the ground from a standing position could cause major injury. Bill looked to have a broken or busted nose, not to mention the bloody mess at the back of his head. He still had a pulse, though. For how long, with Scott standing over him, was the question.

"Bill shouldn't have been here. Neither should you." Scott sighed and smacked a pipe against his thigh. To my surprise, he reached up on a nearby shelf and pulled down Gil's garden trowel, the one Mandy had given him. The one with the sharp edges. "Too many people in this town can't mind their own business."

"Scott?"

"I didn't kill my dad. Or maybe I did." He sighed. "But Joe, now, he was an unfortunate necessity. I had to hand it to him for creativity. He was out to nail the CGC and saw me digging when I'd been so careful not to get caught." Scott smiled, a nasty grin that had me wondering who he really was under the good-guy front. "Problem was, he blackmailed a man who refused to be blackmailed. Bill's not a bad guy. He's a little obtuse, but he's good with computers. Did you know the last code he wrote is worth millions?" Scott barked a laugh. "I work my ass off eighty hours a week for months, and I'm still in the red. And Jan, that moron, keeps spending money like it grows on trees, then has the nerve to complain when I'm not there enough for her. Please."

Not a great time to bring up Matt.

"But why kill your dad?" *Come on, Scott. Monologue for me.*

"I guess that's something you'll die not knowing."

Man, Matt and Jan were right. Scott really was a jerk.

Before he could strike at me, Cookie was on him, growling like a Doberman.

I stared at her in shock, having never heard her make those sounds.

"You should know I called the police," I told him, letting Cookie take point. I looked for a weapon and picked up a butt-ugly ceramic garden gnome. Heck, it hurt just looking at it. But by its weight, it should do some damage.

Scott stepped back, warily looking from Cookie to me. She gnashed her teeth, those fangs sharp, even in the dim light, and continued to growl in a menacing fashion. She was *so* getting a steak later.

"That map wasn't junk, was it, Scott?" I asked, needing answers. "Your dad buried treasure somewhere in town."

"Treasure that wasn't his to bury," Scott snapped. "He lent me money at interest. At interest! His own son! And when I could only afford to pay him back the initial loan, he threatened to tell everyone I wasn't a man of my word. He was going to ruin my business, my marriage—hell, my life."

"I though you paid him back."

"Seriously, Lexi? I lied, okay? Jan and I have been over for a while. I hate my brothers, Matt especially, and Dad was nothing but a mean old bastard who liked to play games. All I had was my work, and it was going south. But with real money, I could start over. I would have too, but my dad could never just leave well enough alone."

I wasn't expecting the move, so when Scott struck at me with the pipe in a sudden lunge, I barely got my arm up in time to block it. And wow, did that hurt when it made contact with my left forearm. Added to that, I tripped backward over some crap on the ground, abusing my posterior as well.

"Get off me, you jerk!" I yelled as Cookie attacked.

Hol-ee Hannah, but Cookie in savage mode was a glorious sight to behold. With Scott off-kilter after striking at me, Cookie managed to wrestle away the pipe and dropped it. She then dodged his strike with the trowel and bit his arm, disarming him. Now weaponless and facing a dog frothing at the mouth, Scott tore for the stairs with Cookie in hot pursuit.

My arm hurt like blazes, but I crawled over to Bill to check his pulse again. Steady, yet he didn't move. I needed to escape and get help, but maybe not upstairs. Gil had a door down here somewhere, I'd bet, so I stood on shaky feet, rubbed my butt knowing I'd have a bruise, and grabbed the heavy ceramic gnome in my good hand before moving deeper into Gil's spooky basement.

I tiptoed but still heard myself sounding like a herd of elephants as I tried to maneuver around random rakes, shovels, and a wheelbarrow. I saw some light ahead, stunned at the size of Gil's basement. It was deep, for sure, but dim light showed a side stairwell leading up, and there, a door leading out on the side of his house facing away from mine.

Before I could take another step, a familiar face moved from out of the darkness.

Bob, the tourist, minus Anna this time, smiled at me while holding a large knife, his fingers wrapped around it. "Well, hello there, Lexi. Fancy running into you here."

It was then I remembered where else I'd seen a crooked finger. On Bob's hand when he'd cupped Anna's shoulder, back when they'd chatted with me in front of the bookshop.

"Claude?"

He nodded. "Claude Robert Cloutier," he said giving the French pronunciation of his name.

"Or Bob for short," I said.

"*Oui*." He gave a mean laugh, and his accent flattened once more. "This has been a huge cluster from the get-go. Finding my nephew and getting him on board was easy. But trying to get my diamonds has been the damnedest thing." He pointed his large knife in my direction. "But you're gonna help me. Fast, before the cops come."

"I lied. They're not coming."

"I know. You're a bad liar." He chuckled. "Once Scott takes care of your mutt, he'll help get to the bottom of this. To be honest, you're going to die. Slow and hard or fast and easy. It's up to you."

"I have no idea where these supposed diamonds are. Gil and I weren't friends."

"No, but he left you a message. Scott and I couldn't make heads or tails of it, but Gil thought you might."

I sighed, not having to swallow down my panic. I was so scared I'd gone numb, which was actually a good thing. Stressing about my lack of a future would be no help whatsoever. "You knew about the message in the dog treat ball."

"Of course we knew. We've been digging all over town for the past month. I found that ball in May right where you found it, under your fence. It wasn't until Gil died and I saw the note he'd written on his garden bench back there"—he nodded behind him—"that I realized he'd been suspicious of me all along. I couldn't figure it out, and when Scott couldn't decipher it either, we realized Gil meant it for you and decided to let you have it. Well? Where are they?"

"I have no idea. I didn't even know there were diamonds to be found until you just told me."

"Yet you knew my name was Claude."

I nodded, wanting him to keep talking until the police arrived. Honestly, the town wasn't that big. They should be here by now! "I overheard the police mention a Claude Cloutier and saw a file about armed robbery and aggravated assault."

"Yeah. I did fifteen years for that. What a crock. I barely tapped that old man. He had a stroke and lived, and they tried to blame me for that. But the diamonds, yeah, I got 'em. And I hid them before the cops found me and dragged me back to California to stand trial. Gil wasn't supposed to know, but he found them and wrote me a letter. Told me we were no longer family and that I had no business making money off of hard-working people.

"What a hypocrite! It was my stealing that gave us the seed money to start our plumbing business in the first place. And he knew it. I staked him enough to get a job at the university. But when I needed help, all the sudden he had a family to support and no time for the dirtier jobs."

I blinked. "Are you saying Gil used to rob people with you?" Wow. In no way had I seen that coming.

"Yeah, I am. And he was pretty good at it too. Till he was too good for the family business. Went straight and put it all behind him, so he said."

"I never knew that."

"That's why I'm telling you. Why protect Gil now? You never liked him. No one did. I still can't believe he got married."

"Are you married? Is Anna your girlfriend for real? Or was that a cover story?"

"Oh, she's real. And she's waiting for her cut. Just as soon as I find the diamonds." He grinned. "Alec fences stuff for us. We really do treasure hunting, you know. But sometimes we find stuff that needs to be discreetly handled. Which is where Alec comes in." He snorted. "You realize I'm only telling you all this because you won't live to share this with anyone else. And if you think you can just not tell me what I want to know, sweet cheeks, think again. Because I'll kill you, your uncles, Cat, Teri, and anyone else you might love before I leave town. They'll never catch me, and you'll die knowing I killed innocent people you could have protected."

I didn't mean to cry, but the thought of him touching anyone I cared about made me so mad I teared up.

"Aw, she's sad." He laughed. "Enough stalling. Where are the diamonds?"

"Fine. But you swear you'll leave my friends and family alone."

"Sure. No sweat. Soon as I have my stash, I'm out of here."

"Without Scott?"

"If he's so pathetic a dog can get the better of him, he doesn't deserve the diamonds. They cost me fifteen years of my life. I paid a heavy price."

I drew in a deep breath and let it out slowly. "Let's see . . . You guys went all over the place looking for roses." I took a step away from him, but he didn't seem to mind. Bill had yet to make a sound. "Can I ask why you killed Gil before getting the location out of him?"

Bob scowled. "If Scott hadn't goaded Gil into an argument, I know I could have persuaded him to be reasonable. I was willing to cut Gil in on some of it. But a week before he died, he got into a fight with Scott, said the boy was letting me influence him. Hell, five minutes after meeting him I could tell Scott doesn't do anything he doesn't want to."

"Oh."

"And Gil, that bastard, wanted half. No way was I going for that. I have expenses, plus I was cutting Scott in. Gil didn't deserve more than a chance to make right with me. He couldn't even do that. We argued Friday night. He threw a few punches. I threw a few back, and somehow I got hold of that trowel and stabbed him. Wish I felt bad about it, but he had it coming."

"How did Scott take it?"

"He's a great kid. He can take anything for a few million." Bob guffawed.

"And Joe?" I wanted to verify Scott's version of the story.

"That was all Scott being sloppy. Joe saw something he shouldn't have, and Scott took care of it. I admit I hadn't thought the kid had it in him." Gil shook his head. "Stupid to use the trowel on the guy, considering I used it on his father. But Scott's deluded about his dad. Still thinks Gil would have wanted him to have it, like he's his father's favorite or something. Said it made him feel closer to his dad to use it digging in the dirt all over town. Kid's a moron, but now his prints are all over the murder weapon. And mine aren't." He gave me an evil grin. "You ready to show me the diamonds? Or do you need persuading?"

I gripped the garden gnome tighter, ready to make my move. "Fine. You want the diamonds? I want an end to all this death."

"That's the spirit."

"They're out back by Gil's white roses."

He frowned. "Gil doesn't have any white roses."

"Um, yes he does. The ones with thorns? The note said roses have thorns. And 'it's all in how you hold it' refers to the shovel.

I used to hear him yelling at Abe to hold the shovel straight up and down, to dig deep eight inches, to accommodate the root ball." I was so talking out of my butt on all this, but hey, it was either get the guy to move outside, where I could run from him and yell for help, or die down in Gil's cluttered basement.

Except Bob didn't seem to be buying what I was selling.

"Look, get Gil's trowel and I'll show you." I nodded behind me, where Scott had dropped the thing.

"Fine, but don't try—"

I swung that gnome as hard as I could and didn't wait for him to fall. It crashed against his skull and shattered as I ran for the stairs leading to the light of freedom into Gil's yard.

Chapter Thirty

I made it up into the backyard and took four steps onto the grass before a hand grabbed my ponytail from behind and yanked.

I shrieked as I fell back into a hard body, and we crashed to the ground, rolling over each other to get the upper hand.

I struggled for all I was worth, but Bob had to outweigh me by a solid hundred pounds at least.

He knelt over my prone body and pulled back a fist. With a furious glint in his eye and blood trickling down his temple, he growled, "Slow and hard it is."

Only to be tackled by a dog and man who seemed to appear from out of nowhere.

Cookie kept growling as she backed to stand over me while Berg punched Bob in the face to subdue him before shoving him onto his belly and cuffing him.

The action seemed to take seconds yet felt like it took forever.

"Lexi? Lexi, are you okay?" Berg was saying as I blinked up into his face.

Cookie kept licking me and whining, so I got a snootful of dog breath and dog slobber before wonder cop lifted me in his arms.

"Oh my gosh, put me down," I said, my voice reedy as I ineffectually struggled in Berg's strong arms.

He gently set me down and helped me get stable. And as I looked up at him, I saw Dash right behind him, easing Cookie's whimpers, muttering, "It's okay, Cookie. We're all good."

Roger and Officer Brown arrived seconds later to take Bob into custody, and I let them know about Bill in the basement. Sirens filled the air, and more cops showed up.

Berg said to the first medical guy on the scene, "We have an injured male, unconscious, in the basement. Head wound."

The EMT nodded. "Got it." He grabbed his partner and they rushed into Gil's house.

"Lexi, let's get you looked at as well."

"I'm better than Bill," I told Berg. "Can we do this next door?"

He nodded for Dash to take hold of me. "I'll be over as soon as I can. In the meantime, I'll send aid over as soon as they get here."

"Scott?" I asked.

"Down and done for," Dash said with relish. "I was walking over to check on your weird phone call when Berg drove up and started questioning me."

That answered the question of why the police hadn't arrived any faster. I must have misdialed.

Berg rolled his eyes. "I was asking a few questions in general, not treating you like a suspect."

"Uh-huh. So then we see Scott running like his hair is on fire with Cookie snarling after him. Your dog is amazing."

"I know." I leaned down to hug her with my good arm, breathing in all her protective goodness. "She saved me twice, though Detective Berg did help."

"Thanks for that," Berg said, a half smile on his face. "Once Scott was in cuffs, I had Dash sit on him until help arrived so I could make my way to you. Cookie was pretty insistent." Berg stared at her. "But still off her leash."

Cookie whined, and Berg cracked a huge smile. "But so brave."

"Yeah. Well, Bill will tell you when he wakes up, but Bob, aka Claude Robert Cloutier, confessed to killing his brother, Gil. Scott confessed to killing Joe, and Gil confirmed it."

"Good to know." Berg nodded to Dash.

"Okay, murder girl, let's get you home. Your arm doesn't look so good."

"It really hurts," I said, realizing it really did.

And then I passed out.

* * *

When I came to, it was in the ambulance on my way to the hospital. A visit that would seriously tax my insurance with its large deductible once the bill came. But my fractured arm got set, my cast was scheduled to go on a few days later once the swelling went down, and I'd been pronounced stressed but otherwise okay. My uncles arrived to take me home—to their home, where they spoiled me rotten for days.

Friends had swung by to visit but hadn't stayed long. I'd slept a good bit, until I just couldn't take the pampering any longer. Four days later, unable to take any more, I sneaked home to find Cat and Teri waiting with the Macaroons. In my house. With my uncles present. Huh.

One surprise breakout party later, after everyone had shared congratulations, well wishes, and a sincere desire to get back to regular Macaroon Mondays, I had the house to myself. Cat and Teri had offered to dog-sit, though I wondered who had become more popular—me or my superdog, who'd recently been given a baked-dog-biscuit key to the city. Right after she got her award, I got my cast. I'm pretty sure she got the better end of the deal.

Fortunately, the cast only covered my forearm. But I had to wear it for six to eight weeks, and I could already feel it itching.

During my days recuperating, Dash had been by several times to make sure I had what I needed. Oddly, his attitude swayed from big brother to solicitous acquaintance to guy who looked at me like he like-liked me. I had no idea what to do about it, so I did nothing.

Detective Berg kept his distance, busy wrapping up the case.

But the good news was that we did find the diamonds. Rather, I found them, thank you very much.

Bob hadn't looked hard enough at Gil's trowel. That rosewood handle did have a thorn. The trowel had a secret pointy catch that released only if I "held it just right" and the handle popped off. Without touching the pointed catch that was exposed after the handle was removed, one couldn't tell that the handle wasn't solid wood after all but had been built with a secret compartment inside. One large enough to house a picture of young Mandy and Gil, standing arm in arm. And to hold a small packet of diamonds worth more than I'd ever see in my lifetime.

Mandy had been beyond surprised, as the trowel hadn't been hollow when she'd given it to him, so Gil must have had it made that way to hide his most prized possessions.

In more unsurprising news, Jan had immediately moved forward on divorcing Scott. Matt had asked her to move in with him in Portland, and Scott went to jail along with his Uncle Bob. Abe planned on moving next door to me just as soon as the police gave him the okay.

To thank me for all I'd done, he'd given me the twin to the garden gnome I'd broken over Bob's head.

This one was a god-awful little thing with green pants, a red hat, and a blue painted shirt over what looked like man boobs. No wonder Abe was eager to part with it.

Still, a week later as I stared at it staring back at me on my dining table, I felt as if the ugly fella was looking over me. Just not as fiercely as Cookie did. She hadn't left my side since I'd gotten my cast, and I felt, to be fair to her, we both needed a little break. Her with Cat and Teri and Teri's famous meatballs. Me alone with my thoughts and a bubble bath and a book. Or bed and a book. I wasn't sure which I'd choose yet.

Just as I readied myself to go read in bed, clad in an oversized T-shirt that said *Careful or I'll Kill You in My Novel*, the doorbell rang.

I opened it to see Detective Berg standing in civilian clothes, both handsome and fierce and unbending. And holding a wrapped present.

"Hello, Detective."

He smirked at my sleep shirt. "Good thing you didn't wear that when in custody, eh?"

"Ha-ha. Did you need something?"

"I came to say thank-you for your help—that wasn't asked for, but the chief is making me be friendly—and to give you this."

"You're welcome." At least Berg was back to normal. Mostly. "What is this?"

He glanced around. "Open it and you'll see. You all alone?"

"Yeah. Cookie's with Cat and Teri tonight. I'm planning to read and sleep in."

He looked at my cast as I struggled with the paper.

"Need help?"

"Please."

He ripped part of the plain brown paper, what looked like it had once been a paper bag, and handed it back.

"Oh, it's a . . . retractable leash?"

"For Cookie." He handed me another slip of paper. "And for you."

"Is this . . ." I just stared. "A citation?"

"Actually, it's several all added into one. But watch." He took it from me and tore it in two before handing it back. "From the city to you. We thank you for helping out a fellow citizen. Bill told us he heard some of what you said, though he was in and out of consciousness. And you probably saved his life by distracting Scott and Claude."

"Oh. Good." I stared at the ripped citation. "I really don't have to pay it?"

"No. And I'm not sure if you heard or not, but both Gil and Scott had a lot to say about the murders, so we have an open-and-shut case."

"Poor Joe," I said, thinking about how being in the wrong place at the wrong time was so unlucky.

"Your 'poor Joe' only saw Scott because he was out at two AM intending to damage the Confection Rose, then incriminate Bill as having done it. That way Joe could blackmail his friend into helping him destroy the other contenders for the Gardener's Purse. Joe wasn't rational about that contest."

"No kidding." I shook my head. "So Scott killed Joe in Central Garden?" Then what about all the blood in Joe's house?

"No. Scott pretended to go along with Joe's plan. The next day, he walked into Joe's house in broad daylight and killed him using Gil's garden trowel, then walked out and joined a garden tour without anyone noticing. Which was really stupid, because if you hadn't heard Gil confess to killing his own brother, we might have convicted Scott for doing so. His prints are all over the murder weapon of two victims. But between the two of them trying to get a lesser sentence, Gil and Scott rolled all over each other."

"Nice." I enjoyed hearing that. So much.

"Now I'll leave you in peace."

"Thanks for the leash, Detective. I'm sure Cookie will just love it."

"Cookie? The leash is for you. The citation was for her."

"Aren't you the comedian," I said drily.

He gave me an honest-to-goodness grin, and it made my whole body tense in anticipation of . . . something.

Berg chuckled. "I'm about as funny as you are a detective. Now go to bed and stop butting into police work."

"Yep. Like I said. This is why you have no friends." I'd better make sure he never learned just how much help I'd had on this case, or what the Macaroons might just turn into—a crime-fighting team the likes of which Central Oregon had never seen.

Berg shot me a sly glance. "By the way, if you need any help with research, let me know. I definitely think your detective should have slate-gray eyes and wide shoulders with the power to decimate his enemies."

I blinked. "You read my laptop!"

"That would be unethical. I just read your journal. And I'm a much better role model for a detective book than Dash Hagen. Just saying."

He turned and left me standing there with my mouth open.

I finally closed the door and went to bed.

But my dreams were of a new kind of detective agency—Lexi's Angels, starring Lexi, the Macaroons, and two promising male leads.

Jinkies.

Acknowledgments

I have to acknowledge several people who helped make this book a reality. First, to the talented people at Crooked Lane. Thank you so much for making this book stand out. To my agent Nicole, without whom *Digging Up Trouble* would not have come to pass. Thank you. To the real Cat for her help with recipes, and to her, Teri, Stefanie, Kathy, and Amy, for inspiration for my characters. (None of you are in the book, by the way. But you did inspire some fun personality types!) To my beta readers, in particular Michele, Sarah, and Mimi; your feedback about characters and plot helped so much. And of course, I must acknowledge Cookie, who really deserves the credit for this book. Without you, Cookie, none of the story would have been possible.